The Best
AMERICAN
SHORT
STORIES
2014

The Best AMERICAN SHORT STORIES® 2014

Selected from
U.S. and Canadian Magazines
by JENNIFER EGAN
with HEIDI PITLOR

With an Introduction by Jennifer Egan

HOUGHTON MIFFLIN HARCOURT
BOSTON • NEW YORK 2014

www.hmhco.com

ISSN 0067-6233
ISBN 978-0-547-81922-8
ISBN 978-0-547-86886-8 (pbk.)

Printed in the United States of America
DOC 10 9 8 7 6 5 4 3 2 1

Contents

Foreword

SOMETIMES IT SEEMS as if the aspiring—and financially well enough endowed—American writer is offered more than the reader. For the young writer, there are a fast-growing number of MFA programs, fellowships, summer workshops, residencies, creative writing centers, endless books that teach about writing and publishing. For evidence of the opportunities and widespread desire to write in our country, note the sheer number of blogs that populate the Internet, the comment sections of said blogs, Facebook and Twitter (where everyone gets to be a published writer, at least within the confines of a status update or tweet), the self-published army on Amazon.com.

This year, I detected a certain uncertainty in short stories, a sense of disorientation, perhaps a reflection of these unsteady times for publishing and readers. A lot of story writers relied on a character's intuition or impulse to fuel the forward motion of their stories. As a result, many stories tended to wander—sometimes intriguingly, often into unsettling territory—rather than accelerate toward some definitive endpoint. While some stories that I read this year were built around or upon some narrative roadway—and many of those appear in this volume—plenty were not.

From my vantage point, there are moments when it seems that more people in this country want to write than read. Many people who read this book are in fact writers in training, reading in order to learn to write better. I myself came to serious reading relatively late, halfway through college, and this was in a class where both reading and creative writing were taught. I soon wanted to give to others the singular high that I felt when reading an Alice Munro or a Margaret Atwood story. I should say that I went to college in Canada.

There is, of course, nothing wrong with wanting to write and seeking help in that endeavor. I am the proud owner of an MFA, a shelf full of books about how to write fiction and how to get published, memoirs by fiction writers, and at least a dozen story anthologies that I bought before I was lucky enough to land this job. But what happens if and when writers begin to outnumber readers? What happens when writing becomes more attractive than reading? Will we become—or are we already—a nation of performers with no audience?

For the reader of books, there are book clubs, many informally initiated by friends or neighbors, a smattering of independent bookstores that serve as meeting places for readers and writers, libraries, some websites. Getting books has become easy—click on Amazon.com, and from the sound of it, a drone will soon be able to deliver a book to your door in the time it takes to say "drone." But I'm talking about accessible, widespread support for reading. Brick-and-mortar bookstores accessible to everyone who would patronize them. Also, a sense in our country that reading fiction is necessary and, dare I say, a wee bit glamorous. Like writing.

I had the good luck to take part in a reading and trivia night the other week at a bookstore in Cambridge, Massachusetts. This was a fundraiser for 826 Boston, a fabulous organization that offers writing support for kids. Four of us were invited to read for a few minutes, and then came a rowdy, rambunctious game of literary trivia for the mostly twenty-something audience. In order to win, players needed to have read things. There were questions about *Mrs. Dalloway* and *Let the Great World Spin* and *Frankenstein*. The place was packed. Drinks were served, fun was had. Reading became a galvanizing force rather than a solitary chore.

Soapbox alert. We—editors, writers, teachers, publishers—need to do whatever we can to enliven readers, to help create communities for them if we want to continue to have readers at all. Our independent bookstores are the frontlines, and many booksellers are fighting the good fight. Here, books stimulate conversation. Conversation stimulates a sense of community. Listening happens. Thinking. The exchange of thoughts.

Here's the thing: I am guilty of spending evenings scrolling through my Facebook and Twitter feeds, telling myself that after a day of reading stories, why not give myself a break? Why on earth would I want to read more fiction? I have a list three miles long of books that I want to read. I have twenty-five books on my bedside table. It's all a little overwhelming. Why not take a few minutes or maybe an hour and see what's going on with all my "friends" and the people whom I "follow"? But then I start to become a little groggy from staring at the screen, a little glum from reading other people's opinions of the day's news, which is so rarely good. I've been trying to spend more time during the evening with books, less online, to keep myself engaged in some book, any book, at all times. Because really, what I've done all day, whether it was reading short fiction or writing longer fiction or shepherding children, does not matter. We're all tired at night. We are all entitled to some self-indulgence, be that taking a self-test on BuzzFeed or smiling at the humorous tweets from the perplexingly enormous number of writers who watch *The Bachelor* each week. But we all know the drill: if we eat only candy, if we cultivate our friendships and relationships primarily online, if we forget to walk to town sometimes instead of drive, a crucial part of us will wither. You don't have to read all the books on your list at once. Just pick up the one that grabs you right now. If you don't love it, put it down. Move on.

This year, I'm not going to vow never to dip into Facebook or Twitter, but maybe I'll go online a little less. I'm going to try to keep reading some book each night. I'm going to start asking people which books they're reading instead of which movies they have seen. I'm going to see if I can't talk a few bookstore people into starting weekly trivia nights at their stores.

One other thing. I was more aware this year than usual that American short fiction, for so long primarily the domain of the privileged white, is becoming even more so. Voices of nonwhite and nonprivileged authors and characters are too rare. We need to do better. The short story has typically been the gateway form for young authors. Our MFA programs, literary journals, summer workshops, and providers of fellowships need to send representatives into different neighborhoods, libraries, and schools to seek a broader range of voices. If there are more proactively diverse magazines that I should be reading in addition to those listed at the back of this book, please let me know. My contact information can be found at the end of this foreword.

Working with Jennifer Egan was an honor, as well as ridiculously easy. She was a thoughtful, serious reader, never satisfied with embellishments of language nor easily tempted by likable characters. She wanted the stories to go somewhere new and strange, to surprise and confound. Every story that she chose for this book achieves these difficult feats.

The stories chosen for this anthology were originally published between January 2013 and January 2014. The qualifications for selection are (1) original publication in nationally distributed American or Canadian periodicals; (2) publication in English by writers who are American or Canadian, or who have made the United States their home; (3) original publication as short stories (excerpts of novels are not considered). A list of magazines consulted for this volume appears at the back of the book. Editors who wish for their short fiction to be considered for next year's edition should send their publications or hard copies of online publications to Heidi Pitlor, c/o *The Best American Short Stories,* 222 Berkeley Street, Boston, MA 02116.

HEIDI PITLOR

Introduction

AS WITH ANY "best of" or "top ten" list—or any prize, for that matter—the authority of an anthology like this one stands in direct contradiction to its essential arbitrariness. Winning, or inclusion, is a matter of managing to delight the right combination of tastes—in this case, that of the series editor, Heidi Pitlor, who superhumanly winnowed the contents of 208 publications to 120 individual stories, and then my own, as chooser of the final 20. In other words, getting into this book is largely a matter of luck.

And yet a volume titled *The Best American Short Stories* casts an iconic shadow—as I know all too well, having published short stories for twenty-one years before I managed to eke one into these pages! The self-endowed authority of a collection of "bests" can feel onerous not just to the many whose work is passed over, but to readers who disagree with the selection of contents—namely, just about everyone who opens this book. Can you recall reading a collection of "bests" and not musing, at least once, of the editor, "Was she out of her mind?" A different sensibility—yours, for example—would doubtless have produced a different volume. So much for authority!

But there are excellent—even crucial—reasons to publish a book like *The Best American Short Stories:* it generates excitement around the practice of writing fiction, celebrates the short story form, and energizes the fragile ecosystem of magazines that sustain it. Worthy goals at any time, and never more so than now, when copyright is hanging in the balance, publishers are beset by uncertainties, and fiction writers are wondering, rightly, how important our work really is to the cultural conversation. True, some of the people gazing at their iPhones on the train may be reading short stories, but a great many more are playing games, listening to music, watching movies, or checking the stock market. I'm struck by how often, even among a gathering of literary folk, the talk turns to television.

However, as anyone who loves reading fiction knows, there is no activity quite like it. In fact, my primary motive for accepting the role of guest editor this year is that I welcome any excuse to call reading work. I had other reasons too: I wanted to explore, systematically, what I think makes a short story great—to identify my own aesthetic standards in a more rigorous way than I've done before. And having spent the past couple of years reading early-twentieth-century fiction, I was eager to get a snapshot of what short fiction writers working in America (120 of them, anyway) are doing and thinking about at present—formally, stylistically, culturally. I wanted to see what I might glean from their preoccupations, both about the state of the contemporary short story and about the wider world, whose synthesis is a writer's job.

To put my biases—and therefore handicaps—directly on the table: I don't care very much about genre, either as a reader or as a writer. To me, fiction writing at any length, in any form, is a feat of radical compression: take the sprawling chaos of human experience, run it through the sieve of perception, and distill it into something comparatively miniscule that somehow, miraculously, illuminates the vast complexity around it. I don't think about short stories any differently than I do about novels or novellas or even memoirs. But the smaller scale of a story is important; the distillation must be even more extreme in order to succeed. It also must be purer; there is almost no room for mistakes.

I read fiction for the same reason I write it: to escape. Don't get me wrong—I enjoy my real life, but I feel about it much the way I do about New York City, my chosen and adored home: I'm always happy to leave, and I'm always happy to come back. It's fair to say that I read in a childlike way, for fun. That sounds frivolous, I know, but I can't find a better word that doesn't sound pretentious (and *entertainment* is too evocative of reclining chairs and surround sound). Classic novels—a vexed category, granted—are, for the most part, incredibly fun to read. Jane Austen? A page-turner.

Charles Dickens? Catnip. George Eliot? Un-put-downable. Wilkie Collins? Prepare to lose a night's sleep.

I recognize, of course, that one person's fun can be another person's slog. We'd probably all agree that we want gripping stories full of characters that move us. For me, that stuff can't be achieved without intelligence, nuance, and fresh language. The fun I'm talking about is fully compatible with fear, discomfort, and great sadness; I weep every time I read Edith Wharton's *The House of Mirth*, but I feel permanently enriched by it. The best fun, for me, comes from reading something that feels different from anything else. Originality is hard to gauge, of course—the fact that *I* haven't seen it before doesn't mean it hasn't been done—but for our purposes, let's say that I'm biased toward writers who take an obvious risk, formally, structurally, or in terms of subject matter, over those who do a familiar thing exquisitely.

If there was a single factor that decided whether a story ended up in my ongoing pile of contenders, it was its basic power to make me lose my bearings, to envelop me in a fictional world. In the case of Molly McNett's "La Pulchra Nota," that world unfolds in the year 1399, when a devout singing teacher named John Fuller narrates his own mystical, heartbreaking downfall. In Laura van den Berg's "Antarctica," it is the end-of-the-earth landscape of the story's title, a setting for grief and forensic investigation. Charles Baxter's "Charity" manages, in three paragraphs, to gyre its protagonist from teaching English in Ethiopia into homelessness and drug addiction in Minneapolis. And Benjamin Nugent's "God" is imbued with the cloistered bonhomie of college fraternity life, made perilous by the homosexual longings of its fraternity-brother narrator.

The vehicle for this transport into alternate worlds is vivid, specific language. Consider Craig Davidson's "Medium Tough," which subsumes the reader in the hyper-medicalized sensibility of Dr. Jasper Railsback, a surgeon of newborns who is beset with a physical abnormality he attributes to his mother's alcohol abuse while he was in utero. Railsback observes, "The air in the NICU was heavy with pheromones: aliphatic acids, which waft from the pores of women who've just delivered. A distinctive scent. An undertone of caramelized sugar." The language is technical, lyrical, and sensory—qualities whose seeming incompatibility makes their fusion even more potent.

It seems silly to continue quoting from stories that are printed in this volume (though I'm tempted), but suffice it to say that there's plenty more where that came from. Karen Russell's "Madame Bovary's Greyhound" is the imagined story of Emma Bovary's lost pet, Djali, told from the animal's perspective. An intriguing conceit, to be sure, but what gives the story its energy and tenderness is the play of Russell's inimitable prose. And Ruth Prawer Jhabvala's "The Judge's Will" owes its idiosyncratic power to the crystalline precision of her sentences.

So: a compelling premise and distinctive language to get in the door. Then what?

I read many stories that met both those requirements at first, but ultimately settled into predictable patterns, or seemed to stop short of something truly interesting. Each one of the twenty stories I chose had at least one move—often several—that genuinely surprised me, pushing past the obvious possibilities into territory that felt mysterious, or extreme. In Joyce Carol Oates's "Mastiff," a dog attack—which the reader half-expects—prompts an unlikely intimacy between the quasi-strangers who undergo it. Stephen O'Connor's "Next to Nothing" has the aura of a modern-day Grimms' fairy tale, featuring a pair of blunt, affectless sisters who insist on ignoring warnings of an impending flood as they summer together with their children.

The surprise in David Gates's "A Hand Reached Down to Guide Me," a story about the long friendship between an alcoholic musician and his one-time devotee, is its final destination: happiness. Gates's protagonist winds up happy—a striking outcome in a year when optimism was in short supply. The stories I read were predominantly dark, even grim, reflecting a mood of anxiety and unease that I guess is no surprise at all, given that Americans have endured six years of recession and eleven years of a war whose point—and endpoint—remain unclear. I'm proud to include two excellent stories that engage directly with the lives of soldiers: Will Mackin's "Kattekoppen," set among American forces in Afghanistan, and O. A. Lindsey's "Evie M.," about a female veteran struggling to function in a corporate workplace as she contemplates suicide. The British Petroleum oil spill in the Gulf of Mexico figured in more than one story I read, including Nicole Cullen's "Long Tom Lookout," included here, about a woman who spirits away the autistic, out-of-wedlock child of her husband, who is working long-term on the Gulf cleanup.

For the most part, the locus of anxiety in the larger pool of stories I read was the domestic sphere: illness and addiction, dead or imperiled children, cheating spouses, dissolving marriages. There was a curious predominance of pivotal roles played by wildlife, including crows, elk, bear (both brown and polar), turtles, deer, fish, and the aforementioned dogs. The prevailing narrative approach was the first-person singular, past tense. It was a year without much humor, but I welcomed the laughs that came, and was reminded that the funniest stuff is usually quite serious. I've included T. C. Boyle's riotous "The Night of the Satellite," in which a relationship's precipitous unraveling culminates in a dispute over whether a mysterious piece of hardware has fallen to earth from outer space. In Nell Freudenberger's "Hover," about a divorcing woman who begins levitating involuntarily, humor offsets a fierce account of a mother protecting her gentle, quirky son. In Ann Beattie's "The Indian Uprising," caustic repartee between a retired professor and his former student masks their shared understanding that he is dying. And the deadpan delivery of Peter Cameron's "After the Flood," in which an elderly couple agrees, at the behest of their pastor, to house a family left homeless by a flood, allows the story's horrific underpinnings to surface very slowly.

Although the majority of the 120 stories I read had contemporary settings, many could as easily have been set twenty years ago without anachronism. This is odd when you consider that a present-day photograph of any American location containing humans—a school, a street corner, a concert, a ball game—would be impossible to confuse with an image of the same scene, circa 1994. I'm not talking about facial hair or width of pants; I'm talking about the devices people walk around with, hold in their hands, and use to communicate—in some cases, almost constantly.

That revolution is the biggest change I've witnessed in my lifetime. Between the year I was born and when I went to college in 1981, I knew of exactly three telephonic possibilities: a busy signal, or a person picking up, or endless ringing. *Eighteen years of telecommunications stasis!* Hard to imagine that happening ever again. I'm not a proselyte; as a parent, journalist, music fan, and believer in copyright, I find my responses to our warp-speed technological change falling mainly on a spectrum from anxiety to terror. But there is no denying that a transformation is upon us, pervasive, dramatic, ongoing. And it is inseparable from many other seismic shifts of the past twenty years: modern terrorism, globalization, climate change.

How can such topics be manifest in a short story? Not all of them can at once, of course—or not directly. But my love of escape notwithstanding, I turn to contemporary fiction seeking a shared awareness with the writer of the cultural moment we both occupy, its peculiar challenges. In each of the twenty stories I chose—even those set in the past—I felt an engagement with the wider world at this specific point in time. It was my last criterion, but possibly the most important.

One way that cultural engagement can show itself is in the form a short story takes. Brendan Mathews's "This Is Not a Love Song" tells of the rise and fall of an early-1990s indie rocker, using artifacts assembled by her self-appointed documentarian: descriptions of photographs and interviews transcribed from cassette tapes. The story's inventive structure allows it to ask what separates homage from exploitation, and its setting in a precise technological moment (about twenty years ago, as it happens) suggests a shared understanding with the reader of all that has changed since then.

Another formally ambitious story I've included is Lauren Groff's "At the Round Earth's Imagined Corners," which begins in the 1940s and reaches to the present. The sweeping tale of a man who spends the bulk of his life in a serpent-infested Florida swamp that gradually becomes surrounded by a university, it vividly juxtaposes primordial mystery with sprawling modernity. Joshua Ferris's "The Breeze" dramatizes a young woman's ineffable craving for intensity and authenticity in her dealings with her new husband. By conjuring the relationship in a series of scenes that don't quite add up—and often seem to contradict each other—Ferris manages, as in a cubist painting, to evoke a larger whole without ever quite pinpointing it.

Of course, there's a long relationship between literary innovation and seismic cultural change: the modernists absorbed the impact of Freud, a world war, and the popularization of film (James Joyce managed a Dublin movie theater); the postmodernists reacted to television, structural theory, and the counterculture. Personally, I could do without any further "isms" (is anyone actually *drawn* to fiction called "postmodern"?), but I'm stirred by the question of how novels and short stories will evolve to accommodate and represent our ongoing cultural transformation. Prose fiction was invented as a means of flexible, eclectic storytelling, after all; from the very start, fiction writers have greedily absorbed whatever forms were around and bent them to their will. *Pamela,* one of the first novels written in English, is epistolary, and *Tristram Shandy* and *Robinson Crusoe* include legal documents, fake autobiography, and (in Sterne's case) weird graphics. It would be uncharacteristic if our literary production *didn't* seek out new ways to embody the novelties of twenty-first-century life: the commingling of online with actual experience; the disappearance of a certain kind of solitude; the illusion of safety that goes along with being in touch; surveillance as a fact of everyday life; the gulf between those who are technologically connected and those still isolated. To name just a few.

All of this brings me back to fiction's relevance to the cultural conversation. Will people continue to read short stories and novels, now that virtually every alternative that exists can fit more easily into our pocket than a paperback? People have been asking this question for a long time now—through the arrival of movies, TV, the Walkman, video games, cable, VCRs, personal computers, the Internet, and smartphones. By the time this introduction is printed (the very word outmoded), there may be some new threat. And while I do occasionally cower before the question, I also know that the answer is finally simple: people will keep reading fiction as long as it provides an experience of pleasure and insight they can't find anywhere else. The twenty stories in this collection did exactly that—for me. Now I cordially invite you to agree, object, call me crazy, and begin the conversation.

JENNIFER EGAN

The Best
AMERICAN
SHORT
STORIES
2014

Charity

FROM *McSweeney's*

I

HE HAD FALLEN into bad trouble. He had worked in Ethiopia for a year—teaching in a school and lending a hand at a medical clinic. He had eaten all the local foods and been stung by the many airborne insects. When he'd returned to the States, he'd brought back an infection—the inflammation in his knees and his back and his shoulders was so bad that sometimes he could hardly stand up. Probably a viral arthritis, his doctor said. It happens. Here: have some painkillers.

Borrowing a car, he drove from Minneapolis down to the Mayo Clinic, where after two days of tests the doctors informed him that they would have no firm diagnosis for the next month or so. Back in Minneapolis, through a friend of a friend, he visited a wildcat homeopathy treatment center known for traumatic-pain-relief treatments. The center, in a strip mall storefront claiming to be a weight-loss clinic (WEIGHT NO MORE), gave him megadoses of meadowsweet, a compound chemically related to aspirin. After two months without health insurance or prescription coverage, he had emptied his bank account, and he gazed at the future with shy dread.

Through another friend of a friend, he managed to get his hands on a few superb prescription painkillers, the big ones, gifts from heaven. With the aid of these pills, he felt like himself again. He blessed his own life. He cooked some decent meals; he called his boyfriend in Seattle; he went around town looking for a job;

he made plans to get himself to the Pacific Northwest. When the drugs ran out and the pain returned, worse this time, like being stabbed in his elbows and shoulders, along with the novelty of addiction's chills and fevers, the friend of a friend told him that if he wanted more pills at the going street rate, he had better go see Black Bird. He could find Black Bird at the bar of a club, the Inner Circle, on Hennepin Avenue. "He's always there," the friend of a friend said. "He's there now. He reads. The guy sits there studying Shakespeare. Used to be a scholar or something. Pretends to be a Native American, one of those imposter types. Very easy to spot. I'll tell him you're coming."

The next Wednesday, he found Black Bird at the end of the Inner Circle bar near the broken jukebox and the sign for the men's room. The club's walls had been built from limestone and rust-red brick and sported no decorative motifs of any kind. If you needed decorations around you when you drank, you went somewhere else. The peculiar orange lighting was so dim that Quinn couldn't figure out how Black Bird could read at all.

Quinn approached him gingerly. Black Bird's hair went down to his shoulders. The gray in it looked as if it had been applied with chalk. He wore bifocals and moved his finger down the page as he read. Nearby was a half-consumed bottle of 7 Up.

"Excuse me. Are you Black Bird?"

Without looking up, the man said, "Why do you ask?"

"I'm Quinn." He held out his hand. Black Bird did not take it. "My friend Morrow told me about you."

"Ah huh," Black Bird said. He glanced up with an impatient expression before returning to his book. Quinn examined the text. Black Bird was reading *Othello,* the third act.

"Morrow said I should come see you. There's something I need."

Black Bird said nothing.

"I need it pretty bad," Quinn said, his hand trembling inside his pocket. He wasn't used to talking to people like this. When Black Bird didn't respond, Quinn said, "You're reading *Othello.*" Quinn had acquired a liberal arts degree from a college in Iowa, where he had majored in global political solutions, and he felt that he had to assert himself. "The handkerchief. And Iago, right?"

Black Bird nodded. "This isn't *College Bowl,*" he said dismissively.

With his finger stopped on the page, he said, "What do you want from me?"

Quinn whispered the name of the drug that made him feel human.

"What a surprise," said Black Bird. "Well, well. How do I know that you're not a cop? You a cop, Mr. Quinn?"

"No."

"Because I don't know what you're asking me or what you're talking about. I'm a peaceful man sitting here reading this book and drinking this 7 Up."

"Yes," Quinn said.

"You could always come back in four days," Black Bird said. "You could always bring some money." He mentioned a price for a certain number of painkillers. "I have to get the ducks in a row."

"That's a lot of cash," Quinn said. Then, after thinking it over, he said, "All right." He did not feel that he had many options these days.

Black Bird looked up at him with an expression devoid of interest or curiosity.

"Do you read, Mr. Quinn?" he asked. "Everybody should read something. Otherwise we all fall down into the pit of ignorance. Many are down there. Some people fall in it forever. Their lives mean nothing. They should not exist." Black Bird spoke these words in a bland monotone.

"I don't know what to read," Quinn told him, his legs shaking.

"Too bad," Black Bird said. "Next time you come here, bring a book. I need proof you exist. The Minneapolis Public Library is two blocks away. But if you come back, bring the money. Otherwise, there's no show."

Quinn was living very temporarily in a friend's basement in Northeast Minneapolis. His parents, in a traditional Old World gesture, had disowned him after he had come out, so he couldn't call on them for support. They had uttered several unforgettable verdicts about his character, sworn they would never see him again, and that was that.

He had a sister who lived in Des Moines with her husband and two children. She did not like what she called Quinn's "sexual preferences" and had a tendency to hang up on him. None of his friends from high school had any money he could borrow; the acquaintance in whose basement he was staying was behind on his rent. His student debt had been taken up by a collection agency, which was calling him three times a day.

Quinn's boyfriend in Seattle, a field rep for a medical supply company, had a thing about people borrowing money. He might break up with Quinn if Quinn asked him for a loan. He could be prickly, the boyfriend, and the two of them were still on a trial basis anyway. They had met in Africa and had fallen in love over there. The love might not travel if Quinn brought up the subject of debts or his viral arthritis and inflammation or the drug habit he had recently acquired.

Now that the painkillers had run out, a kind of groggy unfocused physical discomfort had become Quinn's companion day and night. He lived in the house that the pain had designed for him. The Mayo Clinic had not called him back, and the meadowsweet's effect was like a cup of water dropped on a house fire. Sometimes the pain started in Quinn's knees and circled around Quinn's back until it located itself in his shoulders, like exploratory surgery performed using a Swiss Army knife. He had acquired the jitters and a runny nose and a swollen tongue and cramps. He couldn't sleep and had diarrhea. He was a mess, and the knowledge of the mess he had become made the mess worse. The necessity of opiates became a supreme idea that forced out all the other ideas until only one thought occupied Quinn's mind: *Get those painkillers.* He didn't think he was a goner yet, though.

He could no longer tell his dreams from his waking life. The things around him began to take on the appearance of stage props made from cardboard. Other people—pedestrians—looked like shadow creatures giving off a stinky perfume.

In the basement room where he slept, there was, leaning against the wall, a baseball bat, a Louisville Slugger, and one night after dark, in a dreamlike hallucinatory fever, he took it across the Hennepin Avenue Bridge to a park along the Mississippi, where he hid hotly shivering behind a tree until the right sort of prosperous person walked by. Quinn felt as if he were under orders to do what he was about to do. The man he chose wore a T-shirt and jeans and seemed fit but not so strong as to be dangerous, and after rushing out from the shadows, Quinn hit him with the baseball bat in the back of his legs. He had aimed for the back of the legs so he wouldn't shatter the guy's kneecaps. When Quinn's victim fell down, Quinn reached into the man's trouser pocket and pulled out his wallet and ran away with it, dropping the Slugger into the river as he crossed the bridge.

Back in his friend's basement, Quinn examined the wallet's contents. His hands were trembling again, and he couldn't see properly, and he wasn't sure he was awake, but he could make out that the name on the driver's license was Benjamin Takemitsu. The man didn't look Japanese in the driver's license photo, but Quinn didn't think much about it until he'd finished counting the cash, which amounted to $321, an adequate sum for a few days' relief. At that point he gazed more closely at the photo and saw that Takemitsu appeared to be intelligently thoughtful. What had he done to this man? Familiar pain flared behind Quinn's knees and in his neck, punishment he recognized that he deserved, and the pain pushed out everything else.

He called his boyfriend in Seattle. In a panic he told him that he had robbed someone named Benny Takemitsu, that he had used a baseball bat. The boyfriend said, "You've had a bad dream, Matty. That didn't happen. You would never do such a thing. Go back to sleep, sweetheart, and I'll call you tomorrow."

After that he lay awake wondering what had become of the person he had once been, the one who had gone to Africa. To the ceiling he said, "I am no longer myself." He did not know who this new person was, the man whom he had become, but when he finally fell asleep, he saw in his dream one of those shabby castoffs with whom you wouldn't want to have any encounters, any business at all, someone who belonged on the sidewalk with a cardboard sign that read HELP ME. The man was crouched behind a tree in the dark, peering out with feverish eyes. His own face was the face of the castoff.

Somehow he would have to make it up to Benny Takemitsu.

In the Inner Circle, when Quinn entered, Black Bird did not look up. He was seated in his usual place, and once again his finger was traveling down the page. *Cymbeline,* this time, a play that Quinn had never read.

"It's you," Black Bird said.

"Yes," Quinn said.

"Did you bring a book of your own?"

"No."

"All right," Black Bird said. "I can't say I'm surprised."

He then issued elaborate instructions to Quinn about where in the men's room to put the money, and when he, Black Bird, would retrieve it. The entire exchange took over half an hour, though the procedure hardly seemed secret or designed to fool anyone. When Quinn finally returned to his basement room, he had already gulped down two of the pills, and his relief soon grew to a great size. He felt his humanity restored until his mottled face appeared before him in the bathroom mirror, and then he realized belatedly what terrible trouble he was in.

Two days later he disappeared.

2

That was as far as I got whenever I tried to compose an account of what happened to Matty Quinn—my boyfriend, my soulmate, my future life—the man who mistakenly thought I was a tightwad. I *was* very thrifty in Ethiopia, convinced that Americans should not spend large sums in front of people who owned next to nothing. But to Matty I would have given anything. Upon his return to Minneapolis he had called me up and texted and e-mailed me with these small clues about the medical ordeal he was going through, and I had not understood; then he had called to say that he had robbed this Takemitsu, and I had not believed him. Then he disappeared from the world, from his existence and mine.

Two weeks later the investigating officer in the Minneapolis Police Department (whom I had contacted in my desperation) told me that I could certainly come to survey the city if I wished to. After all, this Officer Erickson said, nothing is stopping you from trying to find your friend, although I understand that your permanent home is in Seattle and you do not know anyone here. It's a free country, so you're welcome to try. However, circumstances being what they are, I wouldn't get your hopes up if I were you. The odds are against it. People go missing, he said. Addicts especially. The street absorbs them. Your friend might be living in a ditch.

He did not say these words with the distancing sarcasm or condescension that straight men sometimes use on queers. He simply sounded bored and hopeless.

Matthew Quinn. First he was Matt. Then he was Matty. These two syllables formed on my tongue as I spoke his name repeatedly into his ear and then into his mouth. That was before he was gone.

This is how we'd met: I had come by the clinic, the one where he worked, to deliver some medical supplies from the company I was then working for, and I saw him near a window whose slatted light fell across the face of a feverish young woman who lay on a bed under mosquito netting. She was resting quietly with her eyes closed and her hand rising to her forehead in an almost unconscious gesture. She was very thin. You could see it in her skinny veined forearms and her prominent cheekbones. On one cheekbone was a J-shaped scar.

Close by, a boy about nine years old sat on a chair, watching her. I had the impression that they had both been there, mother and son, for a week or so. Four other patients immobilized by illness were in other beds scattered around the room. Outside a dog barked in the local language, Amharic, and the air inside remained motionless except for some random agitation under a rattling ceiling fan. The hour was just past midday, and very hot.

That's when I noticed Quinn: he was approaching the woman with a cup in his hand, and after getting himself underneath the mosquito netting, he supported her head as he helped her drink the water, or medicine (I couldn't see what it was), in the cup. Then he turned and, still under the mosquito netting, spoke to the boy in Amharic. His Amharic was better than mine, but I could understand it. He was saying that the boy's mother would be all right but that her recovery would take some time.

The boy nodded.

It was a small, simple gesture of kindness, his remembering to speak to that child. Not everybody would go to the effort. Even when the woman's husband arrived—sweaty, gesticulating, his eyes narrowed with irritation and fear—to complain about the conditions, Quinn smiled, sat him down, and calmed him. Soon the three of them were speaking softly, so that I could not hear what they said.

Young white Americans come to Africa all the time, some to make money, as I did, others in the grip of mostly harmless youthful idealistic delusions. Much of the time, they are operating out of the purest postcolonial sentimentality. I was there on business, for which I don't apologize. But when I saw that this man, Matty

Quinn, was indeed doing good works without any hope of reward, it touched me. Compassion was an unthinking habit with him. He was kind by nature, without anyone asking him to be.

Sometimes you arrive at love before going through the first stage of attraction. The light from the window illuminated his body as he helped that sick woman and then squatted to speak to the boy and his father. After that I found myself imprinted with his face; it gazed at me in daydreams. Here it is, or was: slightly narrow, with hooded eyes and thick eyebrows over modestly stubbled cheeks, and sensual lips from which that day came words of solace so tenderhearted that I thought: *This isn't natural; he must be queer.* And indeed he was, as I found out, sitting with him in a café a week later over cups of the local mudlike coffee. He didn't realize how his kindness and his charity had pierced me until I told him about my own vulnerabilities, and the erotic directions in which I was inclined, whereupon he looked at me with an expression of amused relief. When I confessed how the sight of him had stunned me, he said, very thoughtfully, "I can help you with that," and then he put his hand on my knee so quickly that even I hardly noticed the gesture.

Being white and gay in Ethiopia is no easy matter, but we managed it by meeting on weekends in the nearest city. We'd go to multinational hotels, the impersonal expense-account Hiltons with which I am familiar and where they don't care who you are. In those days, before he got sick, Matty Quinn walked around with a lilt, his arm half-raised in a potential greeting, as if he were seeking voters. His good humor and sense made his happiness contagious. A good soul has a certain lightness and lifts up those who surround it. He lifted me. We fucked like champions and then poured wine for each other. I loved him for himself and for how he made me feel. I wonder if Jesus had that effect on people. I think so.

By the time we both came back to the States, however, Quinn was already sick. I said I could fly out to see him, but he asked me not to, given his present condition. He was living in a friend's basement, he told me, and was looking around for a job, and he didn't want me to visit until his circumstances had improved. That was untrue, about the job. Instead, he was losing himself. He was breaking down. He was particulating. When he disappeared, I resolved to find him.

*

Entering the Inner Circle, the bar on Hennepin that I finally identified as the place that Quinn had described to me, I saw, through
the tumult of louts near the entryway, a man sitting at the back of
the bar, reading a book. He did not have graying black hair, but he
did wear glasses, so I made my way toward him, reflexively curling
my fingers into fists. I elbowed into a nearby space and ordered a
beer. After waiting for a lull in the background noise and finding
none, I shouted, "What's that you're reading?"

"Shakespeare!"

"Which play?"

"Not a play! The sonnets."

"Well, I'll be! When in disgrace with fortune and men's eyes!"
I quoted loudly, with a calculating, companionable smile on my
face. I extended my hand. "Name's Albert. Harry Albert."

The man nodded but did not extend his hand in return. "Two
first names? Well, I'm Blackburn."

"Black Bird?"

"No. Blackburn. Horace *Blackburn*."

"Right. My friend told me about you!"

"Who's your friend?"

"Matt Quinn."

Blackburn shook his head. "Don't know him."

"OK, you don't know him. But do you know where I might
find him?"

"How could I know where he is if I don't know him?"

"Just a suspicion!" Doing business in central Africa, I had gotten
used to wily characters; I was accustomed to their smug expressions of guarded cunning. They always gave themselves away by
their self-amused trickster smirks. I had learned to keep pressing
on these characters until they just got irritated with me.

"Come on, Mr. Blackburn," I said. "Let's not pretend. Let's get
in the game here and then go to the moon, all right?"

"I don't know where he is," Blackburn insisted. I wondered how
long this clown had carried on as a pseudo-Indian peddling narcotic painkillers to lowlife addicts and to upstanding citizens who
then became addicts. Probably for years, maybe since childhood.
And the Shakespeare! Just a bogus literary affectation. He smelled
of breath mints and had a tattoo on his neck.

"However," he said slyly, "if I *were* looking for him, I'd go down
to the river and I'd search for him in the shadows by the Henne-

pin Avenue Bridge." Blackburn then displayed an unwitting smile.
"Guys like that turn into trolls, you know?" His eyes flashed. "Faggot trolls especially."

Reaching over with profound deliberation, I spilled the man's 7 Up over his edition of Shakespeare, dropped some money on the bar, and walked out. If this unregistered barroom brave wanted to follow me, I was ready. Every man should know how to throw a good punch, gay men especially. I have a remarkably quick combination of left jabs and a right uppercut, and I can take a punch without crumpling. Mine is not a glass jaw. You hit me, you hit a stone.

Outside the bar, I asked a policeman to point me in the direction of the Mississippi River, which he did with a bored, hostile stare.

I searched down there that night for Quinn, and the next night I searched for him again. For a week, I patrolled the riverbank, watching the barges pass, observing the joggers, and inhaling the pleasantly fetid river air. I kept his face before me as lovers do, a light to guide me, and like any lover I was single-minded. I spoke his name in prayer. Gradually I widened the arc of my survey to include the areas around the university and the hospitals. Many dubious characters presented themselves to me, but I am a fighter and did not fear them.

One night around 1 A.M., I was walking through one of the darkest sections along the river, shadowed even during the day by canopies of maple trees, when I saw in the deep obscurity a solitary man sitting on a park bench. I could make him out from the pinpoint reflected light from buildings on the other bank. He was barely discernible there, hardly a man at all, he had grown so thin.

Approaching him, I saw that this wreck was my beloved Matty Quinn, or what remained of him. I called his name. He turned his head toward me and gave me a look of recognition colored over with indifference. He did not rise to greet me, so I could not hug him. He emanated an odor of the river, as if he had been living in it. After I sat down next to him, I tenderly took him into my arms as if he would break. But he had already been broken. I kissed his cheek. Something terrible had happened to him, but he recognized me; he knew me.

"I was afraid it was you, Harry," he said. "I was afraid you would find me."

"Of course I would find you. I went searching."

He lifted up his head as if listening for something. "Do you think we're all being watched? Do you think anything is watching us?"

At first I thought he meant surveillance cameras, and then I understood that he was referring to the gods. "No," I said. "Nothing is ever watching us, Matty. We're all unwatched." Then I said, "I want you to come back with me. I have a hotel room. Let me feed you and clean you up and clothe you. I should never have left you alone, goddamn it. I shouldn't have let you end up back here. Come with me. Look at you. You're shivering."

"This is very sweet of you," he said. "You're admirable. But the thing is, I keep waiting for him." He did not elaborate.

"Who?"

"I keep waiting for that boy. Remember? That mother's boy? And then when he shows up, I always hit him with a baseball bat." This was pure dissociation.

"You're not making any sense," I said. "Let's go. Let's get you in the shower and wash you down and order a big steak from room service."

"No, he's *coming*," he insisted. "He'll be here any minute." And then, out of nowhere, he said, "I love you, but I'm not here now. And I won't be. Harry, give it up. Let's say goodbye."

I'm a businessman, very goal- and task-oriented, and I won't stand for talk like that. "Come on," I said. "Matty. Enough of this shit. Let's go. Let's get out of here." I stood before him and raised him by his shoulders as if he were a huge rag doll, and together, with my arm supporting him, we walked along the river road until by some miracle a taxi approached us. I hailed it, and the man drove us back to my hotel. In the lobby, the sight we presented—of a successful well-groomed gentleman holding up a shambling, smelly wreck—raised an eyebrow at the check-in desk from the night clerk, but eyebrows have never inflicted a moment of pain on me.

I bathed him that night, and I shaved him, and I ordered a cheeseburger from room service, from which he ate two bites fed from my hand to his mouth. I put him to bed in clean sheets, and all night he jabbered and shivered and cried out and tried to fight me and to escape. He actually thought he could defeat me physically, that's how deluded he was. The next day, after a few phone calls, I checked him into a rehab facility—they are everywhere in this region, and he was quite willing to go—and I promised to return in ten days for a visit. They don't want you sooner than that.

Matty Quinn was right: he was now a different man, his soul ruined by his dealings with Black Bird, or Blackburn, or whatever that scholar of Shakespeare was calling himself these days, and I did not love him anymore. I felt fairly certain that I had gone through a one-way gate and would not be able to love him again. I can be fickle, I admit. Yet I would not abandon him until he was ready for it. In the meantime, out of the love I had once felt for him, and which it had been my honor to possess, I resolved to kill his enabler.

The next night I lured Black Bird outside the Inner Circle. I informed him that I had brought with me a bulging packet of cash and that I would give it to him for the sake of my friend Quinn's painkilling drugs. But the cash was outside, I said, and only I could show him where. I did my best to look like a sucker.

Once in the shadows, I worked quickly and efficiently on him, and then after some minutes I left Black Bird battered on the brick pavement out of sight of the bar's alley entryway. The man was a drug dealer, and I had administered to him the beating I thought he deserved. I would have beaten Matty's doctor too, the one who first prescribed the painkillers, but they don't let you do that; you can't assault our medical professionals. Black Bird had gotten the brunt of it. But the angel of justice calls for retribution in kind, and since Matty Quinn was still alive, so, in his way, was Black Bird.

When Matty was ready to be discharged, I returned to Minneapolis and picked him up. Imagine this: the sun was blazing, and in broad daylight the man I had once loved folded himself up into my slate-gray rental car, and we drove like any old couple to the basement where he had been staying. We picked up his worldly possessions, the ones he wished to keep and to take with him to Seattle. Remnants: a high school yearbook, photographs of the village where he had worked in Ethiopia, a pair of cuff links, a clock radio, a laptop computer, a few books, and clothes, including a dark blue ascot. Not loving him, I helped him pack, and, not loving him, I bought him a ticket back to Seattle.

Saying very little, we sat together on the plane, touching hands occasionally. Not loving him, I moved him temporarily into my condo and took him around Seattle and showed him how to use its public transportation system and located a job for him in a deli. Together we found him a twelve-step program for drug addicts in recovery.

He lives nearby in an apartment I hunted down for him, and we have gone on with our lives. I call him almost every night, whether I am here or away on business. Slowly, he is taking charge of his life. It seems a shame to say so, but because the light in his soul is diminished, the one in mine, out of sympathy, is diminished too. I cry occasionally, but unsentimentally, and we still take pleasure in bickering, as we always have. His inflammations still cause him pain, and he moves now with small steps like an old man, but when I am in town I bring him dinners from Trader Joe's and magazines from the drugstore, and one night he brought over a sandwich for me that he himself had made at the deli. As I bit into the rye bread and corned beef, he watched me. "You like it?" he asked.

"It's fine," I said, shrugging. "Sauerkraut's a bit thick."

"That's how I do it," he said crossly, full of rehab righteousness.

"And I like more Russian dressing than this." I glanced out the window. "Moon's out," I said. "Full, I think. Werewolf weather."

He looked at it. "You never see the moon," he said, "until you sit all night watching it and you see how blindly stupid and oafish it is. I used to talk to it. My whole autobiography. Looked like the same moon I saw in Africa, but it wasn't. Never said a damn word in return once I was here. Over there, it wouldn't shut up."

"Well, it doesn't have anything to say to Americans," I remarked, my mouth full. "We're beyond that. Anything on TV?"

"Yeah," he said, "junkie TV, where people are about to die from their failings. Then they're rescued by Dr. Phil and put on the boat to that enchanted island they have." He waited. I got the feeling that he didn't believe in his own recovery. Or in the American project. Maybe we weren't really out of the woods.

"OK, here's what I want you to do," he said. "I want you to call up Benny Takemitsu and tell him that I owe him some money." He laughed at the joke. Even his eyes lit up at the prankster aspect of making amends and its bourgeois comforts. "Tell him I'll pay him eventually. I'll pay him ten cents on the dollar."

"That's a good one."

"Hey, even Plato was disappointed by the material world. Me too."

"Gotcha."

"Pour me a drink," he commanded. I thought I knew what he was going to do, so I gave him what he wanted, some scotch with ice, despite my misgivings.

"Here's how you do it," he said, when he had the scotch in his hand. "Remember what they did in Ethiopia, that ceremonial thing?" He slowly upended the drink and emptied it out on my floor, where it puddled on the dining room tile. "In memory of those who are gone. In memory of those down below us."

It felt like a toast to our former selves. I looked out at the silent moon, imagining for a moment that he would be all right after all, and then I remembered to follow along. You're supposed to do it outside, on the ground, not in a building, but I inverted my beer bottle anyway. The beer gurgled out onto the dining room floor, and I smiled as if something true and actual had happened, this import-ritual. Quinn smiled back, triumphant.

The Indian Uprising

FROM *Granta*

"THERE'S NO COPYRIGHT on titles," he said. "It wouldn't be a good idea, probably, to call something *Death of a Salesman,* but you could do it."

"I wanted to see the play, but it was sold out. Tickets were going for $1,500 at the end of the run. I did get to New York and go to the Met, though, and paid my two dollars to get in."

"Two dollars is nicer than one dollar," he said.

"Ah! So you do care what people think!"

"Don't talk like you're using exclamation points," he said. "It doesn't suit people who are intelligent. You've been fighting your intelligence for a long time, but exclaiming is the coward's way of undercutting yourself."

"Cynicism's better?"

"I wonder why I've created so many adversaries," he said, then did a good Randy Travis imitation. "I got friends in . . . high places . . ."

"Maker's Mark interests you more than anyone, every time. We used to come see you and we have a burning desire to talk to you, to pick your brain, find out what to read, make you smile, but by the end of every evening, it's clear who's your best friend."

"But pity me: I have to pay for that best friend. We don't have an unlimited calling plan."

"How can you still have so much ego involved that you hate it that my father's company pays for my cell phone and doesn't—what? Send someone to come rake your leaves for free?"

"The super does that. He doesn't have a rake, though. He refuses to think the maple's gotten as big as it has. Every year, he's out there with the broom and one black garbage bag."

"Made for a good poem," I said.

"Thank you," he said seriously. "I was wondering if you'd seen it."

"We all subscribe to everything. Unless we're as broke as I'd be without my daddy, as you so often point out."

"If the maple starts to go, the super will be thrilled, and as a good citizen, I promise to chop and burn the wood in the WBF, not let it be made into paper. Paper is so sad. Every sheet, a thin little tombstone."

"How's Rudolph?"

"Rudolph is energetic again, since the vet's found a substitute for the pills that made him sleep all the time. I envied him, but that's what the old envy: sleep."

"Is this the point where I try to convince you seventy isn't old?"

"I've got a better idea. I'm about to turn seventy-one, so why don't you get Daddy to fly you here and we can celebrate my birthday at the same restaurant where Egil Fray shot the bottle of tequila, then offered the bartender a slice of lime as it poured down from the top shelf like a waterfall. Egil was funny."

Egil, back in college, had been the star student of our class: articulate; irreverent; devoted to books; interested in alcohol, bicycling, Italian cooking, UFOs, and Apple stock. He'd been diagnosed bipolar after he dove off the Delaware Memorial Bridge and broke every rib, his nose, and one wrist, and said he was sorry he'd had the idea. That was years ago, when he'd had insurance, when he was still married to Brenda, when everybody thought he was the brightest boy, including his doctors. He'd gotten good with a slingshot—none of that macho shooting the apple off the wife's head—but he'd caused a significant amount of damage, even when taking good aim. He was finishing medical school now.

I said, "I wonder if that's a sincere wish."

"It would be great," he said, and for a second I believed him, until he filled in the details: "You'd be in your hotel room on your cell phone, and I'd be here with my man Rudy, talking to you from the Princess phone."

He really did have a Princess phone, and he was no more wrong about that than Egil had been about Apple. Repairmen had offered him serious money for the pale blue phone. His ex-wife (Carrie, his third, the only one I'd known) had asked for it officially, in court papers—along with half his frequent-flyer miles, from the days when he devotedly visited his mother in her Colorado nursing home.

"You know, it would be good to see you," I said. "I can afford a ticket. What about next Monday? What are you doing then?"

"Getting ready for Halloween. Looking in every drawer for my rubber fangs."

"Can't help you there, but I could bring my Groucho glasses and mustache."

"I'll take you to the finest new restaurant," he said. "My favorite item on the menu is Pro and Pros. It's a glass of prosecco and some very delicious hard cheese wrapped in prosciutto. Alcoholics don't care about entrées."

"Then we go dancing?" (We *had* gone dancing; we had, we had, we had. Everyone knew it, and every woman envied me.)

"I don't think so, unless you just wanted to dance around the floor with me held over your head, like Mel Fisher on the floor of the ocean with his buried treasure, or a goat you'd just killed."

"You live in Philadelphia, not Greece."

"There is no more Greece," he said. "They fucked themselves good."

Pretty soon thereafter, he had a coughing fit and my boyfriend came into the kitchen with raised eyebrows meant to ask: Are you sleeping with me tonight? And we hung up.

I took the train. It wasn't difficult. I got a ride with a friend to some branch of Metro going into Washington and rode it to Union Station. Then I walked forever down the train track to a car someone finally let me on. I felt like an ant that had walked the length of a caterpillar's body and ended up at its anus. I sat across from a mother with a small son whose head she abused any time she got bored looking out the window: swatting it with plush toys; rearranging his curls; inspecting him for nits.

The North 34th Street station was familiar, though the photo booth was gone. We'd had our pictures taken there, a strip of them, and we'd fought over who got them, and then after I won, I lost them somehow. I went outside and splurged on a cab.

Since his divorce, Franklin had lived in a big stone building with a curving driveway. At first, as the cab approached, I thought there might be a hitching post, but it turned out to be a short man in a red vest with his hair slicked back. He took an older man's hand, and the two set off, waved forward by the cabbie.

This was great, I thought; I didn't have to worry about parking, I'd gotten money from a cash machine before the trip and wouldn't have to think about that until I ran short at the end of the month, and here I was, standing in front of the imposing building where my former teacher lived. Inside, I gave the woman behind the desk his name and mine. She had dark purple fingernails and wore many bracelets. "Answer, hon, answer," she breathed into her phone, flicking together a couple of nails. "This is Savannah, sending you her 'answer' jujus."

Finally he did pick up, and she said my name, listened so long that I thought Franklin might be telling her a joke, then said, "All right, hon," hung up, and gave me a Post-it note with 303 written on it that I hadn't asked for. I sent him Royal Riviera pears every Christmas, books from Amazon, Virginia peanuts, and hell, it wasn't the first time I'd visited, either. I knew his apartment number.

Though the hallway looked different. That was because (I was about to find out) someone very rich had been irritated at the width of the corridors and had wanted to get his antique car into his living room, so he'd paid to widen the hallway, which had created a God-awful amount of dust, noise, and inconvenience.

It was funnier in Franklin's telling. We clinked shot glasses (mine brimming only with white wine), called each other Russian names, and tossed down the liquor. If everything we said had been a poem, the index of first lines would have formed a pattern: "Do you remember," "Tell me if I remember wrong," "There was that time," "Wasn't it funny when."

When I looked out the window, I saw that it had begun to snow. Rudolph had been the first to see it, or to sense it; he'd run to the window and put his paws on the ledge, tail aquiver.

"I hated it when I was a kid and this happened. My mother made me wear my winter jacket over my Halloween costume and that ruined everything. Who's going to know what gender anybody is supposed to be under their Barbour jacket, let alone their exact identity?"

"The receptionist," he said, "is a guy who became a woman. He had the surgery in Canada because it was a lot cheaper. He had saline bags put in for tits, but then he decided flat-chested women were sexy, so he had them taken out. I asked for one, to put in a jar, but no go: you'd have thought I was asking for a fetus."

The bottle of bourbon was almost full. We might be sitting for a long time, I realized. I said, "Let's go get something to eat before the snow piles up. How far would we have to go to get to that restaurant?"

"You're afraid if we stay here, I'll have more to drink and try to seduce you."

"No, I'm not," I said indignantly.

"You're afraid I'll invite Savannah to come with us and give us all the gory details. Savannah is a former Navy SEAL."

"If you like it when I speak in a monotone, don't tell me weird stuff."

"Listen to her! When the only buttons I ever push are for the elevator. I don't live by metaphor, woman. Don't you read the critics?"

He kicked his shoes out from behind the footstool. Good—so he was game. His ankles didn't look great, but at least they were shoes I'd have to get on his feet, not cowboy boots, and they seemed to have sturdy treads. I knelt and picked up one foot, opened the Velcro fastener, and used my palm as a shoehorn. His foot slid in easily. On the other foot, though, the arch, as well as the ankle, was swollen, but we decided it would work fine if the fastener was left open. It was a little problem to keep the Velcro from flipping over and fastening itself, but I folded the top strap and held it together with a big paper clip, and eventually we got going.

"An old man like me, and I've got no scarf, no hat, only gloves I bought from a street vendor, the same day I had a roasted chestnut and bought another one for a squirrel. I can tell you which one of us was happier." He was holding the crook of my arm. "Only you would take me out in the snow for a meal. Promise me one thing: you won't make me watch you make a snowball and throw it in a wintry way. You can make an anecdote of that request and use it later at my memorial service."

He'd had a triple bypass two years before. He had diabetes. He'd told me on the phone that he might have to go on dialysis.

"Is this the part of the walk where you tell me how your relationship is with that fellow I don't consider my equal?"

"Did I bring him up?" I said.

"No, I did. So is he still not my equal?"

"I feel disloyal talking about him. He lost his job. He hasn't been in a very good mood."

"Take him dancing," he said. "Or read him my most optimistic poem: 'Le petit rondeau, le petit rondeau.' That one was a real triumph. He'll want to know what 'rondeau' means, so tell him it's the dance that's supplanted the Macarena."

"I wish you liked each other," I said, "but realistically speaking, he has three siblings and the only one he talks to is his sister."

"I could wear a wig. Everybody's getting chemo now, so they're making very convincing hair."

We turned the corner. Snow was falling fast, and people hurried along. He wasn't wearing a hat or a scarf. What had I been thinking? In solidarity, I left my little knitted beret folded in my coat pocket.

"Let's go there," he said, pointing to a Mexican restaurant. "Who wants all those truffles and frills? A cold Dos Equis on a cold day, a beef burrito. That'll be fine."

I could tell that walking was an effort. Also, I'd realized his shoes were surprisingly heavy as I put them on.

We went into the Mexican restaurant. Two doctors in scrubs were eating at one of the two front tables. An old lady and a young woman sat at another. We were shown to the backroom, where a table of businessmen were laughing. I took off my coat and asked Franklin if he needed help with his. "My leg won't bend," he said. "That's happened before. It locks. I can sit down, but I'm going to need an arm."

"Seriously?"

"Yes."

The waiter reached around us and put menus on the table and rushed away. I pulled out a chair. How was I going to get it near the table again, though? I was just about to push it a little closer to the table when Franklin made a hopping motion with one foot and stabilized himself by grabbing the edge of the table and bending at the waist. Before I knew it, he was sitting in the chair, wincing, one leg bent, the other extended. "Go get those doctor fellows and tell 'em I swalled Viagra, and my leg's completely rigid," he said. "Tell 'em it's been this way for at least ten hours."

I dropped a glove, and when I bent to pick it up I also tried to move the chair in closer to the table. I couldn't budge it. And the waiter looked smaller than I was.

"Let's see," Franklin said, picking up one of the menus. "Let's see if there's a simple bean burrito for a simple old guy, and our waiter can bring a brace of beer bottles by their necks and we can have a drink and make a toast to the knee that will bend, to Egil our friend, to a life without end . . . at least, let's hope it's not rigor mortis setting in at a Mexican restaurant."

"Three Dos Equis, and you can serve one to my friend," Franklin said to the waiter. "Excuse me for sitting out in the middle of the room, but I like to be at the center of the action."

"You want me to maybe help you in a little closer to the table?" the waiter said, coming close to Franklin's side.

"Well, I don't know," Franklin said doubtfully, but he slid forward a bit on the chair, and with one quick movement, he rose slightly, the waiter pushed the chair under him, and he was suddenly seated a normal distance from the table.

"*Gracias, mi amigo,*" Franklin said.

"No problem," the waiter said. He turned to me. "You're going to have a Dos Equis?"

I spread my hands helplessly and smiled.

At that exact moment, my ex-husband and a very attractive woman walked into the backroom, following a different waiter. He stopped and we stared at each other in disbelief. He and I had met at Penn, but for a long time now I'd lived in Charlottesville. Last time I'd heard, he was living in Santa Fe. He said something hurriedly to the pretty woman and, instead of sitting, pointed to a different table, in the corner. The waiter complied with the request, but only the woman walked away. My ex-husband came to our table.

"What a surprise," Gordy said. "Nice to see you."

"Nice to see you," I echoed.

"I'd rise, but I took Viagra and now I can't get my leg to move," Franklin said. He had settled on this as the joke of the day.

"Professor Chadwick?" Gordy said. "Franklin Chadwick, right? Gordon Miller. I was president of Latin Club."

"That's right!" Franklin said. "And back then, we were both in love with the same girl!"

Gordy blushed and took a step back. "That's right. Good to see you. Sorry to interrupt." He was not wearing a wedding ring. He turned and strode back toward the faraway table.

"Why did you say that?" I asked. "You were never in love with me. You were always flirting with Louisa Kepper. You paid her to cut your grass so you could stare at her in shorts and work boots. She knew it too."

"I wasn't in love with you, but now it seems like I should have been, because where are they now? Who keeps in touch? I never hear, even when a poem is published. It was just a job, apparently. Like a bean burrito's a bean burrito."

"Here you go, three beers. Should I pour for you?" the waiter asked.

"I'll take mine in the bottle," Franklin said, reaching up. The waiter handed him the bottle.

"Yes, thank you," I said. The waiter poured two-thirds of a glass of beer and set the bottle beside my glass. "Lunch is coming," he said.

"I'll tell you what I'd like: a shot of tequila on the side."

"We only have a beer and wine license. I'm sorry," the waiter said.

"Then let me have a glass of red wine on the side," Franklin said.

"OK," the waiter said.

"Take it easy with the drinking. I've got to get you back in one piece," I said. "Also, I don't want to feel like an enabler. I want us to have a good time, but we can do that sober."

"'Enabler'? Don't use phoney words like that. They're ugly, Maude."

I was startled when he used my name. I'd been "Champ" in his poetry seminar. We were all "Champ." The biggest champ had now published six books. I had published one, though it had won the Yale Series. We didn't talk about the fact that I'd stopped writing poetry.

"I hope you understand that he and I"—he tilted his head in the direction of my ex-husband—"had a man-to-man on the telephone, and I told him where we'd be eating today."

"I wonder what he *is* doing here. I thought he lived in Santa Fe."

"Probably got tired of all the sun, and the turquoise and coyotes. Decided to trade it in for snow, and a gray business suit and squirrels."

"Did you see if she had a wedding ring on?" I asked.

"Didn't notice. When I'm with one pretty girl, what do I care about another? Though there's that great story by Irwin Shaw, 'The Girls in Their Summer Dresses.' I don't suppose anyone even mentions Irwin Shaw anymore. They might, if only he'd thought to call his story 'The Amazingly Gorgeous Femme Fatales Provoke Envy and Lust as Men Go Mad.'" He turned to the waiter, who'd appeared with the bean burrito and the chicken enchilada I'd ordered.

"Sir, will you find occasion to drop by that table in the corner and see if the lady is wearing a wedding ring?" Franklin said quietly into the waiter's ear.

"No problem," the waiter said. He put down the plates. He lifted two little dishes of sauce from the tray and put them on the table. "No joke, my brother José is the cook. I hope you like it. I'm getting your wine now."

The first bite of enchilada was delicious. I asked Franklin if he'd like to taste it. He shook his head no. He waited until the waiter returned with the glass of wine, then took a big sip before lifting his burrito, or trying to. It was too big. He had to pick up a fork. He didn't use the knife to cut it, just the fork. I'd studied him for so long, almost nothing surprised me anymore, however small the gesture. I had a fleeting thought that perhaps part of the reason I'd stopped writing was that I studied him, instead. But now I was also noticing little lapses, which made everything different for both of us. I liked the conversational quirks, not the variations or the repetitions. Two months ago, when I'd visited, bringing fried chicken and a bottle of his favorite white wine, Sancerre (expensive stuff), he'd told me about the receptionist, though that time he'd told me she'd had the surgery in Denmark.

The waiter came back and made his report: "Not what I'd call a wedding ring. It's a dark stone, I think maybe amethyst, but I don't think it's a wedding ring, and she has gold rings on two other fingers, also."

"We assume, then, she's just wearing rings."

The waiter nodded. "You want another glass of wine, just let me know."

"He and I had a man-to-man last night and he promised to keep me supplied," he said. "I told you the guy with the Messerschmitt gets drug deliveries? Thugs that arrive together, like butch nuns on testosterone. Two, three in the morning. Black guys, dealers. They're all How-ya-doin'-man best friends with the receptionist. That's the night guy. Hispanic. Had a breakdown, lives with his brother. Used to work at Luxor in Vegas."

"Take a bite of your burrito," I said, and instantly felt like a mother talking to her child. The expression on his face told me he thought I was worse than that. He said nothing and finished his wine. There was a conspicuous silence.

"Everything good?" the waiter said. He'd just seated a table of three men, one of them choosing to keep on his wet coat. He sat at the table, red-nosed, looking miserable.

Leaning forward to look, I'd dropped my napkin. As I bent to pick it up, the waiter appeared, unfurling a fresh one like a magician who'd come out of nowhere. I half expected a white bird to fly up. But my mind was racing: there'd been a stain on Franklin's sock. Had he stepped in something on the way to the restaurant, or was it, as I feared, blood? I waited until the nice waiter wasn't looking and pushed back the tablecloth enough to peek. The stain was bright red, on the foot with the unfastened Velcro.

"Franklin, your foot," I said. "Does it hurt? I think your foot is bleeding."

"My feet don't feel. That's the problem," he said.

I pushed back my chair and inspected the foot more carefully. Yes, a large area of the white sock was bloody. I was really frightened.

"Eat your lunch," he said. "And I'll eat mine. Don't worry."

"It might . . . it could be a problem. Has this ever happened before?"

He didn't answer. He was now using both his fork and knife to cut his burrito.

"Maybe I could run to CVS and find some bandages. That's what I'll do."

But I didn't move. I'd seen a drugstore walking to the restaurant, but where? I could ask the waiter. I'd ask the waiter and hope he didn't know why I was asking. He might want to be too helpful, he might insist on walking us to a cab, I might not get to eat my lunch, though the thought of taking another bite revolted me now. I'd wanted to say something meaningful, have what people think of as *a lovely lunch*. Were we going to end up at the hospital? Wasn't that what we were going to have to do? There was a fair amount of blood. I got up, sure that I had to do something, but what? Wouldn't it be sensible to call his doctor?

"Everything OK?" the waiter said. I found that I was standing in the center of the room, looking over my shoulder toward the table where Franklin was eating his lunch.

"Fine, thank you. Is there a drugstore nearby?"

"Right across the street," he said. "Half a block down."

"Good. OK, I'm going to run to the drugstore," I said, "but maybe you shouldn't bring him anything else to drink until"—and then I fainted. When my eyes opened, my ex-husband was holding my hand, and the pretty woman was gazing over his shoulder, as the waiter fanned me with a menu. The man in the wet wool coat was saying my name—everyone must have heard it when Franklin yelped in surprise, though he couldn't rise, he saw it with his eyes, my toppling was unwise . . .

"Hey, Maude, hey hey, Maude," Wet Coat was saying. "OK, Maude, you with us? Maude, Maude? You're OK, open your eyes if you can. Can you hear me, Maude?"

Franklin, somehow, was standing. He shimmered in my peripheral vision. There was blood on the rug. I saw it but couldn't speak. I had a headache and the thrumming made a pain rhyme: He couldn't rise / He saw it with his eyes. And it was so odd, so truly odd that my ex-husband was holding my hand again, after one hundred years away, in the castle of Luxor. It all ran together. I was conscious, but I couldn't move.

"We had sex under the table, which you were kind enough to pretend not to observe, and she's got her period," Franklin said. I heard him say it distinctly, as if he was spitting out the words. And I saw that the waiter was for the first time flummoxed. He looked at me as if I could give him a clue, but damn it, all I was managing to whisper was "OK," and I wasn't getting off the floor.

"The color's coming back to your face," my ex-husband said. "What happened? Do you know?"

"Too much sun and turquoise," I said, and though at first he looked very puzzled, he got my drift, until he lightened his grip on my wrist, then began lightly knocking his thumb against it, as if sending Morse code: *tap, tap-tap, tap*. He and the pretty woman stayed with me even after I could stand, after the waiter took me into his brother's office and helped them get me into an armchair. For some reason, the cook gave me his business card and asked for mine. My ex-husband got one out of a little envelope in my wallet and handed it to him, obviously thinking it was as strange a request as I did. "She didn't have nothing to drink, one sip of beer," the waiter said, defending me. "She saw blood, I don't know, sometimes the ladies faint at the sight of blood."

"He's such a crude old coot," my ex-husband said. "I should be impressed with your loyalty, but I never knew what you saw in him."

Savannah the receptionist came for Franklin, and he went to the hospital—but not before paying the bill from a wad of money I didn't know he was carrying, and not before taking a Mexican hat off the wall, insisting that he was "just borrowing it, like an umbrella."

"There might be an Indian uprising if we stop him," the waiter's brother said to him. "Let him go." He called out to Franklin, "Hey, pard, you keep that hat and wear it if they storm the Alamo."

I thought about that, and thought about it, and finally thought José hadn't really meant anything by it, that a little shoplifting was easy to deal with, especially when the culprit announced what he was doing.

With the worried transgendered woman beside him, and Franklin holding her arm, it was amazing that he could shuffle in a way that allowed him to bend enough to kiss my cheek. "Awake, Princess," he said, "and thank God our minions were all too smart to call an ambulance."

He refused dialysis and died at the end of April, which, for him, certainly was the cruelest month. I spoke to him the day after I fainted in the restaurant, and he told me they'd put leeches on his foot; the second time, several weeks later, he was worried that it might have to be amputated. "You're the ugly stepsister who crammed my foot into the slipper," he said. "And time's the ugly villain that made me old. I was a proper shit-kicker in my Luccheses. I would have had you under the table back in the day. But you're right, I never loved you. Maybe you'll find something to write about when I'm dead, because you sure aren't kicking your own shit while I'm still alive."

If you can believe it, that Christmas I got a card from the Mexican restaurant, signed by staff I'd never even met. It could have been a crib sheet for remembering that painful day: a silver Christmas tree with glitter that came off on my fingertips and some cute little animals clustered at the base, wearing caps with pompoms and tiny scarves. A squirrel joined them, standing on its haunches, holding sheet music, as Santa streaked overhead, Rudolph leading the way. Rudolph. What had become of Rudolph?

There was no memorial service that I heard of, though a few people called or wrote me when they saw the obituary. "Was he still full of what he called 'piss and vinegar' up to the end? You kept in touch with him, didn't you?" Carole Kramer (who'd become a lawyer in New York) wrote me. I wrote her back that he'd had to give up his cowboy boots, but I could assure her he was still full of piss and vinegar, and didn't say that it was an inability to piss that finally killed him, and that he'd drunk himself to death, wine, vinegar, it didn't really matter.

He'd mentioned squirrels the last day I'd seen him, though, so now when I saw them I paid more attention, even if everyone in Washington thought of them as rats with bushy tails. I even bought one a roasted chestnut on a day I was feeling sentimental, but the squirrel dropped it like it was poison, and I could see from the gleam in the eye of the guy cooking the nuts that he was glad I'd gotten my comeuppance.

Then winter ended and spring came, and I thought, even if I don't believe there's a poem in anything anymore, maybe I'll write a story. A lot of people do that when they can't seem to figure out who or what they love. It might be an oversimplification, but they seem to write poetry when they do know.

T. C. BOYLE

The Night of the Satellite

FROM *The New Yorker*

WHAT WE WERE ARGUING about that night—and it was late,
very late, 3:10 A.M. by my watch—was something that had happened nearly twelve hours earlier. A small thing, really, but by this
time it had grown out of all proportion and poisoned everything
we said, as if we didn't have enough problems already. Mallory
was relentless. And I was feeling defensive and maybe more than
a little paranoid. We were both drunk. Or, if not drunk, at least
loosened up by what we'd consumed at Chris Wright's place in the
wake of the incident and then at dinner after and the bar after
that. I could smell the nighttime stink of the river. I looked up and
watched the sky expand overhead and then shrink down to fit me
like a safety helmet. A truck went blatting by on the interstate, and
then it was silent, but for the mosquitoes singing their blood song,
while the rest of the insect world screeched either in protest or accord, I couldn't tell which, thrumming and thrumming, until the
night felt as if it were going to burst open and leave us shattered
in the grass.

"You asshole," she snarled.

"You're the asshole," I said.

"I hate you."

"Ditto," I said. "Ditto and square it."

The day had begun peaceably enough, a Saturday, the two of us
curled up and sleeping late, the shades drawn and the air condi-
tioner doing its job. If it hadn't been for the dog, we might have
slept right on into the afternoon, because we'd been up late the

night before, at a club called Gabe's, where we'd danced, with the assistance of well rum and two little white pills Mallory's friend Mona had given her, until we sweated through our clothes, and the muscles of our calves—my calves, anyway—felt as if they'd been surgically removed, hammered flat, and sewn back in place. But the dog, Nome—a husky, one blue eye, one brown—kept laying the wedge of his head on my side of the bed and emitting a series of insistent whines, because his bladder was bursting and it was high time for his morning run.

My eyes flashed open, and, despite the dog's needs and the first stirrings of a headache, I got up with a feeling that the world was a hospitable place. After using the toilet and splashing some water on my face, I found my shorts on the floor where I'd left them, unfurled the dog's leash, and took him out the door. The sun was high. The dog sniffed and evacuated. I led him down to the corner store, picked up a copy of the newspaper and two coffees to go, retraced my steps along the quiet sun-dappled street, mounted the stairs to the apartment, and settled back into bed. Mallory was sitting up waiting for me, still in her nightgown but with her glasses on—boxy little black-framed things that looked like a pair of the generic reading glasses you find in the drugstore but were in fact ground to the optometrist's specifications and which she wore as a kind of combative fashion statement. She stretched and smiled when I came through the door and murmured something that might have been "Good morning," though, as I say, the morning was all but gone. I handed her a coffee and the Life section of the newspaper. Time slowed. For the next hour there were no sounds but for a rustle of newsprint and the gentle soughing suck of hot liquid through a small plastic aperture. We may have dozed. It didn't matter. It was summer. And we were on break.

The plan was to drive out to the farmhouse our friends Chris and Anneliese Wright were renting from the farmer himself and laze away the hours sipping wine and maybe playing croquet or taking a hike along the creek that cut a crimped line through the cornfields, which rose in an otherwise unbroken mass as far as you could see. After that, we'd play it by ear. It was too much trouble to bother with making dinner—and too hot, up in the nineties, and so humid the air hung on your shoulders like a flak jacket—and if Chris and Anneliese didn't have anything else in mind, I was thinking of persuading them to join us at the vegetarian place in town for the falafel plate, with shredded carrots, hummus, tabbouleh, and the like, and then maybe hit a movie or head back over to Gabe's until the night melted away. Fine. Perfect. Exactly what you wanted from a midsummer's day in the Midwest, after the summer session had ended and you'd put away your books for the three-week respite before the fall semester started up.

We didn't have jobs, not in any real sense—jobs were a myth, a rumor—so we held on in grad school, semester after semester, for lack of anything better to do. We got financial aid, of course, and accrued debt on our student loans. Our car, a hand-me-down from Mallory's mother, needed tires and probably everything else into the bargain. We wrote papers, graded papers, got A's and B's in the courses we took, and doled out A's and B's in the courses we taught. Sometimes we felt as if we were actually getting somewhere, but the truth was, like most people, we were just marking time.

At any rate, we made some sandwiches, put the dog in the car, and drove through the leafy streets of town, until the trees gave way and the countryside opened up around us, two bottles of marked-down shoppers' special Australian Zinfandel in a bag on the floor in back. The radio was playing (bluegrass, a taste we'd acquired since moving out here to the heart of the country), and we had the windows rolled down to enjoy the breeze we were generating as the car humped through the cornfields and over a series of gently rolling hills that made us feel as if we were floating. Nome was in the back seat, hanging his head out the window and striping the fender with airborne slaver. All was well. But then we turned onto the unmarked blacktop road that led out to Chris and Anneliese's and saw the car there, a silver Toyota, engine running, stopped in our lane and facing the wrong direction.

As we got closer we saw a woman—girl—coming toward us down the center of the road, her face flushed and her eyes wet with what might have been the effects of overwrought emotion or maybe hay fever, which was endemic here, and we saw a man—boy—then too, perched on the hood of the car, shouting abuse at her retreating back. The term "lovers' quarrel" came into my head at the very moment the girl lifted her face and Mallory yelled, "Stop!"

"It's a lovers' quarrel," I said, ever so slightly depressing the accelerator.

"Stop!" Mallory repeated, more insistently this time. The guy was watching us, something like an angry smirk on his face. The girl—she was no more than a hundred feet away now—raised her hand as if to flag us down, and I eased up on the gas, thinking that maybe they were in trouble after all, something wrong with the car, the engine overheating, the fuel gauge on empty. It was hot. Grasshoppers flung themselves at the windshield like yellow hail. All you could smell was tar.

The car slowed to a halt and the girl bent to my window, letting her face hover there a moment against the green tide of corn. "You need help?" I asked, and those *were* tears in her eyes, absolutely, tears that swelled against her lids and dried in translucent streaks radiating out from her cheekbones.

"He's such a jerk," she said, sucking in her breath. "He's, he's"—another breath—"I hate him."

Mallory leaned over me so the girl could see her face. "Is he your—"

"He's a jerk," the girl repeated. She was younger than us, late teens, early twenties. She wore her blond hair in braids and she was dressed in a black tank top, cut-off jeans, and pink Crocs. She threw a look at the guy, who was still perched on the hood of the car, then wiped her nose with the back of her hand and began to cry again.

"That's right," he shouted. "Cry. Go ahead. And then you can run back to your mommy and daddy like the little retard you are!" He was blond too, more of a rusty blond, and he had the makings of a reddish beard creeping up into his sideburns. He was wearing a Banksy T-shirt, the one with the rat in sunglasses on it, and it clung to him as if it had been painted on. You could see that he spent time at the gym. A lot of time.

"Get in the car," Mallory said. "You can come with us—it'll be all right."

I turned to Mallory, blocking her view of the girl. "It's between them," I said, and at the same time, I don't know why, I hit the child lock so the door wouldn't open. "It's none of our business."

"None of our business?" she shot back at me. "She could be abused or, I don't know, *abducted,* you ever think of that?" She strained to look around me to where the girl was still standing on the blacktop, as if she'd been fixed in place. "Did he hit you, is that it?"

Another sob, sucked back as quickly as it was released. "No. He's just a jerk, that's all."

"Yeah," he crowed, sliding down off the hood, "you tell them all about it, because you're Little Miss Perfect, aren't you? You want to see something? You, I'm talking to you, you in the car." He raised one arm to show the long red striations there, evidence of what had passed between them. "You want her? You can have her."

"Get in," Mallory said.

Nome began to whine. The house was no more than half a mile up the road, and he could probably smell Chris and Anneliese's dog, a malamute named Boxer, and maybe the sheep the farmer kept behind the fence that enclosed the barn. The girl shook her head.

"Go ahead, bitch," the guy called. He leaned back against the hood of the car and folded his arms across his chest as if he'd been at this awhile and was prepared to go on indefinitely.

"You don't have to put up with that," Mallory said, and her voice was honed and hard, the voice she used on me when she was in a mood, when I was talking too much or hadn't got around to washing the dishes when it was my turn. "Come on, get in."

"No," the girl said, stepping back from the car now, so that we got a full view of her. Her arms shone with sweat. There were beads of moisture dotting her upper lip. She was pretty, very pretty.

I eased off the brake pedal and the car inched forward even as Mallory said, "Stop, Paul, what are you doing?" and I said, "She doesn't want to," and then, lamely, "It's a lovers' quarrel, can't you see that?" Then we were moving up the channel the road cut through the greenest fields in the world, past the pissed-off guy with the scratched forearms and a hard harsh gloating look in his eyes, down into a dip and up the next undulating hill, Mallory furious, thumping at the locked door as if it were a set of drums and craning her neck to look back, as the whole scene receded in the rearview mirror.

By the time we got to Chris and Anneliese's, Mallory was in full crisis mode. The minute we pulled into the driveway I flicked off the child lock, but she just gave me a withering look, slammed out of the car, and stalked up the steps of the front porch, shouting, "Anneliese, Chris, where are you?" I was out of the car by then, Nome shooting over the front seat to rocket past me even as Boxer came tearing around the corner of the house, a yellow Lab pup I'd never seen before at his heels. The dogs barked rhapsodically,

then the screen door swung open and there were Chris and Anneliese, spritzers clutched in their hands. Chris was barefoot and
shirtless, Anneliese dressed almost identically to the girl on the
road, except that her top was blue, to match her eyes, and she was
wearing open-toed flats to show off her feet. Before grad school
she'd been a hosiery model for Lord & Taylor in Chicago and she
never missed an opportunity to let you know it. As for the rest of
her, she was attractive enough, I suppose, with streamlined limbs,
kinky copper-colored hair, and the whitest teeth I'd ever seen or
imagined. My own teeth tended toward the yellowish, but then
neither of my parents was a dentist and both of hers were.

Mallory didn't say "Hello" or "How are you?" or "Thanks for
inviting us." She just wheeled around in exasperation and pointed
down the road. "I need a bicycle," she said. "Can I borrow somebody's bicycle?"

Anneliese showed her teeth in an uncertain smile. "What are
you talking about? You just got here."

The explanation was brief and vivid and unsparing with regard
to my lack of concern or feeling. All three of them looked at me a
moment, then Anneliese said, "What if he's dangerous?"

"He's not dangerous," I said reflexively.

"I'm going with you," Anneliese said, and in the next minute
she was pushing a matching pair of ten-speed bicycles out the
door, hers and Chris's.

Chris waved his glass. "You think maybe Paul and I should go
instead? I mean, just in case?"

Mallory was already straddling the bike. "Forget it," she said,
with a level of bitterness that went far beyond what was called for,
if it was called for at all. I'd done what anyone would have done.
Believe me, you just do not get between a couple when they're in
the middle of a fight. Especially strangers. And especially not on a
sweltering afternoon on a deserted country road. You want to get
involved? Call the cops. That was my feeling, anyway, but then the
whole thing had happened so quickly I really hadn't had time to
work out the ramifications. I'd acted instinctively, that was all. The
problem was so had she.

Mallory shot me a look. "You'd probably just wind up patting
him on the back." She gave it a beat, lasered in on Chris. "Both
of you."

That was when things got confused, because before I could respond—before I could think—the women were cranking down the drive with the sun lighting them up, as if we were all in the second act of a stage play, and the dogs, spurred on by the Lab pup, chose that moment to bolt under the lowest slat of the bleached wooden fence and go after the sheep. The sheep were right there, right in the yard, milling around and letting off a sweaty ovine stink, and the two older dogs—mine and Chris's—knew they were off limits, strictly and absolutely, and that heavy consequences would come down on them if they should ever slip and let their instincts take over. But that was exactly what happened. The pup, which, as it turned out, was a birthday present from Chris to Anneliese, didn't yet comprehend the rules—these were sheep and he was a dog—and so he went for them and the sheep reacted and that reaction, predator and prey, drove the older dogs into a frenzy.

In that instant we forgot the women, forgot the couple on the road, forgot spritzers and croquet and the notion of chilling on a scalding afternoon, because the dogs were harrying the sheep and the sheep had nowhere to go and it was up to us—grad students, not farmers, not shepherds—to get in there and separate them. "Oh, shit," Chris said, and then we both hurdled the fence and were right in the thick of it.

I went after Nome, shouting his name in a fury, but he'd gone atavistic, tearing wool and hide from one bleating animal after another. I had him twice, flinging myself at him like a linebacker, but he wriggled away and I was down in the dirt, in the dust, a cyclone of dust, the sheep poking at my bare arms and outthrust hands with their stony black hooves. There was shit aplenty. There was blood. And by the time we'd wrestled the dogs down and got them out of there, half a dozen of the sheep had visible gashes on their faces and legs, a situation that was sure to disconcert the farmer—Chris's landlord—if he were to find out about it, and we ourselves were in serious need of decontamination. I was bleeding. Chris was bleeding. The sheep were bleeding. And the dogs, the dogs we scolded and pinched and whacked, were in the process of being dragged across the front yard to a place where we could chain them up so they could lie panting through the afternoon and contemplate their sins. That was the moment, that was what we were caught up in, and if the women were on their bicycles someplace wearing a scrim of insects or stepping into somebody else's quarrel, we didn't know it.

A car went by then, a silver Toyota, but I only caught a glimpse of it and couldn't have said if there were two people in it or just one.

We never did get around to playing croquet—Mallory was too worked up, and besides, just moving had us dripping with sweat—but we sat on the porch and drank Zinfandel-and-soda with shaved ice, while the dogs whined and dug in the dirt and finally settled down in a twitching fly-happy oblivion. Mallory was mum on the subject of the couple in the Toyota except to say that by the time she and Anneliese got there the girl was already in the car, which pulled a U-turn and shot past them up the road, and I thought—foolishly, as it turned out—that that was the end of it. When six o'clock rolled around, we wound up going to a pizza place, because I was outvoted, three to one, and after that we sat through a movie Anneliese had heard good things about but which turned out to be a dud. It was a French film about three nonspecifically unhappy couples who had serial affairs with one another and a troop of third and fourth parties, against a rainy Parisian backdrop that looked as if it had been shot through a translucent beach ball. At the end there was a closeup of each of the principals striding separately and glumly through the rain. The three actresses, heavily made up, suffered from smeared mascara. The music swelled.

Then it was Gabe's and the pounding air-conditioned exhilaration of an actual real-life band and limitless cocktails. Chris and Anneliese were great dancers, the kind everybody, participants and wallflowers alike, watches with envy, and they didn't waste any time, not even bothering to find a table before they were out there in the middle of the floor, their arms flashing white and Anneliese's coppery flag of hair draining all the color out of the room. We danced well too, Mallory and I, attuned to each other's moves by way of long acquaintance, and while we weren't maybe as showy as Chris and Anneliese, we could hold our own. I tried to take Mallory's hand, but she withheld it and settled into one of the tables with a shrug of irritation. I stood there a moment in mute appeal, but she wouldn't look me in the eye, and it was then that I began to realize it was going to be a long night. What did I want? I wanted to dance, wanted joy and release—summer break!—but I went to the bar instead and ordered a spritzer for Mallory and a rum-and-Coke for myself.

The bar was crowded, more crowded than usual, it seemed, even though most of the undergrads had gone home or off to Europe or Costa Rica or wherever they went when somebody else was paying for it. There were two bartenders, both female and both showing off their assets, and it must have taken me five minutes just to get to the bar and another five to catch the attention of the nearest one. I shouted my order over the furious assault of the band. The drinks came. I paid, took one in each hand, and began to work my way back through the crowd. It was then that someone jostled me from behind—hard—and half the spritzer went down the front of my shirt and half the rum-and-Coke down the back of a girl in front of me. The girl swung around on me with an angry look and I swung around on whoever had jostled—pushed—me and found myself staring into the face of the guy from the black-top road, the guy with the distraught girlfriend and the silver Toyota. It took a beat before I recognized him, a beat measured by the whining nasal complaint of the girl with the Coke-stained blouse—"Jesus, aren't you even going to apologize?"—and then, without a word, he flashed both palms as if he were performing a magic trick and gave me a deliberate shove that tumbled me back into the girl and took the drinks to the floor in a silent shatter of glass and skittering ice cubes. The girl invoked Jesus again, louder this time, while the guy turned and slipped off into the crowd.

A circle opened around me. The bartender gave me a disgusted look. "Sorry," I said to the girl, "but you saw that, didn't you? He shoved me." And then, though it no longer mattered and he was already passing by the bouncer and swinging open the door to the deepening night beyond, I added, my own voice pinched in complaint, "I don't even know him."

When I got back to the table, sans drinks, Mallory gave me a long squint through her glasses and said—or, rather, screamed over the noise of the band—"What took you so long?" And then, "Where're the drinks?"

That was the defining moment. My shirt was wet. I'd been humiliated, adrenaline was rocketing through my veins and my heart was doing paradiddles, and what I was thinking was, Who's to blame here? Who stuck her nose in where it wasn't wanted? So we got into it. Right there. And I didn't care who was watching. And when the band took a break and Chris and Anneliese joined us and we finally got a round of drinks, the conversation was strained, to say the least. As soon as the band started up again, I asked Anneliese to dance and then, out of sympathy or etiquette or simple boredom, Chris asked Mallory, and for a long while we were all out on the dance floor, Chris eventually going back to Anneliese, but Mallory dancing with a succession of random guys just to stick it to me, which she succeeded in doing, with flying colors and interest compounded by the minute.

And that was how we found ourselves out in that dark field on the night of the satellite, letting things spill out of us, angry things, hurtful things, things that made me want to leave her to the mosquitoes and go off and rent a room on the other side of town and never talk to her again. She'd just told me she hated me for maybe the hundredth time—we were drunk, both of us, as I've said, the encounter on the road the tipping point and no going back—and I was going to retort, going to say something incisive like "Yeah, me too," when I felt something hit my shoulder. It was a blow, a palpable hit, and my first thought was that the Toyota guy had followed us in order to exact some sort of twisted revenge for an incident that never happened, that was less than nothing—the girl *hadn't* got in our car, had she?—but then I felt whatever it was skew off me and drop into the wet high grass with an audible thump. "What was that?" Mallory said.

I wasn't making the connection—not yet—with the streak of light that had shot overhead as we'd slammed out of the car.

"I don't know."

"Here," she said, pulling out her phone to shine the light on the ground.

The object was right there, at our feet, cradled in a gray-green bowl of broken stalks. It was metallic, definitely metallic, some sort of steel or titanium mesh six inches long and maybe three wide, like a sock, the size of a sock. And it wasn't hot, as you'd expect, not at all. In fact—and this was when it came to me—the heating had taken place twenty-three miles up and by the time it had got here, to earth, to me, it was as lukewarm as a carton of milk left out on the counter.

It was a sign, but of what I wasn't sure. I went online the next day and found an article confirming that the streak in the sky had been produced by the reentry of a decommissioned twenty-year-old NASA climate satellite that scientists had been tracking as it fell out of orbit. The satellite had been the size of a school bus and weighed six and a half tons and that fact alone had caused considerable anxiety as it became increasingly clear that its trajectory would take it over populated areas in Canada and the United States. A picture of it, in grainy black-and-white, showed the least aerodynamic structure you could imagine, all sharp edges and functional planes, the whole overshadowed by a solar panel the size of the screen at a drive-in movie. The article went on to claim that all debris of any consequence had most likely been incinerated in the upper atmosphere and that the chances of any fragment of it hitting a given person anywhere within its range had been calculated at one in thirty-two hundred. All right. But it had hit *me,* so either they needed to recalculate or Mallory and I should get in the car and go straight to Vegas. I brought my laptop into the kitchen, where she was sitting at the table in the alcove, working a serrated knife through the sections of her grapefruit.

"What did I tell you?" I said.

She took a moment to scan the article, then glanced up at me. "It says it was incinerated in the upper atmosphere."

"'Most likely,' it says. And it's wrong, obviously. You were there. You saw it." I pointed through the doorway to the living room, where the piece of mesh—stiff, twisted, blackened from the heat of reentry—occupied a place on the bookcase, where formerly a vase had stood, between Salinger and Salter in the American Lit section. "Tell me that's not real."

The night before, out in the field, she'd warned me not to touch it—"It's dirty, it's nothing, just some piece of junk"—but I knew better. I knew right away. I took it up gingerly between thumb and forefinger, expecting heat, expecting the razor bite of steel on unprotected flesh, and thinking of *The War of the Worlds* in its most recent cinematic iteration, but after we'd had a moment to examine it under the pale gaze of the cell phone and see how utterly innocuous it was, I handed it to her as reverently as if it were a religious relic. She held it in one hand, running her thumb over the braid of the mesh, then passed it back to me. "It feels warm," she said. "You don't really think it came from that meteor or whatever it was?" She turned her face to the sky.

"Satellite," I told her. "Last I heard they said it was going to come down in Canada someplace."

"But they were wrong, is that what you're saying?"

I couldn't see her features, but I could hear the dismissiveness in her voice. We'd been fighting all day, fighting to the point of exhaustion, and it infuriated me to think she wouldn't even give me this. "They've been wrong before," I said, and then I cradled the thing under one arm and started back across the field without bothering to see if she was coming or not.

Now she said, "Don't be crazy. It's just some piece of a car or a tractor or something—or a lawnmower. It fell off a lawnmower, I'll bet anything."

"A lawnmower in the sky? It hit me. Right here, on the shoulder." I jerked at the neck of my T-shirt and pulled it down over my left shoulder in evidence.

"I don't see anything."

"There's a red mark there, I'm telling you—I saw it in the mirror this morning."

She just stared at me.

A week slid by. The heat never broke, not even after a series of thunderstorms rumbled in under a sky the color of bruised flesh—all the rain managed to do was drive up the humidity. We were supposed to be enjoying ourselves, we were supposed to be on vacation, but we didn't do much of anything. We sat around and sweated and tried to avoid contact as much as possible. Dinner was salad or takeout and we ate at the kitchen table, where the fan was, books propped in our hands. It was hard on the dog, what with the complication of his fur, which was made for another climate altogether, and I took him for increasingly longer walks, just to get out of the house. Twice I led him to the park where the satellite had sloughed its skin, and if I combed the grass there looking for evidence—metal, more metal, a screw, a bolt—I never said a word about it to anybody, least of all Mallory. What did I find? A whole world of human refuse—bottle caps, cigarette lighters, a frayed length of shoelace, plastic in its infinite varieties—and the bugs that lived in and amongst it all, oblivious. I came back from the second of these excursions and found Mallory on the couch, where I'd left her, her bare feet and legs shining with sweat, magazine in one hand, Diet Coke in the other. She didn't even glance up at me, but I could see right away there was something different about her, about the way she was holding herself, as if she knew something I didn't.

"I took the dog to the park," I said, looping his leash over the hook in the entryway. "Hotter down there than here, I think."

She didn't say anything.

"You want to go down to Gabe's for a drink? How does a G. & T. sound?"

"I don't know," she said, looking up at me for the first time. "I guess so. I don't care."

It was then that my gaze happened to fall on the bookcase, on the gap there, where the old paperback of *Nine Stories* had fallen flat. "Where's the thing?" I said.

"What thing?"

"The mesh. My *mesh*."

She shrugged. "I tossed it."

"Tossed it? Where? What do you mean?"

In the next moment I was in the kitchen, flipping open the lid of the trashcan, only to find it empty. "You mean outside?" I shouted. "In the dumpster?"

When I came thundering back into the room, she still hadn't moved. "Jesus, what were you thinking? That was mine. I wanted that. I wanted to keep it."

Her lips barely moved. "It was dirty."

I must have spent half an hour out there, poking through the side-by-side dumpsters that served our building and the one across the alley from it. I was embarrassed, I'll tell you, people strolling by and looking at me like I was one of the homeless, a can man, a bottle redeemer, and I was angry too, and getting angrier. She had no right, that was what I kept telling myself—she'd done it just to spite me, I knew it, and the worst thing, the saddest thing, was that now I'd never know if that piece of mesh was the real deal or not. I could have sent it to NASA, to the Jet Propulsion Laboratory, to somebody who could say yea or nay. But not now. Not anymore.

When I came back up the stairs, sweating and with the reek of rotting vegetables and gnawed bones and all the rest hanging around me like a miasma, I went right for her. I took hold of her arm, slapped the magazine away, and jerked her to her feet. She looked scared, and that just set me off all the more. I might have pushed her. She might have pushed back. Next thing I was out the door, out on the street, fuming, the sun still glaring overhead, everything before me looking as ordinary as dishwater. There was a bar down the street—air conditioning, music, noise, people, a change of mood that was as easy to achieve as switching channels on the TV—and I was actually on my way there, my shoulders tense as wire, when I stopped myself. I patted down my pockets: wallet, keys, cell phone, a dribble of dimes and quarters. I didn't have a comb or a toothbrush or a change of underwear, I didn't have books or my iPod or the dog, but none of that seemed to matter, not anymore. A couple in shorts and running shoes flashed by me, breathing noisily. A motor scooter backfired across the street.

We kept the car in the lot out back of the apartment. I went the long way around the building, keeping close to the wall, in case Mallory was at the front window, looking to see where I'd gone off to. The tank showed less than a quarter full, and my wallet held three fives and three singles—along with the change, that gave me a grand total of nineteen dollars and ninety-five cents. No matter. I'd stop at the ATM on the way out of town, and if things got desperate I did have a credit card, which we reserved for emergencies only, because we really struggled just to make the minimum payment every month. Was this an emergency? Mallory wouldn't think so. The geniuses from NASA might not think so, either—or the farmer whose sheep bore crusted-over scabs on their legs and throats and sad white faces. But as I wheeled the car out of the lot I couldn't help thinking it was the biggest emergency of my life.

I didn't know where I was going. I had no idea beyond the vague notion of putting some miles behind me, heading north, maybe, until the corn gave way to forest, to pines as fragrant as the air that went cold at night and seeped in through the open window so that you had to pull a blanket over you when you went to sleep. The car—the rusted-out Volvo wagon Mallory's mother used to drive to work back in Connecticut—shuddered and let out a grinding mechanical whine as I pulled up in front of the bank. I got out, mounted the three steps to the concrete walkway where the ATM was, and waited the requisite six feet six inches away from the middle-aged woman in inflated khaki shorts who was just then feeding in her card. The heat was staggering. My shirt was wet as a dishrag, my hair hanging limp. I wasn't thinking, just doing.

It was then that I glanced up and noticed the silver Toyota parked in the lot of the ice-cream parlor next door. A woman and two kids emerged from the building, licking cones, and went off down the street, and then the door swung open again and there was the blond girl, her own cone—the pale green of pistachio—held high and her face twisted in a grimace as she said something over her shoulder to the guy behind her. He was wearing the same T-shirt he'd worn that day on the road and he didn't have an ice cream of his own, but as he came through the door he twisted his face too, and snatched at the girl's arm. She let out a cry, and then the ice cream, double scoop, which had already begun to melt in green streaks across the back of her hand, slipped from the cone to plop wetly at her feet, just like anything else subject to the law of gravity.

"You creep!" she shouted. "Look what you did." And he said something back. And then she said something. And then I was no longer watching them, because, as far as I was concerned, they could go careering around the world on any orbit they wanted, just so long as it never intersected mine again. Space debris that collides in two wide bands of low Earth orbit, at 620 and at 930 miles up, can fragment and fragment again—things as big as satellites and rocket boosters and as small as the glove the astronaut Ed White lost on the first U.S. space walk. Eventually, it's all going to come down, and whether it'll burn up or crush a house or tap somebody on the shoulder in a dark field on a dark night is anybody's guess.

The woman at the ATM seemed to be having trouble with her card—no bills had yet appeared, and she kept punching at the keys and reinserting the card as if sheer repetition would wear the machine down. I had time. I was very calm. I pulled out my cell and called Mallory. She answered on the first ring. "Yeah?" she snapped, angry still. "What do you want?"

I didn't say anything, not a word. I just pressed my thumb to the off switch and broke the connection. But what I'd wanted to say was that I'd taken the car and that I'd be back, I was pretty sure I'd be back, and that she should feed the dog and pay the rent, which was due the first of the month, and if she went out at night—if she went out at all—she should remember to look up, look up high, way up there, where the stars burn and the space junk roams, because you never can tell what's going to come down next.

PETER CAMERON

After the Flood

FROM *Subtropics*

THE DJUKANOVICS CAME to live with us after the flood because they had nowhere else to go. Well, that's not really true. They had plenty of places to go, they had the whole world to go to, but they came to us, and that was because of Reverend Judy. It was her idea, and Reverend Judy's a very persuasive person. I suppose that's a good quality in a minister, but I have to say I find it somewhat grating. The Djukanovics had to go somewhere because their house was condemned. One wall had buckled and the roof had caved in. Everyone said how lucky it was that they weren't all killed when the house collapsed, but they were not killed. Although they did lose pretty much everything they owned.

The Sunday after the flood, I was leaving church and Reverend Judy was standing in the vestibule saying hello or something cheerful (I suppose) to every person who passed by. This meant it took almost forever to get out of church, especially if you sit up front where Robert and I like to sit on account of the acoustics. Or lack thereof. Anyway, on the Sunday after the flood, when Robert and I finally made it to the vestibule, Reverend Judy clutched my hand—she really clutched it, and sort of shook it, as if it was frostbitten and she was trying to revive it—and told me she had something special to talk about with me and could she stop by our house tomorrow morning? Well, on account of all the people behind us pressing forward, eager to get this part of the day behind them, I agreed, because I didn't have my wits about me to say no.

I am not a fan of Reverend Judy. She has been at the church for about a year, and most people are just crazy about her. For one

thing, it bothers me that she calls herself Reverend Judy. Our last
minister, George Abbott, called himself Pastor Abbott, and that
was just fine. But Reverend Judy thinks she's better than a pastor.
And I don't think the "Judy" goes very well with the "Reverend." I
mean, if you want to be called Reverend, you'd think you'd want
the dignity of your last name, and call yourself Reverend Halliday-
Ortiz (which is Judy's last name). But no. Reverend Judy is part of
this new generation of church folk who are all het up on making
the church contemporary and attractive to young people. Her first
sermon was all about bringing the church into the twenty-first century, as if we had been languishing in the Dark Ages. But as I said, I
am in the minority as far as Reverend Judy is concerned. Everyone
else in the congregation adores her, they think she's just wonderful with her funny glasses (all different colors and shapes, she must
spend a fortune on them) and because she adopted two little girls
from China, or maybe Korea, named Isabelle and Carlotta.

Anyway, on Monday morning Reverend Judy arrived and we sat
down in the living room. I made sure Robert was there because I
didn't want to be alone with Reverend Judy. I know that may sound
silly since she is a minister after all, but I get these feelings about
some people, and I had gotten a feeling about Reverend Judy that
I couldn't shake, so Robert and I sat on the sofa and Reverend
Judy sat in Robert's chair and we chitchatted awhile, and then Reverend Judy said the reason she was there was because the Djukanovics needed a place to live, and since we had this big house all to
ourselves, she thought we would be the perfect refuge for them
and she was sure it wouldn't be long until they were back on their
feet and she knew we were good Christians and would want to do
the Lord's work. Then she got up rather suddenly and said it had
all been arranged, there was nothing for us to do except open our
house and our hearts, and that the Djukanovics would be there
that evening. Apparently there was some sort of ice-cream social at
the shelter that afternoon that they didn't want to miss.

After she had gone, Robert and I just sat there because we didn't
know what had happened or what we should do. I think we honestly both thought about getting in the car and driving away and
leaving our house to the Djukanovics, but of course that wasn't a
very practical response, and Robert is a practical man, so he suggested we clear out the guest room, which he had been using as
a hobby room, and then I remembered that the Djukanovics had

one child and maybe more, but I was sure they had one because my friend Dorothy who teaches second-grade Sunday school told me that the Djukanovic girl was an odd little fish. She didn't elaborate, but I thought it so uncharacteristic for Dorothy to call a girl a fish, and so it had stuck with me.

Could we put them all in the guest room? We did have a roll-away cot up in the attic we could bring down that would work just fine for the little girl, but Robert felt that since Alice's room was right there across the hall from the guest room, and empty, and even though we always kept the door closed, they'd probably open it at some point and wonder why we had crowded all three of them (or more, if they had more children) into the guest room. So we decided we'd put the little girl in Alice's room (Alice was our daughter) and her parents in the guest room (twin beds) and Robert and I would have to share the master bedroom. I forgot to mention that Robert had been sleeping in his hobby room ever since he'd had his hip-replacement surgery and needed to keep his leg at a ninety-degree angle, which he said was impossible with someone else in the bed, and by the time he was back on his feet (so to speak), I think we both realized it was really much nicer having our own bedrooms, and so we just pretended it had always been that way and continued. I find this often happens in long marriages. Robert and I have been married fifty-three years.

The other reason I was apprehensive about the Djukanovics moving in with us is that I felt I had gotten off on the wrong foot with them. Or at least with Mr. Djukanovic. They moved to our town about six months ago and showed up at our church soon after that, and one Sunday morning during the "Care to Share" part of the service that Reverend Judy had initiated, she made them stand up and then introduced them to the congregation and asked us all to welcome them to our town and church. Or something like that. Well, at the coffee klatch after the service, I saw Mr. Djukanovic standing all by himself in a corner of Fellowship Hall, and although it was not in my nature, I decided to go over and chat with him. I have been trying to be a better Christian ever since what happened to Alice happened, because I read somewhere that adversity often turns people bitter, but if you make an effort and keep a watchful eye on yourself, you can turn in the other, better direction. So I went up to Mr. Djukanovic and introduced myself. He shook my hand, and I noticed that his hand was very warm, not unpleasantly warm, not moist, just warm and surprisingly soft. He was a big man. I suppose I was a bit unnerved by the pleasantness of his touch, for instead of saying something kind and welcoming, I said, "What kind of a name is Djukanovic?" Now, I meant this in a very nice way, not at all like it was a suspicious or bad or foreign name, but I know that's how it sounded because Mr. Djukanovic looked at me oddly and said, "Well, what kind of name is Evarts?" And I said, "I think it's just a plain old American name, but your name is so interesting and I wonder what it means." "Means?" asked Mr. Djukanovic. "It's a name, it doesn't mean anything." I realized by his hostile tone that my question had offended him, even though I had meant it in the friendliest possible way, so I tried to think of how to restore the balm of fellowship to our conversation. "Is it European?" I asked him, because no one can be insulted for being taken for a European, but this seemed to only annoy Mr. Djukanovic further, for he said, "No, it's not European," and he turned away and walked over to the doughnut table and grabbed a fistful of Pop'ems. And that was the extent of my relationship with any of the Djukanovics, and now they were coming to live in my house.

I was born and raised in this town. I always thought I would move away at some point, there are so many things that can take a person somewhere else, but none of those things ever happened to me, so here I am. It's not that I want to live somewhere else; this is a very nice town and I can't imagine a nicer place to live except perhaps someplace where it doesn't snow so much, but I suppose every place has its good things and bad things. Robert also comes from here, and we live now in the house he grew up in (which we have renovated twice). My sister lives in the house I grew up in, but I have nothing to do with her for reasons that don't really pertain at all to the matter at hand, which is the Djukanovics. I suppose in a way that everything is connected in some fashion, but I'd rather just leave Valerie (my sister) out of this. She'll only spoil the story, like she spoils everything. I don't know why I said that about her living in the house we grew up in, so just forget it.

   This is not very nice, but I am going to tell it anyway. When I was a little girl in this town, we called all the folk who lived down along the spillway "river rats," on account of the fact that their houses were always being flooded and if, after a flood, you'd drive along the River Road, you'd see them huddled beneath tarpaulins, shivering and surrounded by the waterlogged furniture they'd managed to drag out of their bungalows. It wasn't until I was much older that I realized how insensitive this was; in fact I thought "river rat" was a term of endearment because my father's pet name for me was Minnie Mouse, and there's not much difference between a mouse and a rat. And besides, we weren't insensitive because we'd always bring old blankets and canned vegetables and powdered milk and things like that to the fire station where the people who were flooded out could just come and take what they wanted for free, no questions asked.

But nevertheless, even though we meant no harm and actually did some good, I have come to feel guilty about our attitude toward those folk who lived in the flood zone, and I suppose one of the reasons I didn't resist the arrival of the Djukanovics was that I thought it might serve as an expiation of any sins of pride or selfishness I had (unwittingly) committed in my youth. So I put fresh linens on the beds in the guest room (once Robert had cleared all his junk off them) and then I went into Alice's room to do the same. I don't often go into Alice's room. It's not a shrine or anything, although it is exactly as it was when she left for college, but I do vacuum and dust in there once a week, although it's amazing when you keep the windows closed how little dust accumulates. Although I suppose that makes perfect sense and isn't amazing at all. I have trouble sometimes distinguishing between the two: what is normal and what is amazing. Anyway, even though the sheets on the bed were clean I took them off and put on fresh ones. They were an old set of Holly Hobbie doll sheets Alice had loved when she was little, and I thought the Djukanovic girl might like them, despite being odd. I cleared out the top two drawers in Alice's dresser and moved all her cheerleading and field hockey trophies off her desk. I couldn't quite bring myself to open her closet. I don't know why, really, but I figured that a little girl who had been flooded out of her home wouldn't have much to hang up. Girls hardly ever wear dresses these days.

The Djukanovics arrived about five o'clock, and despite the ice-cream social at the shelter, they seemed ready for supper. I showed them all to their rooms (there was only one little girl after all, named Wanda) and left them to settle in, which didn't take them

long at all because by six o'clock they were sitting in the den, looking hungry. Mr. Djukanovic had put on the TV news without asking me if he might turn the TV on, which I thought was a bit pre-
sumptuous (maybe I didn't like the TV, or news, or something),
but I was determined to be a gracious host. After all, it would only
be a few days: the county was arranging to have those emergency
mobile-home shelters set up behind the high school, and supposedly they were on their way from wherever they came from, from
wherever the last disaster was.

The moment the Djukanovics pulled into the driveway, Robert
had disappeared down into the basement, where he had lugged
his leather-working equipment. Robert "tools" leather belts and
sells them through the website handtooledleatherbeltsbyrobert
.com, which they helped him set up at the senior center. They're
always bringing young people in to teach seniors about technology and the Internet and what have you, and Robert is very keen
on it. I stay out of it. I was disappointed by Robert's subterranean
defection, but I wasn't surprised, as he doesn't really interact with
people anymore. He worked forty-five years as a car salesman and
did very well for himself (and me too, for that matter) (and Alice),
but he never really liked it and it didn't come naturally to him,
and when he retired five years ago, he said he was never going
to talk to anyone ever again. I don't think he included me and a
few other people in this resolution, I think he meant he reserved
the right to never again talk to anyone he didn't want to talk to,
including, apparently, the Djukanovics.

So there they were in the den, listening to the TV news, or at
least pretending to listen. Mrs. Djukanovic was wearing sunglasses
for some reason I could not figure out and had fallen back into
the cushions of the sofa in a way that suggested she might be sleeping. Her mouth was open. Wanda was sitting on the floor, playing
with what looked like a Barbie doll with no arms. She wore pink
eyeglasses that had those thick magnifying lenses and they did
make her look a little like a googly-eyed fish. Only Mr. Djukanovic
was watching the television. He sat with a disconcerting alertness,
holding the remote in his hand, pointed at the TV screen as if the
minute the news didn't agree with him he would click it off.

I stood in the doorway for a moment, and when it became clear
that my presence—or if not presence, for I rarely feel present
anywhere these days, my existence—was not likely to be acknowl-

edged in any way, I cleared my throat, which is of course a terribly schoolmarmish thing to do, and said, trying for a happy brightness, "Well, is anyone hungry for some supper?"

Because Reverend Judy had arranged matters in such an expeditious, not to say careless, way, there were several aspects of the Djukanovics' living with us that befuddled me. Were we merely providing shelter, or were we expected to feed them three meals a day? (By "we" I mean "I.") Was it a sort of bed-and-breakfast, lunch-and-dinner type of arrangement, or was I meant to let the Djukanovics fend for themselves?

Anyway, this question seemed to be answered by Mr. Djukanovic. He said, "Yes, very hungry in fact."

I thought Mrs. Djukanovic might pipe up at this moment and suggest that she could cook her family whatever type of supper they liked to eat, but perhaps she was really sleeping because she made no movement whatsoever.

"Well, how about some spaghetti?" I suggested spaghetti for several reasons. The first was that I knew I had lots of it, as it's one of the few things that Robert still likes. As he's gotten older, he's been having some problems with his digestion, and his appetite isn't anything like it was. He now refuses to eat any dish that can be considered even remotely foreign or exotic. The second was that so many people don't eat so many things these days. Alice was a special type of vegetarian, I forget which kind, but it made things very difficult when she and Charlie (her husband) and Laila (their daughter) came over for supper, and thirdly because spaghetti is one of the few things I feel confident about cooking. If you can call it cooking. I used to think I was quite a good cook, what with Shake 'n Bake and fried chicken and a nice meatloaf once or twice a week, but now that everything is supposed to be local and organic and good for you, I'm afraid to do more than scramble some eggs (which I do very well, but I didn't think I could offer scrambled eggs to the Djukanovics for supper, even though Robert and I often eat them in the evening).

My suggestion of spaghetti was met with a sort of shrug from Mr. Djukanovic, which I chose to interpret as a yes, so I made a big pot of spaghetti (a whole box) and heated up a whole jar of sauce and it's funny, like hot dogs and hot dog buns, how the quantities never correspond, there was far too much spaghetti, but I figured better too much than too little, and made a pathetic salad from some tired lettuce and a bag of those little baby carrots that are all peeled for you that I find a bit creepy because for some reason I associate those peeled baby carrots with babies being flayed alive, which I know is just horrible and I don't know why I think that but I do. I also wonder if they really are baby carrots or if they are really big carrots that are just cut into pieces and shaped to look infantile. Anyway, despite these reservations, I bought them because I thought they might make a nice healthy snack for Robert and me, but like so many things I bought hoping to brighten or at least alter our life in some way, the carrots had been ignored and their expiration date loomed. (In fact it had passed, but only by a few days.)

That night, something strange happened. Well, I suppose just about everything that had been happening for the past day or two, ever since Reverend Judy had clutched at me in the vestibule of the church, had been strange or at least abnormal, but what happened that night was stranger still. Or perhaps not; you know I have trouble distinguishing the strange from the normal.

After I had prepared the spaghetti/salad supper and set it out on the kitchen table and set three places and told the Djukanovics that supper was ready, I went down into the basement and told Robert we were going to Gully's. Robert doesn't like to go out to dinner because he doesn't like spending money on things he thinks he can get cheaper. In restaurants he's always calculating the "markup" on everything that we order and comparing the price of the meal in the restaurant with the price of the meal had we prepared it at home (and by "we" I mean "I"), but I think he was upset by the arrival of the Djukanovics and just wanted to avoid them at all costs, so he agreed to dinner at Gully's with uncharacteristic enthusiasm.

And then he ordered a bottle of wine with dinner, which I don't think he's ever done before. We don't drink liquor at home, but Robert usually has two glasses of wine with dinner when we go out and I usually have one (and maybe two), but I don't think it has ever occurred to either of us to order a full bottle of wine in a restaurant even though it is commonly done (and much cheaper that way, a bottle costs the same as three glasses, which come to think of it would make it appealing to Robert). It just seems somewhat brazen, the way they just plonk the bottle right on your table for all the world to see.

When we got home, the Djukanovics had gone to bed, and the kitchen was spotless. Things had been cleaned that had nothing to do with their supper. I supposed Mrs. Djukanovic did it (I couldn't picture Mr. Djukanovic or Wanda doing it), and it made me feel a little bit bad for thinking poorly about Mrs. Djukanovic when she was sleeping on the sofa. Of course she was exhausted, what with being flooded out of her home and living in the high-school gymnasium and then moving into a strange person's house. She had every right to fall asleep like that on the sofa. I was glad I had made the spaghetti and was sorry that the carrots had expired, although they seemed fresh enough. Everything was cleaned up and put away. Some things were put away in the wrong places, but you couldn't blame her for that. People have different ideas about where things should go.

But none of that was the strange thing I'm talking about. That happened later. It happened in bed. Bed! Imagine anything happening in bed at my age. Except for dying, I suppose. But no, it will probably seem like nothing to you, but what had happened was that after Robert and I had gotten into bed—and it was awkward, because we hadn't gotten into the same bed together since he had his hip replaced, since what had happened to Alice happened to Alice—but we went about it as if we did it every night, getting into the same bed together, which when you think about it is an extraordinary thing to do. I mean, I know it's perfectly natural but if you step back just a little bit and look at the anthropological aspect of it, it does seem odd, doesn't it? Two people getting into the same bed, at least two people our age, although perhaps it's not odd at all, for you hear about those couples from the Old World who slept together in the same bed for a hundred years and died within minutes of each other, but it was odd for Robert and me. That's all I'm saying. I didn't know what to do or how to behave, so I turned away from Robert and pretended to fall asleep. I was aware of Robert lying there beside me, lying on his back, very still but somehow tense, awake, alive, and alone, somehow alone. Perhaps I shifted a little, I don't really know, but Robert turned toward me and pressed himself against my back and reached over me and drew me closer to him and I could feel his breath and maybe his lips on the back of my neck, and then I felt him shaking, gently shaking, and his mouth was pressed against my neck, and I realized he was crying. Robert was crying. Oh, it's all too much for him, I thought. And I turned over and pushed him a little and he turned too, and then I held him like he had held me, held him close against me, until he stopped crying.

The next morning, I slept much later than I normally do, and by the time I came downstairs, Wanda had gone off to school and the Djukanovics were back on the sofa in the den, watching television. They were watching the show about the little bossy cartoon girl who is some sort of explorer. That was one of Laila's favorite shows. It's odd what children like. For some reason this particular show just set my teeth on edge. When Mr. Djukanovic heard me in the kitchen, he quickly clicked the TV off as if he had been watching one of the pornographic channels. (Of course we don't get any of them, we have the no-frills, very basic cable package, and we only have that because you need it to get reception. I do miss the old days when there were just a few channels and just about everything was worth watching.) Mrs. Djukanovic got up and slunk out of the room and went upstairs. She was wearing a headscarf along with the dark glasses and looked quite—well, not frightening, because I know it's wrong to be frightened of people who wear headscarves and sunglasses indoors, but it was a little spooky. Or maybe I just don't get out enough.

Usually I put the coffee and water in the coffeepot before I go to bed each night, so when I come down in the morning all I have to do is switch it on—it seems like such a timesaver, but of course it isn't—but I hadn't done this when we'd gotten home from Gully's, I suppose because I was a bit discombobulated by everything and perhaps a bit tipsy, because Robert and I did drink the entire bottle of wine, a fact which in the clear light of day seemed quite shocking to me.

"Some coffee, Mr. Djukanovic?" I asked, as if I were in a television commercial.

He pushed himself up off the sofa—he was a big man, not fat really, but just large in a way that made our house and everything in it seem small. He sat on one of the stools at the counter that separates the kitchen from the den and said, "Yes, please. We could not find the coffee."

"Oh, I keep it in the freezer," I said, and realized how silly that sounded. But Alice had told me I should keep it there because it kept better, but I suppose anything keeps better if it's frozen. I certainly would. Why not just have done with it and put everything in the freezer?

Mr. Djukanovic and I watched the Mr. Coffee with undivided attention as if it were some sort of miraculous alchemical invention making gold and not Chock full o'Nuts. When it was finished, I filled two mugs and opened the refrigerator and poured some milk into a creamer because I grew up thinking it wasn't nice to put bottles on the table (or the counter in this case), and lifted the lid from the sugar bowl and slid it toward Mr. Djukanovic. For some reason I was very curious as to how he took his coffee, as if this would reveal something to me, something clarifying and comforting about the entire situation we found ourselves in, and I watched as he poured in milk and spooned two spoonfuls of sugar into the mug, and I thought, Oh, he takes it light and sweet, light and sweet. But I didn't know what, if anything, that meant.

Mr. Djukanovic sipped at his coffee and said, "You are very kind to invite us into your house. We are very grateful. Thank you."

"Why, you're most welcome," I said. "I'm so glad you can stay here with us." I realized that this made it sound as if they were friends or family popping by on a holiday and not homeless refugees, so I said, "I am so sorry about your home, and your misfortune."

"Yes," he said. "It is bad. Very bad."

"Terrible," I said. "Just terrible."

"I must apologize for my wife," he said. "She is very ashamed. Because she is very proud, you see. She is so ashamed."

"Ashamed?" I said. "Ashamed of what? There is nothing for her to be ashamed of."

"Losing our house," he said. "Our house in America. She loved it so much. She was proud of it. And so losing it, and having to come here. It is shaming to her. Also, she does not speak English."

I wanted to ask him what language she did speak, but I remembered how we had got off to the wrong start with my question about his name, and things seemed to be going so beautifully now, so I thought it best to hold my tongue.

"It was not a good house, I know, but it was the only house we could afford," he said.

"Well, I'm sure with the insurance money you can buy a nice new house," I said.

"No," said Mr. Djukanovic. "Because the house was in the flood place we could not have insurance. So it is just lost. Gone. Our house in America."

"Well, I don't think that's fair," I said. "Didn't the county condemn it? If they do that, I should think they'll have to give you something for it."

"Something, perhaps, but not enough for a new house."

"Well, you're welcome to stay here just as long as you'd like," I said.

"Thank you," said Mr. Djukanovic, "but we'll go as soon as we can. And live in a trailer."

"Well, you have a home here," I said. "There's no need for that. It isn't right, my husband and me all alone in this big house."

"You have no children?" Mr. Djukanovic asked.

"Yes," I said. "Or no. We had a daughter but we don't have her anymore. Well, in our memories we do, of course, but not—not here."

"She is dead?" asked Mr. Djukanovic.

"Yes," I said. "Her name was Alice."

"Like in Wonderland," he said.

"Yes," I said. "Exactly like that."

Of course Robert had sneaked down into the basement. I brought him a mug of coffee and a powdered-sugar doughnut. He sat at his worktable looking dejectedly at his belts. He had somewhat optimistically bought three hundred plain leather belts, which he intended to personalize and decorate with his leather-tooling kit and then sell on his website, but so far he had sold only three, and those were to people at church and only because of the Christmas Craftmart (another idea of Reverend Judy's, come to think of it, with half of his proceeds going to the church).

"You can't hide down here forever, you know," I said. I cleared a place on the table and put down the coffee and doughnut.

"I'm not hiding," said Robert. "This is my house. You can't hide in your own house."

"Oh, I think you can hide in any house," I said, but I didn't want to argue about it. "Are you warm enough down here?"

"Yes," he said.

"Would you like me to bring down the space heater?"

"No," he said.

He broke the doughnut in half, and then into quarters, and dunked one of the quarters into the coffee and then ate it. He brushed some of the powdered sugar that had come loose onto the floor. I was aware of him wanting me to go, to leave him alone, but something kept me standing there beside him. Since we moved the washer and dryer up into the breezeway (it really isn't a breezeway anymore since it was winterized), I hardly ever go down into the basement. One half of the basement—the dark side—was full of all the things we kept when we sold Charlie and Alice's house. It isn't very much, most of the things we donated to Goodwill (they will come and clean a house out; they'll take everything, anything), but there were some things I just couldn't bear ending up at Goodwill or in some unknown person's house.

"What are we going to do with all of that?" I asked.

"What?" Robert asked. He dunked another piece of doughnut into his coffee.

"That," I said, and nodded toward the dark part of the basement. "Alice's things. Alice's and Charlie's and Laila's things."

"I don't know," said Robert. "You're the one who wanted to keep them."

"Yes," I said. "That's true."

"It's ridiculous," said Robert.

"Yes," I said. "You're probably right."

"Ridiculous," Robert said again, but this time he said it gently.

After a moment he picked up an awl or something and banged it with a hammer onto a belt, but I knew he was only pretending. He'd probably ruin the belt, but it didn't matter, did it, because he had 296 more.

"I just had a nice chat with Mr. Djukanovic," I said.

Robert said nothing, but continued to randomly (it seemed to me) tool the belt. Surely you had to draw some design on it first and not just whack away at it like a madman?

"They didn't have insurance on their house," I said. "On account of it being in a flood zone. So they won't get any insurance money. And what will they do? How will they buy another house?"

"How should I know?" Robert said. "They should never have bought that one in the first place. You don't buy a house in a flood zone."

"Some people do."

"Yes, some crazy people."

"I don't think the Djukanovics are crazy," I said. "It was the only house they could afford."

Robert said nothing, just tooled some more.

"Do you wish they weren't here?" I asked. "Do you wish they would go away?"

"Of course I do," said Robert. "I wish nothing bad ever happened to anyone."

"But it does," I said.

"I know it does," said Robert.

"So we should help them," I said. "Shouldn't we help them?"

"Yes," said Robert. "We should help them. We are helping them."

"Maybe we can give them this house," I said. "Maybe we should."

"And where will we go?"

"I don't know," I said. And I didn't. I couldn't picture us living anywhere else, not in another house, or an apartment, or a retirement home. But it did seem wrong, somehow, that we, and not the Djukanovics, should have this house. It seemed almost a crime.

"Isn't that what good Christians do?" I asked. "Take the coat off your own back and give it to someone who needs it?"

"Well, maybe a coat, because you can buy another coat. But not a house."

"It shouldn't matter," I said. "It's the principle."

Robert sighed. "Then give them our house," he said. "Give the Djukanovics our house. And we'll go live in the street. Is that what you want?"

"No," I said. "No. Of course not."

Robert said nothing. I wanted to say something nice about the belt, something encouraging, but it really did look ruined, so what could I say?

"Would you like some more coffee?" I asked. "Another doughnut?"

"No, thank you," said Robert.

I stood there for a moment, and then Robert picked up his tools and attacked the belt again, and I went upstairs.

It turned out that both Mr. and Mrs. Djukanovic worked at Odd Lot Warehouse & Liquors but because they had missed work the day of the flood, they were suspended and couldn't work again for a week. This didn't make much sense to me, but then it has been such a long time since I had a job (I used to work in the gift department at Downer's Pharmacy during the Christmas season, but it closed when the CVS arrived, and that must have been at least twenty years ago), so I don't really know what the rules are nowadays. I did suggest to Mr. Djukanovic that perhaps if he explained about the flood and their house to the Odd Lot, explained that it was an act of God, they might make an exception in his case, but he told me he had already done that. I thought about calling Reverend Judy and asking her to look into it, but Robert told me it was none of my business and to stay out of it. Despite our tender moment in bed the first night that the Djukanovics arrived, Robert had become rather snippy with me, but I suppose it was just the strain of having strangers in the house and him spending too much time down in the basement.

I was trying to be especially friendly and kind to Mrs. Djukanovic because I felt so bad about her feeling ashamed, but it was difficult to do much of anything since she always scurried away when she saw me and didn't speak English. So I just tried to be extra nice to Mr. Djukanovic and Wanda. I went down into the dark part of the basement and found Laila's Barbie Dreamhouse and her huge collection of Barbies. They were all a little moldy, but I wiped everything down with Lysol and then left them in the den, and Wanda did seem to enjoy playing with the Dreamhouse, although she ignored all of Laila's fully intact Barbies and only played with her own armless doll. It all ended rather badly, though, because Wanda liked to reenact the flood and make the house collapse and by smashing it so often that it finally fell apart. That was fine with me, I had no use for it of course, but Mrs. Djukanovic was terribly upset about it and actually smacked Wanda, which shocked and upset me although I know in some cultures it's perfectly all right for parents to hit their children. (I never laid a finger on Alice; in fact all you had to do was give her a stern look and she'd be in tears.) So we had to throw the Dreamhouse out in the garbage, and I tried to give all the Barbies and their clothes and furniture and junk to Wanda, but Mrs. Djukanovic wouldn't let her have any of it, and she even took Wanda's own handicapped Barbie away for a day or two as a punishment. It all just seemed so mean and terribly unfair to me.

Robert said if I was going to get upset about every little thing
that happened with the Djukanovics, they should leave, and if I
cried one more time he would throw them all out, so after that I
tried to look on the bright side of everything and keep my spirits
up, and I made sure I cried only when I was alone.

The Djukanovics stayed with us for eight days, and then the emergency trailers arrived and were parked in the outfield behind the
high school even though the baseball season was about to begin,
but apparently no one thought about that. I'm surprised that it occurred to me, but it's the first thing I thought of when I saw them
there, all lined up as if the circus had come to town. Alice used
to play on the softball team and I did enjoy going to all the home
games. The girls looked so pretty in their white uniforms, and the
green grass and sunny afternoons. Alice was the pitcher.

I wasn't home the morning the Djukanovics moved into their
trailer because it was a Wednesday, and I volunteer at the hospitality shop at the hospital on Wednesdays. When I was ready to leave
that morning, they were up in the bedroom with the door closed
and I didn't know what to do. Robert was down in the basement,
of course. It felt wrong to just leave the house without saying goodbye to them, but I had always respected their privacy and never
disturbed them when they were in their room, and I wasn't sure
that I should start now. But then I decided I certainly had the right
to say goodbye to them in my own house, so I went upstairs and
knocked on their door.

There was a muffled kind of sound from inside and what
sounded like a grunt and I jumped back, shocked. Had I disturbed
them in a private, intimate moment? Oh, how horrible, I thought:
this is why you should never knock on closed doors. God only
knows what's going on inside. They were a young couple after all.

But then after a moment, Mr. Djukanovic opened the door and
he had all his clothes on and looked perfectly normal, and I could
see Mrs. Djukanovic sitting on the bed near the window, and I realized I was just being silly.

"Oh, Mr. Djukanovic," I said. "I'm off to the hospital but I just
wanted to say goodbye and good luck with your move."

"The hospital?" he asked. "What is wrong?"

"Oh, no, no. Everything is fine. I volunteer there, in the hospitality shop, on Wednesdays. I probably just get in everyone's way, but it makes me feel like I'm contributing something."

I wasn't sure how well Mr. Djukanovic understood any of this—I doubted he knew about hospitality shops; they seemed so quaint and old-fashioned—but he appeared as though he did.

"Thank you for everything you have done for us," he said. "There is no way for us to thank you."

The inherent contradiction in these two statements baffled me for a moment; it seemed so odd that one person would say them both in the same breath. But I suppose life is full of contradictions like this, and I admired Mr. Djukanovic for embracing them (so to speak).

"There is no need to thank us," I said. "Both Mr. Evarts and I were very happy to have you stay with us."

"You are both too kind," said Mr. Djukanovic.

I didn't think Robert had been very kind at all, but I let that pass. I suppose in some large abstract way his willingness to let them stay with us was kind, even if he wasn't a very good sport about it. "Well, goodbye," I said, "and good luck. If there's anything you need, or anything we can do, please let us know."

"You have done too much already," said Mr. Djukanovic.

I felt we could go on and on in this ping-pongy way, so in an effort to put an end to it all, I said, "Goodbye Mrs. Djukanovic."

She had been gazing fixedly out the window, ignoring the two of us, but when I spoke to her, she looked over at me. And then she did something very upsetting, very odd. She stood up and walked over to us and took my hand in both of hers and then knelt on the floor and pressed her forehead against my hand. She kissed my hand and then she stood up.

Of course I was terribly, terribly flustered. I don't know what I said, but I remember shaking Mr. Djukanovic's hand and then shaking Mrs. Djukanovic's hand and then rushing down and into the garage and driving to the hospital in a sort of a daze.

River rats, I thought, the words coming back to me from when I was a little girl, and I felt ashamed.

A few days after the Djukanovics left, Reverend Judy paid us a visit. She rang the doorbell one morning at about eleven. Unfortunately it was a warm day and I had the front door open, and we saw each other through the storm door, so I couldn't pretend I wasn't home, and then I thought, *What's wrong with you? You have no reason to hide from Reverend Judy.*

She brought me a pound cake, and even though it was wrapped in tinfoil and had what looked like a recycled Christmas bow on it, I could tell it was store-bought, and I thought it was a little duplicitous of Reverend Judy to try to pass off an Entenmann's pound cake for homemade, but then I realized she made a dozen of these calls a day and she'd be up all night baking pound cakes, and besides it's the thought that counts. So I made a pot of coffee and we sat in the living room and drank coffee and ate pound cake and Reverend Judy chatted about various irrelevant things, like she was considering adopting another little Chinese baby and should dogs be allowed off their leashes in Jaycee Park even if a child had been bitten, and I forget what all else because I was thinking about the Djukanovics, and I knew we would talk about them sooner or later.

I'd heard nothing from them since they'd moved into their trailer. Of course I hadn't. Why would I think that I would? It wasn't as if we were friends or anything, or there was any reason for them to stay in touch with me. I was just a stranger who'd helped them a little bit. But for some reason I couldn't stop thinking about them. I suppose that just goes to show how little I have to think about. So I wasn't really paying attention to Reverend Judy, and then I heard her say Alice. Alice!

"What?" I said.

"I know you've had your share of sadness. Of tragedy," Reverend Judy said.

I looked at her. Another thing I didn't like about Reverend Judy was the way she dressed. She looked fine in church on Sundays, she wore traditional vestments, different colors at different times of the ecclesiastical calendar (which seemed a bit pagan to me, like dressing up for Halloween), but when she wasn't in church she dressed very casually, very sporty, and you'd never know she was a minister, you might think she was an aerobics instructor or a golf pro. She was wearing a T-shirt that said JESUS IS MY MVP and some black stretchy pants that didn't come all the way down to her ankles and expensive-looking sneakers. For some reason nothing bothers me more than these sneakers people wear as if they're all going to run the Olympic marathon instead of cross the street. I know this is all very superficial and it doesn't matter what people wear, what matters is who they are inside, but I think a minister should look a certain way. Otherwise it's just all too confusing.

"Alice?" I said.

"It is a terrible thing to lose one's child," said Reverend Judy. "And one's grandchild as well."

This didn't seem to be the kind of statement one should either agree or disagree with, so I said nothing. I thought it was interesting she didn't mention Charlie, but I suppose that under the circumstances, even a minister wouldn't think it was terrible to lose Charlie.

"I'm sure you are still grieving," said Reverend Judy.

I realized that I felt very far away from Reverend Judy, far away from my living room, and it was a lovely feeling, like being at the movies, where everything that matters doesn't really exist.

"Does your faith sustain you?" asked Reverend Judy.

I wanted to say no, but that felt like I was blaming my faith, as if faith *should* sustain you. And of course that assumed I had some faith to blame. It's not that I don't have faith, I do, I think I do, I mean I think it's a little pointless to be alive without faith, but I knew it was not a faith like Reverend Judy's. It wasn't a faith that did anything, really. But I think that's the point of faith, for if you felt that your faith did something, of course you would believe, it would be obvious, it would not be faith.

"I read about what happened in the newspapers while I was still in Lansing," said Reverend Judy. I didn't know she had worked in Lansing before she came here. "But I forgot about it."

"I'm sure you have too many tragedies to keep track of them all," I said.

"When I met with Pastor Abbott, he told me about what had happened to your family, and then I remembered, I remembered reading about the terrible tragedy here in Hurlock. It was remiss of me not to visit you sooner."

"Well, I know how busy you are," I said. "Always racing here and there." I looked down at her sneakers.

"He had lost his job, your son-in-law, wasn't that it? And couldn't find another?"

"He was pretending he had a new job," I said. "Going I don't know where every day." No one ever found out what Charlie did all of those days, where he went when he drove away in the morning. He was very clever though, he never drove more than thirty miles,

which was the distance to and from Manatus, where he was supposedly working.

"And so they lost their house?" Reverend Judy asked.

"It was about to be foreclosed. We didn't know. About losing the
house, I mean. We could have helped them, if we had known."

"Of course," said Reverend Judy. "And that's when he did it?"

I didn't say anything. I was listening, of course, but in the way
that you listen to a conversation from the booth behind you at a
restaurant. I was thinking that the Djukanovics were a mother, a father, and daughter just like Alice and Charlie and Laila had been,
or just like me and Robert and Alice, although I didn't equate Alice with Mrs. Djukanovic, even though they were both the mothers,
but with Wanda. I suppose that's because Alice was my daughter.
I remembered Mrs. Djukanovic smacking Wanda when she broke
the Dreamhouse, and I must have made a strange face or perhaps
even some sort of noise, because Reverend Judy leaned forward
across the coffee table and touched my knee and said, "Would you
like to pray?"

For a second I thought she meant did I want to go up to my
bedroom and pray but then I realized she was asking me to pray
with her, right there in the living room. I wondered if she would
make us get down on our knees, but then I realized of course she
wouldn't, we didn't even do that in church.

"Shall we pray?" Reverend Judy asked.

I realized I had let things go too far. "No," I said. I stood up. I
picked up the plate with the pound cake on it and went into the
kitchen and took it off the plate and wrapped it up as neatly as I
could in the tinfoil. It still had the bow taped to it, and because
we had eaten some of it the bow wasn't in the center anymore, but
I couldn't help that. Back in the living room, Reverend Judy was
standing up, looking at the photograph of Alice and Laila that is
on the mantelpiece. She turned to me but before she could say
anything I held out the rewrapped pound cake and said, "Thank
you so much for visiting and for the pound cake, but since Robert
is diabetic I'm afraid we can't have it in the house."

"Oh," she said. "I didn't know."

"Of course you didn't know," I said. "How could you?"

She looked a little confused, and for a moment I felt sorry for
her. It was a hard job, butting into people's lives day after day, trying to fix all the things that were broken. I gave her the pound

cake and put my hand on her shoulder. "It's all right, Judy. Robert and I are fine. You don't have to worry about us."

She looked down at the pound cake as if she had never seen it before and wasn't sure what it was or what she should do with it.

"Why don't you take that to the Djukanovics?" I said. "I think they'd really appreciate a nice homemade pound cake like that."

When Reverend Judy was gone, I sat for a while in the living room, which I never do, but every once in a while it's nice to sit in there and look out at the street, although nothing much ever goes by. (We live on a cul-de-sac.) The dog from next door, I think his name is Rolly, a sort of beagle-basset mix, waddled over and calmly did his business on our front lawn, and then returned home, and I hoped that Robert, who was of course up in his hobby room, wasn't looking out the window because that dog infuriates him. It was very quiet in the house, and I listened to see if I could hear Robert doing anything up in his hobby room, but I couldn't. He was probably napping. I think he naps a lot up there, and that may be why he was so cranky while the Djukanovics were here, because he couldn't nap down in the basement. I should have brought the rollaway cot down there for him.

I went upstairs and knocked at his closed door, and I felt as wary and daring as I had the last time I had knocked on it, the morning the Djukanovics left.

"What?" Robert said.

"She's gone," I said.

"I know," he said. "I heard her go. What did she want?"

"To talk," I said. "And pray."

"Pray?" Robert said.

"Yes," I said.

"Did you?" Robert asked.

"No," I said. "I told her you were diabetic."

"What?" asked Robert. "Why?"

"Oh," I said. "It's a long story. But I lied to a minister. Were you asleep?"

"No," said Robert.

"I thought you might be napping," I said.

After a moment, Robert said, "Why did you lie to Reverend Judy?"

"I don't know," I said. I put my hand up against the door, my palm flat against it. "I miss Pastor Abbott," I said.

"He knew when to leave well enough alone," said Robert.

"Yes," I said.

"Maybe it's time to stop."

"Stop what?"

"Going to church," said Robert.

"Oh," I said. It had never occurred to me to stop going to church. Robert and I had always gone to church. If we stopped, people would think it was strange, but that didn't really seem a good reason to keep going.

"What do you think?" Robert asked.

"I think you're right," I said. "It's a good idea."

"Because you can still go if you want," said Robert. "But I want to stop."

"No," I said. "Me too. I want to stop." It felt a little silly talking through the closed door like that, and I thought about opening it, but then I realized there was no reason to. I knew what Robert looked like. I didn't need to see him. "Are you ready for lunch?" I asked.

"I suppose," said Robert.

"What would you like? I could heat up that lasagna. Or would you like a sandwich? I have turkey and ham."

"You have the lasagna," Robert said. "I'll have a sandwich. Turkey. With cheese, if you have it."

NICOLE CULLEN

Long Tom Lookout

FROM *Idaho Review*

LAUREN DRIVES until she can't drive anymore. She pulls to the side of the road and a dust cloud rolls over the windshield and into the dark. It's five o'clock in the morning. The headlights flood an irrigation canal black with water, a jack fence, and the beginnings of a field. The boy sleeps in the passenger seat. He's five years old and too small to ride in the front, but Lauren is too tired to fight. He wears a bicycle helmet and her husband's old high school letterman jacket, the letter decorated with four gold winged-foot pins. Lauren places her hand on the boy's back to know he's breathing, and she thinks what she's been thinking since they left Texas—that she has no intention of being his mother.

The boy's name is Jonah, but her husband calls him The Boy. He calls his affair with the boy's mother The Mistake. For five years the boy was no more than a dollar amount paid in child support each month. Then last week his mother was convicted of drug possession, and Child Protective Services showed up on Lauren's doorstep. Mr. Lyle had been contacted, the caseworker said, and he'd provided this address. Was Lauren not Mrs. Lyle, the boy's stepmother and legal guardian? Lauren answered with a hesitant yes, and the caseworker explained in no uncertain terms that Jonah would be otherwise placed in foster care. He had nowhere else to go.

Now Lauren and the boy are in Idaho, and her husband Keller is on a skimming vessel on the Gulf of Mexico. He left Galveston six months ago to work on a commercial fishing boat out of New

Orleans. In the midst of the Deepwater Horizon oil spill he's since gone to work for British Petroleum, laying oil booms off the coast of Louisiana. Lauren hasn't heard from him in weeks. She imagines Keller adrift in a rainbow of oil-slick waters, separated from his paternal responsibility by nautical miles, and she thinks, Fucking perfect: we're both cleaning up someone else's mess.

The last few days on the road have been an experiment in cause and effect—the boy's inability to communicate, his self-destructive behavior, his obsession with maps. In Kansas, when Lauren pried the road atlas from the boy's hands, he banged his head against the passenger window. That's when she bought him the bicycle helmet. When he wet himself in the tumult of a Colorado hailstorm, she put him in Pull-Ups and he's worn them every day since. She's ashamed to admit that for three days the boy has eaten only french fries, that for the past three hundred miles he's been doped up on NyQuil.

Wind buffets the truck, and the boy stirs in his sleep. Through the dark, through her own ragged reflection, Lauren can picture the barren, windswept rangeland of eastern Idaho. She can picture her younger self too, stooping to pass through the barbed wires of a fence. Years ago, Lauren's father brought Lauren and her sister, Desiree, to hike the route of the Gilmore-Pittsburgh Railroad—the ghost of a railroad, once connecting Idaho and Montana—and she thinks back to the rare find of a buried railroad tie, the smell of wet sagebrush, her father bending to touch the pink of a bitterroot flower.

That day feels so long ago she wonders if it ever happened. Nine years have passed and now she's back with sixty-four dollars in cash, a truck in her husband's name, and a boy that isn't hers. Yesterday she called her mother from a pay phone in Denver—their first conversation in six years—and for once her mother had the decency not to ask any questions. Lauren studies the boy in the wake of the interior lights. He doesn't look like her husband but then people change. Lord, do they ever change.

The Beaverheads are backlit by dawn when Lauren arrives in the town of Salmon. She drives down Main Street, the only road with a stoplight, taking in the changes. Savage Circle, the hamburger joint, is now a used-car lot. The old used-car lot is now a real estate office. The hospital is new, complete with a helicopter landing pad for Life Flights over the mountain to Missoula. She passes a Wonder Bread truck, then a flatbed hauling hay bales, and two barking dogs. On the hillside above town, houses begin to wake.

Lauren's sister calls twice a year—on Lauren's birthday and Christmas Eve—and only now does Lauren understand Desiree's concern. Their mother has become a recluse, and the property has gone steadily downhill: warped cedar shingles, rusted wrought-iron fence, flowerbeds usurped by star thistle. The front windows are covered in plastic from last winter. Two signs hang from the front door: FRESH EGGS $3 and NO SOLICITORS.

The boy is awake. He has sleep in his eyes, a ketchup stain on his shirt. Lauren positions the letterman jacket over his shoulders and he wears it like a cape. She nearly closes his hand in the door when he reaches back for the road atlas.

Her mother stands in the side yard, dressed in a mud-hemmed housecoat and muck boots, throwing feed to the chickens. Lauren waves, and her mother goes through the backdoor and reappears at the front. Through the grain of the screen Lauren sees a woman impossible to please—dirt-caked knuckles and a gray braid. Glasses hang from a gold chain around her neck. She raises the glasses and studies Lauren and the boy as if they're a pair of Democrat campaigners, or worse: Mormon missionaries.

"Well now," she says at last, "this must be the child."

Lauren says, "Say hello, Jonah," and the boy says, "Say hello, Jonah."

The house smells of onions and overcooked eggs. It appears in order, but Lauren knows it's merely clutter in a clever arrangement—stacks of old magazines, baskets of yarn and crochet needles, crystal bowls filled with bank pens and buttons and pennies. Lauren prods the boy and he steps inside but stops at the entry rug, and for the first time she and the boy share a moment: neither wants to go any farther.

Her mother turns on the television, and the boy's head snaps forward. Cartoon voices cut the silence of the old house. She places a box of Cheerios on a pillow in front of the television, and the boy goes to it, sits, and digs his hand into the box.

"Dry cereal," Lauren says. "Why didn't I think of that?"

Her mother says, "When was the last time you ate something?" She measures Lauren's waist with the eyes of a seamstress. "You're skinny."

It isn't a compliment, but Lauren says thank you. It takes everything she has, but she says what her mother wants to hear: "Thanks
for having us on short notice." And then, because it isn't just Lauren but also the boy, she adds, "I really appreciate it."

After breakfast they drink tea, Lauren watching her mother and
her mother watching the boy. "I know what you're thinking," Lauren says.

"Oh? And what am I thinking?"

"That I should have left him a long time ago."

Her mother takes a drink. The teacup rattles in the saucer.
She's aged in her voice and hands and both are shaky. "And now
you've left Keller but taken his son?"

The paradox is not lost on Lauren. What she doesn't tell her
mother is that Keller was the one who did the leaving. He called
the move to New Orleans a temporary separation, but as the
months passed their relationship didn't tip toward reconciliation
or divorce but evaporated into a state of apathy. Keller claimed
he was living with his parents, but Lauren knew it was a lie even
before she arrived in New Orleans. His mother took one look at
the boy, balanced on Lauren's hip, and apologized. She said she
hadn't heard from Keller since the oil spill and handed Lauren his
forwarding address.

Lauren drove across the Mississippi River to St. Bernard Parish,
to a white house with sun-faded toys in the yard, Christmas lights
still hung from the gutters. A mailbox shaped like a catfish—its
mouth on a hinge—stood at the curb. Keller's truck was parked in
the driveway, a new F-150 they couldn't afford. A woman came to
the door.

"No, Keller isn't home," she said. "He'll be on the Gulf for another few weeks."

It was the way the woman said *home*, the way she answered the
door in an oversized T-shirt and a pair of men's boxers. A phone
rang somewhere in the house, and the woman excused herself. By
the time she returned, Lauren had unwired the key from behind
the license plate of Keller's truck and loaded the boy and their
bags inside. She hadn't intended to steal the truck, or the boy,
but she wanted to take something away from Keller. It wasn't until
she reached the Texas border—a moment of clarity after the boy
dropped her cell phone in a truck-stop toilet—that she realized

she was truly alone. There was nothing, and no one, waiting for her in Galveston.

"I had to bring Jonah," Lauren says. "It was this or foster care."

The cuckoo clock chimes seven times on the hour. Lauren rubs both fists against her eyes. Her mother says, "And now what are you going to do?"

"Stay and work through the summer, if it's all right with you. I thought I'd start by calling Daniel Walker. Is he still working for the Forest?"

"He's married, Lauren. He has a family."

"Good, because I need a job, not a date for the prom."

"And I suppose you expect me to watch Jonah while you work?"

"Just until Keller gets off the Gulf. Then he can come get his son."

They both look at the boy. The cereal box sits upended, crushed Cheerios dusting the carpet. He's pulled the paperbacks from the bookshelf and stacked them on the floor, and now pencils across the cover of a Larry McMurtry novel. Lauren says the boy's name, and her mother says, "He's fine, Lauren. They're only books."

"They're Dad's books."

"Your father isn't alive to read them."

"Yes, Mom, I know."

"Mom," the boy repeats. "Mom."

Lauren gets up from the table and sits cross-legged on the floor. She opens the boy's road atlas and turns the page to Texas. "Here," she says, pointing to Houston. "Your mother is here." She points to herself. *"Lauren."*

The next morning Lauren drives to the Forest Service office to see Daniel Walker. She brings the boy along to prove a point to her mother. He's sleepy and soft-limbed, and Lauren, wearing a pencil skirt and wedge sandals, struggles to carry him. Her fake snakeskin purse is weighted with baby wipes and Ziplocs of dry cereal, a juice box, Pull-Ups, and the boy's road atlas. The boy wears footed pajamas, a milk mustache, and the bicycle helmet. What he lacks in normalcy, Lauren hopes to gain in Daniel's sympathy.

When she asks for Daniel, the receptionist looks her over and says, "You'll have to wait right here while I call him." Lauren's silver bangles clank as she lowers the boy and raises her sunglasses.

She pretends not to notice when the boy scatters a stack of pine beetle brochures, studies her fingernails as he pushes over a cardboard Smokey the Bear.

The receptionist hangs up and gives Lauren a look, and Lauren says, "Isn't he cute? He wants to be a wildlife biologist when he grows up."

Daniel meets her in the lobby dressed in khaki pants, a collared shirt, and a ball cap with a red fly hooked to the bill. He's the wildland fire dispatcher for the Salmon-Challis National Forest. Lauren knows from their brief phone conversation that he's responsible for organizing supplies and personnel for wildland fire efforts. He's filled out through the chest and shoulders but retained the same boyish face, the same crooked gait he's had since being thrown from a horse when they were sixteen.

They hug, and the weight of his arms feels good on her shoulders. "You'll have to excuse Gina for the high security," he says. "She's new around here."

Lauren looks behind her for the boy. He's halfway down the hall, trying to open a locked door. "Jonah," she says, "come and meet my old friend." When the boy doesn't respond, Lauren picks him up in a bear hug and carries him to Daniel's office.

The room is small and cramped with boxes and filing cabinets. The walls are covered in maps. Daniel says, "This is more of a closet. I work out of dispatch most of the time." He taps the boy's helmet. "Hey, kiddo. You going for a bike ride?"

Lauren picks up a framed photo from the desk. A woman, small girl, and twin boys are dressed in matching Christmas sweaters. "Is this your family?"

"That's Carol, my wife. Anna's six. Evan and Oliver are eight."

"They're beautiful."

"They get that from my wife. How old is your son?"

Lauren thinks back to the year of Keller's affair, the same year as Hurricane Katrina. She considers telling Daniel that her husband fathered a child with another woman and named his trawler after Lauren as consolation. That subsequently, the *Lauren Marie* sank them into bankruptcy. She looks at the boy, standing at the wall tracing the contour lines of a topographic map with his finger. Lauren has never wanted children, but now she wants desperately to show something for the years of her marriage. "Jonah's five," she says. "We've just been so busy since he was born. You know how it is with kids."

"And your husband? Is he here with you?"

"He's working on the oil spill. That's why we're here. I thought it would be nice to spend the summer in the mountains while Keller's away. But"—Lauren brings her hand to her brow—"nobody's seen any money from BP yet, and our funds are a little tight. I was wondering if you knew of any, well, any summer jobs."

Daniel takes off his ball cap and rubs his head. "I'm afraid the application period for seasonal jobs was back in February. As far as I know everything's taken."

Lauren waves away the disappointment. "Of course, of course. I don't know what I was thinking, bothering you at work like this." From the corner of her eye she catches the boy reaching across Daniel's desk. She snaps his name—"Jonah, no!"—and the boy startles, knocking over a ceramic mug. Coffee bleeds through a stack of papers, spills over the desk and onto the carpet. Lauren apologizes while digging through her purse. She kneels awkwardly in her skirt, trying to absorb the coffee with a Pull-Up.

"It's OK," Daniel says. "Leave it." He takes her hand to help her up, and she feels the slightest jolt at his touch, a feeling she remembers from the summer they spent together before Daniel broke his back, the summer before her father passed. A time before she understood the power of a place to bring you down and keep you there.

Daniel pulls his hand away. Lauren says, "We should go. I'm sorry for the mess."

She herds the boy toward the door and is halfway down the hall when Daniel calls her name. "Wait. Don't leave yet." He hitches up one pant leg and limps toward her, his chest heaving, Lauren senses, more from anxiety than physical strain.

"You know the lookout tower on Long Tom Mountain?" he says.

"The *fire* lookout?"

Daniel nods. "The job is reporting wildfires and collecting weather data. Twelve days on, two days off, and overtime in peak fire season." He pauses. "Interested?"

Back in the lobby, the boy jangles the handles on the candy dispensers. The receptionist says, "No-no. Don't touch that." Lauren imagines waiting tables at the Salmon River Coffee Shop, cleaning

coffeepots with ice cubes and salt, collecting fifty-cents-and-a-wink
tips from old cowboys. She imagines her mother waiting up at the
kitchen table night after night, and the seasick feeling of stepping
back in time.

"If it gets me out of this town," Lauren says, "then yes, I'm interested."

Daniel laughs. "Well, it'll get you out of town all right, about
four thousand feet *above* town. Of course there's no electricity or
plumbing, so you'd have to haul your water from the spring and
use the outhouse. But the good news is you could bring your son.
The last lookout brought her kids every summer and they got on
just fine up there."

Lauren wants to say, "But I don't know anything about being a
mother." Instead, she says, "But I don't know anything about being
a lookout."

"You ever seen smoke in these mountains?"

"Of course."

"You ever sighted a rifle?"

"Yes."

"We can teach you the rest. Take a day to think about it and I'll
make some calls. If you can tolerate the isolation it's not a bad way
to spend the summer."

Three days of fire lookout training: how to read a map, how to
use a belt weather kit, how to deploy a fire shelter. Then: first aid
and lookout safety, dispatch and communications, the seven signs
of hazardous fire conditions. The instructor demonstrates how to
use the Osborne Firefinder—a circular map and sighting device
used by lookouts to determine the directional bearing of a fire. It's
not as simple as sighting a rifle, as Daniel suggested, and Lauren
wonders what strings he had to pull.

The instructor says, "You are the eagle's eyes." She says, "It takes
a certain kind of person to be a fire lookout. You must be quick
and decisive. You must be patient and steadfast. And you *must*
know how to be alone." Lauren does not know if she is any of these
things, but she writes down everything the woman says.

After the last day of training, the instructor hands Lauren a yellow rain slicker and a used pair of hiking boots. "Sweetheart," she
says, "you're going to need these."

On the drive home, Lauren stops at the place they call Island Park, a narrow strip of land that splits the river. The Salmon has overflowed its banks, and the island is flooded in places. Grown men in lifted trucks charge deep puddles, disappear behind twin walls of water. The old public swimming pool has been converted into a skate park, and teenagers gather here to smoke cigarettes and grab-ass after school. Lauren approaches, and the kids grow quiet. "Hey," she says to one of the boys. "You smoke?" He's hesitant to answer but reaches into his pocket, shakes a cigarette from the pack.

Nearby, the picnic tables are under water, only the tops showing, like a chain of docks. Lauren takes off her shoes and jumps from one table to the next until she reaches the raised pavilion. She sits and smokes, watches cars pass on the bridge above. Daniel has told her about the woman who raised her sons at the lookout, from infants to teenagers, summer after summer, and how the boys thrived in the wilderness. He said Lauren could bring Jonah, no problem. But Lauren has her doubts. Surely Daniel was being kind. Surely he noticed the boy's bruised forehead, his darting eyes.

Back at her mother's, the house is quiet. "Hello?" she calls. "I'm home." The kitchen table is cluttered with game pieces—Monopoly money and Battleship pegs and LIFE station wagons. When Lauren left this morning her mother and the boy were playing a game of Memory. Her mother had altered the game. She left the cards face up and asked the boy to pick one. Then they went looking for the image on the card: apple, watch, fish, keys. Her mother said the word and the boy said it back.

Lauren picks up two red dice and rattles them in the cage of her hand. She doesn't know what bothers her more—the way the boy responds to her mother, or the way her mother responds to the boy.

In the living room, Lauren finds her father's tackle box emptied on the floor: flies, spinners, jig heads, hellgies, weights, bobbers. Rusted three-aught hooks are snagged in the carpet. She rights the box and slides the drawers into place. When she picks it up, its weightlessness feels like something being taken away.

Her father's fishing license, in its plastic sleeve, is wedged in a top compartment. Lauren unfolds the papers and reads the handwritten dates of every steelhead he caught in the months leading up to his death. It hurts to see so many blank spaces, to know how many fish he had left to keep.

From down the hall, Lauren hears her mother's voice. She listens outside the bathroom door. "That's a good boy," her mother says. "Sit very still for Grandma."

When Lauren opens the door her mother and the boy look up at the same time. Her mother's face is flushed; the ropes in her neck tighten. She lowers a pair of wire cutters. Lauren looks from her mother to the boy. His hand is decorated with tackle, hooks deep in the meat of his palm and fingertips. Colored fishing lures jingle and sing as he tries to get down from the counter. He doesn't seem to register the pain, but Lauren feels it acutely in her own hands, and she stands holding them out, speechless, paralyzed.

Her mother says, "I don't know how it happened."

Thirty minutes later, Lauren sits in a hospital room. They've given the boy a local anesthetic, a tetanus shot, and a small dose of Ativan, and she watches his face begin to soften. The doctor comes in and adjusts a light over the bed. He explains the process. For some he'll insert a needle to lift the skin away from the barb and pull the hook free. For others, he'll have to push the hook through the skin, cut the barb, and back the flank out.

Lauren lowers her eyes to the floor. She counts as the doctor drops each retrieved hook into a metal pan with a *clink*. Nine times, nine hooks.

Afterward the doctor says, "Try not to blame yourself." He hands Lauren a white bag with antibiotic ointment, extra bandages, and children's Tylenol. He says the boy will be fine, and he pats her on the back, as if she too is a child who needs comforting.

It's dark when Lauren begins packing for Long Tom Lookout. She goes to the garage for a lantern and sleeping bags but finds herself sitting on the cool concrete, breathing in the smell of oil and grass clippings. The last time she stood in this garage was the last time she saw her father. She helped him spool his fishing reel by holding a pencil through the spool's center while he reeled in the line. They were, in those moments, so gently tethered by the glint of the monofilament strung between them.

On her way back inside, arms full of camping gear, Lauren

passes her mother on the porch swing. "Can you open the door?" she says, and her mother says, "I just talked to Keller. He didn't even know you were here."

"What? You called him?"

"I had to. To tell him about Jonah's accident."

"Shit," Lauren says. "Did he want to talk to me?"

"He said to call when you get back to Texas."

"I'm not going back to Texas. Did you tell him that?"

Her mother brings a tissue to her nose, and Lauren realizes she's crying. "Keller's not upset about the accident, and he's not mad at you for leaving with Jonah."

"He's not mad at *me*?" Lauren drops everything on the porch. The lantern rolls down the steps, breaks when it hits the sidewalk. "CPS dumped his kid on my doorstep. What was I supposed to do? Sit around changing diapers while he fucked some woman?"

Her mother stands and opens the door. "I don't know what's going on between you two," she says, "but running away isn't going to fix it."

The screen slams shut. Lauren collects the pieces of broken lantern, sits on the steps with the shards of glass in her hands. What did Keller see in the boy's mother? Or the woman who answered the door in New Orleans? What do they have that she doesn't? She hears the woman say, "No, Keller isn't home." She remembers the woman standing barefoot in the yard. "Who do you think you are?" the woman shouted, and Lauren called back, "We're the same fucking person, you and me. Exactly the same."

Lauren doesn't tell her mother good night. She doesn't say a word. At first light, she and the boy are in the truck, headed for Long Tom Mountain.

The road to Colson Creek follows the Salmon River like a smoke plume. Lauren takes the corners fast, and the boxes in the truck bed slide from side to side. The boy closes his eyes. Pavement turns to dirt. The canyon narrows. The river runs wide and passive in sunlit stretches, then fast and bawdy with whitewater rapids. High-water season, and there are none of the usual rafters, no fishermen lining the banks. A sandhill crane bends to drink, pauses, raises its head. They pass the skeletons of mining cabins, a rusted cable car, the remains of the Moose Creek dredge. The tires hammer over washboards.

When they stop at the Shoup Store—a log cabin that serves as a restaurant and convenience store—the boy gets out and vomits on his shoes. The cashier takes one look at him and says the bathroom is for paying customers only. Lauren counts three dollars in nickels and dimes from the glove box and buys the boy a huckleberry milkshake, cleans him up in the bathroom with the cashier scowling behind the counter.

Twenty minutes later the boy vomits huckleberry milkshake in the passenger seat. Lauren stops again. A three-hour drive becomes four. At Colson Creek they leave the river and head up the mountain. Dust glints and flits about their heads like a million gold-winged gnats. She's long ago lost the battle of the seat belts, and the boy rides wide-eyed and shirtless, both hands on the dashboard. Daniel has warned her about the condition of the road, and now she thinks "road" is a bit of a stretch; it rides like a goddamn creek bottom. Twice she stops to roll boulders from the road, watches them crash through the sagebrush below. Twice she stops to wait for bighorn sheep, slow to move and unafraid.

Finally the truck crests a rise half a mile from the summit of Long Tom Mountain. The lookout tower stands on a rocky knob like a marooned boat, a relic of the past. The sixteen-by-sixteen-foot cab is a glass box perched atop a ten-foot concrete base. Lauren knows from the training course that four lookout towers have been built and rebuilt here since 1923, staffed every summer since. Yesterday Daniel called in a favor, and a forest ranger dewinterized the cab—replaced the battery in the fixed weather station, stacked a cord of wood, turned on the propane, and removed the shutters. Lightning rods rise from every corner of the roof. The windows gleam with sunlight.

Lauren gets out and takes a deep breath. After nine years in Texas it feels like she's emerged from the depths of a lake. She surveys the land with a hand drawn over her brow and has the sensation of driving through a long, dark tunnel and coming out the other side. From here she can see six national forests and deep into the two million acres of the Frank Church–River of No Return Wilderness: towering granite gorges, slopes of sagebrush, dense pine and fir forest. And below, the confluence of two wild rivers, like a millennia-old handshake, negotiating a path to the Pacific.

"What do you think, Jonah?" she says. "Home sweet home?"

Lauren begins the tedious task of keeping the boy in her sights while unpacking the truck. The boy's hair is windblown into a cowlick; his left-hand bandage is soiled. He strips naked and runs between the lookout and the outhouse, wearing only a pair of white sneakers, and Lauren thinks, Why the hell not? For an instant she is struck by the boy's freedom, not just childhood but also the unknown workings of his mind, the strange and quarantined world he lives in. Maybe, she thinks, we're not all that different. We both exist in an isolation of our own making.

The lookout is furnished with a propane refrigerator and cookstove, a wood-burning stove, a long counter, and a single bed. In the middle of the room, on a table of its own, sits the Osborne Firefinder and a pair of binoculars. Last year's calendar hangs on the wall, a black X drawn through every day in September. Lauren searches the cupboards and finds first-aid and snakebite kits, maps, log books, cloud charts, mousetraps, birdseed, batteries, bug spray, an alarm clock, a single stainless-steel wineglass, *The Firefighter's Handbook,* and a dog-eared copy of *A River Runs Through It.*

Late that afternoon, after everything has been cleaned and their belongings put away, Lauren and the boy eat grilled cheese sandwiches and baked beans while dark clouds push up the Salmon River corridor. The boy looks from side to side as Lauren closes the windows. The trees sway and creak; the birdfeeder tips, spilling arcs of seed. The temperature drops ten degrees in ten minutes. Lauren doesn't want to miss her first radio transaction with dispatch, and, with some reluctance, unpacks the belt weather kit and ventures outside in a yellow slicker to take the weather statistics.

Inside, the boy sits in a cardboard box, hands over his ears. Lightning dances on distant ridge tops. Thunder rumbles overhead. Lauren comes in with a small spiral notebook in her hand, rainwater dripping from her fingers and nose.

She goes to the radio. "Dispatch. Long Tom Lookout."

For a time, there is nothing. Then: "Long Tom. Dispatch."

Daniel's voice is a small comfort. She reads the statistics slowly: wind speed and direction, precipitation, air temperature, relative humidity, Haines Index. There is a moment, after she finishes, when neither speak. The radio sizzles with static.

"Dispatch. Long Tom," Daniel says. "Do you copy?"

"Long Tom. Affirmative."

"Everything OK, Long Tom?"

"We've got a storm blowing in."

"Copy that. Is there lightning?"

"Affirmative."

"Is it close?"

"It's getting closer."

"You know what to do. Turn off the propane and get off the radio."

Lauren takes a deep breath to keep from crying.

Daniel says, "You're going to be all right, Long Tom."

She wishes he would say her name. Rain lashes the windows. The boy begins to whimper. "Copy," she says. "Clear."

All night thunderstorms pass overhead, one after another, like the ghosts of a recurring dream. Lauren wakes after midnight to the air charged with electricity, her hair on end, something like a whisper at the nape of her neck. The forest shudders into view, collapses into darkness. The boy is jolted awake by thunder. Lauren holds him on one hip, whispers *one-potato-two* under her breath. She knows to account one mile for every five seconds between flash and thunder, knows it's getting closer. She thinks of the story the instructor told in training, how lightning once struck a chimney, coursed down the flue, jumped through the damper, and killed a lookout in his sleep.

Lauren extinguishes the lantern, turns off the propane, and drags the glass-insulated stool to the center of the room. She sits with her feet on the bottom rung, the boy on her lap. Together they wait. It is the waiting, she knows, that will kill her in the end. The hours upon hours of contemplation, of looking out the window for smoke, her thoughts knitting back to Keller. She is eight thousand feet above sea level and has never felt so alone. She thinks back to their last night together, and how, when he touched her hip beneath the sheets, she said, "How can you want to be with me when I am so far away?"

All at once the room fills with white light and the simultaneous boom of a thunderclap—the sound of an enormous whip being snapped—and she knows the lookout has been hit by lightning. The boy screams, and Lauren screams. He wants nothing more than to escape, and she wants nothing more than to let him go. She places her hands over his ears and forces him to stay put through the worst of it.

"We're OK," she sings, her voice shaking.

The days press forward. Cloudbursts blow out the road and cut new creek channels. Wildflowers bloom without worry. Lauren checks in with dispatch and Stormy Peak Lookout twice a day. She suffers headaches from eyestrain, struggles to stay awake through the long northern days. It is a slow start to the fire season. Some days she listens to radio traffic if only to hear a voice that isn't hers, or the echo of the boy, who has taken to repeating her every word. At night, coyotes call from ridge to ridge. The sky is a graveyard of lights. She tells the boy there is a star for every ship lost at sea.

Three times a week Lauren ties one end of a rope around the boy's waist, the other around her own, and like two mountain climbers they make their way to the spring and back. It's a three-mile round trip with Lauren hauling buckets of water, and the boy tugging as he runs ahead. They bathe from a bucket of spring water warmed on the stove. So intent is the boy on examining the flecks of pyrite that shimmer and shift that he tips headfirst into the bucket, comes out spitting like a cat. Lauren stops shaving her legs, then her armpits. She wears sunscreen instead of makeup, pulls her hair into a ball cap, longs for a manicure, a grocery store, air conditioning.

Five days in a row they see the same domestic goat roping up the trail, a Nubian goat with a golden coat and a bell around its neck. It climbs the stairs of the lookout, rattles along the catwalk, bleating at the windows. Lauren radios dispatch, and they ask the few residents along the river if anyone has lost a pet. No one claims the goat. When at last the goat wanders off, the boy says only *goat* for two days. How about some lunch, Jonah? *Goat.* Are you tired, Jonah? *Goat.* Finally, they go out looking for the goat. Lauren tethers it to a twenty-foot rope and it mows everything from balsamroot to cheatgrass to Canada thistle around the lookout's perimeter. The boy feeds it snowberries from the palm of his hand.

In the evenings, the boy studies the road atlas, turning the pages, state after state, the way another child might study a picture book. Lauren takes his finger and traces their route from Texas to Idaho by way of Louisiana. She draws a little boat in the Gulf of

Mexico. That night the boy begins tracing roadways in the atlas.
He pencils over Interstate 80, from Cheyenne to Rock Springs, the
road now a silver river on the map. He lies propped on his elbows,
his hand curiously steady. His hair is fine and fair as a dandelion
gone to seed, so unlike her husband's, which is thick and dark.
And yet they resemble each other in many ways—the boy's domi-
nant left hand, his cleft chin, the apples of his cheeks. Lauren
reaches down and touches him on the head.

Other days are a fight. The boy resists eye contact and any recognition of Lauren's presence, her voice. He empties a bag of rice
on the floor, feeds their cache of chocolate bars to the goat. He
has taken to collecting rocks—nothing special by her eye, but to
the boy they are gems—and arranging them into winding paths
across the floor. If, and when, Lauren disrupts his roadway of
rocks, the boy beats his head against the floor. He will take any
map she leaves within reach. He will refuse to eat for no discernible reason. She must keep one eye on the horizon, one eye on
the boy. She comes back from the outhouse and finds him flying
the fire shelter like a kite. It catches in an updraft, snags in a pine
bough, glinting like a three-hundred-dollar Christmas ornament.

Then it's July, bordering on hot after so many days of rain, the
sun drawing slats of light across the concrete floor. Crickets sing,
welcoming the heat. The boy sleeps red-faced and sweating, both
arms above his head. Daniel arrives in a white Forest Service truck,
a cloud of dust winding up the road. Lauren puts on deodorant
and a clean shirt and helps him unload a roll of woven wire, a
dozen lodgepole fence posts, and two bales of hay. "I figure I better
get a pen built for that goat," he says. "I don't want to scare you, but
I've seen what a wolf can do to a calf. Believe me, it ain't pretty."

He holds up a paper bag. "My wife made me bring these. I don't
know if Jonah needs clothes, but I tried to take out everything
pink."

Lauren says, "He does, thank you. And thank Carol for thinking
of us."

They walk to the east side of the lookout where the goat works
a sunflower between its teeth, root and all. The sky is stained lavender and coral and soon it will be dusk. Daniel reaches into his
pocket, hands her a piece of folded paper. "It's from your mother,"
he says. "If you need to go home, I can send up a replacement."

Lauren reads the message once, then a second time. Her

mother explains in perfect cursive that Keller is coming for the
boy. Lauren looks across the valley and wonders if she didn't have
the boy, would Keller come for her? She remembers an afternoon
they spent on South Padre Island when she and Keller were newlyweds. A surf fisherman had hooked a seagull by mistake. The
more the gull fought, the more it became entangled in the line,
and soon the flock had moved down the beach without it. Eventually, the fisherman cut his line. The gull lifted, flew a few feet, and
crashed back into the water. It carried on like that until Lauren
couldn't watch anymore.

She asks Daniel, "Did you read this?"

He looks at his shoes. "We've all got our troubles."

On the third of July, Lauren and the boy leave Long Tom Mountain for town. Lauren's sister, Desiree, and brother-in-law, Ted,
and their four children are visiting from Coeur d'Alene. They're
all camped in the backyard as Ted does something he calls grill-
ing, but it smells a lot like burning. They've mowed a clearing in
the grass, and the children have laid out a slat of plywood and an
arsenal of illegal fireworks they picked up in Missoula. The two
older boys light firecrackers in the chicken coop, cover their ears,
and run.

Desiree is eight months pregnant. She has named her children
after places she has never been: Branson, Lincoln, Trenton, and
Madison. Lauren suggests Houston as a joke, and Desiree says
it with different middle names: "Houston Lee? Houston Hope?
Houston Marie?" No one says Keller's name, but Ted puts an extra
burger on the grill. The women share looks of anticipation, simultaneously turning when a car door slams.

After dinner the children scatter, playing a game of hide-and-
seek. The yard backs up to a calm stretch of river, but to either
side the property is littered with junk cars, tires, broken bee boxes,
a shed, and the chicken coop. They are waiting for true dark, for
fireworks to pop and explode over Old Dump Hill. Desiree props
her swollen feet on a stump. Lauren's mother brings out a transis-
tor radio and tunes in the only station in town, and they listen to
songs with "America" in the title. Ted struggles with the campfire,
eventually dousing logs with lighter fluid and throwing in a match.

Desiree raises a hand to the flames, says, "Lordy, Ted. You trying
to burn the place down?"

The boy darts across the yard in a red sweatshirt with RODEO PRINCESS spelled in rhinestone studs, a hand-me-down from Daniel's daughter. Lauren knows he isn't playing along so much as hiding from the other children, and she's surprised when Madison, Desiree's youngest, takes him by the hand. They crawl into an old drift boat, Lauren's father's boat, now overgrown with skeletonweed. Their small heads peek over the bow, and in that moment Lauren's life carries the semblance of normalcy. A calm before the storm, she thinks. Before she loses Keller to the boy, and the boy to Keller.

No, she thinks, they were never mine in the first place.

Ted retrieves a beer from the cooler and hands it to Lauren. "So your mother tells us you've been working at a lookout tower. Long John—"

"Long *Tom*," Lauren says. "It was named after a miner that drowned."

Desiree shudders. "I think I drowned in a previous life. That's why I'm scared of water. Ted doesn't believe in past lives, do you, Ted?"

"It's fire that scares me," Ted says. "Burning to death."

"Actually," Lauren says, "the miner's real name was Joe Lockland. They packed his body upriver and ordered a coffin from town, but when it arrived it was too short."

"A child's coffin?" Desiree says. "Oh, that's the worst. Remember the time we caught all those baby moles and put them in a shoebox and they died in the night? Remember, Lauren? And Daddy held a funeral in the backyard. Oh, bless his heart."

"No, not a child's coffin. It's just that Tom was too long."

"*Long* Tom," Ted says. He looks to Desiree. "Get it, honey?"

"I get it," Desiree says. "Why wouldn't I get it?"

Lauren makes slits of her eyes. It's after nine o'clock and twilight lingers. She scans the yard, searching for the boy's red sweatshirt. The children are hiding. It's eerily quiet. She thinks it's too late for them to play so close to the river.

Ted says, "So what'd they do with the body?"

Lauren stands, both hands on her hips. "They cut the tendons under the dead man's knees, bent his calves over his thighs, and nailed the coffin shut."

Desiree gasps. Their mother says, "That's a terrible story. Just awful."

Lauren doesn't see the boy anywhere. She walks into the yard. Trenton and Madison appear from behind a pile of tractor tires. Trenton holds Madison's hands behind her back like a caught criminal. The other two boys wait for the game to begin again. Lauren nearly yells when she says, "Where's Jonah?"

The children look at Lauren and then each other. Madison points. "He's in the tires," she says. "He won! Jonah won the game!"

The adults clap and cheer. The boy runs out from behind the tires, keeps running across the yard, and Lauren chases after him, pretending he's too fast.

After everyone has gone to bed, Lauren turns on the television for any news about skimming vessels off the coast of Louisiana. It's Day 73 of the Deepwater Horizon disaster: over 140 million gallons of crude oil along 423 miles of coastline. Cleanup workers in Louisiana have reported symptoms from exposure to oil chemicals. CNN loops images of ruined beaches. There's a message drawn in the sand: *Spill, baby, spill.* Last week a charter-boat captain in Alabama put a gun to his head and pulled the trigger.

Lauren begins to worry. Four days ago Hurricane Alex forced boats to port in the Gulf of Mexico. Four days ago Keller called Lauren's mother, but nobody's heard from him since. For the first time Lauren admits that leaving Keller wasn't so much about leaving, but wanting him to acknowledge her absence, and now she feels like a child. She doesn't know if Keller is traveling by car, or by plane and then by car. The closest airports—Idaho Falls and Missoula—are both three hours away. Her mother gets up for a glass of water and says what Lauren is thinking: "What if something happened?"

Lauren steals a pack of cigarettes from Ted's coat pocket, smokes, pacing the dark garage. She raises the glowing ember to her father's ghost, says, "Would you look at us now?" Then she does what she promised herself she wouldn't do. She calls Keller.

His voice sounds small and far away. "Where are you?" she asks.

"Laurie?" A pause. He clears his throat. "I'm in New Orleans. Where are you?"

Lauren cups her hand around the phone and yells in a whisper: "I'm in *Idaho* at my goddamn *mother's* with your *son*, which you know perfectly well."

She can hear Keller breathing, wheezing. He discharges the in-

haler, takes a deep breath. His asthma has worsened over the years
and it's easier to imagine him on the deck of a trawler clutching
his chest than as a high school athlete setting pole-vault records.
"Are you OK?" she says. "My mother said you were coming."

"I said I would try, and I am. They've got us working fourteen-
hour days. Someone has to pay the rent while you're on vacation."

"Vacation? Is that what you think this is?"

"No one told you to go to Idaho. I mean, really, what were you
thinking?"

Keller's voice fluctuates with his movements, and she imagines
him stepping into his jeans. She wonders how many women have
seen him do this. Sometimes he touches her in a familiar way, other
times as if he's trying to please another woman. Lauren doesn't
know if this other woman is a younger version of herself—the person he still believes her to be—or someone she's never met.

"I drove to New Orleans, Keller."

"I know. Margot said some crazed woman took off in my truck.
You're lucky she didn't call the police and report it stolen."

"Is that her name? Margot?"

"She's Doug's wife. Doug and I work together. I rent the guest
bedroom."

"Do you really expect me to believe that?"

"Come on, Laurie. Don't do this."

"I thought you were staying with your parents. Why would you
lie to me? Why did that woman—Margot—look at me like *I* was
the other woman?"

"Christ," Keller says. "Is that what this is about?"

Lauren slumps against the counter. She doesn't know what to
believe.

"Hello? Laurie? When are you coming back?"

"I'm not coming back. Come get your son."

Lauren hangs up the phone. Her mother appears at the end of
the hallway. Lauren says, "He's not coming." She gathers the sleeping boy in her arms and carries him to the truck. Her mother follows in her housecoat and slippers, asking Lauren to leave Jonah.

"What if Keller comes for him?" she says. "What am I supposed
to tell him?"

Lauren starts the engine. "Tell him he can come to me."

"But Lauren," her mother says, "this isn't about you."

*

By mid-July, temperatures in the Salmon River Canyon break one hundred. Beetle-infested trees turn new shades of red, ribbons of rust among the dense green. Noxious weeds carry their seeds easily on the wind. A Forest Service helicopter flies over Cache Bar drainage, dropping purple streamers in honor of two fallen firefighters. The lookout at Stormy Peak complains of yellow jackets; Lauren complains of horseflies. They talk, always, of weather. It's the closest thing Lauren has had to a friendship in a long time.

For two days lightning storms ignite a series of spot fires, and for two days Lauren paces the windows with binoculars, glassing for phantom fires—sleeping fires that creep across the forest floor, waiting for a gust of wind or a snag of fuel. She stands at the Osborne Firefinder and looks through the vertical slot of the front sight, targets smoke in the cross hairs of the rear sight. Of the fires she reports, four still burn: the Spring Fire, the Bighorn Fire, and two smaller fires near the Corn Creek Boat Launch.

Lauren's head aches; her hands tremble. It's four o'clock in the afternoon and she hasn't looked in a mirror in two days. On the counter beside her a cup of coffee grows cold. She goes to the stove to heat more water, finds the kettle already near boil. These are the twenty-hour days Daniel has warned her about.

The boy goes to the door, as he has all day, and turns the locked handle. Lauren lowers the binoculars. "I know, buddy. We can't go out just yet." She tries to sit him down with the road atlas, only to find he's penciled across all fifty states. She thumbs the pages quickly, like a flipbook, and sees an endless maze, a web of confusion.

That evening, Lauren straightens a wire clothes hanger and she and the boy roast marshmallows over the propane flame. Afterward, the boy lets the goat lick his sticky hands. They sit outside on a sleeping bag with the wind at their backs. Lauren has taken the four track pins from Keller's letterman jacket and attached them to the boy's sweatshirt, and the boy sits with his head bowed, examining the gold.

It's a cool night made warmer by the sight of the Bighorn Fire. From this distance the two-hundred-foot flames make the ponderosa appear as small as matchsticks, the flames extinguishable with the pinch of a finger. Steep terrain and high winds have kept firefighters out of the Bighorn Crags, and there's nothing to do but watch it burn.

In Lauren's pocket is a message from her mother, already a week old: *Keller says please come home.* The paper has worn soft between her fingers. This is something she's learned: nothing is safe, nothing is sacred. There is always another fire on another mountain. The boy closes his eyes. Wind shifts through the trees like the sound of cars passing, and it's easy to believe she's back in Galveston, she and Keller together with so much undone between them.

Lauren sleeps without dreams. And when she wakes, the boy is gone.

The sun is not yet over the ridge, the sky gritty with smoke. Lauren staggers to the edge of the bluff and peers into the rocky depths, hoping to see, and hoping not to see, the boy's red sweatshirt. She finds the goat pen open, the goat gone. The outhouse is empty; the storage unit is locked. The front door to the lookout squeaks on its hinges. She turns over a cardboard box, searches under the bed. She runs down the dirt road, cups her hands around her mouth, and yells the boy's name in every direction.

Finally, she radios dispatch. "He's gone," she says. "I've lost him."

Forty minutes later a Forest Service helicopter begins a search pattern around the lookout. Canyon winds surge up the draw and the helicopter tips, then rights itself again. Watching from the catwalk, her neck craned, Lauren feels on the verge of fainting. It is dangerous country, as steep as it is rugged, with nowhere to go but down. She thinks of Keller, of the boy's mother, her own mother, and she leans over the railing and vomits.

Daniel arrives with the deputy sheriff, two officers, and two tracking dogs. The deputy explains that the dogs are trained to sniff out drugs and cadavers. Lauren holds her knees at the sound of *cadavers*. The officers let themselves into the lookout and begin organizing a search grid. A red Suburban full of search-and-rescue workers arrives, with a trailer of ATVs and medical equipment. Behind them: a caravan of volunteers in their own vehicles. One of the volunteers looks to be the same age as Lauren. Their eyes meet, and Lauren sees what the woman sees—tangle of blond hair, swollen eyes, quivering jaw. She says to Lauren, "Why don't we go inside and talk, OK?"

Lauren tells her the boy is wearing a red sweatshirt, denim overalls, and a pair of white sneakers with heels that light up when he steps down. She tells her about the goat's golden coloring, its bell.

She spells Keller's name, the boy's mother's name, and the name of the caseworker in Texas. She feels a pain in her ribs when she says, "We fell asleep outside." The woman asks what time, and Lauren says, "After dinner, but before dark." She tries to explain the boy's behavior by showing the woman the road atlas. The woman nods and writes everything down. It looks so small on the page.

They search until nightfall. The moon glows red behind a haze of smoke. Search-and-rescue teams rotate shifts. Forest Service trucks come and go. Wildland firefighters arrive with packs on their backs, ready to search at dawn. Someone has brought up a gas generator, and it rumbles outside, two floodlights illuminating a path. On the patch of grass where Lauren and the boy last slept, rescue workers set up pup tents.

A dozen people occupy the lookout. Lauren doesn't know where to sit or what to do with her hands. Styrofoam coffee cups litter the counter. Maps are unfolded on the bed and taped to the windows. The area left to cover appears an infinite number of acres. The deputy tries to comfort Lauren by saying a five-year-old boy can only get so far. "He'd never make it to the river," he says, and Lauren cups her face in her hands.

Daniel unwraps a granola bar, says, "Eat something. It'll help." Her voice is raw and tight. "I can't call Keller," she says. "I can't." "We already contacted him. He's on his way."

That night Lauren sleeps in the back of Daniel's truck, parked beside the lookout with the tailgate lowered. She slips in and out of dreams, sees a beach lined with gulls, hears the beating of a hundred wings: helicopters, truck engines, window hinges, the kettle screaming, doors closing, the boy's laugh like a whisper. She opens her eyes. Over a two-way radio, someone refers to the boy as Lauren's son.

At the start of the second day, search-and-rescue workers meet outside the lookout to reevaluate their plan. Lauren cannot bear to listen. She knows they found the goat eating sunflowers on Long Tom Creek. She knows they found the boy's red sweatshirt on the trail to the spring. Lauren knows after twelve hours, the chances of recovering the boy begin to diminish. No one says as much, but she knows they are searching for a body.

Daniel asks everyone in the lookout to leave, holds the door as they file out. He turns down the volume on the radio, pours

Lauren a cup of coffee. He says, "I'm sorry, Lauren," and she says, "Don't say that. Don't make me hate you for saying that."

He sits beside her on the bed, holds out his hand. Resting in the center of his palm is a single winged-foot pin. "I thought you might want this," he says. "It was on the sweatshirt we found."

Lauren looks away. To touch it feels like acceptance—of her mistakes, and of the boy's fate, which she so easily took into her own hands. He places the pin on the bed between them, and Lauren knows it will always be between them, that after today she'll have to bury this place, and this part of herself, all over again.

Daniel stands and faces the window, his silhouette a mountain among mountains. He says in a whisper, "Where are you, Jonah?"

In the corner of the windowpane, Lauren sees the boy's tiny handprints. She remembers holding the binoculars to his face, and how, when she lowered them, he put both hands to the pane, eyes roving the mountainside as if to say, "Something very fascinating is happening here." Sometimes he looked at Lauren the same way, would reach out and touch her face, and she wondered what he saw that she couldn't—the fabric of her thoughts, circuitry of her nerves, blood coursing the chambers of her heart.

Lauren goes to the window and rips down the search maps. Daniel holds up his hand in protest. "Don't"—he starts to speak but falls silent. She empties a drawer on the floor and picks through the mess for a roll of tape. On her hands and knees she reaches under the bed for the boy's road atlas and pulls it toward her. She tears out the pages, state after state, the paper thudding against the spiral binding like tires on a rumble strip, a car veering from its path, and she doesn't stop until she reaches Texas, sees the little boat she drew for the boy in the Gulf of Mexico. A moment of hesitation, and then she tears it out too, the paper leafing to the floor.

Lauren adheres the first road map to the window and sunlight bleeds through the paper. The room dims one map at a time until she's covered every pane. She turns in a circle, following the boy's pencil from Alabama to Wyoming. The darkened lines resemble the electrocardiograms of a thousand heartbeats, the tributaries of a thousand rivers. It is as beautiful as it is haunting. There's a particular logic to the boy's work, a complex network of intersecting routes, and yet, even now, he remains a mystery to Lauren. She thinks, He is only a child. She thinks, This is as close as I will ever be to him again.

Medium Tough

FROM *Agni*

THE NEEDLE: 21 gauge, 1.5 inches. A hogsticker. I'd liberated it from the thoracic care unit—they stock cannulas for emergency chest decompression, hammer one of those big-bore pins between the fourth and fifth intercostal to vent compacted air and blood. The contents of the syringe run as follows: 1 cc of Equipoise, a veterinary drug injected into cattle to render them fat and juicy, plus an additional 2 ccs of testosterone cypionate—i.e., roughly twenty times the testosterone a man my size produces in a week. I've never been one for half-measures.

I tried hormone replacement therapy. Creams, patches, gels, slow-release subdermal pellets sunk into my flanks. Only adrenaline can I produce regularly; the rest of my hormones are flatlined. The doc gawped at my T-levels and said: "Sure you weren't born a woman, Jasper?" We're old pals; he can joke. But HRT is the bailiwick of geriatric dynamos and middle-aged graspers. Plus you're rubbing that goo on your hands so the "T" can seep in—problematic, seeing as I handle loads of babies. Skin-to-skin transference, yeah? Good Dr. Railsback lays hands on little Janie Sue Macintosh and next she's growing a beard.

Shortly I'd be pumping the stuff into my rear end. A fine pincushion. But the sciatic nerve radiates from your hips—if the needle raked the nerve stem, I'd be doing the noodle-legged cha-cha. And if I dumped the stuff directly into a vein, it'd slam me into cardiac collapse. But fortune favors the brave, so tallyho.

I pierced the skin, aspirated, saw only the thinnest thread of blood, and bottomed the plunger. *Yeeeeessss*—there's the heatseeker.

I slipped the needle into a sharps bin and located the blister pack of capsules. *Fludara.* An anti-metastatic; it attacks the RNA, rots the helix, and kills the spread. The label read: *Avoid inhaling the dust from a broken caplet.* The urge to crack one and snort it up my nose was awesomely powerful. I swallowed two, then two more. My tongue flitted absently around my mouth; its nodules rasped against my incisors, but they were too dense to burst. My name went out on the PA. "Dr. Railsback to pediatrics . . ."

The vulcanized orthotic spacer on my left shoe made a jazzy *dunka-dunka-dunk* on the hospital tiles. Up to the fifth floor. The air in the NICU was heavy with pheromones: aliphatic acids, which waft from the pores of women who've just delivered. A distinctive scent. An undertone of caramelized sugar.

"Are we prepped?" I asked the nurse, Sandy, who herself smelled of cherry sanitizer. She nodded with remote calmness. Sandy was the one you wanted intubating a preemie with a blocked airway.

"OR 5, Dr. Railsback. Dr. Beverly's finishing up with an epidural."

I prepped in a deep-basined metal sink. Shirtless—a quirk, but you really can't be too clean with surgery. One hand washed the other. The right: huge, thick-knuckled, bones lashed by a meshwork of heavy ligatures. The left: long and bony like the hand of Nosferatu, metacarpals projecting beneath the thinnest stretching of skin—the bones in a bat's wing. The right arm: a bowling-pin-like forearm roped with freaky striations, a grapefruit-bulge of biceps. The left, a pair of sticks jointed at the elbow.

There's a line where the two halves of my body intersect. It begins to the left of my throat, centers itself between the points where my collarbones meet, cleaves the breastplate and rib cage, then snakes to the left down my abdominals and carves right again before finishing at my groin. To the right: densely muscled, proportionate. To the left: austere devastation. The line of demarcation is plain: the vascular round of my right pectoral dips into a trough where it meets my breastbone and fails to rise again, in a flat expanse so devoid of muscle that every thump of my heart shivers the flesh. The ribs on my right are banded by stout tendons. The left stick out like the spars of an unfinished boat.

My left side still *works.* The muscle, what there is, flexes. The nerve clusters fire. My left foot is 2.12 inches shorter than my right, and my left arm 2.84 inches shorter than its mate—I had a colleague take the precise measurements. My face is unaffected. Should you see me walking down the street in trousers and long sleeves, you would not notice much amiss. Were we carnally acquainted, however, you might wonder if I'd not been born so much as *fused* from separate selves. During maiden intimacies it's my habit to disrobe slowly, explaining things. An educational striptease.

Dr. Beverly waited in the OR. Our patient lay on the surgical table. Wracked with tremors—brainstem release phenomena. Isla, pronounced *Eye-la*. Beverly set her on the digital scale. 3.55 pounds.

"I'll start on inhalants," he said. "Nitro to speed the uptake, then something with a slower wash-in. You looking for total bodily torpor?"

"I'll be inside her head, Bev. Can't have her squirming."

"Run with a quarter milligram of hydromorphone, but if she reverts to a pattern fetal circulation we'll risk acute hypoxemia."

Hypoxemia: CO_2 chewing black holes into Isla's brain. Beverly painted a Mercurochrome square on her back and located the L3 caudal space between her spinal discs. The epidural catheter—a shiny segmented tapeworm—pierced the flesh in the square's center. The girl's eyes, set in wrinkled webs of flesh, did not open.

Bev slipped a tiny mask over Isla's face, pumped in nitro to open her bloodpaths. He switched the drip to isoflurane, a powerful analgesic. Isla's chest shuddered. Infant breathing patterns can be random. You had to ignore it. The number 12 scalpel rested in my left hand, classic pencil grip.

In med school the question had been: "Is Jasper Railsback surgeon material?" I wasn't the prototypical specimen, but I did possess the physical basics and the intangibles: force of will, self-confidence. Plus there was the matter of my hands . . .

True surgeons, or "blades" as we're known, are defined by our hands. Look at our fingers: willowy and tapered, seemingly possessed of an extra joint. A concert pianist's hands. A surgeon must possess extraordinary dexterity and be steady in the cut. You could eke by as an orthopedic surgeon with so-so digits—that's basically meatball surgery. But if you go blundering around in an infant's skull, things die. In school we'd practiced on bananas. Draw a dotted line on the skin, carve out the "lesion" using the slide cut technique. I'd bought bananas by the bushel—green specimens first, working my way up to speckly black ones. While my fellow students

were exceeding the bursting strength threshold and slicing into the
banana "meat," my dynamite left was popping out perfect plugs.

My right is a bricklayer's hand. It can be taught blunt-force
tasks. But I can feel music through my left hand. The right is my
hammer. The left, an instrument of God.

I began at the supraorbital node, five centimeters above Isla's
nasal shelf. One must remember that an infant's bones are porous
or, in some cases, nonexistent. Soft heads, flabby gizzards. In many
ways they are only token humans. The scalpel bisected the fontanel. I avoided the cortical veins running bluely under the skin and
checked the incision before hitting the transverse sinuses. A brief
freshet of arterial blood. A lateral incision bisected the first: an X.
I tweezed back the flesh, pinning the flaps down.

"Suction."

Sandy removed the occluding blood with a vacuum wand. Isla's
brain shone within its encasement of cerebrospinal jelly. I searched
for what I'd seen on the ultrasound: a tumor developing within
the runneled folds. A teratoma, as it's known: a congenital defect
composed of foreign tissue such as muscle, hair, or even teeth.
Teratomas are rare; normally I'm looking for cortical dysplasia—a
mutation of the brain cells—or pre-epileptic markers.

"That's a lot of blood," said Beverly.

"Coagulant, then, Bev."

He said: "Getting close to peak toxicity already, Jazz."

"Suction."

I switched to the harmonic scalpel; it'd coagulate any severed
vessels. Sandy slipped a pair of magnifying spectacles over my eyes;
Isla's brain expanded in intimate detail. Spread the hemispheres
with a pair of forceps; they pierced the cerebrospinal sac soundlessly. Oxygen licked at the pink loaves of her brain, tinting the
surface cells gray. I snipped nerve clusters, avoiding the corpus
callosum, spreading the spheres until I could make out the Vein
of Galen.

There's an instant in any procedure when you understand that
you hold everything. The God Moment. Each surgeon feels it differently. For me this was a moment of awesome, near-paralyzing
love. For the child beneath my blade, for its life and its capacity to
do great things—or if not great, then productive, *valuable*.

"Light, Sandy."

She illuminated the cranial vault. Below the hub of the angular gyrus sat a foreign mass: off-white, oddly ribbed, crushed between the thalamic folds.

"I'm titrating up," Beverly said. "But I can't hold this level for long. She's nearing catatonic shock. Sandy, give me four and a half ccs of plasma replacement."

She handed Beverly a syringe with a tablespoon of crystalloid plasma 3:1. I reached in with the forceps. The metal brushed Isla's olfactory bulb; her nostrils dilated involuntarily. I gripped the foreign mass. Teased it out.

"What in God's . . ."

A tiny, stunted foot. My forceps gripped its big toe. I grasped its neighbor and pulled gently. The toe released from the medullar fold with an audible *plik!* The entire foot came out slick with glia—brain glue, essentially. No calf, no knee. Just a disembodied foot, no bigger than a vitamin lozenge.

"Parasitic twin," I said. "Consumed in utero."

"Signs and wonders," said Beverly.

Two nights later I busted a poor guy's arm. Classic greenstick. Radius and ulna bones. Three percussive pops as the flexor and brachii muscles unshackled from their moorings. Then the first of two wet, fibrous snaps: the ulna, which sounded like a pistol fired into wet sand. There's something madness-inducing about the sound of breaking bone. A rip in the fabric of things, a glimpse into a vast realm of polar whiteness. Sounds silly, I know . . . In the operating theater I break bones *purposefully:* incise with a number 5 scalpel, slit the silverskin-like fascia, spread the overlapping musculature, and split the bone with a surgical chisel called an osteotome. A controlled break, but still: always that glimpse.

But this happened at the Ontario Arm Wrestling Association's Arm Melter event, the semifinals of which were held in the basement of the K of C Hall on North Street. Low popcorn ceiling, steel cistern of rotgut. A passel of old Knights with pale suety faces slapping down dime bets on the Crown and Anchor wheel. A pair of padded arm-wrestling tables set up on the warped parquet. The type of crowd you'd expect when roller derby passes through town.

I'd been arm wrestling for years. My right arm—*the gorilla,* I like to call it—is the perfect weapon: a grapefruit bulge of biceps, bowling-pin forearm, vise-grip fingers. The battering ram to my left hand's lock-pick set.

My opponent was your standard Barbell Billy: fireplug-squat, vein-riven biceps jutting from a sheer wife-beater. He stuck his arm out as if he was *giving* me the damn thing. I only pull right-handed. I'm a specialist—plus, you know, the left is my moneymaker. Can't let one of these big goons crush my livelihood.

The ref cinched our hands with a leather thong to keep us gripped. When he said "Go!" the guy hit hard sideways, head down and snorting. Technique? Forget it! I fixed my elbow on the pad and let my shoulder absorb his thrusts; I felt the joint straining, idly concerned that he'd pop the humerus knob out of its cup of bone and destroy that fragile arrangement, but it held and I was able to hook his wrist, get my knuckles pointed skyward, and gradually peel his wrist backward—which was when his forearm went kerflooey.

The shock wave juddered through my body, dissipating into the skeletal muscle. But my veins were blitzed on adrenaline; I kept trying to pin his wrist. The guy wasn't aware of the trauma he'd sustained: the signals weren't routing through the proper synapses, so his body kept fighting. Twin tusks of white where the bone had shorn through. He stared at his assways-hanging arm and gave a quizzical half-laugh, as if his arm were a riddle I'd unceremoniously solved.

There was something terribly intimate to that moment. Your instinct is to pull back, give the man space to bleed—but we're strapped together, right?

"I'm a doctor," I told him. Pointlessly.

He hiccuped in shock. I elevated his arm. We were still lashed together so I looked like a ref holding up a boxer's hand post-victory. One of the Knights humped into the kitchen. He came back with paper towels in one hand and a roll of aluminum foil in the other.

"This is all we got," he said. "We do Friday Fish Fries, not busted arms."

Afterward everyone gathered outside in the cooling night. The guy sat on the steps, arm mummified in bloody paper towels. His wife showed up.

"What the hell did you do to yourself?" she said.

Everybody laughed. That was how women were around here—you do something idiotic, something *male*, your lady gives you both barrels.

The last light of day—briefly intensified as it slipped below the curve of the earth—softened through the roadside firs, a blade edge of light limning the car's contours and turning the woman's face a mellow gold. I thought about the coming hours: the two of them under the stark halogens of the ER, the bonesetter's tray, the crisp *snik!* as the carpals locked back in place, dissolvable sutures, coagulant, and pain meds. Maybe she'd drive him home to their small, clean house, and by then she may've softened, forgiving him for the bizarre things men do. She'd lead him to the bedroom as she might a child—he'd have a goofy oxycodone smile—settle him into bed, and work her body against his with concerned control. Hell, I'd suffer a broken arm for that. I'd suffer a dozen.

A Knight came over. Red fez cocked on his skull at a jaunty angle, face like a bowl of knuckles.

"One hell of an arm you've got, son. Too bad they aren't a matching pair."

His face shattered in laughter. The old prick.

"State your name for the record."

"Dr. Jasper Railsback."

"Place your right hand on the Bible and repeat after me: I swear to tell the truth, the whole truth . . ."

Niagara Regional Courthouse. Youth Services Court. Three pewlike benches. Penny Tolliver, a Children's Aid Society worker, the only spectator. One Crown attorney, one for the defense. The object of discussion: a ten-year-old boy with slight facial malformations. I sat in the witness box, having been summoned by the Crown.

"You operated on this boy shortly after he was born, Dr. Railsback—is that correct?"

"It is."

"Explain the nature of the operation—what did it address?"

"The boy's mother is a meth head."

"Objection," the defense council said. "Irrelevant."

The judge cocked her head at me. "Sustained."

"I operated on the boy, Randall, because his mother suffered a placental abruption. She suffered this because she smoked methamphetamine for the duration of her pregnancy."

"Objection. Conjectural."

"Sustained. Dr. Railsback . . ."

I returned the judge's look evenly. "Due to the placental abruption, the boy was delivered early. He exhibited tremors, sleeplessness, and muscle spasms, which are symptoms consistent with infant narcotic withdrawal."

"*Objection.* Conjectural."

"Overruled. Could these be symptoms of other conditions, Doctor?"

"It's doubtlessly possible. Due to his being delivered early, Randall's brain was not properly formed. He suffers from lissencephaly—*smooth brain.* His lacks the normal folds and grooves. The most common side effect is severely retarded motor skills. My procedure split the corpus callosum, severing the hemispheres in hopes of addressing those issues."

The Crown said: "Was it a success?"

"Most children with lissencephaly die before they turn two. If you're asking if the operation *cured* Randall, then no."

Crown: "Doctor, you mentioned his mother's substance abuse."

Defense, tiredly: "Objection, your honor. What bearing?"

"I'll allow it."

"In your experience, Doctor, what are the—"

I said: "My mother was a juicehead."

Crown: "I'm sorry?"

"You must understand: a mother will never have more direct physical contact with her child. What she eats, the baby eats. What she drinks or smokes or inhales. They share the same blood. The fetus's circulatory system is patched into hers. My mother was—*is* an alcoholic. My father too, though that has less bearing."

The defense rose. "Your honor, what bearing does *any of* this have—?"

"Yes, Dr. Railsback," the judge said. "Where are you going with this?"

I rolled up one sleeve, then the other. Laid my bare arms on the witness box. The judge eyed them with interest. We're all rubberneckers, deep down.

"My mother drank enough to float a coal ship while I was inside her. What people fail to grasp is how *sensitive* it is. A billion chemical reactions. A trillion tiny hurdles to clear. What happened to me was hormonal. A hormone is a key, you see: our cells are locked doors. If you've got the right key to fit the lock, the door opens. Well, one side of my body is all locked doors."

The judge said: "And this was a result of . . . ?"

"Of my mother pickling me in the womb. And listen, I've . . . *surmounted*. I'm a surgeon. A healer of men! But there's that line where love and basic concern butt up against weakness and addiction."

"Your Honor, could we please—"

"This being a custody case," I spoke over the defense attorney, "my opinion on a personal and professional level is that anyone who falls on the wrong side of that line ought to forfeit their child. Simple math."

Afterward I stood on the courthouse steps in the ashy evening light. Penny Tolliver stepped out with Randall. The boy's facial features were consistent with lissencephaly: the thin lips, temple indentations. His arm was wrapped around Penny's thigh, his head vibrating on the swell of her pregnant stomach.

"Thanks," she said simply.

"No prob, Pen. Part of the job."

I knelt before the boy. His left eye was foggy with cataracts.

"You grow funny," I told him. "That's what a girl in elementary school once said to *me*. Greta Hillson with the golden curls. What a jerk, huh? But you know, she was right. I grew funny. But guess what, Randall? It's OK to grow a little funny."

Literal truth? Truth is twisty. The boy pressed his face into Penny's belly.

"Can I see you tonight?" she said.

"My door's always open."

I left Penny sleeping while I got up to medicate. My bare feet slipped across the hardwood to the window overlooking the city. The Falls rumbled ceaselessly down the streetlighted thoroughfares, into Cataract City's pocketed dark: the sound of earthbound thunder. Clifton Hill shone like a strip of tinsel. Tonight at honeymoon haunts with names like Lover's Nest Lodge and Linked Hearts Inn, couples would bed down on motel sheets with the texture of spun glass. I liked the idea—that people I did not know, strangers I'd never meet, were happy and in love in the city of my birth.

To the south I could make out the oxidized metal roof of my old elementary school. In grade six Ernie Torrens busted my left arm. Yanked it between the bars of the bike rack, held me there as I squirmed. Took just one good kick. Ernie was a pig-ugly, brutish creature—fingers constantly stained Popsicle-orange. Nowadays he's a grease monkey at the Mister Lube on Stone Road; he stands in the pit, eyes webbed in grease-smeared flab, as my Volvo's chassis blots out his sun.

As I'd sat on the crinkly butcher paper with a doctor setting my arm bones, I knew I'd have to act. Lie down too many times—make a habit of showing your soft belly—and you forfeited the spine it takes to get up. I brought a tube of airplane glue to school and ran a thick bead around the toilet seat Ernie always sat on just before recess. His confused bellowings were auditory honey to me. He tore skin off his backside trying to stand. The firefighters were called, but before they arrived the janitor attempted to loosen the bond with some manner of chemical solvent; it reacted with the glue, scalloping Ernie's thighs with a first-degree heat rash. The firemen unscrewed the seat from the bowl and led him out to the truck. Ernie didn't get a chance to wipe.

We were both summoned to the principal's office. Ernie glared at me, eyes reflecting dull, smokeless hate. I whispered: "You're strong, but I'm smart. I'll hurt you worse."

Ernie laid off, but others didn't. My childhood was a procession of bowl-cut, feeble-minded tormentors who earned harsh, quixotic reprisals. Eventually the message disseminated among our city's bully population: *Don't bother with Jasper. Seek easier meat.* But it was a message writ in blood, as much mine as theirs. The hospital's staff psychologist had once asked, during my mandatory annual appointment, if the years of bullying had compelled me to make one side of myself as powerful as possible.

"Look at Ziggy Freud over here," I'd said. "You've pinned my id to the wall."

I turned from the window, headed into the kitchen. I always medicated on the polished granite of the butcher block—clean and sanitary like the OR. My pills were in the fruit bowl. I popped four Nolvadex, an anti-estrogen med, two Proviron, two Fludara.

I cracked open the fridge, found the pre-mix of HCG behind the cocktail olives. I was unwrapping an insulin needle when Penny came in. The harvest moon fell through the east-facing window to gloss the swell of her stomach.

"What's that?"

I said, "Truth serum."

"Oh?" she said. "You'll tell me all your secrets?"

"It's human chorionic gonadotropin," I said. "Testosterone regulator."

"I love when you talk shop, Jazz."

"It's derived from the urine of pregnant women. I take 250 IUs weekly, spread out in 50 IU doses. The synthetic testosterone I inject converts into estrogen. *Aromatizes* is the word."

"I like the sound of that. Aromatize."

"Gotta take my meds so I don't get gynecomastia. Buildup of breast tissue, yeah? Otherwise I'd develop a lush set of man-cans. Except I'd only get one, on my right side."

Penny cupped her own breasts. "Mine are huge."

"They'll get bigger. Wait until your milk drops."

She took the needle. "Where do you want it?"

"Deltoid. Medial head."

She swabbed my shoulder with rubbing alcohol, jabbed the needle.

"It could be yours, Jazz."

"Pen, please."

"What?"

"You may as well be fucking a eunuch. I've been playing silly buggers with my body chemistry and I still produce barely enough testosterone to put hair on my nuts. Plus I was tested. You know that."

"You say so, but—"

"My swimmers are not viable, Pen. Mutation levels sky-high. Two-headed swimmers. Or no heads at all."

Put my sperm under an electron microscope and you'd see platoon on platoon of headless, legless, useless soldiers. Sometimes an image hits at the instant of release: a flood of broken-limbed bodies and horribly mutated forms sheeting over an austere landscape. Unmuscled arms and sightless eyes and corkscrewed appendages divorced from their husbanding bodies—no connectivity, no purity of form. A tidal stew of sexless, mismatched parts.

If I've somehow been robbed, karmically speaking—well, then only if considered in juxtaposition to normal people, the average life possibilities. But I've never been normal. Not one moment of my life. The word "miraculous" has tagged too many of my life-markers. Since birth, every second of my existence has been borrowed against fate. We're all on extinction vectors anyway; some vectors are simply more acute than others.

"It only takes one," Penny said. "You'd make a good dad." Her fingers traced her belly. Her bellybutton had popped out. "Anyway, I could lose it."

"Don't talk that way, Pen."

I'd met her when she'd lost the first one. Then later, when the second one passed. A third survived a few days. Gastroschisis: born with its organs outside its body. I never got a chance to operate. It would've taken an act of God anyway.

"You'd make a good dad," she said again.

I plucked an orange from the fruit bowl, squeezed it convulsively. The rind ruptured, spilling juice down my forearm. A funny trick I pulled out at parties—I'd get drunk, pulp a whole sack of them. The Juicer.

"You know who else'd make a good dad, Pen? Your husband."

"Cruel."

Why dispute it?

The Arm Wars Classic Finals took place in the parking lot of the Americana Motor Lodge, a hop-skip from the flesh pits at the ass-end of Stanley Avenue. The night was humid. I felt the high-hat beat of my heart where my throat met my jaw.

I'd been training on a jury-rigged pulley system in my garage: one end of the cable was attached to a U-handle, the other to a milk crate. I'd loaded the crate with weight plates, gripped the handle, and pinned it down. I worked out after my graveyard shifts at the NICU, inching my way to nearly three hundred pounds and only quitting when my wrist made poppy-grindy noises.

I bought a Labatt Blue from an old Mexican selling them out of a picnic cooler, and scanned the contestants. Everybody was wearing yellow T-shirts that read I'M PULLING FOR YOU. I milled with the crowd, relishing the tightening sensation inside my chest: a thousand disparate threads pulled from each muscle group, gathering toward a singular purpose.

My opponent was a cask-bellied brute in a John Deere cap. He set his elbow on the pad, tendons protruding from his neck. Didn't matter if a guy had sweeping back muscles or a striated chest—arm wrestling required a specific kind of strength, concentrated in the wrist and fingers, the biceps and shoulders. I had that. Beyond that I had a grinding, golemlike power to demoralize my opponents.

I dusted my hands with chalk. We locked up. The guy grooved

deep into the webbing between my thumb and fingers, trying to preemptively break the plane of my arm — if he could peel back the wrist and come over the top, the match was won.

I disengaged, shaking my arm out. The adrenaline was jacked into me now — that familiar ozone tang at the back of my throat. We locked up. The grip was pure. Spectators clustered round. The ref straightened our wrists.

"Go!"

My opponent pulled hard, sank in the hook, dropped his thumb, and came over in a smooth, quick move. My arm bent back. The cartilage in my shoulders shrieked. My hand was two inches from the pad, but it held. The big bastard torqued his shoulder, bearing down, screaming: "Reeeeagh!"

I hissed between my teeth, popped my opponent's thumb, and broke the hook. My biceps were spiderwebbed with veins, flushed pink with pressure. I jerked my arm in a series of hard upward pops, each one budging the guy's arm. I shifted instinctively, slipping my thumb over his first knuckle and finding my own hook, bearing down with ceaseless pressure. This was my element: the slow and steady grind. The big man's wrist folded back, steel gone out of it. His shoulder gave out next. His whole body went from a power posture to a crumbling one. I worked steadily, inching him down.

A comber of teeth-splitting coldness broke over me, something awful happening in my chest, as if each organ was unlocking itself from my body. The big guy folded his wrist back over and cranked my arm back. I let out a pitiful yelp.

"Winner," the ref said, holding up the big man's hand.

I wiped spittle off my chin. "Good pull," I told him.

Ten seconds later I was humping across the road, squinting against the glare of onrushing headlights, over the crushed gravel of the breakdown lane to The Sundowner. I tipped the tuxedoed bouncer and settled into a seat on Pervert's Row.

The girl on stage had rudely chopped dark hair and lean, articulate limbs that seemed to swivel on finely tuned servos. She had an android's aura: a futuristic pleasure model — all ballistic rubber, frictionless nylon, and silicon grease. As she rode the brass pole, her expression was one part boredom mingled with two parts existential despair. When the song ended she stepped off the stage and took the chair next to mine. Her hand fell on the baguette of flesh and bone that was my left thigh.

"Buy a gal a drink?"

The waitress took my twenty and returned with a glass of water for the girl.

"Pricey agua," I said.

"It's from a glacier."

"I don't normally come to places like this."

"Nobody ever does, man."

She asked if I'd like to have sex. I said yes without giving it much thought. She disappeared behind the tinselly curtain and came back in a tracksuit. The night sky was freckled with clear, cold stars. We walked to the Double Diamond motel, past its leaf-strewn swimming pool hemmed by a waist-high chainlink.

Her room was small and neat and smelled of carpet freshener. She threw herself on the bed in a childlike way: her butt hit the mattress, bouncing her up. She sloughed her sweatshirt off in a manner some might've found simply unpretentious but to me seemed sloppy and careless.

"Three hundred bucks," she said.

"For what?"

She explained what it would buy. Seemed reasonable enough.

I said: "What do we do now?"

"Do you need a refresher on the birds and bees? You can tell me what to do if you'd like."

"Just give me the usual."

"Ah. A traditionalist."

She gripped my hips. Unbuttoned my pants, slid them down.

"Your legs . . ."

She seemed fascinated rather than horrified—either that, or she was the consummate pro's pro. I slid my shirt up to show her my stomach.

"You're like that all the way up?"

"To my neck, yes."

She fished her hand through the fly of my boxers. Her touch was dry but gentle. "Feels like the standard apparatus."

A fragile voice said: "Mom?"

The boy had stepped through a door that connected to the adjacent room. At first sight I understood he'd been dealt a common genetic indignity. His chest had that telltale shrunken quality. The girl snatched up her top and went to him. I pulled up my trousers.

"What's wrong?" she asked the boy, who was perhaps six.

"Thirsty."

She gave me a tight smile and held up one finger—*give me a minute.*

"Take your time," I said. "In fact, I could use some water myself."

I walked into the next room, which clearly they shared. Open suitcases, the smell of cough syrup and body butter. In the bathroom I unpacked two motel glasses from their paper wraps. I smiled at my reflection. Blood climbed the chinks of my teeth. I swished water around in my mouth, spat it red-tinged down the drain.

The boy rubbed sleep-crust from his eyes and accepted the glass. He drank, coughed a little, breathed heavily.

"CF?" I asked his mother.

"How can you tell?"

"I'm a children's physician. Saw the medicine bottles on the nightstand."

Cystic fibrosis. A gene mutation. Hallmark symptoms: poor growth, low muscle tone, high incidence of infertility. The boy and I were practically brothers.

"Show him," she said to me.

I sipped water, regarding her over the glass's rim.

"Please."

I peeled off my shirt, flexed my right biceps. A single ticket to the gun show.

The boy said: "Are you sick?"

"Aaron. That's not nice to ask."

"Yes. I'm sick."

"You're not going to die, are you?"

"Aaron."

"Not right here in front of you. I'll hold on a bit longer, I promise. Do you know where I was tonight, Aaron? An arm-wrestling contest."

The boy said: "Did you win?"

"Not this time, but I've won before. Here, I'll show you how."

I had him sit on one side of a small table while I sat on the other.

"Lay your arm on the table."

Obediently, he did so.

"Let's work on your form, Aaron. Your butt's stuck way out for starters; scoot up, get closer. Now your arm's too straight. Bend your elbow, get your hand closer to your chin." I gripped his hand, the bones birdlike. "Now you've got all the leverage and I've got none. Technique is what evens the odds. It doesn't matter how strong or fast your opponent is if you've got him beat on technique."

I wanted to tell him: *Life is* all *technique. The world is full of us, Aaron. The mildly broken, the factory recalls and misfit toys. And we must work a lot harder. Out-hustle, out-think . . . out-technique.*

"Now if your opponent cranks your arm, don't panic. You can rest with your hand nearly pinned—the shoulder joint will prop you up." I pushed his arm gently backward, demonstrating. "Feels stable, doesn't it?"

"Yeah."

"Let your opponent exhaust himself, right? Then it's your turn. Concentrate on rotating your hand, pointing your knuckles at the sky. Try it, OK?"

The boy turned his hand over, peeling my wrist back.

"See? Now *you're* in control. And your opponent wants to quit. So make him."

The boy bent my arm back. "You let me win," he said.

"I did. But I'm an adult and I've been doing this a long time."

His mother tucked him back in bed. She cocked her head at the neighboring room and said, "Still want to . . . ?"

"It's OK."

I reached for my wallet. She trapped my hand in my pocket. We stood in the gauzy half-light. My cell phone chimed. Code blue at the hospital. So I hotfooted it back to the strip club and got into one of the taxis queued there. It wended down Stanley Ave., through pools of streetlight incandescence. I dialed the NICU, got Sandy on the line.

"Premature birth," she said. "Signs of IVH."

Intraventricular hemorrhage. Excessive pressure on the preemie's skull causes blood vessels to burst.

The cab dropped me at the ER. I shouldered through the swinging doors, moving fast, blitzed with adrenaline, stripped off my shirt in the prep area, and lathered my hands and arms with carbolic soap. A short hallway connected the prep area to the main surgical suite. The route took me past a series of glass-fronted rooms. In the final one, I saw Penny. I got only a flash of the delivery room—the blood, Penny's husband gripping her hand—before stepping into the surgical suite.

Penny's baby lay on the operating table. It—*he,* a boy—was covered in cottage-cheese-like vernix; his cheeks were feathered with lanugo hair. Dr. Beverly had strapped a mask over his mouth and nose.

"I've got him on a low dose of desflurane," Beverly said. "There's not a lot of brain activity."

The buildup of blood may've been screwing with the neurological rhythms. I selected the thinnest cannula, its gauge just wide enough to let the platelets out single-file. The procedure was tricky: pierce the fontanel and thread between the hemispheres into the ventricle shafts. Release the blood and bleed off the pressure without forfeiting too much cerebrospinal fluid—otherwise the unprotected brain would bounce against the skull case, killing motor function and the acute senses. Purely a "feel" operation—the equivalent of searching for water with a dowsing rod.

I positioned the needle in the center of the fontanel "diamond," the four corners where the skull bone had yet to join. The tip dimpled the skin and slid in without resistance. I crouched, training my gaze tightly. It always amazes me just how wonderful a newborn baby smells. The skin so unlined. The world hasn't yet laid its marks on it.

"He's spasming, Bev," I said. "You've got to stabilize."

The rubber hose feeding into the baby's mask was kinked. Gingerly, Beverly straightened it.

"Dr. Railsback?" Sandy's voice: distant, tinny. "You OK?"

The slope of the child's nose . . . The fingers of my left hand tightened ever so slightly around the needle's shaft. The fast-twitch fibers vibrated like overtuned piano wires. It only takes one. Jesus. Signs and wonders.

"Jazz, pressure's building."

I unscrewed the stent-clamp. A pressurized stream of blood jetted out. I willed myself to calm down—*begged* my body to do as it was told.

"Pressure's climbing," Beverly said. "We're getting spikes on the EEG."

I pulled the needle back half an inch, adjusted the angle, and reinserted. I'd be flirting with the pituitary gland.

We are all children of eggs. Old Ashanti proverb. And yes, we start that way. Flawless at conception. But consider all the ways it can go wrong: a defect within the zygotic membrane, an erroneous replication in the DNA chain, a chromosomal hitch, a slight misexpression of a critical peptide . . . imperfections so tiny that the strongest electron magnification reveals but a shadow of it. They are immeasurable in the truest sense; too often we measure them the wrong way, and they take on the weight of fate. The progenitor's sins passed down the bloodline. Such flaws are pearl-like: a body shapes itself around that tiny speck of grit. The pure mathematics of a healthy body and mind are staggering.

"We're black-spotting," Bev said. "We're going dark in there."

I gave the cannula the gentlest half-twist, hunting for the pocket. The steel slipped effortlessly through the folds, through storms of neurons snapping between those awakening synapses but going dark now, dimming . . . slowing now, going dark . . .

You've got to be tough for contingency's sake. My mother was tanked to the gills when she told me this. She had left a stove element on and I'd touched it. My right hand still bears the concentric scar. She pressed ice to the burn cavalierly, never setting down the jelly jar in her free hand. *You're only medium tough, kiddo,* she'd told me. *Right in that meaty part of the curve.*

There was weakness inside me. Some nights I felt it as a discrete entity, shifting and ungrippable. It was nothing I could seek out or eradicate—as much part of me as my organs and flesh, inseparable from whatever goodness of character or strength of will I might possess. I am simply not built to true. And my witching-hour fear is that this inborn weakness—marrow-borne and incurable—will find its deepest groove at the worst possible instant.

I bloodhounded that phantom pressure, grappling with my own rising terror that found its outlet through my fingertips—be *still,* for God's sake, please—the needle's tip inching through the dark forever inside the boy's skull as one pure, clean thought blitzed through my own furied brainpan:

O my son my boy my son my baby baby boy—

The Breeze

FROM *The New Yorker*

SHE WAS IN THE BRIG when her husband came home. Below her, neighbors reclined on their stoops, laughing and relieved, shaking off winter with loud cries and sudden starts. Someone unseen scraped a broom over a little courtyard, the rhythmic sound of brownstones in spring.

"In the brig!" Sarah called out and, with her wineglass at a tilt, looked down on the neighborhood. They called their six feet of concrete balcony overlooking the street the brig.

The children's voices carried in the blue air. Then the breeze came. It cut through the branches of the trees, turning up the silver undersides of the young leaves, and brought goosebumps as it went around her. The breeze, God, the breeze! she thought. You get how many like it? Maybe a dozen in a lifetime . . . and already gone, down the block and picking up speed, or dying out. Either way, dead to her, and leaving in its wake a sense of excitement and mild dread. What if she failed to make the most of what remained of this perfect spring day?

She finished her wine and went inside. Jay was thumbing listlessly through the mail.

"Hey," he said.

"What do you want to do tonight?" she asked him.

"Oh," he said, and paused over what looked like a credit-card offer. "I don't care. What do you want to do?"

"There's nothing you want to do?"

"I want to do whatever you want to do," he said.

"So it's up to me to come up with something?"

He looked at her at last. "You asked me to come home so we could do something."

"Because I want to do something."

"I want to do something too," he said.

"OK," she said, "so let's do it."

"Let's do it," he said. Then he said, "What is it you want to do?"

She wanted to have a picnic in Central Park. They bought sandwiches from a place in the neighborhood and took the train into Manhattan. He unfurled a checkered blanket in the breeze and spread it under a tree whose canopy would have spanned the length of their apartment. In the mild wind, the leaves ticked gently back and forth, like second hands on stuck clocks. She wore a shimmery green sundress, with a thin white belt, slipped on quickly in the few minutes she gave them to get ready. His knees looked as pale as moons in last year's shorts. They ate their sandwiches and drank a little wine, and then they stood and tossed a Frisbee until it was just a white underbelly floating in the darkness. Before leaving, they walked into a little wooded area and with barely a sound brought each other off in two minutes with an urgency that had hibernated all winter, an urgency they both thought might have died in its hole. It was all right now; they could go home. But it was early, and he suggested going to a beer garden where they'd spent last summer drinking with friends. There was a flurry of texts and phone calls, and before too long their friends showed up—Wes and Rachel, Molly with her dog. They drank and talked until closing time. Sarah skipped ahead down the street on their way to the subway and then skipped back to him, leaping into his arms. It stayed warm through the night.

On their way into Manhattan, he told her that they had tickets to a movie that night. It was the 3-D follow-up to the sequel of a superhero blockbuster. He had gone online the day before only to learn that the IMAX showings were already sold out. He couldn't believe it. How far in advance did this city make movie tickets available for pre-purchase, and how much cunning did it take to get your hands on them? He hadn't even been able to get tickets to the early show at the regular theater, which would have been preferable—it had been a long week and he was tired, and, for God's sake, who thinks they need to plan more than a day in advance to see a movie? It was just a movie, it wasn't—

She put a hand out to stop him. "Jay," she said. "I'm sorry, sweets. I can't see a movie tonight."

"Why not?"

"It's too predictable," she said. "Aren't you tired of movies? All we've done all winter long is go to movies."

"But I bought the tickets. They're bought and paid for."

"We'll get a refund," she said. "I can't see a movie."

"You're always telling me you like it when I plan things."

"It's a movie," she said, "not a weekend in Paris. I can't sit in a movie theater tonight, Jay. I'll go bonkers."

"It doesn't start until eleven. The night's practically over by then."

"Whose night is over?" she said. "Whose particular night?"

He didn't understand. "What are you getting so excited about?"

Her focus shifted, and she didn't answer. The train had slowed to a crawl and was now stopped altogether. Why had it stopped? They were sitting dead still in the bowels of the subway while the last hour or two—not even, not two—the last hour and change of daylight and breeze died out on the shoulders of those who had known better than to lock themselves inside the subway at such a delicate moment. Here was the underworld of the city's infinite offering: snags, delays, bottlenecks, the growing anxiety of never arriving at what was always just out of reach. It was enough to make you stand and scream and kick at the doors. Their ambitions should have been more modest. They could have walked over the Brooklyn Bridge and stopped midway to watch the sun go down.

She stood.

"Sarah?" he said.

The train started to move—not enough to jolt her, but enough to get her sitting again. She didn't answer or look at him.

She left the table and started toward the ladies' room of the beer garden. She walked under a sagging banner of car-lot flags weathered to white, past a bin of broken tiki torches. A thick coat of dust darkened a stack of plastic chairs growing more cockeyed as they ascended a stucco wall. Open only a week or two after the long winter and already the place looked defiled by a summer of rough use.

In the brig a few hours earlier, she had come to believe that in all the years she had lived in the city, this was the most temperate and gentle day it had ever conferred. Distant church bells had rung out. The blue of the sky had affected her deeply. A single cloud had drifted by like a glacier in a calm sea. Looking down, she had paid close attention to the tree nearest the brig, picking out a discrete branch. It ended in a cluster of dark nubs, ancient knuckles sheltering life. Now, breaking through, surfacing blindly to the heat and light, pale buds had begun to flower. Even here, in rusted grates, down blocks of asphalt, spring had returned. Then the breeze touched her flesh. A tingling ran down her spine to her soul, and her eyes welled with tears. Did she have a soul? In moments like this, absolutely. The breeze! She spent the day at her desk, all the light of day spent while she kept her head down, and the snack pack convinced her it was OK—the snack pack and the energy drink, the time stolen to buy shoes online. Then this reminder, this windfall. As thrilling and irretrievable as a first kiss. This was her one and only life! It would require something of her to be equal to this day, she had thought at that moment in the brig, and now, looking at herself in the mirror of the ladies' room, scrutinizing her eyes, her veined and clouded eyes, she was afraid that she had made a series of poor choices and failed.

She left the bathroom. Jay was quietly drinking, surrounded by livelier tables. Their friends had not been able to come on such short notice.

"Can we go?" she asked.

He stood. She was dozing in the cab before they reached the bridge.

When they came up the subway stairs, she took one look at the light and said that it was too late. By the time they found food for the picnic and bought the wine, walked the rest of the way to the Park, and laid everything out, they would be eating in darkness.

"What are you after?" Jay asked.

"Let's cross," she said.

"What am I supposed to do with this stupid blanket if we're not going to the Park?"

They left the curb late and found themselves marooned on an island of concrete between two-way traffic. Cars zipped by in a steady stream. They didn't give them an inch to maneuver.

"What do you want to do?" she asked him.

"No, no," he said. "You just killed the picnic. You're in charge."

"I came up with the picnic," she said.

She needed an alternative, something to salvage this vital hour. But what? And this fucking traffic! A hundred million lights and every one of them stuck on green.

"What about that hotel?" she asked.

"What hotel?"

The drinks would be overpriced, and there would be no breeze, but the hotel lounge had a fine view of Central Park. It'd be better than waiting in a badly lit bodega for sandwiches to be made. They could eat later.

It was a short walk. They took the elevator up. The lobby, like the lounge, was on the thirty-fifth floor. Receptionists were checking guests in with hushed efficiency, as if, behind them, the first act of a play were just getting under way. Through the window in the distance, the Park was divided in two: the westernmost trees, hunkered beneath the tall buildings, were sunk below a line of shadow, while the rest, looking fuller, rose up in the light. Their leaves shivered in the breeze with more silver than green.

They had to sit at the bar first. Then the hostess came and got them. Once seated in the tiered lounge, they faced outward, as in a Paris café, and watched as the remaining trees were claimed by the shadow. They drank crisp white wine. Night settled grandly.

It still felt like winter down in the subway. There were hot gusts, weird little eddies of cold, the steel burn of brakes poisoning the platform—but never a breeze. Nothing so limpid and delicate as spring could penetrate here. Even inside the car, they were breathing last century's air. Salt tracks stained the floors. Soon winter would give way to hell: the subway's two seasons.

The train pulled into the station. Passengers rose from their seats and stood before the silver doors. They waited and waited. At last the doors opened and off they went, given early release; she still had time to serve. People from the front cars walked by, and then the platform was empty, and yet the doors didn't close. The purgatorial train seemed to be breathing, taking in air and letting it out, pointlessly. The automated voice announced, "Ladies and gentlemen, we are being held momentarily by the train dispatcher." A ludicrous little god at play with switches. One station after another it was like that, and, between each station, a maddening stop-and-go.

The warning *ding* of the closing doors sounded, but nothing happened, and the train failed to move. She was out on the edge of the bench. She turned, offering him only her profile. Slowly she said, "I would literally rather kill myself than go to a movie tonight."

He raised his brows, as if, at his desk on some Wednesday afternoon, the peal of a fire alarm had brought him to sudden life. It was an exaggeration, but her level voice was soft and frighteningly sincere.

"OK," he said. "We won't go to the movies."

Traffic eased. They stepped off the median and hurried across the street. But they didn't know where they were going or what they were doing, so they idled under the shade of a building. Passersby ignored them in a push toward known destinations, fixed plans, the city's eight million souls seeming to conspire against her, joining in something mysterious and urgent.

"Sarah," he said. "What is it you want to do?"

"I don't know," she said. "But don't put it like that."

"Like what?"

"What *should* we do, Jay?" she said pointedly. "What *should* we do?"

"Don't they come to the same thing?"

"They don't."

She spent ten minutes searching for something on her phone. He retreated a few feet, squatting near a scrawny tree planted in a little cell. When she gestured, he rose to his feet and followed her, keeping a step behind. At the next corner, they waited as taxis bounced by on their shocks. They caught every red light thereafter. They reached the building she wanted, the one with the lounge with a floor-to-ceiling view. She kept hitting the button as the elevator made its way down to them.

They were the last ones out when the doors opened. The window just past the reception area showed the buildings down Fifty-ninth Street checkerboarded with lights in the dimming hour. Bankers in their brigs, she thought. A canopy of shadow was slowly rolling across the silver treetops, settling the leaves into their darkest green.

All the tables were occupied or reserved. The hostess took Jay's name.

"Should we be here?" Sarah asked him.

"Isn't this where you wanted to be?"

The hostess watched them. "You're welcome to sit at the bar," she told them.

"Thank you."

"How long until a table is free?" Sarah asked.

The hostess didn't know. She couldn't guarantee one at all. They went to the bar, where they drank in silence.

She had wanted a picnic, then the subway had defeated her. Then they'd been stranded on the median bickering over nothing, the all-consuming nothing of what to do. Was it she, she alone, who made that question so inscrutable and accusing some nights, like a stranger leveling a finger at her from across a room? Or was it the haltings and blinders of an entwined life: the fact of Jay, the disequilibrium of having to take what he wanted into consideration, whatever *that* might be? Because he kept it to himself, or it remained alien to him, and so how could she hope to name it? Or maybe there was no mystery at all. Maybe he just wanted to see a movie.

The last of the daylight disappeared as they waited, and all the possibility that had arrived with the breeze was reduced to yet another series of drinks at a bar. By the time a table opened up, she felt drunk and unfocused. They had a final drink and left.

They tried having dinner at a cheap Italian joint downtown, but they got into a fight and left before he would even enter the restaurant. When they got home, they were no longer speaking. They lay in the dark for a long time before he broke the silence. "I could have gone to the fucking movie," he said.

She grabbed him when they reached the bottom of the stairs, turned, and, with his hand in hers, raced back the way they'd come, up the stairs into the mellow night. She breathed the spring air in deeply, shedding the subway stuff, the still blue sky confirming her good judgment. But he was confused.

"What are we doing?"

"Let's not get on the subway," she said. "I can't stand it down there, not right now. Let's just walk."

"Walk where?"

She led him west toward the Brooklyn Bridge. On the pedestrian walkway, she skipped ahead, then waited for him, then skipped ahead, then swung around and smiled. They came to a stop midway between Manhattan and Brooklyn just as the sun was setting. The wavelets in the bay turned over in little strokes, scaling the water silver before it darkened to stone. She looked straight up. Just to see the towering spires of the bridge climbing to a single point in the sky was to affirm that nothing more could be asked of this hour, nothing better apprehended in this life. She took hold of a steel cable in each hand and gazed out again at the setting sun. The burn-off against the buildings grew milder, its colors deeper; for a minute, the certainty that it would die out was in doubt. The sun dropped away, and a blue shadow settled over everything—the bridge, the water. It mirrored the cool ferric touch of the suspension cables. She let go, and the blood came back to her hands in heavy pulses. Her eyes filled with tears for the second time that night.

When the last of the sunlight was gone, she turned to him and said, "What did you think of that?"

He looked at her with perfect innocence. "Of what?" he said.

It was before midnight when she found herself sitting on the edge of the tub, fully dressed, doubting the future of her marriage.

They waited a long time for their drinks to arrive. The bar was situated—stupidly, to her mind—far from the view, and they were facing the wrong way. They had nothing to look at but liquor bottles and wineglasses, while outside the sun was disappearing and shadow was unfurling swiftly across the trees.

It had been a terrible idea to come up here, thinking they'd fall miraculously into a table. She wanted the city to be full of exclusive places turning people away, as long as they always accommodated her. It didn't work like that. What a stupid place to live—stretched thin, overbooked, sold out in advance. And, as if choosing the wrong place weren't bad enough, there were all those alternatives, abstractions taking shape only now: a walk across the bridge, drinks with Molly at the beer garden. Lights, crowds, parties. Even staying put in the brig, watching the neighborhood descend into darkness. The alternatives exerted more power over her than the actual things before her eyes. What had she been thinking, penning them in a bar on a night like this?

Knees fixed between the stool and the bar, she turned to him as best she could. "I'm sorry, Jay," she said.

"For what?"

"For rushing us out of the apartment, and for how I acted on the subway. And it was a mistake to come up here. Let's do something," she said.

"OK," he said. "Like what?"

The second he asked, the desire came over her to be in the Park, obscured by trees and bent over with her fingertips dug into the earth, and to feel him push her panties down to her ankles. As she worked it out in her mind, they would not be perfectly secluded, so that he would feel rushed, and as a result would be a little rough with her, dispense with the considerate sheets-and-pillows concerns of their weekend sex life and just fuck her, fuck her hard and fast. Then let the passersby ignore them, ignore the flash of white skin inside a clot of trees in the near-dark. She'd feel no sense of exclusion then. The minute she felt him coming, she would come too. Then she would right herself as he was buckling, straighten the sundress, smile at him, and, just like that, all the stale tenement air of married life would disperse.

"Sounds like you have something in mind, Sarah," he said, taking her hand under the bar. "Tell me what it is."

She dared herself to lean in and whisper it.

"I'm up for anything," he said.

But she lost the nerve.

"I don't really know," she said. "What do you want to do?"

He suggested they buy sandwiches before getting on the train, from the neighborhood place. But the neighborhood place! She was so sick of it. They had lived off that menu for as long as she could remember. Then she climbed out of the subway and knew they'd made a mistake. Finding food for a picnic would take time, time they didn't have. But if she called off the picnic because there was no time to find food, then what did they have if not time? Time to squander and squander until the night was over. One night after another until her life was over. A night in spring could make her go a little crazy, start thinking her options were either a picnic or death. Jay was charging forward, blanket under his arm, toward the picnic he believed was still on, when she stopped. It took him a minute to notice. He turned, then walked slowly back to her.

It wasn't in him to see what made this day different from other days. He didn't pick up on breezes and breaks in weather, or they came upon him as the natural course of events too common to celebrate. If he had had his druthers, even today he would have worked into the night, feeding at his desk from some Styrofoam trough, then hurrying to meet her for the late-night showing of the follow-up to the sequel. Once home, he would have collapsed on the bed as if all the adventurous excursions of the day had depleted him of everything but the delicious aftertaste of exhaustion. She wanted to be a different person, a better person, but he was perfectly happy being his limited self.

She had made a series of bad decisions, and now she traced them back to their source. It was not forgoing the sandwiches, or stepping onto the subway, or heading into Manhattan at the wrong hour. It was not leaving the brig where she had fallen into a fragile harmony with the day, or foolishly breaking that harmony to seek out something better. It was asking him to come home early. That was the mistake that had set everything else in motion.

"What is it?" he asked.

She was about to tell him. She had overcome her fear and was about to tell him everything when she said, "Thanks for carrying the blanket."

He looked at the blanket in his hands. "Sure," he said.

By the time they found food and made it into the Park, the shadow had overtaken the spaces between the trees. She could see vaguely that it was him as they laid the food out on the blanket, but, when the time came to pack up, it was so dark that he could have been anyone.

Molly looked up from the general laughter just as Sarah hurried past the tables in the distance. Sarah disappeared through a rusted steel trellis festooned with lights that served the beer garden as entrance and exit. "Uh, Jay?" Molly said.

She was a block away by the time he caught up with her.

"Hey," he said. "Hey!"

"It's over!" she cried. "It's over!"

"What's over?" he said, trying to take hold of her. "Stop. Stop!"

She stopped resisting and pressed her head against him and sobbed. Tears came through his shirt. Passersby, intrigued by the sight of another life on fire, skirted around them, turning back to stare.

"Spring," she said.

"Over?" He lifted her off his chest and looked at her. "Sarah," he said, "spring just started."

He was wrong. Spring was a fleeting moment, and it blew past like the breeze on the brig. Then summer rushed in, hot and oppressive as car exhaust, and she couldn't take another summer in the city. It was followed by another single moment, the instant the leaves changed color, and then it was winter again, the interminable winter, one after another endured and misspent until they came to an end with a final hour that she would never be prepared for.

"Tell me you get it," she said. "Please tell me you get it, Jay." She shook her head into his chest. "I'm scared to death," she said.

"What just happened?" he asked. "What went wrong?"

"What are we doing? Why did we come here?"

"Where?"

"What else could we have done?"

"We did a lot," he said. "We had a picnic, now we're with friends. Why are you so upset?"

"Should I not do the thing I do?" she asked. "Or should I do the thing I don't do?"

"What thing are you talking about?" he asked.

She didn't want to go back to the beer garden. She made him go. He said goodbye to their friends and reassured them that everything was OK. Then he returned to the corner where he'd left her. She was already in a cab on her way back to Brooklyn. She gathered some things from the apartment—her pills, her toiletries—and an hour later she was in Molly's apartment falling apart again.

The hostess came for them at the bar and led the way to a table in the lounge. The buildings down Fifty-ninth Street brought midtown to an abrupt end; the trees filling the Park had tumbled over the sheer blue cliffs of their mirrored surfaces.

Now night was rapidly resolving the green from the trees. A minute later, it seemed, the dark knit them together, and they were all one. Yellow taxis lost their color and became lights floating on air. The mysterious figures they were picking up and dropping off at the curb, those shadows: what were they seizing hold of at this hour, that would escape her grasp? She had to do something.

"Jay," she said. "Do you know what I've always wanted to do in the Park?"

He was idly picking at the label on his bottle of beer. "What's that?" he asked.

"Lean in," she said. "I have to whisper it."

The hostess never rescued them from their tight squeeze at the bar. They had a final drink and left. Out on the street, in the shadow of the Park, he asked, "Are you in the mood for dinner?"

"Sure," she said.

"Yes or no?"

"I said sure."

"Should we stay here, or go downtown?"

"Either way."

They took a cab downtown. This was the best they could imagine: another dinner downtown. She opened the cab door and stepped onto the curb just as a loud pack of strangers came through a foyer and out to the street. They were aimed half drunk at the center of the night. She wanted to abandon Jay and his blanket and dinner plans and follow them into another life.

Jay shut the door, and the cabbie drove off. "Do you have a taste for anything in particular?" he asked.

"No."

They stopped at a place to look at the menu. "Looks good to me," he said.

"It's fine."

"You're not crazy about it."

"Do I have to be crazy about it? It's dinner, who cares. It's fine."

"It should be more than fine if we're going to drop a hundred bucks in there," he said. "It should be a place you want to go."

"Oh, for fuck's sake," she said, and opened the door and walked inside.

It was an Italian place with checkered tablecloths, not likely to be anything special. And air-conditioned! There was no breeze here, only a recycled stream of arctic air. She would have walked out if Jay had been beside her. It was an affront to time. The first day of spring, and this place had it in a choke hold, waiting for its legs to stop kicking.

She requested a table for two, then turned and gestured Jay inside. He didn't move. She followed the hostess to the table and sat down. He glared at her through the window. *Unbelievable.* She picked up the menu and began to study it. So this was how the night had settled: in a squalid little showdown at a cheap Italian restaurant that was as far from a picnic in the Park as—

She didn't see him open the door. He raised his voice above the din.

"I'm not fucking eating in there!" he yelled.

Startled, she watched his head disappear and the door swing slowly shut. In that second, she was more determined to stay than ever, but people turned to stare at her, and she felt embarrassed, and so at sea compared with them, in their perfect little parties of friends and lovers, unburdened by the possibility of different companions, competing appetites, alternative pursuits of a finer life, as their dishes arrived at the appointed hour like destiny.

They left the bar excited. This was unexpected. *This* was being equal to the night. Not just watching the Park from afar, admiring its trees. Heading straight for them, into a different life. She hardly recognized him in the elevator. He kept looking over with a smile she'd never seen before. It was nearly enough to release them from the sentence of a long winter and its dull bedroom strain.

Outside, the last of the sunlight was gone from the sky. They were led into the Park by the silver light of old-fashioned streetlamps. Her heart pounded with uncertainty: Where would they do it? Would they be seen? How was it even done? Like a rush job, or something more deliberate, slowed down to expand the risk, intensify the thrill, feel anew the audacity of what two people can do?

They went deeper and deeper into the Park, until they were lost in it. They stopped and looked in both directions. Then she took his hand and rushed him into a dark knot of trees.

He unbuckled in a hurry as they kissed. She had to slip her panties down herself. Then she turned, planting her hands on the ground, and waited.

She waited and waited.

"Do you need help?" she whispered.

"Sh-h-h," he said suddenly. "Do you hear that?"

"What?"

He was quiet.

"Jay?"

"I need some help," he said.

She turned. A few minutes later, she brought her hands back to the ground. She waited.

"I lost it again," he said.

She stood and dusted herself free of earth.

"That's OK," she said. He was quickly buckling up. She reached out and touched him on the head.

There was an essential difference between them—what he might have called her restlessness, what she might have called his complacency—which had not surfaced before they were married, or, if it had, only as a possibility, hidden again as soon as it revealed itself. When they pointed out their shortcomings to each other, often in an argument, they both treated them as implausible accusations. But, if there was some intractable self in her that could be identified and accused, she thought, it was one in search of more life, more adventure, of the right thing to do at the given hour. It was not a homebody. It was not a moviegoer.

But suddenly she stopped. What made her any less predictable, she wondered, than she accused him of being? Night after night she was anxious not to miss out on . . . what? She didn't know. Something she couldn't define, forever residing just on the other side of things. It must be so tiresome for him, she thought. He must be convinced by now that she would never find it, that indeed there was nothing to find.

She was no longer beside him. It took him a minute to notice. He turned, then walked slowly back to her.

She reached out and took his hand. "Jay," she said. "What do you want to do tonight?"

"I thought we were having a picnic."

"Is that what you want?"

"Sure," he said. "Isn't that what you want?"

"Am I too predictable, Jay?"

"Because you like picnics?" he asked.

He put his arm around her, and they walked the rest of the way to the Park. After they ate, they lay on the blanket in the dark and talked again about having kids.

He was gloomy on the ride downtown, and gloomy when they stepped out of the cab. He was gloomy going from restaurant to restaurant while she studied the menus posted outside.

"Do you have a taste for anything in particular?"

"No," he said.

"Do you just want to go home?"

"Whatever," he said. "Up to you."

"Well, I don't want to go home," she said.

She chose a harmless Italian place. She wanted to turn to him to express her outrage that they were blasting the air conditioning on the first day of spring, but she knew that he wasn't in the mood. The place was louder than she had anticipated, a fact that became clear only after they'd been seated. They looked at the menu, keeping whatever impressions it made on them to themselves. Finally, he set his down on the checkered tablecloth, on top of the checkered blanket he'd brought for the picnic.

"Do you know what you're getting?"

He shrugged.

"Jay," she said, "it doesn't matter, it really doesn't."

"Maybe not to you," he said.

"I'm sorry that I even suggested it," she said.

"Why did you touch my head?" he asked.

"What?"

"Did you have to pat me on the head?"

She returned to studying the menu. Had she patted him? She hadn't meant to. She was just trying to make him feel better. When she looked up, sometime later, she found Jay staring intently across the room. She tracked his gaze to a table and to the man there, who was, she thought, his opposite in every way: charismatic at a glance, holding the table rapt with some expansive conversation. He was the handsomest man in New York. He would know what to do with her in the Park. Jay's fixation on him, she thought, while sullen and violent with envy, was also possibly at root pure curiosity, a reflection, a desire. He wanted to be the man, or at least someone like him: someone poised, commanding, rapacious. He would never change, but in his way, he wanted to, as she had always wanted most to be someone else.

They waited for their meal in silence, in muted unhappiness, the odd ones out in that lively place. They ate quickly, but it took forever. He went to bed when they got home. She went back out on the brig. What breeze came had no effect on her, and she understood that the night had been over several hours earlier, when everything she was seeking in the world had been brought out from inside her. If it had not lasted long, was it not enough? It had been an error to go in search of something more. If she had just told Jay about the breeze, shared that stupid fleeting moment with him—why hadn't she? He might have understood. Everything that came after was a gift that she had squandered.

They walked out of the Park and hailed a cab. The driver let them out with plenty of time to kill. They had dinner, then found a bar where they nursed their drinks. They didn't say much.

"Are you sure you want to do this?" he asked her.

"I told you."

"I know, but why? You were so adamant on the subway."

"It's what you want to do," she said.

It was time to leave. She stood up from the bar.

"OK," he said. "But it was never that big a deal to me."

"I know," she said.

"And what you wanted to do," he said, "we couldn't do."

"I told you it doesn't matter," she said.

They left the bar and walked to the theater. They watched the follow-up to the sequel, and then they went home.

Hover

FROM *Paris Review*

IT STARTED A FEW WEEKS after we separated for good. In this line of work, the symbolism wasn't lost on me. But to call it "flying" might be to misrepresent it. It wasn't as if I were soaring above the housetops, gliding west over the wide boulevards to see the sun setting over the Santa Monica Pier. If it was anything, it was a hovering: a little lift, when I least expected it.

You'd think it would have happened when I was feeling most free. Jogging around the tar pits early on a clear morning, which is something I do to get myself out of the house on the very quiet weekends when Jack is with his father. Or even sitting at my computer, as I am now, looking at the flat roof below my window, where the wind rolls a basketball, bleached white, back and forth across a damp depression in the tar paper. But this isn't the case. Instead, it's during the times I am doing those jobs I used to complain about to Drew: cooking or laundry or sorting the recycling, tasks I had imagined would be shared in a contemporary marriage and which automatically fell to me because I was the one whose work yielded a smaller and more erratic income, and who was home all day.

I was standing over something on the stove, a quick-cooking grain like bulgur or amaranth that requires constant stirring—something my mother would never have bothered with—when I noticed that I had to bend to reach the pot. And then that the stove seemed to be receding as well, and I remember thinking that the floor was collapsing under our feet, and that a stove that fell that way would surely explode. I lunged toward Jack, who was sitting at the kitchen table, eating cheddar-cheese crackers shaped like rabbits, and my feet, without traction, simply pedaled the air before I landed with an awkward stumble. My son looked up in mild surprise—I am always asking him not to stomp, because it's a duplex and there's a single woman below us—his mouth edged in brilliant orange.

"Amy," he said, which is the name of the other tenant.

That was the first time.

It's true that I've been doing yoga for the past three years. In fact, the yoga was one of the things that bothered Drew, something about my enthusiasm for something that everyone else is enthusiastic about too. Well? Yoga is good for your body, and it calms you down, and maybe the herd is sometimes right. On the other hand, even I have to admit that I enjoy talking about it more than I actually like doing it, and that I'm not one of the shining stars of the class—not the worst, certainly, but somewhere in the bottom third. I have trouble getting myself from chaturanga dandasana back to downward dog, and so it seems unlikely that I have learned to levitate, which rules out the only vaguely plausible explanation for the thing that started happening to me since we agreed to a divorce.

I can't help feeling that other people had better reasons for their breakups than we did. (This is characteristic of me, Drew would say, the way I am always comparing. "How can you be happy if you're constantly measuring your life against the lives of others? And not even examining," he would say. "Inventing . . . fictionalizing! How can you know what anyone else's life is like?") I think of Helene, a woman I used to teach with at the Y, who married a Czech architect she met on vacation in Prague. Life in the United States didn't suit him and he moved back after eighteen months. Or Drew's old friend Jim, whose wife left him for her high school boyfriend, with whom she reconnected through social media soon after the birth of their second child.

With Drew and me there was nothing so concrete to explain it: one night last spring we sat down in the living room after dinner, looked at each other, and knew.

"When was the last time you were happy?" he asked me.

I was indignant. "Just this afternoon," I told him. "Jack asked if I wanted him to zip or button my jacket for me."

He shook his head. "Not with Jack," he said, and it was one of those moments in an argument when you know it's very important to respond quickly, but you don't respond, and the length of the pause makes the question irrelevant.

"Well, what about you," I said, and he just shook his head. One of the things I've always liked about Drew is that he doesn't have any trouble crying, and his crying then made me want to take him in my arms and promise it would be fine. I did do that, with the predictable result that we had sex, and it was so clearly the last time, even while it was happening, that I cried too.

My friends have gently suggested that Jack's attachment to a bag of King Arthur unbleached self-rising flour has something to do with his parents' separation, that he sensed it coming, and it's the kind of allegation you can't dispute without sounding defensive. But I know for a fact that Jack had no inkling of our problems until we told him his father was moving out and that his relationship with the flour began several months earlier, coinciding exactly with the time he began asking questions about death.

"What do people do after they die?"

"How do dead people pee?"

"Will you die?"

And then one afternoon when we were pulling into the parking lot at Gelson's, me looking in the side-view mirror to make sure I didn't hit one of those giant concrete columns and Jack watching me from his booster seat:

"Will *I* die?" His face white like a mushroom in the gloom of the back seat.

"Not until you're very, very, very old—not for almost a hundred years." Drew and I had agreed on this answer, and that time I think I did it perfectly, turning around to face Jack, saying it in an upbeat way but without any false heartiness. He waited until we were getting the cart from the line outside the door, wrenching it away from its fellows.

"I am really afraid of dying."

And so I put him in there, hoping I wouldn't get stopped by a manager; he's a skinny kid, but tall, more than forty pounds now. People glanced at him, but I thought this was one of those times when you give in, as long as the request isn't too unreasonable.

"Can I have something?"

"From the grocery store?"

"Just one thing?"

"Nothing junky."

"I don't mean that," he said. Maybe if he hadn't been up in the cart, he wouldn't have noticed the flour, with the knight waving his pennant: a Greek cross, red on a white ground.

"There," he said, grabbing the metal shelf so that I had to stop.

"But we're not baking anything."

"Not to use. Just to keep."

"Keep where?"

"In my room."

So I bought him the flour. It sat on the shelf with the books he'd outgrown. Sometimes it was incorporated into a building made of Bristle Blocks or a playground for the Lego people, who used it for a trampoline. He named it Malfin, which he pronounced to rhyme with *dolphin*. Drew didn't notice Malfin, and uncharacteristically Jack didn't mention it to his father, and so it didn't come up, at least until he started sleeping with it.

"No," I heard him say. I was in the kitchen making dinner, and Drew had come home early enough to put Jack to bed, as he used to do most nights. Their voices escalated, and then Jack was in the kitchen, close to tears, his arms around the bag of flour. There was a dusting on the front of his navy-blue pajamas, the pair that features dogs in spaceships, and a faint white trail on the carpet behind him.

"Daddy says I can't sleep with Malfin."

"He's leaking," I said weakly.

"I slept with him last night."

"Here." I gave him a Ziploc gallon bag and sealed it up. He didn't like having the flour under plastic like that, but I could see he was going to compromise. "But when he starts to come out of this bag, he's going to have to go back on your shelf."

He nodded. "Just don't throw him away while I'm at school."

"I promise."

"How long will he last?"

I almost said "Forever," and then changed my mind. "As long as you need him."

The year he was three, when he wanted to wear one of my necklaces to school every day for several months, everyone thought it was sweet, including the teacher. I give Drew credit, because he was born in the sixties. The idea that Drew's father would've allowed his son to wear a necklace to school is laughable, but Drew went right along with it, talking about how well Jack was negotiating separation. I don't know why the flour didn't work the same way, but it didn't—with the teacher or with Drew.

When she called to make an appointment, I figured it was about the flour. Either that or his problems with another boy in the class who seemed to be picking on him. I hoped it was Malfin, and I tried to make a joke about it. But the teacher didn't laugh.

"Nothing serious, but I think we should talk about it. If you can come in?"

"Just me?" I'd asked, but she said it would be better if we could both come.

The boy whom he was having problems with was also called Jack: Jack H. They have a playground with a climbing structure that incorporates round, wooden "barrels" elevated off the ground and big enough for five or six children to sit inside. One day our Jack had come home saying that Jack H. had told him he couldn't come into the barrel, even though there was room, and when he'd tried to go past him, Jack H. had pinched his ear.

I looked at the ear, which did seem a little red. Then I tried to distract him, since these things usually blow over quickly. But I kept hearing about Jack H., who organized games of bad guys/good guys in which Jack wasn't allowed to take either role.

"Can't you go play with someone else?"

Jack let out an exasperated sigh. "I told you—if I go somewhere else, he follows me." This was on a Sunday night, when we try to have dinner in a restaurant, all three of us, in order to ease Jack's transition from me to Drew, or vice versa.

"Maybe he likes you," Drew suggested. "He just doesn't know how to show it."

Jack looked at his father with disgust. "The problem is our names are the same. Why did you give me this name?"

"Why did his parents give *him* the name?" Drew said. "It's your name—you had it a long time before you met Jack H."

Jack shook his head. "You don't understand. His birthday is March, and mine is July, so he had it first."

"It's actually very impressive," I told Drew when he called me later for our weekly scheduling talk. "Most kids his age don't have a sense of time like he does. Some of them don't even know the order of the months. His abstract-reasoning skills are strong—that must be from you."

I thought a little flattery would help, but Drew didn't go for it. "Do you know the kid?"

"No. I've met his parents at school, but that's it. They've never played together."

"There was this bully, Christopher, in middle school," Drew said. "A big Irish kid who took lunch boxes. He'd throw them up in a tree, and they'd get stuck there. Then he said he'd break your nose if you told—he did break one kid's nose. My dad told me Italians were tougher than Irish, but I knew we weren't real Italians. I was so scared of that kid, I couldn't sleep at night."

"Jack H. is Chinese," I said.

"Chinese?"

"Half."

"Can you imagine a Chinese bully when we were in school?"

"I can't really remember." I have trouble remembering the details of my childhood, which Drew used to say was strange. I remember the setting: the bougainvillea over the garage, the smell of the Santa Anas, the fact that it was a coyote that killed our black-and-white cat when he wandered onto the golf course across the street. But I have to think for a moment to remember that the cat's name was Fletcher.

"Of course not—the Asian kids were all first-generation then. That's where our stereotype comes from, but you see Jack's going to have a completely different set of references." Drew is the HR director of a midsize technology company, but as an undergraduate he studied anthropology; he has always loved an explanation, particularly when it overturns some piece of empirical evidence.

"What does the teacher say?"

"I thought I'd wait until the conference. I'm not crazy about her."

"Why?"

"She's a little cold. Like with Malfin—the first day he brought him in to share, she just gave me this look. Like, 'Flour?'"

Drew was incredulous. "He brings the flour to school?"

"Just for the past week or so."

"Jesus," he said, and used my name, which he never does. "Why the fuck do you let him do that?"

"Because he wants to. And I didn't want him to feel embarrassed about it."

"You're supposed to feel embarrassed about things that are embarrassing! How else do you learn?"

"Learn what?"

"What's embarrassing!" Drew sighed, as if someone had just sent him a big assignment that hadn't previously been part of his workload. "Of course he's getting bullied by a Chinese kid. Christ."

I ran into Jack H.'s mother a few days before the conference, standing outside the one-way mirror through which we could look into the classroom and see our children. They weren't supposed to be able to see us, but Jack said that he could see "my shadow," and he often looks up near the end of the school day and gives the window his patented half-smile. That day, I was relieved to see, he was nowhere near Jack H. but was sitting on the floor with a three-year-old named Ava, one of the younger children in his mixed-age classroom. Ava was lying rigid on a small red carpet, and Jack was measuring her with a wooden stick. Malfin was sitting (if that is the right word) by his left hip.

Jack H.'s mother greeted me by name, and I wondered for the millionth time what it is about me that keeps me from remembering the names of people I don't know well. I'm always afraid I'll make a mistake, and usually I don't risk it.

"I love when I can be here early to watch them." She was beautifully dressed in a gray silk pencil skirt and heels. I did remember that she worked at Google.

"I'm usually early."

"Oh, you're lucky," she said, but not in an unkind way. If she noticed that I was wearing exercise pants and a hooded cotton sweatshirt, she didn't show it. "I'm taking him to the dentist today. Here he comes." The teacher opened the door and Jack H. bounded out, a wiry, handsome kid, a little shorter than our Jack. He didn't know who I was and ignored me, throwing himself on his mother and burying his face in her elegant skirt. She suggested that he go to the bathroom before they left, and he obligingly went.

"That's great that he goes alone."

"Yeah," she said. "But you wouldn't want to use it after him."

We laughed, and I thought that I should suggest a playdate. Maybe if it was just the two of them.

We could hear the water running on the other side of the door,
going off and on again. Jack H.'s mother rolled her eyes in the direction of the bathroom and then suddenly put a hand on my arm.

"I've been meaning to say, I'm so sorry about—whatever it is."

"Oh, it's OK," I said, too quickly. "They'll probably be best
friends by next week."

"Maybe—but it's still not OK." She looked suddenly flustered,
and I felt an unexpected sympathy.

"Jack told me—I'm *so sorry*."

One thing I hadn't expected about getting divorced was the
way everyone wants to talk to us about it. There's a predictable
voyeurism in it, but also a sense of duty. I wonder sometimes if it's
a particularly American thing, an obligation to probe the domestic
upheavals of strangers.

"Oh," I said. "It's OK—really. It wasn't for a while, but now it is."

Jack's mother gave me a searching look and lowered her voice.
"I can imagine it would never be OK. And now you're going
through this too."

Did she mean the bullying? "Um—I hope not. I mean, I hope it
will all be OK."

She nodded uncertainly. "I can see how the flour . . . helps.
Do you think if he stopped bringing it, though, it might be easier
for him?"

"For my Jack?" The other Jack was coming out of the bathroom,
drying his hands on his T-shirt, and so his mother lowered her
voice:

"I was just thinking, maybe the other kids would tease him less?"

That night at bedtime I sang "God Rest Ye Merry, Gentlemen,"
even though it was nearly March. Jack drinks a cup of warm milk,
followed by a bath, toothbrushing, books, peeing one last time,
and then a song. I used to alternate among a few favorites: "Baby
Beluga," "This Land Is Your Land," "Puff, the Magic Dragon," Si-
néad O'Connor's "The Emperor's New Clothes"—the first three
because he knows them from school, and the third because I happen to remember all the lyrics. But last Christmas when he was
four, we heard "God Rest Ye Merry, Gentlemen" in Rite Aid on
Wilshire, and we've been singing it ever since. I'd always understood it as a sort of prayer to God for some merry gentlemen who
might be suffering from fatigue, perhaps even the Wise Men, but

it turns out that it's "rest" in the sense of "keep" the gentlemen merry, and that they aren't any particular gentlemen, but all of us—at least those of us who are members of the church.

The other night, Jack stopped me near the beginning.

"Was Mary a witch?" he asked unhappily.

"Did she have special powers, you mean?"

"The which His mother Mary did nothing take in scorn," Jack repeated. I still need the iPhone to get started with each verse, but he knows all the words by heart.

I explained that it was the other *which,* and what it meant: that Mary didn't mind giving birth to Jesus in an animal's stall, because Mary was a special kind of mother. I hoped he wouldn't ask why Mary was special, since we haven't yet gone into detail about conception, much less immaculate conception.

"But Jesus is dead."

"No!" I said. "That's the magic thing about Jesus. He was dead, but then he came back to life and went to heaven."

"Do you believe in heaven?" Jack asked.

I started in on the thing I always say about my grandmother and how I still kind of feel her near me sometimes. Jack has heard this before and didn't let me finish.

"I want to believe in it."

"You can!" I told him. "Definitely. When you grow up—and I mean, now too. You can just believe in it."

I waited, but he didn't say anything else, and so I kept singing:

> The shepherds at those tidings rejoiced much in mind,
> And left their flocks a-feeding in tempest, storm, and wind,
> And went to Bethlehem straightway, the son of God to find,
> O tidings of comfort and joy . . .

Comfort and joy, comfort and joy, until the end of the song. When I finished I thought he was asleep, but then he turned over so that he was facing the door.

"Sit by the door," he said.

We waited outside the classroom until they were ready for us. The children had just gone to the playground.

"I wouldn't mention the Chinese thing," I told Drew. "They'll take it the wrong way, I guarantee."

"You think I'm a total moron," Drew said. "And by the way,

there's no reason to go into any more detail about our situation."
We had already met with both the teachers and the principal to
discuss how best to handle the thing we were inflicting on our son.
"We don't even have to mention it, unless they bring it up."

"You think *I'm* a moron."

Then the pretty, young assistant teacher waved us in.

"Welcome," said the head teacher, whose name was Janine.
"Thanks so much for coming in."

We sat down on the tiny wooden chairs.

"I don't think it's too serious, but we want to make sure we understand what's going on."

The assistant, who couldn't have been more than twenty-four,
gave us a sympathetic look. She had doll-like features and round,
green eyes, accentuated by expertly plucked brows; she was wearing a loose-knit white sweater-vest over a pink T-shirt and corduroy
pants, an outfit that managed to look both whimsical and stylish.
Jack adored her and once had asked if she could come over to
take a bath with him.

One of the nice things about Drew is that if he finds another
woman attractive, he doesn't show it in front of me. He also tends
to seek out the source of authority in a room and speak exclusively to that person—something he did with Janine, who looked
appropriately teacherly, with a grayish brown braid and a pair of
tortoiseshell glasses.

"We thought maybe you were concerned about Malfin," Drew
said, mispronouncing the first syllable to rhyme with *pal*. "That's
his name for the flour."

"Oh—we know about Malfin," Janine said, getting it right.

Drew smiled companionably. He can be charming when he
wants to. "He probably wanted to make cupcakes, and then when
you said no"—he looked at me—"he started using it in his con-
structions. He likes to build cities—maybe you've noticed. Civilizations."

"Civilizations," the teacher repeated neutrally.

"Jack D. does love building," the assistant piped up, and I
thought that "Jack D." was a person I didn't know, who existed
only in this classroom, and that Jack must undergo a metamorpho-
sis every weekday morning. I thought of how he must spend those
quiet drives to school, during which he stares out the window and

insists on my playing Adele's "Rumor Has It" on repeat, shedding Jack for Jack D. Molting.

"He knew we weren't making cupcakes," I said. "He's attached to the flour—the way another kid might be attached to a stuffed animal."

The teacher glanced down at a piece of paper, hidden in a manila folder, and frowned. "I'm sorry to ask something so personal—but since Jack has only been with us a year—"

"It's OK," Drew and I said at the same time. We've answered every question enough times that it's almost a relief to field them.

"You didn't have any kind of tragedy in your family?"

I was confused, and I looked at Drew. Of course they knew about the tragedy already.

"Tragedy?" Drew asked politely.

"You've never had any other children?"

"Of course not," Drew said.

Both teachers smiled with relief. "I don't want you to be alarmed," Janine said. "Jack has a vivid imagination, and sometimes kids with a lot of imagination make things up. For example—Jack said he had a sibling who died."

"He said *what?*" Drew exclaimed. But I could picture it: Jack sitting in the block area with two or three other kids, Jack H. among them. Raising his voice in the strident way he does when he feels he's being ignored.

"He told other children?"

The teacher nodded apologetically, and I remembered Jack H.'s mother, how I had understood her to be talking about the divorce: *I can imagine it would never be OK.*

"It was a little brother named Peter."

I maintained a serious expression, but a tiny part of me was proud. He had a sack of flour, and he named it Malfin, but when he wanted someone to buy his story, he knew how to hew to reality.

"A lot of the kids are having little siblings," Gemma explained. "And so we've been reading *Peter's Chair*—he could have got the name from the book."

"We'll talk to him," Drew said.

"I wouldn't make a big deal about it. He's been doing very well otherwise—we saved some of his work for you to see." Janine handed Drew a sheaf of papers, many of them finger paintings.

Drew looked through them, pretending interest, although the paintings were a mess. Then he tried to fold them, but the dried paint began to flake off onto the carpet.

"Here," I said, and rolled them together to put in my bag, since Jack likes to show us each production. Then I reached down to pick the paint chips out of the industrial carpeting.

"Can we talk about the bullying?" Drew asked, and at that very inconvenient moment, I had a peculiar carbonated sensation, as if I'd been treated by one of those countertop soda makers everyone has now. I could feel the tug of whatever force propelling me upward, and so I hooked my feet around the base of the chair. Whether the chair was too light or the force too strong, I didn't know—all I could tell was that I was taking the chair with me. I put my hand on the table next to me, a low round table they used for art projects, and was relieved that it remained stable; unfortunately that movement made me appear to be purposely tilting my chair in that direction, like a provocative teenager.

"*Bullying* is too strong, I think," Janine said. "But Jack H. is excluding Jack D. He's keeping him out of the barrels."

I wanted to explain to Drew about the barrels, which I thought he might have failed to notice, but I was distracted by my predicament: Janine was staring at me, her natural eyebrows furrowed, and at any moment that tiny chair was going to lift off the floor. I couldn't see any other option, and so I pitched myself forward onto the floor, right in the center of the impromptu circle the four of us had made with our chairs, landing on my stomach with my face very near Janine's substantial leather clog. The sound that escaped from me obviously suggested I was hurt, although it was pure relief—that the impact of my fall seemed to have returned me to the realm of gravity.

"Are you OK?" Gemma exclaimed.

"Jesus," said Drew. "Are you?"

"No broken bones," I said. "Sorry. I'm a klutz." I sat back down in the chair, reassuringly anchored once again to the floor.

"The chairs are treacherous," Janine said drily. I could tell that she thought I'd engineered my bizarre fall in order to divert the conversation from our family's multifarious problems.

I turned to Gemma, whose sympathy suddenly struck me as genuine. "He's afraid of dying," I told her. "He's been asking a lot of questions."

"Sex and death," Gemma said cheerfully. "That's what it's all about—when you're four."

"Sex?" Drew asked.

"Their bodies," said Janine. "Not sex per se. What I recommend is lots of clear information. Not detail, but clarity."

"About sex and death," Drew said.

"About everything," Janine insisted. "Your custody agreement, especially. Does Jack have a calendar in both his rooms? It's very important that he be able to visualize the time he's spending with each of you."

"We did that," Drew said, although we hadn't.

"Of course we'll keep an eye on the situation with Jack H.— that's *our* job." Janine smiled meaningfully at us to remind us of our job: the clear information. Then she got up and thanked us for coming.

"He takes after you," Drew said.

"What do you mean?"

"Storytelling."

"All kids do that."

"Lie for fun?"

I had a sinking feeling as we descended the cinder-block stairwell, painted glossy white, our feet silent on the rubberized stairs. I thought of another thing we had told Jack, about how each of us would be happy to exchange his or her work for his days in school. That one I hadn't realized was a lie until this moment, when the thought of being at the beginning of a long school career, as Jack was, filled me with dread.

"I'll be there Saturday at noon," Drew said without expression, when we reached the first floor. Then he raised his hand cheerfully to the receptionist in the outer office and greeted her by name, before stepping out into the fierce sunlight. He put on his sunglasses, took out his phone, and then stood there in front of the school, e-mailing or texting with someone, a faint smile on his face.

I walked down the long hallway, where a pair of glass doors led to the playground. There were several classes out there, and for a few moments I didn't see him. It was a hot day, the sky big and white over their heads, and the children seemed to be running

in spurts, and then resting. Their voices rose to sharp, brief cre-
scendos, mimicking this frantic movement. Then I saw Jack in the
sandbox, still playing with Ava.

Sometimes I imagine a different child, although I've never ad-
mitted it to Drew. The one I picture is active and sun bronzed, a
little wild maybe, a big eater and a hard sleeper. Not crazy about
books, except for the kind that identifies types of construction vehicles or dinosaurs. It would've been unlikely for Drew and me to
have a kid like that, but there was something about Jack's position,
crouched so intently over whatever imaginary game they were playing, that disappointed me. Suddenly he looked up: someone had
called his name. I watched him stand up and make his way toward
the barrels, where, sure enough, one bare leg hung out of the
rectangular opening, the foot dangling in an army-green Keen.

There was no explicit rule about parents on the playground,
but we were obviously meant to wait and show ourselves to the
children when the school day was finished. I thought they probably had only ten or fifteen minutes left. I glanced back at the
exit, where Drew had finished with whatever conversation he'd
been conducting and disappeared. Then I stepped out onto the
playground and identified myself as Jack D.'s mom to the teachers on duty. Both of them nodded distractedly, each one shading
her eyes with her left hand. I headed toward Ava and Jack, who
had reached the barrel and were negotiating. It pleased me that
Ava was pretty in such a conventional way: long blond hair and
large, round blue eyes, slightly too close together, like one of those
molded plastic dolls. It occurred to me, absurdly, that she could
protect him.

"This is only for the good guys," I heard Jack H. say, as I came
up behind them.

"We're bad guys!" said Ava, not getting it.

"I'm not a bad guy," my Jack said, with disgust.

"How old are you?" Jack H. asked, ignoring Ava.

Lie now, I thought, but Jack gave his age correctly.

"I'm five," Jack H. said. "I had my bouncy-castle party. Ava was
invited, and Henry—but not you."

Jack started to climb the ladder to the barrel. The other Jack
stuck out his leg: "NO." Then he looked up and saw me. My Jack
turned around, and his surprise was replaced almost immediately
by pleasure.

"I'm a little early today." I realized that I'd been thinking of them as older than they were when I saw the twin expressions of envy on the faces of the other two children.

"He can't come in," said Jack H. My Jack looked at me.

"Why not?" I asked.

"You have to say a secret."

"I have a secret," my Jack said.

Jack H. ignored him. "Ava, you can." Ava scampered up the ladder: a turncoat in butterfly socks.

"I have a secret," I said. Jack H. considered this.

Ava laughed. "Let Jack's mommy come in."

"Only four kids in the barrel."

"And one mommy!"

"There's three kids," my Jack corrected. But when he climbed the ladder, the other Jack didn't stop him. All three children peered out at me from the rectangular opening. My Jack was smiling broadly. On the other side of the playground, the teachers were distributing balls from a nylon sack.

The inside of the barrel was dim, even warmer than outside. The air was thick with glittery bits of dust. You sat with your feet at the lowest point, your back resting against the wooden curve. It was intimate and uncomfortable. The children looked at me with wonder.

"You go first," Ava said.

"I'll go last," I said.

This made sense to Jack H. "Ava goes first, she's youngest."

"I have two dogs!"

"That's not a secret," the two Jacks chorused together.

Ava examined the lace on her socks.

"Jack, you're next."

Jack looked at me. "Daddy has a girlfriend," he said.

"Barbie has a girlfriend," Ava said. "It's Ken."

"Now me," said Jack H. "I had a wart, but the doctor burned it right off."

"Now the mommy!" Ava exclaimed.

"Your turn, Mommy."

"I can fly," I said. "I couldn't always, but I can now."

Jack H. was already shaking his head. "Nobody can."

"I know," I said. "That's why it's so strange."

My Jack looked at me nervously. "Is that a story?"

"No."

"Fly," said Ava.

"I don't know if I can do it now," I said. "It only happens when I'm doing mom stuff—taking care of the house and cooking and things."

"Do mom stuff," Ava said. "Do something for Jack."

Jack put his leg over mine and undid his sneakers. "Velcro my shoes."

I thought of Drew in the sunlight, one hand in his graying hair. I thought of the smile on his perfect mouth, which is also Jack's. Brilliant needles of light came through the cracks between the boards, streaking our arms and legs. I reached down and fastened my son's shoe, breathing deeply at the same time. The barrel smelled powerfully of cedar. There was a moment of perfect quiet, when even the voices outside on the playground seemed to fall away. Suddenly Ava screamed:

"She did it! I saw it!"

Both Jacks turned to correct her, but the expression on Ava's face was so genuinely awed that neither one of them spoke. She was so convincing—so convinced—that they both looked back at me, questioning.

"What's going on in there?"

One of the teachers was standing underneath the barrel on the other side, where we couldn't see her.

Jack H. put his finger to his lips. "Don't tell," he said. "Say you're coming out."

My Jack and Ava obeyed. "I'm coming out!"

"Time to line up," the teacher said.

Jack H. descended the ladder first, then Ava, and finally my Jack.

"See you upstairs." I didn't whisper these words because I thought that would implicate me further. I planned to tell the teacher that the kids had invited me in. Then I would take her aside and say I was getting a divorce. I would tell her how I didn't like to say no to any of Jack's requests and that I knew I was being too indulgent. I thought it would be almost no effort to cry, if I could do it without being detected by Jack.

But the teacher never came around to the opening of the barrel. She had moved off, presumably to corral more children, and so I sat there looking at my phone, which did not have any new messages. I stared at a picture of Jack inside a giant soap bubble at the Discovery Science Center until the children's voices got fainter. Finally I could tell that they were inside the building. I waited until two-forty, five minutes before pickup, before I climbed out of the barrel. Now I had my story down perfectly, and I thought I could do it convincingly without crying. I was almost disappointed by the time I got upstairs, to realize that no one had even seen me.

A Hand Reached Down to Guide Me

FROM *Granta*

THE NAME PAUL THOMPSON won't mean any more to you than my name would, but if you'd been around the bluegrass scene in New York some thirty years ago, you would have heard the stories. Jimmy Martin had wanted to make him a Sunny Mountain Boy, but he'd refused to cut his hair. He'd turned Kenny Baker on to pot at Bean Blossom and played a show with Tony Trischka while tripping on acid. Easy to believe it all back then. The first time I actually saw him he was onstage, wearing a full-length plaster cast on his—give me a second to visualize this—his left leg, holding himself up by a crutch in each armpit, playing mandolin with only his forearms moving. And someone had Magic-Markered the bottom of the cast to look like an elephantine tooled-leather cowboy boot. This was at an outdoor contest in Roxbury, Connecticut, in 1977, the summer I turned eighteen. The band I'd come with had finished its two numbers, and we were behind the stage, putting instruments in cases, when Paul kicked off "Rawhide." I heard our mandolin player say, "OK, we're fucked."

His band—older longhairs, except the fiddle player, a scary guy with a marine buzzcut—won first prize, as they had the year before. But we placed second, and he lurched over to me on his crutches and said he'd liked the way I'd sung "Over in the Gloryland." It was *Paul Thompson* saying this. I suppose I was a good singer, for a kid just out of high school; I thought of Christian songs simply as genre pieces in those days, but I had the accent down. I said,

"Thanks, man," and refrained from embarrassing myself by complimenting him back. We ended up singing a few songs together out by the cars—I remember him braced up against somebody's fender—and I think it surprised him that I knew so much Louvin Brothers stuff: "Too Late," "Here Today and Gone Tomorrow," "Are You Afraid to Die?" I let him sing Ira's tenor parts; now that he'd stopped smoking, he said, he could get up there in the real keys. He was taller than me, and his cheekbones made him look like a hard-luck refugee in a Dust Bowl photograph; he had white hairs in his sideburns, though he must only have been in his thirties. He told me he'd broken the leg playing squash; naturally I thought it was a joke.

We'd both come up from the city that afternoon, me in a van with the banjo player in my band and his wife and kids, Paul driven by his girlfriend. As we were packing up, he asked me how I was getting back, and could I drive stick. The girlfriend got pissed at him, he said, and went off on the back of somebody's motorcycle, and now here he was up in East Buttfuck, Connecticut, and no way to get himself home. His car turned out to be an old TR6, with so much clutter behind the seats we had to tie my guitar to the luggage rack with bungee cords; all the way back to New York he played the Stanley Brothers on ninety-minute cassettes he'd dubbed from his LP collection. We didn't talk much—I had to wake him up to ask directions once we hit the West Side Highway—but I did note that he said *man*dolin, not mando*lin,* and I've taken care to say *man*dolin ever since.

He lived in a big old building on West End around 86th; because it was Saturday night I had no trouble finding a space on his block. He said he'd figure out some way to deal with the car on Monday. Did I want to come up, have a few more tunes, smoke some dope? He hadn't given *that* up. But it was late to be taking my guitar on the subway, and I already had enough of a Paul Thompson story to tell.

Most of us were just weekend pickers, and only little by little did you learn about other people's real lives. Our banjo player taught calculus at Brooklyn College; the fiddler in Paul's band (the one native southerner I ever ran across in New York) managed a fuel-oil business in Bay Ridge; another guy you saw around, good Dobro player, was a public defender. I was working in a bookstore that summer before starting NYU, where I planned to major in English. And Paul Thompson turned out to be a science writer at *Newsweek*. One day I saw him in the subway at Rockefeller Center, and I had to think a minute to figure out where I knew him from: he was wearing a blue oxford shirt and a seersucker blazer, with jeans and cowboy boots. Somebody told me he'd published a novel when he was in his twenties, which you could still find at the Strand.

A couple of years later, Paul brought me into his band when their lead singer moved to California, and we also played some coffeehouses as a duet, calling ourselves the Twofer Brothers. I went to the University of Connecticut for graduate school but I drove down to the city a couple of times a month, and every so often Paul would put the band back together for some party where they'd place hay bales around the room. After these gigs we'd go up to his place, get high and listen to music, or drink and talk books. He told me he loved "Jimmy Hank" and gave me a copy of *The Ambassadors* from his collection of pristine old Signet paperbacks; it had a price of fifty cents. By then I'd decided to specialize in the nineteenth century, and I resented Jimmy Hank for his review of *Our Mutual Friend*— "poor with the poverty not of momentary embarrassment, but of permanent exhaustion." But I've still got that book: the cover illustration shows a top-hatted gent seen from behind in a cafe chair, with wineglass and cane. I imagine it'll be on my shelves, still unread, when I die.

While I was finishing my dissertation, I got married to the first woman I'd ever lasted with for more than a month. Diane, I might as well admit, was my student when I was a TA, and why bother trying to extenuate it, all these years later, by telling you that we started sleeping together only after the semester was over? Or that in our History-of-Us conversations, we could never decide who'd made the first move? She'd go to festivals and parties with me to be the cool girlfriend with the cut-off jeans, and we promised each other that when we got out of married-student housing we'd live in the country somewhere, in a house full of books, no TV, and raise our own food. I'd grown up in Park Slope, but my father was an old folkie—he used to hang around Washington Square in the fifties—and when I was twelve or thirteen I began listening to his LPs and fixating on the photos of ruined grampaws on their falling-down porches; even the mean, sad bluegrass guys in business suits and Stetsons, holding thousands of dollars' worth of Martins and

Gibsons, had been posed by abandoned shacks in the mountains. Everybody in our little scene thought of themselves as secret country boys. My old banjo player, the one I rode up to Roxbury with, quit his teaching job and moved to the Northeast Kingdom, where I hear he makes B-string benders in his machine shop and plays pedal steel in a country band. Our bass player left the East Village for Toast, North Carolina, to sit at the feet of Tommy Jarrell. Even my father, in his bourgie-folkie way. He was an engineer at Con Edison for thirty years; when he retired he and my mother built a solar house up near Woodstock.

I found a teaching job at a small college in New Hampshire and Diane got accepted at the Vermont Culinary Institute. We bought a fixer-upper farmhouse, with a wood stove, a barn, and twenty acres, on a dirt road, equally inconvenient to my school and hers. I put a metal roof on the old henhouse—Diane had always wanted to keep chickens—rototilled our garden patch every spring, and bought a chainsaw and a splitter, as well as a rusty Ford 8N, the pretext being that we needed to keep the fields from growing back to brush. Our neighbor, a man in his seventies, kept the thing going for me; he liked us because I was so helpless and Diane was so pretty. In the spring he and I would work up the next winter's wood together, sharing my splitter and running his buzz saw off the tractor's PTO. I don't know how I did all this while teaching three and three and working on my book; when the old man finally went into a home I started buying cordwood. My parents drove up a couple of times a year, and my father always brought his single-O Martin, the guitar on which he taught me my first chords. He and I would sit around playing the half-dozen finger-picking songs—"Lewis Collins," "Spike Driver's Moan"—that he'd never cared to get beyond. They seldom stayed more than a day or two. The wood stove didn't keep the guest room warm enough in fall or winter, and my mother got bitten to death by mosquitoes in the summer.

Every July Diane and I threw an outdoor music party and pig roast; she'd cook the whole week before, and her friends from Boston and my friends from New York brought tents and sleeping bags and tried to dance to the ad-hoc bands that formed in the corners of the field behind the house. Paul Thompson always turned up with his mandolin, some good weed, and a younger woman, never the same one twice.

For a few years, he'd drive that summer's woman to catch a bus in White River Junction and stay on until Tuesday or Wednesday. Diane liked him—what woman didn't, at first?—and he was no trouble to have around. He took walks in the woods by himself; he spent hours reading in the hammock on the porch, and didn't mind when we went up to bed and left him downstairs with his weed and his headphones. "A man could die happy up here," he used to say. He told me he liked hearing the rooster at first light, because it made him feel safe to go back to sleep. When he finally got up, he'd go out to the henhouse, gather eggs, and cook his own breakfast—and clean up afterward. Diane usually picked eggs early in the morning, but she'd leave a couple for him to find. Once, when he'd been out there for what seemed like a long time, I went to check on him, and I saw him through the window, squatting on his hams, his cowboy boots the only part of him touching the floor. He was talking and nodding to himself, or to the hens, who came right up to him as they never did for me. I sneaked back to the house and I don't think he heard me.

But most of the time, Paul wasn't anybody I thought about much, though I know now that he was thinking about me.

For whatever reason, I never wanted children. Not a crime against humanity—arguably quite the opposite—but of course this became an issue when Diane turned thirty. That and suspicions about me and my students, which I should have seen coming as well, and about one student in particular. (The wrong one, as it happened.) Diane and I lasted ten years, and after she left I drank myself to sleep every night for a month. Didn't that argue that I wasn't cold-hearted? She's remarried now, has her own catering business, and her older daughter's applying to colleges—better schools than the one where I teach. We're on good enough terms these days that she sends me pictures. At the time of the divorce, though, she held out for money in return for her share in the house, and I had no prospect of a better-paying job. My book, *Cathy's Caliban: Sex, Race, and the Sublime in Wuthering Heights*—a rewrite of my dissertation—got only one notice, in *Victorian Studies*, whose reviewer (from some other no-name college, in Missouri) called it "by turns perverse and pedestrian." The book got me tenure, since nobody else in the department had published in the past ten years, but only a two-thousand-dollar raise. So I went back to working up my own wood, until—God, must we? Until I was able to sell my father's house.

Diane had already left the last time he came up, the fall after my mother died. He had his Martin with him, as usual, but he didn't feel like playing. Could he leave it with me? The strings felt stiff; maybe I could take it to the guy who worked on my guitar? It didn't feel any different to me, but I told him I'd see if Brad could bring the action down a little. Hell, I thought, he's seventy-eight, his fingers might not be as strong as they used to be. This turned out to be what Harold Bloom might call a weak misreading.

I set the chessboard up on the wooden factory spool Diane and I had used for a coffee table—he mostly kicked my ass—and poured glasses of the Jameson he always brought. While I was considering whether or not to move a rook, he picked up a photo from the table beside the sofa: Diane and I sitting at a café in Barcelona, the one time we went to Europe.

"What are you, running a museum?" he said. "Look, I liked Diane. Your mother had her opinion, fine. Me, I think you were crazy to let her go. But you made your choice, right?"

"You *could* call it that."

"And you still got all her hair shit in there." He flipped his thumb in the direction of the bathroom, where Diane had left behind mostly empty bottles of conditioners, moisturizers, and lotions.

"Don't think I don't see what you're up to."

"What, throw you off your game? You fucked yourself two moves back." I looked the board over again, then got up and put another couple of logs in the stove.

"What I'd do?" he said. "Find some sucker who wants to be—who'm I trying to think of? Thoreau. Then buy yourself a nice little place where you don't have to do *that* nine months a year. You want to be living like this when you're my age?"

"I seem to recall you couldn't wait to get out of the city."

"Not to live like a sharecropper. You even get cable up here?"

"We don't have a TV." I sat down again and took another look at the board.

"Interesting," he said. "And who's the 'we'?"

"Yeah, OK. I get it."

"Anyway, now your mother's gone and I'm staring at trees all day. You could have a life. You meeting anybody?"

I laid my king on its side. "Pop. It's been a month."

"That's my point." He looked out the window. "These trees are gonna kill you."

By the time Janna moved in, I'd been living in New Hampshire for longer than I had in the city, though I still wasn't fooling the locals any. You could see another house by then: an A-frame up on the rise catty-corner across the road. Diane and I could have bought that parcel along with the land on this side, but we hadn't been able to come up with the extra ten thousand dollars. I hated to look over there.

Janna worked at Century 21, near my college in the old downtown. Yes, I met her at the bar where I'd started going after classes. She'd gotten her job just by walking in and asking for it, and her boss liked the tricks she'd picked up on some website: putting bowls of lemons and Granny Smith apples on kitchen counters, fanning out copies of *Country Journal* on coffee tables. I thought she was too bright to have ended up here: she had an MA in political science from Tufts. But she said she'd found her place in the world. I suppose I had too.

She told me right from the beginning that she didn't want to be the Second Wife, and she'd put a bumper sticker on her Subaru reading COPULATE, DON'T POPULATE.

Her apartment had track lighting, good oriental rugs, and a gas fireplace, but she seemed to feel at home in my house. Aside from repainting the living room—a yellow she said would feel warmer than the white Diane and I had gone with—all she did was move the sofa over to where the armchair had been and find us a pine blanket chest for a coffee table. She was fine with dial-up and no TV—she'd let corporate media waste too much of her time, she said—and she even claimed the rooster didn't wake her, though she refused to go into the henhouse herself. After five years, we still had sex more days than not: I'd made peace with her chubby knees; presumably she'd made peace with my loose belly and my too-small hands.

Janna played guitar—another point in her favor—and we sang together once in a while. I'd back her up on her songs—Ani DiFranco, Michelle Shocked, the Indigo Girls, some of it not as bad as you might think—and she knew "Silver Threads and

Golden Needles" and the usual stuff by Emmylou Harris. I tried
to teach her a couple of Porter and Dolly songs, though she didn't
have much of a range and we could never hit on the right key for
her. It was Janna, in fact, who talked me into having the music parties again. She hated to cook, so we'd lay in beer and Jack Daniel's
and chips, get pizzas delivered, and tell people to bring whatever.
She hung back most of the time and let the bluegrass guys do
their inside-baseball thing—*Yeah, "Rank Strangers." Who's gonna do
Ralph's part?*—but late at night I could sometimes get her to step
into a circle of pickers and sing "Sin City."

"We could probably make this work," she'd told me when we'd
been together for a month. "If neither of us turns into an asshole."

"How likely is that?" I said.

"Well," she said, "if people aren't willing to change. I mean
when things call for it."

"But you're happy *now*."

"You would've heard," she said.

When I sent the notice out for the party that last summer—we
were having it early, since we were going to Yorkshire in July, to
see Brontë country—Paul e-mailed back that he'd taken a buyout
from *Newsweek* and was "living on Uneasy Street" but that he'd try
to make it. He was working on a book proposal, he said, about
mountaintop removal, which would get him some time in eastern
Kentucky—where maybe he'd be able to play some music too, if
he didn't show up in a car with New York plates.

The Friday night of the party, he rolled into the dooryard
just after dark, in a Jeep Wrangler, with a woman at the wheel.
She looked to be Janna's age and not quite up to Paul's standards—maybe too much nose and too little chin—but with a slender body and straight, dyed-black hair down to her shoulders. He
got out, stretched, and looked off at the hills. "Shee-*it!*" he said to
the woman. "Just smell the air. I ever tell you? This is my favorite
place in the world."

"Several times," she said.

"I want y'all to meet Simone," he said. He always talked more
southern when he was around the music. "My last and best."

"Until the rest of the ass parade comes around the corner." She
ran a finger down his arm.

"Never happen," Paul said. He looked even lankier than usual, and when he turned to me I saw dark pouches pulling his eyelids down, exposing red below his eyeballs. "Hey, listen, we gotta do 'Hit Parade of Love.' But first off—what do you say?" He opened his mandolin case and took out a pipe and a plastic bag of buds.

After one hit, I knew I'd had plenty, and that a beer might help and might not; even Paul stopped at three. He kicked off "Hit Parade of Love," and somehow I found myself singing the first verse, whose words I thought until the last instant wouldn't come to me—*From what I been a-hearin', dear, you really got it made*—but when we got to the chorus, with the tenor part, his voice cracked on the word *top*, and he asked if we could take it down to A. Well, hell, he had to be what, pushing seventy by now? If I was fifty-one?

He gave up before midnight—he said the drive had done him in—and we put him and Simone in the big guest room at the far end of the hall. When the music petered out around two-thirty and people retired to their tents and RVs, Janna and I came upstairs and saw their light was still on; Janna thought she heard him coughing. The rooster woke me for a few seconds as the windows began to show gray; I hoped that if Paul was hearing it too he'd fall back safe asleep.

In the morning I put on one of the knee-length white aprons Diane had left behind, cooked up enough scrambled eggs, along with kale from the garden, to fill the turkey-roasting pan, set out paper plates and plastic forks, and clanged the triangle she'd always used to get the party guests in. Paul and Simone didn't come down until the others were finishing up. "You sleep OK?" I said.

"Never better," he said. The pouches under his eyes looked darker in daylight. "Once I got my *nightly obligations* taken care of." He put a hand on Simone's ass and squeezed. "This is the one that's gonna be the death of me."

"You'll scandalize your friend," she said. "Look how he's blushing."

Paul reached down, lifted the hem of my apron, and peeked under. "What's fer breakfast, Maw?"

They took plates out onto the porch, and when I came out after a preliminary cleanup, I found Janna sitting next to him while Simone was on the lawn, trying to get up into a headstand, her black hair splashed out on the grass. He hadn't touched his eggs. "Hey, the Iron Chef," he said. "Listen, did I tell you I'm playing bass in a rock band? Like one of those daddy bands? I fuckin' love it—we missed so much shit being hillbillies." He speared a forkful of egg, but set it down. "I might have to quit, though."

"What's going on with the book?"

"Yeah, well, that too. Story for another time." Simone had gotten both feet in the air, muscled legs straight, toes pointed, black-polished toenails. Paul clapped his hands and called "Brava!" He turned back to me. "I can't believe I finally got it right," he said. "In the bottom of the ninth. Check her the fuck out."

"She seems great," I said. The legs of Simone's shorts had fallen just enough to expose about that much of black lacy underwear.

"Listen, I might call you pretty soon to ask you a favor," he said. "I *might*. It would be a *big* favor." He looked at Janna. "From both of you."

"*You're* being mysterious," she said.

"Sure," I said. "Whatever whenever."

"I appreciate it." He stood up and called to Simone. "You going to stay like that all day, babe? Come on, I want to show you the gals."

He took her hand and led her along the path to the henhouse. He was limping worse than usual—that broken leg had never healed properly—and I noticed that he was wearing Nikes instead of boots.

Janna touched my arm. "I don't think he's OK."

"He's just in love," I said.

"I could see that little display wasn't lost on you." I was thinking of how to deny it, but she put a finger to my lips. "I mean, you know him better than I do," she said, "but *I* think she's got a situation on her hands."

That summer was the first time Janna and I had traveled together. The Brontë Trail turned out to be a five-hour trudge through British badlands—"No wonder the brother was an alcoholic," Janna said—and back in Haworth we found our rental car had a yellow metal clamp on the front wheel. At Whitby it was too cold to swim, and neither of us had any interest in joining the fossil-hunters at low tide, or in taking the Dracula tour. When we got home, I found a package Janna had sent me from Amazon—she'd found an Internet café in Whitby—with a book of Doré's illustrations of the *Divine Comedy,* and a note reading *It's time we got you interested in writers from Tuscany.*

A week later, I got the e-mail.

This is Simone, Paul's friend. I hope you remember me from your party. He doesn't know I'm writing this (truly), but I was afraid he never would ask you. I'm sure you must have seen that he wasn't well, and the truth is that he's been diagnosed with liver cancer, stage 4, though he still seems like his old self most days. Anyway, I know that his wish is, and I apologize if this is just too much to ask, that you could let him be in your home for the very last part of this—he says he will know when. He has always told me your home was his favorite place ever to be. I can take care of all the arrangements, home hospice and etc. (truth is, I've already made some calls to places in your area). Not really knowing you, I hope I've explained all this in the right way. Do you think you could in any way do this for him?

"What?" Janna said. We were propped up together on the bed. One thing I'd learned from being married to Diane was not to be furtive about e-mail.

"Here." I turned the screen her way. "I guess you called it."

I watched her face as she read, but Janna didn't give much away. "He put her up to this," she said.

"She says not."

"Well of course," she said. "That's the tell."

"I just have no idea what to say to something like this."

"He's your friend," she said. "What time is it?"

"So you're saying I should call?"

"I don't even know this man," she said. "But I'd do this with you."

They came late on a Sunday afternoon in October. Simone helped him out of the Jeep, then reached behind the seat and handed Janna a gallon of cider, just as she might have done if they'd been normal lovers up for a country weekend. The label showed it was the catchpenny orchard on the state highway, where kids could feed donkeys with pellets from dispensing machines at a quarter a handful. Paul had let his beard grow in, entirely white; he looked like the last pictures of Ezra Pound. "And here he is," he said. "Appearing for a limited time only."

"He rehearses his lines," Simone said.

Janna put him on the sofa with the afghan over him while Simone and I went back out to get his stuff. "It's just a few clothes," Simone said, "and a couple of pictures he wanted to be able to look at. He didn't want to take up your space. I think he's planning to give you this." She held up the mandolin case.

"That's crazy," I said. "It's got to be worth a fortune." Paul's F-5 wasn't a Lloyd Loar, but I remembered that it was from the thirties.

"Welcome to my life," she said. "He tried to leave *me* his apartment. He's turned into the Bill and Melinda Gates Foundation. I have to get with his brother tomorrow in the city and figure out what to do. Paul won't talk to him."

"You're not driving down again tonight?"

"Breakfast 8 A.M. The brother's a freak too."

"But you're coming back."

"And you've known Paul for how long? I mean, I wanted to. He's got it all plotted out, like each of us with our own little jobs—I mean, not that yours is little. He's just putting everybody away, away, away. Fuck *him,* you know? I was a good girlfriend."

"Would you like us to disappear for a while? We do need to go to the store at some point."

"No, it's fine. He already got the last sweet blowjob. Under this fucking apple tree—sorry. I just feel like *somebody* should know. And all the way up here, he keeps finding these sports-talk stations. Did you know that the World Series begins next week? It's going to be quite a matchup."

We found him sitting up on the sofa, propped up by pillows under his back, looking at *The New York Review of Books.* "So," he said, "did she tell you what a dick I'm being to her?"

"I can imagine how hard this must be for both of you," I said.

"Ah, still the slick-fielding shortstop," he said. "But we're into serious October baseball here."

"Can you just *stop?*" Simone said.

"Isn't that the whole idea?" he said.

Janna came downstairs with her arms full of sheets and blankets. "We're going to put you guys in the den tonight," she said. "I thought it would be easier than having to do stairs."

"She has to go back," I said.

"You know," Paul said. "Stuff to do with the, ah, e, s, t, a, t, e."

Simone turned to me. "They said they'd be coming with the bed tomorrow morning. And the nurse should be here. You have my information, right?"

Paul shook his finger at her. "Now *that* should have been said sotto voce."

"Let me make you some coffee," Janna said. "I don't know if anything's open between here and the interstate."

"She'll be cool," Paul said. "My guy brought over some Adderall before we left. He gets the *real* stuff. Made from adders."

I walked Simone out to the car. She opened the driver's door, then turned back and came into my arms, taking deep breaths. "He's been lucky to have you," I said.

"And now he's lucky to have you," she said. "There's just no end to his luck."

In bed that night, I said to Janna, "Can we really do this?"

"What's our choice at *this* point?" We were lying on our backs, and she rolled over, her breasts against my arm. "Did you two talk at all?"

"I don't want to, you know, press him." I worked my arm over her shoulder and pulled her closer. Her belly into my hip. She sighed and moved her palm up my thigh.

"Why didn't he ever, you know, find somebody?" she said. I felt myself beginning to get hard—could we really do *this*? "That woman loves him."

"He never had any trouble *finding* them," I said.

"Do you ever wish you were like him?"

"What, you mean dying?"

She jerked away and rolled onto her back again. "I hate when you pretend to be stupid."

"No," I said. "Who would ever want a life *that* lonely?"

"It's even more obnoxious when you try to figure out the right thing to say."

I shoved a pillow against the headboard and sat up. "Are we fighting?" I said. "Because this is a hell of a time for it."

"For the record, I don't blame you for getting us into this. I just hope it gets over with quickly. Is that horrible to say?"

"No, it's actually the *kindest* thing you could say."

"But would you say it about me? If *I* were in the situation?"

"Come on," I said. "Nobody can ever—"

"OK, I need to go to sleep," she said. "Obviously I'm not going to get laid tonight. Why don't you go down and check on your friend and see if he's still breathing. Then you can get yourself a drink and forget all about it."

I put my legs over the side and got to my feet. "I bring you one?"

"I'll be asleep," she said. "You don't even listen anymore."

The rooster woke me at six. I heard Janna breathing away and couldn't get back to sleep. But when I came downstairs Paul had already dressed himself, except for shoes and socks—he'd told us it hurt to bend down—and had managed to get from the den, where Janna had made up the fold-out, to the living room sofa, and was stretched out listening to something through earbuds. He flicked them out when he saw me.

"How are you?" I said. "You hurting? I can get you another Vicodin."

"Just took a couple. They're coming with the real shit this morning, right?"

"They should be here by ten," I said.

"What we like to hear. Listen, did I even thank you for this?"

"You'd do it for me."

"*There's* a hypothetical we won't be putting to the test. Man, I have been such a shit. To everybody in my life."

"You were never a shit to me," I said.

"You weren't *in* my life. Well, who the fuck was. Not to be grim. How did I get onto this? That Vicodin must work better than I thought. Your lady still asleep?"

"She was."

He nodded. "She's going to need it."

I was in the kitchen cutting up a pineapple when I heard Janna come downstairs. She must have smelled the coffee brewing. "You boys are up bright and early," she said.

"Only way to live a long and healthy life," Paul said. "Get up, do the chores, plow the north forty—I don't mean anything sexual by that."

"No, I'm sure that's the *last* thing you'd think of." She came into the kitchen and put a hand on my arm. "Did you get enough sleep? I'm sorry I was being . . . whatever I was."

I set the knife down and put an arm around her. "I think you get a free pass, considering."

"I hope I was just getting it out of my system early." She poured a cup of coffee and put in milk for me. "Will you be OK with him if I go in for a while? I should get some stuff done while I can."

"Hey," Paul yelled out. "Why's everybody talking behind the patient's back?"

"Shut up, we're having sex," she called back. She poured a cup for herself. "He seems pretty chipper this morning."

"Yeah, I don't know what to hope for," I said. "Quality, I guess. And then not too much quantity."

A little after nine they came with the hospital bed, and the guy helped me move the sofa into the corner so we could set the bed up in the living room, by the window looking out at the hills. Janna and I would take the fold-out in the den when it became clear that we had to be nearby. Paul watched us from the armchair, his bare feet on a footstool, his earbuds back in, his eyes on us. When the guy left, he turned the iPod off, plucked out the earbuds, and said, "Why am I reminded of 'In the Penal Colony'?"

The FedEx truck delivered a cardboard box with the drugs, then the nurse from the hospice showed up. She had thick black hair, going gray, down her back in a single braided pigtail, and hoop earrings—not what you'd expect with the white uniform. Her name was Heather. I brought her a mug of herbal tea—she wasn't a coffee drinker, she said—and she showed me the spreadsheet-looking printed forms, on which we were to record dosage and time, then opened the FedEx box, picked up her clipboard, and took inventory. She wrote down Paul's temperature and blood pressure, listened to his heart. "So, Paul," she said, "how would you say your pain is right now?"

"One to ten? Let's give it a seven. Good beat and you can dance to it."

"We can improve on that," she said.

"Can you do less than zero?"

"That's going to be up to you. And your caregivers. I'm a believer that you keep on top of the pain. This shouldn't be about you being in any discomfort." She got up and put on her jacket—wool, with a Navajo design. "I'll be by tomorrow, but if you have any concerns or questions, any emergency, someone's always there."

I took my jacket off the coat rack. "Here, I'll walk you out. I've got to feed the hens."

"Smooth," Paul said. "Jesus Christ, why don't you just ask her how long?"

"I knew I was going to like you," she said to him. "I'll be seeing you tomorrow—that much I think we can count on."

I followed her to her car. "I'm not asking you to make a prediction," I said. "But just from your experience."

"OK, based on nothing? I think he'll move fast."

When I came back in he was sitting on the edge of the hospital bed, bare feet dangling, pushing the button and making it go up and down. "So, we going to break out the good stuff?"

"Should you wait till what she gave you kicks in?"

"Don't start *that*," he said. "You heard the lady." He lay back, stuck out his tongue, and pointed at it.

He dozed—call it that—until the middle of the afternoon, while I sat in the armchair, checking from time to time to make sure his chest was rising and falling, and making notes in my new paperback copy of *Middlemarch;* the covers had finally come off my old one. If Janna could hold the fort tomorrow while I went in to campus, that's what I'd be teaching.

"Let's go for a ride." I looked up: Paul's eyes were open. "I want to see some trees, man. And can we bring some music? I got weed."

"If you're up to it," I said. "Stanley Brothers? You remember driving back from Roxbury that time?"

"Not really," he said. "Did I have that fucked-up Triumph?"

"Yeah. Whatever became of that?"

"Whatever became of anything? I should've kept a journal. Fucking *years* of fucking lost days."

The truck had a handle above the door frame that you could grab to pull yourself up onto the seat; Paul used both hands, but I still had to take his legs and hoist. I could feel the bones.

We took back roads, dirt roads when I could find them. Cornfields with ranks of tubular stubble, falling-down barns, with Holsteins standing outside in the mud. Hunting season had started—that morning I'd heard gunshots in the woods—and we passed a double-wide where a buck hung from a kids' swing set, one front hoof scraping the ground.

"My kind of place," he said. "You know, when they say you're dead meat—like isn't meat dead by definition?" He snapped the buck a salute. "Shit, *I* should have settled up here. Come to think of it, I *have* settled up here."

"I always thought *you'd* get a place out of the city. At least for weekends."

"I think it would have ruined it," he said. "I was really just into the songs. Hey, can we have the Stanleys?"

"I just want to say," I said. "I admire the way you're dealing with this."

"Yeah, wait till the screaming starts."

I put in a Stanley Brothers CD—*Can't you hear the night bird crying?*—and he began packing a bowl. He blew out the first cloud of skunky smoke, then held it out to me. I put up my hand and opened my window.

"You mind cracking yours just a little?" I said. "If this is that shit you had last summer . . ."

"That? That was fucking ditchweed." He exhaled again. "Yeah, actually I wouldn't advise you." He closed his eyes. "OK. Better. I haven't heard this for fucking ever."

After a few miles, he packed the bowl again. "What's so weird," he said, "I can't tell if something's beautiful anymore. Like, is *that* beautiful?" He pointed at the CD player: the Stanley Brothers were singing "My Sinful Past"—where the harmony comes in on *a hand reached down to guide me.*

"Well," I said. "I mean I'm not always in the mood."

"OK, you don't want to talk absolutes," he said. "Can't blame you there."

We stopped at the convenience store outside West Rumney—we'd run out of milk. "Anything I can get you?" I said.

"I'm disappointing you," he said. "You want to know what this is like."

"Not unless you want to tell me," I said. "This isn't about me."

"Right, see, that's my point," he said. "Listen, would they have eggnog this early? I mean in the year?"

"That's a thought."

"Yes it is," he said. "Good for me, right? Could you leave the thing on?" We'd switched over to the King recordings; the Stanley Brothers were singing "A Few More Years."

But when I came out with the milk and a half-gallon of eggnog, already with holly wreath and red ribbon on the carton, he was sitting in silence. "I didn't want to run down your battery," he said. Could he have been crying? His eyes had looked red all day. And of course he'd been smoking. I had to help him get the egg-nog open and hold the carton up so he could sip. "How did Bob Cratchit drink this shit?" he said. "Guess I can cross this off too."

Back at the house, he lay on the sofa for a while, then got up, bent over, groaned, and picked up the mandolin case. "You know, I haven't played since your thing," he said. "I want you to have this."

"Come on, buddy. I could never play mandolin for shit. There must be somebody who could really—"

"Fuck *somebody*," he said.

Just two days later, he'd gotten so weak that Heather brought him a walker, which he used to get back and forth to the armchair and the bathroom. Then he stopped going to the armchair, and she brought in a commode; he could get his legs over the side of the bed, and if you'd bring the walker over he could get to his feet, go the two steps by himself, turn, and sit, in his open-backed hospital johnny. And then Janna had to help him; he wouldn't let me. And then the bedpan. And then the day Heather came to catheterize him. He said to Janna, "Here goes our last chance." That was the same day Heather hooked him up to the morphine. Think of this as the baseline, she told us, and then you give him more by mouth. This is in your hands, she told us. You understand what I'm saying?

After our car ride, he never wanted music again. He'd brought pictures in stand-up Plexiglas frames: a photo of Simone, a postcard reproduction of Scipione Pulzone's *The Lamentation* (1591)—I looked at the back—and a snapshot of the two of us, standing in front of my house. I set them up on the table by his bed, but I never saw him look at them.

He screamed when we turned him to prevent bedsores—it took me and Janna together—but still insisted on being turned, until he didn't. When he could no longer drink, we swabbed the inside of his mouth with supposedly mint-flavored sponges, the size of sugar cubes, on plastic sticks. At first he'd made faces at the taste of the morphine; then he was sucking at the dropper.

One day, the day before the last day, he motioned for me to bend down and whispered, "Why will you not just *do* it? They're not gonna say shit to you. *She* knows."

"Buddy," I said, "you know I can't." Which she was the *she?* He'd gotten to a point where he was conflating Heather and Janna.

"I'm not your buddy," he said. "You cocksucker."

On his last night, we both slept in the living room with him—*slept,* I guess, isn't the word—Janna on the sofa, me on the floor, and took turns getting up every half-hour to dose him again. I'd stopped drawing the morphine up to the exact line on the dropper: just squirted in as much as it would hold, then watched the tip of his tongue touch at the green crust on his lips. I'd write down the time and *20 mg,* hoping they wouldn't check my chart too carefully against what drugs would be left. When the light finally started going gray outside, I turned on his bedside lamp—I saw his eyelids tighten—gave him the next dropper, ten minutes early, then another one for good measure. In a while, the moaning quieted down; I turned the lamp off, went to the window, and saw pink above the mountains. I pulled my fleece over my sweatshirt and went out to feed the hens. Frost on the grass, a faint quarter-moon still high.

Walking back to the house, I saw the light go on in the living room. Janna was standing over his bed, holding his hand, the one with the needle taped to it. "Where *were* you?" she said. "He was asking for you."

I leaned over him; he was still breathing, but shallow breaths. "Should we call them?" I said.

His eyes came open and he said, "I've never been *here* before."

"Don't be afraid," Janna told him.

He rolled his head an inch one way, an inch the other. "I don't know how to do this."

"You can just let go," she said.

"Oh fuck," he said. "You are one stupid twat."

Janna's head jerked back, but she kept hold of his hand.

"Is there anything you want us to do?" I said.

He closed his eyes. "You won't." He began drawing harder, deeper breaths. "I keep being mean," he said.

"Rest," I said. I took his other hand.

He rolled his head again. "I need to get this right."

Janna put her other hand on his, over where the needle went in.

"We both love you," she said. "It's OK to go."

"I don't know," he said.

We watched him breathe. It took longer and longer for the next one to come, and then there wasn't a next one.

I looked at Janna. She pointed back at him. You could see it: there was nobody in there anymore.

I let go of the hand. "I better call them."

"Can't you take a *minute?*" she said. "This is what he came to give you."

After Heather left and the guy from the funeral home took the body away in the back of his black Escalade, I drove Janna into town for breakfast. It was still only ten in the morning. There was a family in the next booth, so it must have been Saturday. Or Sunday. One of the kids was playing games on his phone or whatever; I could hear the little beeps and the snatches of metallic music. How could this not be driving the parents crazy? Janna ordered a grapefruit that she didn't eat; I had pancakes and no coffee. They were supposed to pick up the bed around noon, and I planned to sleep away the rest of the day.

"How are you holding up?" I said.

"He was absolutely right," she said. "I *am* a stupid twat. At least you kept your mouth shut. *We love you we love you we love you it's all right to go.* I'm going to be hearing that the rest of my life."

"He didn't know what he was saying. We did the right thing for him."

"So that's what you'd want? Somebody doing the *right thing* for you?"

"You're beating yourself up," I said. "We're both exhausted."

"This has to change." She pushed the grapefruit away and waved to get the waitress. "Can you take me back to the house so I can get my car? Shit's been piling up at my office."

"They can spare you for one more day."

"You don't get what I'm telling you," she said. "I'm not spending another night there. You can do what you want. Wear her fucking aprons, feed her fucking chickens. Sing your dead-people songs, whatever. Read your dead-people books. You're going to kill yourself one of these days, making that drive in the winter. Look, this is my fault—I should have helped you. But you don't even know who I am."

*

These days the summer parties happen in other people's fields, behind other people's farmhouses. So far this year I've been to one near Ludlow, Vermont, and another one an hour south of Albany. It's always the same people, give or take, and the same songs, said to be timeless. Our crowd isn't old enough yet to be dying off; they don't even seem to age that much year by year. But their kids, whose names I never remember, keep getting older, until you don't see them anymore.

When I go, I go alone: Janna says if she has to hear a banjo one more time she'll shoot herself, and I'm grateful to her for saying so. I've given Paul's mandolin to the son of that banjo player, the guy I used to play with all those years ago. He's nineteen or twenty, the son, loves the music and has the gift; he'd been playing some hopeless Gibson knock-off. You still see one or two like him. He makes it to some of the parties and we'll do a song or two, I hope not just because he feels obliged. I suppose I'm getting too old to be standing out in a field on a summer night as the dew makes the strings slick, but I can still sing; having some age on me, maybe I sound more like the real thing.

It only took Janna two months to sell the old house on the dirt road. She got us our asking price, enough to buy a three-bedroom Craftsman-style bungalow—an office for her, a study for me—ten blocks from campus, four blocks from the health-food store. I walk to class, except on the coldest days, and Janna rides her bicycle to work. I play squash once a week with my department chair. We've bought a flat-screen television, forty-six inches, high definition, for my ball games and her shows. I'm making notes toward a second book. If I can ever finish, it could get me invited to a conference or two; despite that trip to Brontë country, Janna says she wants to travel with me. You see all this as a defeat, I know. I would have. But I can't begin to tell you.

LAUREN GROFF

At the Round Earth's Imagined Corners

FROM *Five Points*

JUDE WAS BORN in a cracker-style house at the edge of a swamp that boiled with unnamed species of reptiles.

Few people lived in the center of Florida then. Air conditioning was for the rich, and the rest compensated with high ceilings, sleeping porches, attic fans. Jude's father was a herpetologist at the university, and if snakes hadn't slipped their way into their hot house, his father would have filled it with them anyway. Coils of rattlers sat in formaldehyde on the windowsills. Writhing knots of reptiles lived in the coops out back where his mother had once tried to raise chickens.

At an early age, Jude learned to keep a calm heart when touching fanged things. He was barely walking when his mother came into the kitchen to find a coral snake chasing its red and yellow tail around his wrist. His father was watching from across the room, laughing.

His mother was a Yankee, a Presbyterian. She was always weary; she battled the house's mold and humidity and devilish reek of snakes without help. His father wouldn't allow a black person through his doors, and they didn't have the money to hire a white woman. Jude's mother was afraid of scaly creatures and sang hymns in the attempt to keep them out. When she was pregnant with his sister one August night, she came into the bathroom to take a cool bath and, without her glasses, missed the three-foot albino alligator her husband had stored in the bathtub. The next morning, she was gone. She returned a week later. And after Jude's sister was born dead, a perfect petal of a baby, his mother never stopped singing under her breath.

Noise of the war grew louder. At last, it became impossible to ignore. Jude was two. His mother pressed his father's new khaki suit and then Jude's father's absence filled the house with a kind of cool breeze. He was flying cargo planes in France. Jude thought of scaly creatures flapping great wings midair, his father angrily riding.

While Jude napped the first day they were alone in the house, his mother tossed all of the jars of dead snakes into the swamp and neatly beheaded the living ones with a hoe. She bobbed her hair with gardening shears. Within a week, she had moved them ninety miles to the beach. When she thought he was asleep on the first night in the new house, she went down to the water's edge in the moonlight and screwed her feet into the sand. It seemed that the glossed edge of the ocean was chewing her up to her knees. Jude held his breath, anguished. One big wave rolled past her shoulders, and when it receded, she was whole again.

This was a new world, full of dolphins that slid up the coastline in shining arcs. Jude loved the wedges of pelicans ghosting overhead, the mad dig after periwinkles that disappeared deeper into the wet sand. He kept count in his head when they hunted for them, and when they came home, he told his mother that they had dug up 461. She looked at him unblinking behind her glasses and counted the creatures aloud.

When she finished, she washed her hands for a long time at the sink. "You like numbers," she said at last, turning around.

"Yes," he said. And she smiled and a kind of gentle shine came from her that startled him. He felt it seep into him, settle in his bones. She kissed him on the crown and put him to bed, and when he woke in the middle of the night to find her next to him, he tucked his hand under her chin where it stayed until morning.

He began to sense that the world worked in ways beyond him, that he was only grasping at threads of a far greater fabric. Jude's mother started a bookstore. Because women couldn't buy land in Florida for themselves, his uncle, a roly-poly little man who looked nothing like Jude's father, bought the store with her money and signed the place over to her. His mother began wearing suits that showed her décolletage and taking her glasses off before boarding the streetcars, so that the eyes she turned to the public were soft and somewhat misty. Instead of singing Jude to sleep as she had in the snake house, she read to him. She read Shakespeare, Hopkins, Donne, Rilke, and he fell asleep with their cadences and the sea's slow rhythm entwined in his head.

Jude loved the bookstore; it was a bright place that smelled of new paper. Lonely war brides came with their prams and left with an armful of Modern Library classics, sailors on leave wandered in only to exit, charmed, with sacks of books pressed to their chest. After hours, his mother would turn off the lights and open the back door to the black folks who waited patiently there, the dignified man in his watch cap who loved Galsworthy, the fat woman who worked as a maid and read a novel every day. "Your father would squeal. Well, foo on him," his mother said to Jude, looking so fierce she erased the last traces in his mind of the tremulous woman she'd been.

One morning just before dawn, he was alone on the beach when he saw a vast metallic breaching a hundred yards offshore. The submarine looked at him with its single periscope eye and slipped silently under again. Jude told nobody. He kept this dangerous knowledge inside him where it tightened and squeezed, but where it couldn't menace the greater world.

Jude's mother brought in a black woman named Sandy to help her with housework and to watch Jude while she was at the store. Sandy and his mother became friends, and some nights he would awaken to laughter from the veranda and come out to find his mother and Sandy in the night breeze off the ocean. They drank sloe gin fizzes and ate lemon cake, which Sandy was careful to keep on hand, even though by then sugar was getting scarce. They let him have a slice, and he'd fall asleep on Sandy's broad lap, sweetness souring on his tongue and in his ears the exhalation of the ocean, the sound of women's voices.

At six, he discovered multiplication all by himself, crouched over an anthill in the hot sun. If twelve ants left the anthill per minute, he thought, that meant 720 departures per hour, an immensity of leaving, of return. He ran into the bookstore, wordless with happiness. When he buried his head in his mother's lap, the women chatting with her at the counter mistook his sobbing for sadness. "I'm sure the boy misses his father," one lady said, intending to be kind.

"No," his mother said. She alone understood his bursting heart and scratched his scalp gently. But something shifted in Jude; and he thought with wonder of his father, of whom his mother had spoken so rarely in all these years that the man himself had faded. Jude could barely recall the rasp of scale on scale and the darkness of the cracker house in the swamp, curtains closed to keep out the hot, stinking sun.

But it was as if the well-meaning lady had summoned him, and Jude's father came home. He sat, immense and rough-cheeked, in the middle of the sunroom. Jude's mother sat nervously opposite him on the divan, angling her knees away from his. The boy played quietly with his wooden train on the floor. Sandy came in with fresh cookies, and when she went back into the kitchen, his father said something so softly Jude couldn't catch it. His mother stared at his father for a long time, then got up and went to the kitchen, and the screen door slapped, and the boy never saw Sandy again.

While his mother was gone, Jude's father said, "We're going home."

Jude couldn't look at his father. The space in the air where he existed was too heavy and dark. He pushed his train around the ankle of a chair. "Come here," his father said, and slowly the boy stood and went to his father's knee.

A big hand flicked out, and Jude's face burned from ear to mouth. He fell down but didn't cry out. He sucked in blood from his nose and felt it pool behind his throat.

His mother ran in and picked him up. "What happened?" she shouted, and his father said in his cold voice, "Boy's timid. Something's wrong with him."

"He keeps things in. He's shy," said his mother, and carried Jude away. He could feel her trembling as she washed the blood from his face. His father came into the bathroom and she said through her teeth, "Don't you ever touch him again."

He said, "I won't have to."

His mother lay beside Jude until he fell asleep, but he woke to the moon through the automobile's windshield and his parents' jagged profiles staring ahead into the tunnel of the dark road.

*

The house by the swamp filled with snakes again. The uncle who had helped his mother with the bookstore was no longer welcome, although he was the only family his father had. Jude's mother cooked a steak and potatoes every night but wouldn't eat. She became a bone, a blade. She sat in her housedress on the porch rocker, her hair slick with sweat. He stood near her and spoke the old sonnets into her ear. She pulled him to her side and put her face between his shoulder and neck and when she blinked, her wet eyelashes tickled him, and he knew not to move away.

His father had begun, on the side, selling snakes to zoos and universities. He vanished for two, three nights in a row, and returned with clothes full of smoke and sacks of rattlers and blacksnakes. He'd been gone for two nights when his mother packed her blue cardboard suitcase with Jude's things on one side and hers on the other. She said nothing, but gave herself away with humming. They walked together over the dark roads and sat waiting for the train for a long time. The platform was empty; theirs was the last train before the weekend. She handed him caramels to suck, and he felt her whole body tremble through the thigh he pressed hard against hers.

So much had built up in him while they waited that it was almost a relief when the train came sighing into the station. His mother stood and reached for Jude, and he smiled into her soft answering smile. Then Jude's father stepped into the lights and scooped him up. His body under Jude's was taut.

His mother did not look at her husband or her son. She seemed a statue, thin and pale. At last, when the conductor said "All aboard!" she gave an awful strangled sound and rushed through the train's door. The train hooted and slowly moved off. Though Jude shouted, it vanished his mother into the darkness without stopping.

Then they were alone, Jude's father and he, in the house by the swamp.

Language wilted between them. Jude was the one who took up the sweeping and scrubbing, who made their sandwiches for supper. When his father was gone, he'd open the windows to let out some of the reptile rot. His father ripped up his mother's lilies and roses and planted mandarins and blueberries, saying that fruit brought birds and birds brought snakes. The boy walked three miles to school where he told nobody he already knew numbers better than the teachers. He was small, but nobody messed with him. On his first day, when a big ten-year-old tried to sneer at his clothes, he leapt at him with a viciousness he'd learned from watching rattlesnakes and made the big boy's head bleed. The others avoided him. He was an in-between creature, motherless but not fatherless, stunted and ratty-clothed like a poor boy but a professor's son, always correct with answers when the teachers called on him, but never offering a word on his own. The others kept their distance. Jude played by himself, or with one of the succession of puppies that his father brought home. Inevitably, the dogs would run down to the edge of the swamp, and one of the fourteen- or fifteen-foot alligators would get them.

Jude's loneliness grew, became a living creature that shadowed him and wandered off only when he was in the company of his numbers. More than marbles or tin soldiers, they were his playthings. More than sticks of candy or plums, they made his mouth water. As messy as the world was, the numbers, predictable and polite, brought order.

When he was ten, a short, round man that the boy found vaguely familiar stopped him on the street and pushed a brown-paper package into his arms. The man pressed a finger to his lips, minced away. At home in his room at night, Jude unwrapped the books. One was a collection of Frost's poems. The other was a book of geometry, the world whittled down until it became a series of lines and angles.

He looked up and morning was sunshot through the laurel oaks. More than the feeling that the book had taught him geometry was the feeling that it had showed the boy something that had been living inside him, undetected until now.

There was also a letter. It was addressed to him in his mother's round hand. When he sat in school dividing the hours until he could be free, when he made the supper of tuna sandwiches, when he ate with his father who conducted to Benny Goodman on the radio, when he brushed his teeth and put on pajamas far too small for him, the four perfect right angles of the letter called to him. He put it under his pillow, unopened. For a week, the letter burned under everything, the way the sun on a hot, overcast day was hidden but always present.

At last, having squeezed everything to know out of the geometry book, he put the still-sealed envelope inside and taped up the covers and hid it between his mattress and box springs. He checked it every night after saying his prayers and was comforted into sleep. When, one night, he saw the book was untaped and the letter gone, he knew his father had found it and nothing could be done.

The next time he saw the little round man on the street, he stopped him. "Who are you?" he asked, and the man blinked and said, "Your uncle." When Jude said nothing, the man threw his arms up and said, "Oh, honey!" and made as if to hug him, but Jude had already turned away.

Inexorably, the university grew. It swelled and expanded under a steady supply of air conditioning, swallowing the land between it and the swamp until the university's roads were built snug against his father's land. Dinners, now, were full of his father's invective: did the university not know that his snakes needed a home, that this expanse of sandy acres was one of the richest reptile havens in North America? He would never sell, never. He would kill to keep it. Safe and whole.

While his father spoke, the traitor in Jude dreamed of the sums his father had been offered. So simple, it seemed, to make the money grow. Unlike other kinds of numbers, money was already self-fertilized; it would double and double again until at last it made a roiling mass. If you had enough of it, Jude knew, nobody would ever have to worry again.

When Jude was thirteen, he discovered the university library. One summer day, he looked up from the pile of books where he'd been contentedly digging—trigonometry, statistics, calculus, whatever he could find—to see his father opposite him. Jude didn't know how long he'd been there. It was a humid morning, and even in the library the air was stifling, but his father looked leathered, cool in his sunbeaten shirt and red neckerchief.

"Come on, then," he said. Jude followed, feeling ill. They rode in the pickup for two hours before Jude understood that they were going snaking together. This was his first time. When he was smaller, he'd begged to go, but every time, his father had said no, it was too dangerous, and Jude never argued that letting a boy live for a week alone in a house full of venom and guns and questionable wiring was equally unsafe.

His father pitched the tent and they ate beans from a can in the darkness. They lay side by side in their sleeping bags until his father said, "You're good at math."

Jude said, "I am," though with such understatement that it felt like a lie. Something shifted between them, and they fell asleep to a silence that was softer at its edges.

His father woke Jude before dawn and he stumbled out of the tent to grainy coffee with condensed milk and hot hush puppies. His father was after moccasins, and he gave Jude his waders and himself trudged through the swamp, protected only by jeans and boots. He'd been bitten so often, he said, he no longer brought antivenom. He didn't need it. When he handed his son the stick and gestured at a black slash sunning on a rock, the boy had to imagine the snake as a line in space, only connecting point to point, to be able to grasp it. The snake spun from the number one to the number eight to a defeated three and he deposited it in the sack.

They worked in silence all day, and when Jude climbed back up into the truck at the end of the day, his legs shook from the effort it took him to be brave. "So now you know," his father said in a strange holy voice, and Jude was too tired to take the steps necessary, then, and ever afterward until he was his father's own age, to understand.

His father began storing the fodder mice in Jude's closet, and to avoid the doomed squeaks, Jude joined the high school track team. He found his talent in the two-hundred-meter hurdles. When he came home with a trophy from the State Games, his father held the trophy for a moment, then put it down.

"Different if Negroes were allowed to run," he said.

Jude said nothing, and his father said, "Lord knows I'm no lover of the race, but your average Negro could outrun any white boy I know."

Jude again said nothing but avoided his father and didn't make him an extra steak when he cooked himself dinner. He still wasn't talking to him when his father went on an overnight trip and didn't come back for a week. Jude was used to it and didn't get alarmed until the money ran out and his father still didn't come home.

He alerted the secretary at the university who sent out a group of graduate students to where Jude's father had been seen. They found the old man in his tent, bloated, his tongue protruding from a face turned black; and Jude understood then how even the things you loved most could kill you.

At the funeral, out of a twisted loyalty for his father, he avoided his uncle. He didn't know if his mother knew she'd been widowed; he thought probably not. He told nobody at school that his father had died. He thought of himself as an island in the middle of the ocean, with no hope of seeing another island in the distance, or even a ship passing by.

He lived alone in the house. He let the mice die, then tossed the snakes in high twisting parabolas into the swamp. He scrubbed the house until it gleamed and the stench of reptiles was gone, then applied beeswax, paint, polish until it was a house fit for his mother. He waited. She didn't come.

The day he graduated from high school, he packed his clothes and sealed up the house and took the train to Boston. He'd heard from his uncle that his mother lived there and so he'd applied and been accepted to college in the city. She owned a bookstore on a small, dark street. It took Jude a month of slow passing to gather the courage to go in. She was either in the back, or shelving books, or smiling in conversation with somebody, and he'd have a swim of darkness in his gut and know that it was fate telling him that today was not the day. When he went in, it was only because she was alone at the register, and her face—pouchy, waxy—was so sad in repose that the sight of it washed all thought from his head.

She rose with a wordless cry and flew to him. He held her stoically. She smelled like cats, and her clothes flopped on her as if she'd lost a lot of weight quickly. He told her about his father dying and she nodded and said, "I know. I dreamed it."

She wouldn't let him leave her. She dragged him home with her and made him spaghetti carbonara and put clean sheets on the couch for him. Her three cats yowled under the door to her bedroom until she came in with them. In the middle of the night, he woke to find her in her easy chair, clutching her hands, staring at him with glittering eyes. He closed his own and lay stiffly, almost shouting with the agony of being watched so.

He went to see her once a week but refused all dinner invitations. He couldn't bear the density or lateness of her love. He was in his junior year when her long-percolating illness overcame her and she too left him. Now he was alone.

There was nothing but numbers, then.

Later, there were numbers, the great ravishing machine in the laboratory into which he fed punched slips of paper, the motorcycle Jude rode because it roared like murder. He had been given a class to teach, but it was taken away after a month and he was told that he was better suited for research. In his late twenties, there were drunk and silly girls he could seduce without saying a word, because they felt a kind of danger coiled in him.

He rode his motorcycle too fast over icy roads. He swam at night in bays where great whites had been spotted. He bombed down ski slopes with only a hazy idea of the mechanics of snow. He drank so many beers he woke one morning to discover he'd developed a paunch as big as a pregnant woman's belly. He laughed to shake it, liked its wobble. It felt comforting, a child's pillow clutched to his midsection all day long.

By the time he was thirty, Jude was weary. He became drawn to bridges, their tensile strength, the cold river flowing underneath. A resolution was forming under his thoughts, like a contusion hardening under the skin.

And then he was crossing a road, and he hadn't looked first, and a bread truck, filled with soft dinner rolls so yeasty and warm that they were still expanding in their trays, hit him. He woke with a leg twisted beyond recognition, a mouth absent of teeth on one side, and his head in the lap of a woman who was crying for him, though she was a stranger, and he was bleeding all over her skirt, and there were warm mounds of bread scattered around them. It was the bread that made the pain return to his body, the deep warmth and good smell. He bit the hem of the woman's skirt to keep from screaming.

She rode with him to the hospital and stayed all night to keep him from falling asleep and possibly going into a coma. She was homely, three years older than he, a thick-legged antiques dealer who described her shop down a street so tiny the sun never touched her windows. He thought of her in the silent murky shop, swimming from credenza to credenza like a fish in an aquarium. She fed him rice pudding when she came to visit him in the hospital and carefully brushed his wild hair until it was flat on his crown.

He woke one night with a jerk: the stars were angrily bright in the hospital window and someone in the room was breathing. There was a weight on his chest, and when he looked down, he found the girl's sleeping head. For a moment, he didn't know who she was. By the time he identified her, the feeling of unknowing had burrowed in. He would never know her; knowledge of another person was ungraspable, a cloud. He would never begin to hold another in his mind like an equation, pure and entire. He focused at the part of her thin hair, which in the darkness and closeness looked like inept black stitches in white wax. He stared at the part until the horror faded, until her smell, the bitterness of unwashed hair, the lavender soap she used on her face, rose to him and he put his nose against her warmth and inhaled her.

At dawn, she woke. Her cheek was creased from the folds in his gown. She looked at him wildly and he laughed, and she rubbed the drool from the corner of her mouth and turned away as if disappointed. He married her because, during the night, to not marry her had ceased to be an option.

While he was learning how to walk again, he had a letter from the university down in Florida, making a tremendous offer for his father's land.

And so, instead of the honeymoon trip to the Thousand Islands, pines and cold water and his wife's bikini pressing into the dough of her flesh, they took a sleeping train down to Florida and walked in the heat to the edge of the university campus. Where he remembered vast oak hammocks, there were rectilinear brick buildings. Mossy pools were now parking lots.

Only his father's property, one hundred acres, was overgrown with palmettos and vines. He brushed the redbugs off his wife's sensible travel pants and carried her into his father's house. Termites had chiseled long gouges in the floorboards, but the sturdy cracker house had kept out most of the wilderness. His wife touched the mantel made of heart pine and turned to him gladly. Later, after he came home with a box of groceries and found the kitchen scrubbed clean, he heard three thumps upstairs and ran up to find that she had killed a blacksnake in the bathtub with her bare heel and was laughing at herself in amazement.

How magnificent he found her, a Valkyrie, half-naked and warlike with that dead snake at her feet. In her body, the culmination of all things. He didn't say it, of course; he couldn't. He only reached and put his hands upon her.

In the night, she rolled toward him and took his ankles between her own. "All right," she said. "We can stay."

"I didn't say anything," he said.

And she smiled a little bitterly and said, "Well. You don't."

They moved their things into the house where he was born. They put in air conditioning, renovated the structure, put on large additions. His wife opened a shop on the ground floor of the one building in town over four stories tall, though she had to drive to Miami and Atlanta to stock it with antiques. He sold his father's land, but slowly, in small pieces, at prices that rose dizzyingly with each sale. The numbers lived in him, warmed him, brought him a buzzing kind of joy. Jude made investments so shrewd that when he and his wife were in their midthirties, he opened a bottle of wine and announced that neither of them would ever have to work again. His wife laughed and drank but kept up with the store. When she was almost too old, they had a daughter and named her after his mother.

When he held the baby at home for the first time, he understood he had never been so terrified of anything as he was of this mottled lump of flesh. How easily he could break her without meaning to, she could slip from his hands and crack open on the floor, she could catch pneumonia when he bathed her, he could say a terrible thing in anger and she would shrivel. All the mistakes he could make telescoped before him. His wife saw him turn pale and plucked the baby from his hands just before he crashed down. When he came to, she was livid but calm. He protested, but she put the baby in his hands.

"Try again," she said.

*

His daughter grew, sturdy and blond like his wife, with no flash of Jude's genius for numbers. They were dry as biscuits in her mouth; she preferred music and English. For this, he was glad. She would love more moderately, more externally. If he didn't cuddle with her the way her mother did, he still thought he was a good father: he never hit her, he never left her alone in the house, he told her how much he loved her by providing her with everything he could imagine she'd like. He was a quiet parent, but he was sure she knew the scope of his heart.

And yet his daughter never grew out of wearing a singularly irritating expression, one taut with competition, which he first saw on her face when she was a very little girl at an Easter egg hunt. She could barely walk in her grass-stained bloomers, but even when the other children rested out of the Florida sunshine in the shade, eating their booty of chocolate, Jude's little girl kept returning with eggs too cunningly hidden in the sago palms to have been found in the first frenzy. She heaped them on his lap until they overflowed and shrieked when he told her firmly that enough was enough.

His fat old uncle came over for dinner once, then once a week, then became a friend. When the uncle died of an aneurysm while feeding his canary, he left Jude his estate of moth-eaten smoking jackets and family photos in ornate frames.

The university grew around Jude's last ten-acre parcel, a protective cushion between the old house and the rest of the world. The more construction around their plot of land, the fewer snakes Jude saw, until he felt no qualms about walking barefoot in the St. Augustine grass to take the garbage to the edge of the drive. He built a fence around his land and laughed at the university's offers, sensing desperation in their inflating numbers. He thought of himself as the virus in the busy cell, latent, patient. The swamp's streams were blocked by the university's construction, and it became a small lake, in which he installed some bubblers to keep the mosquitoes away. There were alligators, sometimes large ones, but he put in an invisible fence and it kept his family's dogs from coming too close to the water's edge and being gobbled up, and the gators only eyed them from the banks.

And then, one day, Jude woke with the feeling that a bell jar had descended over him. He showered with a sense of unease, sat at the edge of the bed for a while. When his wife came in to tell him something, he watched in confusion at the way her mouth opened and closed fishily, without sound.

"I think I've gone deaf," he said, and he didn't so much hear his words as feel them vibrating in the bones of his skull.

At the doctors', he submitted to test after test, but nobody understood what had gone wrong in his brain or in his ears. They gave him a hearing aid that turned conversation into an underwater burble. Mostly he kept it off.

At night, he'd come out into the dark kitchen, longing for curried chicken, raw onion, preserved peaches, tastes sharp and simple to remind himself that he was still there. He'd find his daughter at the island, her lovely mean face lit up by her screen. She'd frown at him and turn the screen to show him what she'd discovered: cochlear implants, audiologic rehabilitation, miracles.

But there was nothing for him. He was condemned. He ate Thanksgiving dinner, wanting to weep into his sweet potatoes. His family was gathered around him, his wife and daughter and their closest friends and their children, and he could see them laughing, but he couldn't hear the jokes. He longed for someone to look up, to see him at the end of the table, to reach out a hand and pat his. But they were too happy. They slotted laden forks into their mouths and brought the tines out clean. They picked the flesh off the turkey, they scooped the pecans out of the pie. After the supper, his arms prickling with hot water from the dishes, they sat together, watching football, and he sat in his chair with his feet propped up, and everyone fell asleep around him and he alone sat in vigil over them, watching them sleep.

The day his daughter went to college in Boston, his wife went with her.

She mouthed very carefully to him, "You'll be all right for four days? You can take care of yourself?"

And he said, "Yes, of course. I am an *adult*, sweetheart," but the way she winced, he knew he'd said it too loudly. He loaded their bags into the car, and his daughter cried in his arms, and he kissed her over and over on the crown of the head. His wife looked at him worriedly, but kissed him also and climbed inside. And then, silently as everything, the car moved off.

The house felt immense around him. He sat in the study, which had been his childhood bedroom, and seemed to see the place as it had been, spare and filled with snakes, layered atop the house as it was, with its marble and bright walls and track lights above his head.

That night, he waited, his hearing aid turned up so loud that it began to make sharp beeping sounds that hurt. He wanted the pain. He fell asleep watching a sitcom that, without sound, was just strange-looking people making huge expressions with their faces and woke up and it was only eight o'clock at night, and he felt as if he'd been alone forever.

He hadn't known he'd miss his wife's heavy body in the bed next to his, the sandwiches she made (too much mayonnaise, but he never told her so), the smell of her body wash in the humid bathroom in the morning.

On the second night, he sat in the black density of the veranda, looking at the lake that used to be a swamp. He wondered what had happened to the reptiles out there; where they had gone. Alone in the darkness, Jude wished he could hear the university in its nighttime boil around them, the students shouting drunkenly, the bass thrumming, the noise of football games out at the stadium that used to make them groan with irritation. But he could have been anywhere, in the middle of hundreds of miles of wasteland, for as quiet as the night was for him. Even the mosquitoes had somehow been eradicated. As a child, he would have been a single itchy blister by now.

Unable to sleep, Jude climbed to the roof to straighten the gutter that had crimped in the middle from a falling oak branch. He crept on his hands and knees across the asbestos shingles, still hot from the day, to fix the flashing on the chimney. From up there, the university coiled around him, and in the streetlights, a file of pledging sorority girls in tight, bright dresses and high heels slowly crawled up the hill like ants.

He came down reluctantly at dawn and took a can of tuna and a cold jug of water down to the lake's edge, where he turned over the aluminum johnboat his wife had bought for him a few years earlier, hoping he'd take up fishing.

"Fishing?" he'd said. "I haven't fished since I was a boy." He thought of those childhood shad and gar and snook, how his father cooked them up with lemons from the tree beside the back

door and ate them without a word of praise. He must have made a
face because his wife had recoiled.

"I thought it'd be a hobby," she'd said. "If you don't like it, find
another hobby. Or *something*."

He'd thanked her but had never had the time to use either the
rod or the boat. It sat there, its bright belly dulling under layers of
pollen. Now was the time. He was hungry for something indefin-
able, something he thought he'd left behind him so long ago. He
thought he might find it in the lake, perhaps.

He pushed off and rowed out. There was no wind, and the sun was
already searing. The water was hot and thick with algae. A heron
stood one-legged among the cypress. Something big jumped and
sent rings out toward the boat, rocking it slightly. Jude tried to get
comfortable but was sweating, and now the mosquitoes smelled
him and swarmed. The silence was eerie because he remembered
it as a dense tapestry of sound, the click and whirr of sandhill
cranes, the cicadas, the owls, the mysterious subhuman cries too
distant to identify. He had wanted to connect with something,
something he had lost, but it wasn't here.

He gave up. But when he sat up to row himself back, both oars
had slid loose from their locks and floated off. They lay ten feet
away, caught in the duckweed.

The water thickly hid its danger, but he knew what was there.
There were the alligators, their knobby eyes even now watching
him. He'd seen one with his binoculars from the bedroom the
other day that was at least fourteen feet long. He felt it somewhere
nearby, now. And though this was no longer prairie, there were still
a few snakes, cottonmouths, copperheads, pygmies under the leaf-
rot at the edge of the lake. There was the water itself, superheated
until host to flagellates that enter the nose and infect the brain, an
infinity of the minuscule, eating away. There was the burning sun
above and the mosquitoes feeding on his blood. There was the silence. He wouldn't swim in this terrifying mess. He stood, agitated,
and felt the boat slide a few inches from under him, and sat down
hard, clinging to the gunwales. He was a hundred feet offshore on
a breathless day. He would not be blown to shore. He would be
stuck here forever; his wife would come home in two days to find
his corpse floating in its johnboat. He drank some water to calm

himself. When he decided to remember algorithms in his head, their savor had stolen away.

For now there were silent birds and sun and mosquitoes; below a world of slinking predators. In the delicate cup of the johnboat, he was alone, floating. He closed his eyes and felt his heart beat in his ears.

He had never had the time to be seized by doubt. Now all he had was time. Hours dripped past. He sweated. He was ill. The sun only grew hotter and there was no respite, no shade.

Jude drifted off to sleep, and when he woke he knew that if he opened his eyes, he would see his father sitting in the bow, glowering. Terrible son, Jude was, to ruin what his father loved best. The ancient fear rose in him, and he swallowed it as well as he could with his dry throat. He would not open his eyes, he wouldn't give the old man the satisfaction.

"Go away," he said. "Leave me be." His voice inside his head was only a rumble.

"I'm not like you, Dad," Jude said later. "I don't prefer snakes to people."

Even later, he said, "You were a mean, unhappy man. And I always hated you."

But this seemed harsh and he said, "I didn't completely mean that."

He thought of this lake. He thought of how his father would see Jude's life. Such a delicate ecosystem, so precisely calibrated, in the end destroyed by Jude's careful parceling of love, of land. Greed; the university's gobble. Those scaled creatures, killed. The awe in his father's voice that day they went out gathering moccasins; the bright, sharp love inside Jude, long ago, when he had loved numbers. Jude's promise was unfulfilled, the choices made not the passionate ones. Jude had been safe.

And here he was. Not unlike his father when he died in that tent. Isolated. Sunbattered. Old.

He thought in despair of diving into the perilous water, and how he probably deserved being bitten. But then the wind picked up and began pushing him back across the lake, toward his house. When he opened his eyes, his father wasn't with him, but the house loomed over the bow, ramshackle, too huge, a crazy person's place. He averted his eyes, unable to bear it now. The sun snuffed itself out. Despite his pain, the skin on his legs and arms blistered with sunburn and great, itching mosquito welts, he later realized he must have fallen asleep because when he opened his eyes again, the stars were out and the johnboat was nosing up against the shore.

He stood, his bones aching, and wobbled to the shore.

And now something white and large was rushing at him, and because he'd sat all day with his father's ghost, he understood this was a ghost too, and looked up at it, calm and ready. The lights from the house shined at its back, and it had a golden glow around it. But the figure stopped just before him, and he saw, with a startle, that it was his wife, that the glow was her frizzy gray hair catching the light, and he knew then that she must have come back early, that she was reaching a hand out to him, putting her soft palm on his cheek, and she was saying something forever lost to him, but he knew by the way she was smiling that she was scolding him. He stepped closer to her and put his head in the crook of her neck. He breathed his inadequacy out there, breathed in her love and the grease of her travels and knew he had been lucky; that he had escaped the hungry darkness, once more.

RUTH PRAWER JHABVALA

The Judge's Will

FROM *The New Yorker*

AFTER HIS SECOND HEART ATTACK, the judge knew that he could no longer put off informing his wife about the contents of his will. He did this for the sake of the woman he had been keeping for twenty-five years, who, ever since his first attack, had been agitating about provisions for her future. These had long been in place in his will, known only to the lawyer who had drawn it up, but it was intolerable to the judge to think that their execution would be in the hands of his family; that is, his wife and son. Not because he expected them to make trouble but because they were both too impractical, too light-minded to carry out his wishes once he was not there to enforce them.

This suspicion was confirmed for him by the way Binny received his secret. Any normal wife, he thought, would have been aghast to learn of her husband's long-standing adultery. But Binny reacted as though she had just heard some spicy piece of gossip. She was pouring his tea and, quivering with excitement, spilled some in the saucer. He turned his face from her. "Go away," he told her, and then became more exasperated by the eagerness with which she hurried off to reveal the secret to their son.

Yasi was the only person in the world with whom she could share it. As a girl growing up in Bombay, Binny had had many friends. But her marriage to the judge had shipwrecked her in Delhi, a stiffly official place that didn't suit her at all. If it hadn't been for Yasi! He was born in Delhi and in this house—a gloomy, inward-looking family property, built in the 1920s and crowded with heavy Indo-Victorian furniture inherited from earlier generations. Binny's high spirits had managed to survive the somber atmosphere; and, when Yasi was a child, she had shared the tastes and pleasures of her Bombay days with him, teaching him dance steps and playing him the songs of Hollywood crooners on her gramophone. They lived alone there with the judge. Shortly after Yasi was born, the judge's mother had died of some form of cancer, which had also accounted for several other members of the family. It seemed to Binny that all of the family diseases—both physical and mental—were bred in the very roots of the house, and she feared that they might one day seep into Yasi's bright temperament. The fear was confirmed by the onset of his dark moods. Before his first breakdown, Yasi had been a brilliant student at the university, and although he was over thirty now, he was expected shortly to resume his studies.

More like a brother than like a son, he had always enjoyed teasing her. When she told him the news of his father's secret, he pretended to be in no way affected by it but went on stolidly eating his breakfast.

She said, "Who is she? Where does he keep her? I don't know what's wrong with you, Yasi. Why can't you see how important this is for us? Why are you asking me why? Because of the *will*. His will."

"And if he's left it all to her?" Yasi asked.

"He'd never do that. Oh, no." Better than anyone, she knew the pride the judge took in himself and his ancestral possessions. "I'm sure she's a you-know-what. He must have taken her out of one of those houses—he owns half of them, anyway," she said, stifling her usual wry amusement at that sector of her husband's substantial family properties.

A day or two later, the judge had to be returned to the hospital. He stayed there for a week, and when they sent him home again he began to spend all his time in his bedroom. Apart from a few irritated instructions to Binny, he accepted her ministrations in silence; now and again, he asked for Yasi—reluctantly, as if against his own inclination. It took him some time to overcome his pride and demand a visit from his son.

Binny was so excited. It was probably to do with his will, with the woman. "You have to go! You must!" she urged Yasi. He agreed, on condition that she not listen at the door. "As if I would!" she cried indignantly, though both of them knew that she would be crouching there—and, in fact, when he emerged from his father's bedroom he found her hastily scrambling up from that position.

"What is it? What did he say?"

On the rare occasions when the judge had tried to talk alone with his son in the past, Yasi had recounted the conversations to his mother, with some embellishments: how the judge had had to clear his throat several times and had still been unable to come out with what he wanted to say, and instead had babbled on about his student days in London and the wonderful English breakfasts he had enjoyed, bacon and eggs and some sort of fish—"kippers, I believe they are called," Yasi had repeated, in the judge's own accent, to entertain his mother.

But now it was as if he was protecting his father: he wouldn't tell her anything. It wasn't until she challenged him, "Whose side are you on?," that he said, "He wants to see her."

"He wants to bring her *here?*"

"He's sending the driver."

"The fool, the first-class *idiot,*" Binny said. Her scorn for the judge soon turned to angry defiance: "What do I care? Let him bring her—bring all the women he's been keeping for twenty-five years." But, beneath it all, there was a sort of thrill—that at last something dramatic was happening in their lives.

There was nothing dramatic about the woman the driver brought the next day. She arrived in a plain white cotton sari and wearing no jewelry—"as if she were already a widow," Binny commented. Binny herself was a far more appealingly feminine figure: short and plump, in tight-fitting harem pants and very high heels, draped with the costume jewelry she preferred to the family jewels; at the salon they had bobbed and curled her hair and made it gleam with golden streaks. By contrast, Phul—that was her name, Phul, meaning "flower"—was as austere as a woman in constant prayer. Leaving her shoes at the threshold, she glided into the judge's bedroom; and though Binny lingered outside, no sound reached her to indicate what might be going on.

This performance, as Binny called it, was repeated the next day, and the next. After the fourth visit, she declared to Yasi, "This can't go on. You have to do something."

She had always depended on Yasi to get her out of difficult situations. In earlier years, when she still had a few women friends, Yasi had helped her cover up some secret expenditures—such as losing at cards, which she and her friends had played for money. She appreciated the way Yasi had circumvented the judge's disapproval. She had always been proud of her son's intelligence, which he had inherited, she had to admit, from his father.

Friends had asked her why she had married the judge, who was in every way so different from her. But that was the answer. Before meeting him, she had lived in an adolescent world of flirtations carried on in the cafés and on the beaches of Bombay. The judge, some twenty years older than she, was already a highly regarded lawyer with a private practice in Delhi when she met him. He was working on a professional assignment in Bombay with Binny's father, an industrialist, who had invited him to the family table—usually the dullest place in the world for Binny. But, with the judge there, she had sat through every course, not understanding a word but understanding very well that the guest's attention sometimes strayed in her direction. Afterward, she lingered in the vestibule to give him the opportunity to talk to her, though all he did was ask, in the weighty tones of a prosecutor in court, about her studies. A tall, heavy person, he habitually wore, even in the humid heat of Bombay, a suit, a waistcoat, and a tie, which made him stand out from everyone else, especially from her friends, who floated around in the finest, flimsiest Indian garments. She loved describing him to these friends, who exclaimed, "But he sounds *awful!*" That made her laugh. "He *is* awful!" By which she meant that he was serious, somber, authoritarian—everything that later oppressed her so horribly. One day, after posing his usual question about her studies, he went to her father to ask for her hand—for her hand! How she laughed with her friends. Wasn't it just like an old-fashioned novel—Mr. Darcy and Elizabeth Bennet! Or, from another book on their matriculation list, Heathcliff. In fact, she began to refer to him as Heathcliff, and to think of him as the gypsy lover who had come to steal her away.

The driver was sent to Phul every day, and every day she remained with the judge in his bedroom. Although this bedroom had meant nothing to Binny for many years, now her thoughts were concentrated on it, as they had been at the beginning of the marriage. The judge had been an overwhelming lover, and those nights with him had been a flowering and a ripening that she'd thought would go on forever. Instead, after about two years, the judge's presence in their bed was changed into a weight that oppressed her physically and in every other way. It had been a relief to her when Yasi was born and she could move with him into her own bedroom. She never returned to the judge's, and when he came to hers, she was impatient with his need. Mostly she used Yasi as an excuse—"Sh-h-h! The child is sleeping!"—ignoring her husband's protest that a boy that age shouldn't still be in his mother's bed. The judge's visits became less and less frequent, and finally they ceased altogether.

She hardly noticed and, until Phul came, thought nothing of it. On his good days, Yasi was always there for her, and she for him. He had a large group of friends and went out most nights. She would wait up for him, and, however late he came home, he would perch on the edge of her bed to tell her about the music festivals he had attended, the poetry recitals, the places where he had dined and danced. He was quite frank with his mother about the girls he slept with—she knew the sort of modern, fashionable girls who formed his social circle and had even learned to recognize the subtle Parisian perfumes that clung to him.

Then there were his bad days, when he didn't get out of bed, and when he did, he was silent and somber—yes, just like his father. But whereas the judge's anger was always contained, controlled, Yasi's was explosive—sometimes he would hurl a glass, a vase, a full cup of coffee, not caring where it landed. A few times he had struck her, suddenly, sharply. Afterward she pretended that it hadn't happened, and never spoke of it to anyone, and certainly not to him. This silence between them was a mutually protective one. Living so close together, perpetually intent on each other, each was wary of disturbing the other's balance, so precariously achieved, of anger and resignation, revolt and submission.

Alert to every sound from Yasi's room, one night she heard voices from there that made her tiptoe to his door. She found it open and the judge standing inside, ghostlike in his long white nightshirt. He was talking to Yasi, but as soon as he saw her he shut the door in her face. She had every right to open the door, to know what her husband was saying to their son, but it was not only the judge's prohibition that prevented her, it was Yasi's too; for there were times when he was as forbidding as his father.

The next day, she impatiently waited to question him. But he had hardly begun to speak when she interrupted him. "Probably he's left her everything. Very good! Let her have everything. Only don't think I won't get the best lawyer in the world to see that she has nothing."

"He knows how difficult it will be for you to accept the will. To accept her. He says she has no family at all."

"She doesn't? Then where did he find her? Wasn't there a whole tribe of them, in one of those rooms where they play music and people throw money?"

"He took her away before she was fifteen, and she's stayed all those years where he put her. So now he thinks she's like some tame thing in a cage—with a wild creature waiting to get her as soon as she's released. He made me promise to protect her."

"Against *me?*"

She shouted so violently that he shushed her. They were speaking in English but they knew the servants would be listening and, even without understanding the language, would be perfectly aware of the drift of the conversation. Now she spoke more quietly, and more bitterly. "That's what he's wanted from the day you were born. To turn you against me. To have you on his side—and now on hers too."

Tears, rare for her, streamed from her eyes, streaking her makeup, so that she did at that moment look like a wild creature. At first, Yasi felt like smiling, but then he felt sorry for her, as he had felt sorry for his father, that proud man pleading for a promise.

Binny had never allowed her circumstances to depress her. She had been very impatient with her women friends' constant complaints about unreliable servants, bad marriages, worse divorces. By the time she was in her fifties, she had dropped all of them except one. And finally there came the day when this friend too had to be abandoned. It happened over cocktails in their favorite hotel lounge. Binny was speaking about her close relationship with her son when the other woman interrupted her: "It's all Freud, of course."

"I see," Binny said, after a long silence. "Freud."

She got up. She took out her purse and deposited her share of the check on the table. She gave a brief, cold laugh. "Freud," she repeated. It was the last word she ever spoke to this friend.

So nowadays she comforted herself with her own amusements: shopping for new outfits and jewelry, intense sessions at a salon run by a Swiss lady. Her last stop was always Sugar & Spice, for Yasi's favorite pastries. If the judge warned her that Yasi was getting too fat, she suppressed her own observation that Yasi *was* getting too fat. She countered that it was the judge himself who should be careful: a man with two heart attacks, she reminded him.

But that morning when she arrived home with the pastries and said to the servant, "Call Yasi Baba," she was told that he had gone out. "In a taxi?" she asked casually, licking cream off her fingers. The servant said no, Judge Sahib had sent Yasi in the car—and by the way he said it, with lowered eyes, she realized that it was something she wasn't supposed to know. She stood fighting down a flush of anger, then suddenly she shouted, "Don't we have any light in this house?" All the shutters and curtains were closed to keep the sun out. The servant turned on the chandelier, but its luster was absorbed by the Turkish rugs, leaving only a thin shaft of silver light. Binny alone illumined the dark room, with her embroidered silks and the golden glints in her hair.

The judge's longtime driver was always at her disposal, and she had arranged with him that some of her destinations should be kept secret from his employer. She hadn't realized that the judge had made a similar arrangement. It didn't take her long to persuade the driver, to whom she had always been generous, to reveal the address where he had taken Yasi, as well as his instructions to take him there again the following night. She called for a taxi for the same time and went there herself.

It was across the river, in one of the first new colonies to be built in the area some twenty-five years before, far from the judge's prestigious neighborhood of shady old trees and large villas. Binny's taxi took her into a lively bazaar—the open stalls lit up with neon strip-lighting, the barrows of fruit and nuts with Petromax lanterns. Radios played film songs; chickens hung in rows from hooks. Opposite Phul's residence was a clinic, with patients waiting inside, and next to it a shoe shop, where Binny could try on a variety of ladies' footwear. This absorbed her so much that she almost missed Yasi's arrival. She glanced up at the opposite house when she heard the downstairs tenant assuring Yasi that the upstairs tenant was at home. Then she quickly returned her gaze to her feet, which were being fitted into a pair of bright blue sandals with silver heels, which she liked so much that she bought them there and then.

Yasi returned home very late, and as usual he perched on his mother's bed to tell her where he had been and what he had done. He had attended a music festival, he told her, and he sang her a phrase and swayed to it, his eyes closed. He loved music, which was something he'd got from Binny, though for him it was classical music, whereas she loved swing and jazz.

"So that's where you were all night?"

Alerted by her tone, he opened his eyes.

She said, "That's not what I was told."

Yasi said, "He sent me with the driver. I couldn't say no. She played her harmonium and sang. It was horrible, and I left as soon as I could."

"Then where were you until two in the morning?"

"I told you: I was at the music festival. You always think the worst of me. Oh, I'm sick of it! No, don't talk to me! My head's bursting!" And, indeed, his face had changed in a way she knew and had dreaded since the first breakdown.

The next day he slept late, and she sat beside him in his bedroom, where he lay with the tousled, tortured look of his sickness. She blamed herself for having been angry at him. She looked at the array of medicine bottles on his bedside table—she didn't know which were his sleeping pills and which were those prescribed for his moods, or how many he had taken. Usually so particular in his personal habits, he hadn't even changed out of the shirt he had been wearing the night before. A faint smell rose from it, not the delicate scent of his girlfriends but the heavy bazaar perfume she smelled whenever Phul entered the house.

Her pity for him turned into rage against his father. In earlier years, whenever she had felt her life to be intolerable, she had packed her suitcase and announced her decision to return to Bombay. At first, the judge had used a defense attorney's arguments to dissuade her; later, he had said nothing but simply waved his hand dismissively over the packed suitcase. And after a while she had unpacked it again. But this time she would not do so, would not retreat from her decision; for now it was not she who had to be considered but her son.

Leaving Yasi asleep, she walked through the house, through the many unused rooms, some shrouded, others shuttered, and before she had even closed the judge's door behind her, she announced, "I'm taking him to Bombay."

These days, she hardly ever entered the judge's bedroom. Everything was still in its place—his colonial armchair with the extended leg rest, his big bed and bigger chest of drawers, its brass handles too heavy for her to pull, and the mirror too high for her to look into—but there was a subtle change of atmosphere. Well, not so subtle! For there was Phul squatting on the floor by the judge's feet, massaging them as any devoted wife might do. He was gazing down at her with a look that Binny recognized as the expression—of father as much as of lover—that had so thrilled her in her youth.

When Binny entered, Phul turned and smiled—partly in apology but also with some pride at fulfilling a duty that she clearly felt was her right. She was a woman in her early forties, but her smile was peculiarly childlike: her teeth were as small as milk teeth and her gums showed up very pink against her complexion, which was much darker than Binny's. When she noticed that her sari had slipped off her shoulders, she tugged it back, though not before Binny had seen that she was very thin and with no breasts worth mentioning.

"Get up, child," the judge told Phul, his voice as tender as his gaze on her.

Child! Binny thought. Never since the day of their marriage had he called her anything except Bina—never Binny or Baby, as everyone had called her at home in Bombay. And now, as he shifted his eyes from Phul to her, his expression changed completely: for Binny was not at his feet but standing upright and facing him in hostility. She said, "We're taking the evening plane."

"The boy stays here," the judge pronounced.

"Here with you? And with *her?*"

Since the judge's last return from the hospital, a carved Kashmiri screen had been placed around the washstand installed for his minor ablutions. Although husband and wife were speaking in English, which she couldn't understand, Phul had quietly retreated behind this screen. Her absence made no difference to Binny, who continued, "And now you're sending him to her house at night! Shame on you—your own son! To take her off your hands and do what with her, with a woman old enough to be his mother?"

"You're an educated woman," the judge said. "You can count.

You know that she would have had to be a very precocious seven-year-old to become a mother."

"Not a day longer in this house! We're going to Bombay. He has to see a doctor."

"We have very good doctors here."

"And what have they done for him, stuffing him full of drugs meant for psychos. He's nervous, high-strung, like his mother—yes, I know you think I'm strong as a horse and yes, I've had to be, to bear almost forty years of marriage with you. But now—today, he and I . . ."

The judge was facing the door and he saw Yasi before she did. "Your mother wants to take you to Bombay," he told their son.

Binny spun around. "Tonight. The seven-thirty plane."

"Why do I always have to be caught between the two of you?" Yasi said. "Between a pair of scissor blades." He spoke in Hindi, and his parents looked warningly toward the screen. There was no sound or movement from behind it. Binny said, "Come out," but it was not until the judge repeated the command that Phul emerged.

Yasi made a sound that was not like his usual laugh but was meant to express amusement. "I think we're in the middle of an old-fashioned French farce."

"This is what your father has become, an impotent old man in a farce with his young what's-it, except this one isn't young." She smiled grimly, expecting Yasi to smile with her.

Instead he was looking at Phul, as was the judge. She stood humbly, wrapped from head to foot in her widowlike sari, and she pleaded in a low voice, "Send me home."

"Home?" Binny cried. "You *are* home. This is your home. You can move in right now with my husband—please, I beg you, the house will be empty. I'm taking my son to Bombay."

Before she had finished speaking, Yasi had sunk to a footstool, embroidered years ago by a great-aunt now deceased. He buried his head in his hands and sobbed.

His parents exchanged helpless looks. Binny said, "He's not well. It's his headaches. He mustn't be upset."

And the judge said, "You're right. We mustn't upset him." United in concern like any two parents, they spoke as though they were alone in the room.

Now Phul came up behind Yasi and laid her hands on his forehead, pressing it as she had done with the judge's feet. He seemed to relax into her touch, and his weeping stopped.

Binny noticed—and hoped the judge did too—that Phul's fingers were thick and coarse, unlike Binny's own, which were adorned with several precious rings, some of them inherited from the judge's mother.

Yasi resumed his lively social round and soon became so preoccupied with helping one of his girlfriends with a private fashion show that he was often out all night. So he was absent the morning the driver returned alone from his daily mission with the report that Phul was sick. At once, the judge asked for his three-piece suit, but when Binny found him trembling with the effort of getting his thin legs into his trousers—how frail he had become!—she put him back into his nightshirt and forced him into bed again. He pleaded with her to ask Yasi to take a doctor and some medicine to Phul. "She's alone," he told his wife. "She has no one." Binny regarded him with angry concern, then turned away. "Yes, yes, yes," she agreed impatiently to his request.

It was almost night when she called for the car and driver. The bazaar was even more alive than on her previous visit—music and lights and announcements on megaphones, vegetables trodden into the gutters, bits of offal thrown for the overfed bazaar dogs. She took the outside staircase that Yasi had climbed as she watched him from the shoe shop. The room she entered had a very different ambience from the one in which Phul presented herself in the judge's house. Gay and gaudy, with little pictures and little gods, and hangings tinkling with tiny bells, it seemed more innately Phul's, as though arising from memories of the places and the people among whom she had lived before meeting the judge. A garland of marigolds had been hung around an image of a naked saint with fleshy breasts. Amid the few bolsters scattered on the floor, there were only two pieces of furniture, both large: a colonial armchair, the twin of the one in the judge's bedroom, and a bed, on which Phul lay. She wore a sort of house gown, as crumpled as the bed and with curry stains on it. When she saw Binny, she started up, and her hand flew to her heart—yes, Binny thought, she had every reason to fear the judge's wife, after he had kept her holed up in this secret den for twenty-five years.

But it turned out that her fear was for the judge—that there was bad news about him that would leave her forever penniless, alone, unprotected. She let out a wail, which ceased the moment she was reassured. Then her first words were of regret for her inability to serve a guest. She blamed her servant boy, who regularly disappeared when needed. She spoke in a rush and in a dialect that Binny found hard to follow.

When the servant boy reappeared, Binny sent him for the doctor from the clinic next to the shoe shop. Phul lay resigned and passive on her bed, though her moaning grew louder at the doctor's arrival. He was dismissive—some sort of stomach infection, he said. It was going around the city; he saw dozens of cases every day. He scribbled a prescription, ordered a diet of rice and curds. To Binny, it seemed that the room itself was a breeding ground for fevers and infections, with sticks of smoking incense distilling their synthetic essence into the air shimmering with summer heat. There was only one window, which was stuck. Watching her visitor wrestle with it, Phul got up and tried to help her and in her weakness almost fell, before Binny caught her. Struggling then to free herself—"No, no!" she cried—she threw up in a spasm that spattered over Binny's almost new blue-and-silver shoes. Then she allowed herself to be carried to the bed and lay there with only her lips moving. What she seemed to be saying was the English word "sorry"—Binny thought how typical it was of the judge that among the few English words he had taught her was this abject one of apology.

Binny was wiping the judge's face after his meal when he asked, quite shyly, "Is she better?"

"For all I know, she may be, but not well enough to come here and infect us all."

She wrung out the facecloth in the basin behind the screen. When she emerged, she saw that he was deep in thought. He made a gesture as though communicating with himself; his hand was unsteady but his voice was determined.

"Yasi must take care of her. He promised. Send him again; send him every day."

"If you go on fretting this way, you'll have another attack and kill the rest of us with having to nurse you."

But it was she herself who went every day, with specially prepared dishes of healthy food. She ascribed the slowness of Phul's
recovery to the unfresh air in her room. With the one window now
propped open, the incense and the bazaar perfume blended with
the street smells—wilted produce, motor oil, and a nearby urinal.
And what was worse were the unhealthy thoughts in Phul's mind,
the despair that kept her moaning, "What will happen to me?"
One day, Binny found her up and dressed and ready to go to the
judge; she sank back only when Binny asked her, did she really
want to expose that sick old man to her infection? Then, for the
first time, Phul spoke of Yasi and begged to see him.

It was also the first time that Yasi was told about her sickness.
"Oh, the poor thing," he said. "I'd go to see her, but you know as
well as I do that I catch everything."

"No, no, of course you mustn't."

He promised to go once the danger was past. Binny couldn't
help warning, "Only don't stay with her all night and then tell me
lies about music and poetry."

"If you'd just listen for once in your life!" His exasperation
lasted only a moment and he continued patiently, "I never stayed
all night. I tried to get away as soon as I could, but she's very clinging. And she's also very stupid. And her singing, oh, my God, I
wanted to pay her to stop. It's his fault. It was her profession to
entertain but he took her away to keep for himself before she
could learn anything. Would you believe it, she can hardly read
and write. I'd try to teach her, but it would be hopeless. Poor little
Phul, and now's she's over forty." He had accumulated a fund of
feeling, first for his mother and then for all women whom he considered to have had a raw deal.

In the early years of their marriage, the judge had taught Binny to
play chess. Now, alone with him in his convalescence, she brought
out the neglected chessboard and set up a table in his bedroom.
He was a keen player, but that day his mind was not totally on the
game. Instead of deploring her wrong moves, he asked if Yasi was
looking after Phul. She said, "He's done enough for you. Send
someone else."

"There is no one else. I have no one."

"No one except her? And all she's thinking is: What will happen to me? That's all I ever hear from her—Yasi ever hears," she corrected. "That is what she thinks about. Not about you, about herself."

"I've told her about the will and the boy's promise, and still she's afraid."

"Of me? Tell her she can vomit all over me and still there's no need."

The judge clicked his tongue in distaste. He pointed at her castle, which she had just stupidly exposed. He wouldn't allow her to take the move back, but scolded her for not keeping her mind on the game. It was true: she was distracted. If she hadn't been, she wouldn't have made her next move, which put his bishop in jeopardy. She was usually more careful—she knew how much he hated losing. Intensely irritated, he reproached her, "It's as impossible to have a serious game of chess with you as it is to have a serious conversation."

She reared up. "Then let me tell you something serious. Whatever happens, God forbid, she's safe in her cage: there's no wild creature waiting for her outside. She can have everything. Tell her! Yasi and I want nothing." Without a qualm, she took his bishop.

In a voice like thunder, the judge shouted, "Call him! Call your son!" He had leapt up and with one sweep of his hand he scattered the chess pieces, so that some fell in her lap, some on the floor. This sudden strength frightened her. She grasped his shoulders to make him sit in the chair again and, though withered, they still felt like iron under her hands. She had to match her strength against his; it didn't take her long to win, but what she felt was not triumph.

She bent down to pick up the pieces from the floor and tried to replace them on the board. He waved her away, as though waving everything away.

"You can't do this," she said. "In your condition."

"Yes, my condition," he echoed bitterly. "Because of my condition, I lose my bishop to someone with no notion of the game."

He allowed her to lead him from the chair to his bed. She brought him water, and after he had drunk it he gave the glass back to her and said, "I'm sorry."

"Oh, my goodness!" she cried in shock. He had often done this—scattered the pieces when he was losing—but he had never before apologized for it. She understood what this was about and tried again to reassure him. "Everything will happen as you want it, the way you've written it. You have my promise, and Yasi's promise."

"The boy is weak. It's not his fault—no, not yours, either. You've done your best."

"Who knows what is best and what is not best," she said. Freud, she thought, bitter in her mind against her friend.

"Fortunately, you're strong enough for both of you. Sometimes too strong." He smiled, though not quite in his usual grim way.

He was looking at her, *considering* her, as she was now, as she had become; and though what she had become was not what she had been in her youth, he showed tolerance, even affection. It made her put her hands to her hair; she could guess what it looked like, what *she* looked like to him, how wild. She was overdue at the salon. She had been meaning to go for weeks—but what time did she have, between the judge and Yasi and this home and the secret one across the river, day after day, running from here to there?

Evie M.

FROM *Iowa Review*

TODAY I PHONED and had a cup of coffee, created/distributed a handful of B-20s, then phoned and had a cup of coffee. We ran out of powder creamer, but there were creams from McDonald's in the break area mini-fridge, which I just disinfected. Around 4:40, I decided to cruise hyperlinks until close. There was something about the president, and news that a small plane had crashed somewhere in Illinois. A sullen pop diva will guest-star on a Thursday night prime-time. It's sweeps. Her crimson mouth was parted in the photo, and for an instant I couldn't help but picture myself ejaculating—I guess. Accurate or not, I felt despicable, and quickly went to scrub my hands. I must remember to remember her name, to purchase her recordings. I drove home.

Home, where the shows are on. Between five-thirty and seven: utter contentment. The reruns allow me to nod off for a few and then rejoin any story without worry. They showed these same shows in the women's barracks, and again at base camp, and you could even watch them at forward operations. Usually a nap, followed by a quick Swiffering of the apartment, will help me to unwind before the new episodes come on at seven. I know everything, until the new episodes come on, at seven.

Today, though, someone had called and the red light blinked. No one ever calls. I was terrified to check the message, so I did not, and then did not sleep.

*

Back to work. Somebody left the coffee machine on all night, so the break area smelled burnt, and the pot had a veneer of tar-stuff on the bottom. I picked it up and looked into it, considered scrubbing it, considered smashing it into the brushed-steel sink, my knuckles grinding the shards, but then put it back and trod down the long hall to another break area, where I poured a cup. There were pyres everywhere in the desert. There was plenty of powder cream, here. Near my partition, a thin clerk shrugged his shoulders at the scorched pot. His khakis were wrinkled from having been worn too many times without a wash. I told him about the other break area, but he just stared at me. I told him there was plenty of cream.

Later, my supervisor stood at the edge of my workspace and flashed his perfect, glazed teeth. It made me nervous, which I think he enjoyed. Enjoys. He's younger than I am but doesn't act it. He told me he's been listening in on my customer calls and that I needed to master the Art of Inflection. Told me that I had a lovely voice, but that if I didn't sound interested in our product, I could not expect anyone else to get interested in it. Could I? Huh?

At lunch, my hands and face were filmy from a french dip. I finished half of it before I had to rush to the bathroom to wash. There was only an air dryer, so I used toilet paper to pat myself and ended up with tissue pills all over my chin. After that, I drove through McDonald's for coffee. I asked the woman for a handful of extra creams, and she glared at me as if I were the cause of something awful, like a tumor. She spoke into a headset, then slammed the window. As I pulled away, my exhaust made a grumbling sound, like rocks tumbling in a pipe, like the collision of track gears on an M113A3 personnel carrier. I simply cannot afford any extra expenses, car repair or anything. I put the car in park and sat in the lot, rubbing my thumbs against the corrugated thimbles of cream, rubbing and rubbing until another headset person knocked on my window and ordered me away.

Supervisor came by again. He stood over my shoulder, breathing through his nose. At some point, I had to turn and look up at him. His smile made me feel like a schoolgirl humiliated by her teacher. (I was given remedial teeth-brushing lessons after the red pill polluted my mouth.) The Art of Inflection, Evie, he said to me again. He then squeezed my neck, kneaded it, and walked off. I spent the rest of the day refreshing my in box. Someone sent a joke e-mail that showed a fat cartoon woman in black lingerie. Her beet-red nipples were spilling over the top, and her vagina was bisected by the panties. A stick-thin bald man dressed only in an undershirt and with a small, limp cock said that Victoria's secret was out: models were one thing, but nobody's *wife* looks good in these outfits. It wasn't funny. I sent it on to my account reps.

The red light was a message from Helen—I finally checked; I had to sleep. We broke up because she took a job elsewhere. Maybe this wasn't the end of the world, but it wasn't so goddamn good either. The thing is, we sat Indian-style on the wooden floor in her empty living room, the window light gentle and lemony, the moving trucks already gone, and she promised that *she* would hang in there if *I* hung in there.

I have to stop thinking about it—her—now. If you heat an individual serving (two) of Rich's frozen glazed doughnuts for 29 to 42 seconds, they'll be as hot and fresh as fresh. We had this little bitch dog in the desert, this black-and-white mutt that found us, just wandered into camp out of nowhere. We fed it chunks of dehydrated pork patty and whatever from our MREs, and someone named it Sheeba—that name, my God I hated that name. Growing up I'd never been allowed to have a dog, so I gave it every leftover from my meal packet, gum and salt and powdered cream and everything, and it began to sleep under my cot every night, and I'd dangle my hand down there on its ribs for as long as I could stay awake, and . . . And you'd pat it—her—Sheeba, and puffs of dust would fly from her fur, it was so funny, so dirty, and once she was outside the compound berm, out there in the sand, pawing at a beetle, springing back from a tiny bug or something, crouching on her front paws and growling at it like a puppy, and a few of us laughed and then went in the tent, and some guys from the motor pool took bets and shot it. Her. It depends on how frozen the doughnuts are. You can tell they are ready when they are spongy but not hard as you test them with the tines of your fork. Then: stop. Any longer in the microwave and the dough seizes up, and the glaze will coagulate. I know this.

*

Supervisor's teeth are only clean on the front. He uses those gro-
cery-store whitening strips instead of going to the dentist. I want to
tell him about his yellow side-teeth. Wanted to tell him today when
he smiled and told me to remember—told me twice—that Annual
Evaluations are upon us.

I was sitting on the floor next to the copier. I can't bear it when
the copier spool gets dry because of too much usage. It's precari-
ous, because you'd think you could just relubricate the plate glass
with a wipe of oil, like greasing a cookie sheet. But you absolutely
cannot put an abundance of copier oil on it, or it won't feed right.
Just a film, a light au jus. Unfortunately, if you're out of copier oil
and still have to bundle stapled and sorted sets of product logs
for supervisors with white front teeth, you know that this will take
your entire day: press the green button, get through (at best) one
set, deal with the jam. Repeat repeat repeat. Empty Duplicator.
Replace Last Two Originals In Document Feeder. Repeat repeat
repeat. Close Document Feeder. Repeat. It kills you after about an
hour. Finally, you just sit on the floor, dying over the fact that if you
wait for the repairman to arrive and relubricate, your ass is over.
Annual Evaluations are here.

Home again, though I can't seem to break off. The D-20 is for
requisition and the B-20 is for back order and the Service Order is
for the copy machine and the T-sheet is for time off and the PTO
sheet is for paid time off and the P-sheet is for parts order and
the O-sheet is for order in stock. I've seen this episode a thousand
times. I know all the dialogue by heart. Helen called again, and
her voice is . . . She hopes I'll call her back, hopes I'm still talking to the counselor woman at the VA. The box says that in seven
and one-half minutes my sirloin steak will be perfect. Yet I know
the mashed potatoes will be icy in the middle. It will take a precise balance of extra microwave and stirring to get them just warm
enough to eat without completely ruining the steak. I realize about
six minutes in that I am going to kill myself. At seven minutes, I
determine that I will not die with the guilt of making anyone feel
bad. I must start writing my notes.

The potatoes are not done. The extra minute ruins the sirloin.

*

Father—

I cannot begin to describe how sorry. My action is against everything you believe, and I know. . . . I think of your lifetime behind the desk, in the office. Honor and strength and poise—and you never once complained. I love and envy you. I am not strong. I am not obliged. I am not . . .

Jesus Christ, the shows are on.

You must adore digital cable. The search options have revolutionized me and everybody. Technology marches, no matter. You can be groped inside the hot metal gut of a troop carrier, or you can see things die and see pieces of dead things. I promise you it will not affect the remote control. Though I forgot to write down the name of the pop singer, with digital cable I can see into the future, and I will find her. This is amazing. She will come back.

Supervisor *yelled* at me today. So close I could smell his cologne. He barked that I wasn't "into it" the way I needed to be. Sandalwood. In consequence, I couldn't finish my first note, to my father. What if everyone counted on someone else to locate the clerical errors? he demanded. What if everyone produced reports whose pages crinkled because of a stupid copy jam? What if the whole damn order of things broke down?

Before he escorted me into his office, I was thinking about the salty taste of frayed baseball glove. After the Little League coach lets you on the team but still won't play you—save once, two innings in right field—things get quiet. In the corner of the dugout, wrapped in chainlink, your cleats sucking into mud and mangled seed husks, sometimes you chew on the leather strips that welt your glove. Dad realized things real early, and he showed me how to field with two hands, how to keep my elbow up when I was batting, and above all how to always run over and back up the throw on any given play. We knotted my hair under my ball cap. He said hustle was supreme, beyond even talent or background. I was going to revise my note to him from those principles of ambition, of compassion. I want him to know that I believed in them, that I learned.

Inside the supervisor's office is an L-shaped hardwood desk and a plastic *Ficus benjamina* in a dark wicker pot. He has no windows, but he does have three titanium-white walls and a white drop ceiling and fluorescent overheads and one glass wall that faces the general office. On the wall behind his desk is a diploma for business administration, alongside a membership certificate for Sigma Alpha Epsilon, and a Kiwanis Club award and a Young Entrepreneurs Intramural Softball group photo.

As he screamed, I stared past him, to those certificates—at least, until he yelled the words "copy machine," at which point I made the mistake of snapping focus. I then remembered my baseball glove and realized how fucked everything was. He says they're also going to check and see who's doing what online and deal with that, pronto. He left the mini blinds open, and the office could see everything. I thought of Helen, who, when she worked here, would have been waiting for me in the break area. I guess he saw my eyes start to water, because he eased his tone, said something about everybody's respecting my time in the service and all, etc. This prattle allowed me to again focus on the certificates. I have got to finish my notes immediately. I have got to finish my notes.

She called four times. She's coming into town this week and *really wants to see me* and says I *need to stop worrying*. Her box-dye auburn hair is dry to touch. Her eyelids sag and have tiny folds. I wonder if I should add her to my list of notes. Dad, Mom, Carla and Ray, and Helen. Maybe. What can I say? Can I say that she shouldn't worry about those road-to-nowhere veins on her legs? That I feel like I'm breathing under the ocean when she's around? I don't know. *Just call me back,* she says. The shows are on in seven minutes, and I've got a broccoli and cheddar that must sit for 120 additional seconds before the cellophane can even be removed.

Mother—

How difficult for you. Chocolate milk on the yellow sofa? Sabotaged cotillion? But you taught me so much. I'm sorry I was. I am proud at least that you would be proud of my home. Perhaps you can . . .

Heart-red, quivering sun on white talc sand. Crimped emerald blade of fern. Chocolaty plowed earth. Ice sheet blinding, sunlit snow traversed by knotted tree shadow. Salty gray ocean smashes rocky shore in fall.

The phone on my desk rings. I pray it is Helen. I answer, and our West Coast rep screams that I was supposed to get a boxful of promos to Brendel's, then asks where the hell they are. I tell him

that I sent them two-day; he yells at me and calls me a dumb asshole for not overnighting. I tell him that the Employee Handbook
says No Overnight Packages Are to Be Sent unless either (A) an
error has been made by the supplier's (our) end of things, thus
causing a delay in shipment, or (B) the recipient provides his or
her personal shipping account code for forward billing. He tells
me that I should fuck the Employee Handbook, because as I very
well know, Brendel's sells approximately 29 percent of all of our
merchandise to all of the United-fucking-States, and that if product sales and revenue and placement like that are not important
enough for overnight promos, he'll suck my dick. We fall silent.
Seconds later he says, Well, you get my point anyway, Evie, then
tells me he's calling my supervisor and hangs up.

   These phrases are no kind of note for Helen. I'd been looking
at the nature photos on my screen saver, desperate to list something pure.

On the way into work, the gravelly sound beneath my car broke
into a roar. The front end shook, and the gas pedal mudded. I
made it into the lot, hazards flashing, and told my supervisor I had
to take my car to the dealership service shop immediately. (Only
the dealership service shop requires annual certification of every
mechanic.) He said that this was not a company problem and that
I had to do it on my own time. I called him Sir and reminded him
that the dealership service shop would not be open on my own
time until Saturday, and that I was sure the car wouldn't make
it that long. He told me that I should look for a ride from a co-
worker. Or rent a car.

   I had to sit down. I had to sit down as he took the last of the coffee from our station and then walked away, leaving the empty pot
spitting on the machine. I could almost *feel* myself on the shoulder
of the tar-stinking road, choking on the emissions of commuters,
all of them able to get home and watch the shows. I can't stomach
the hot smells of anyone else's car. I won't ride in someone else's
baby-seated, taco-wrappered, cola-ringed, faded-upholstery, dust-
caked vehicle. And my rent is due and my cable bill is due and my
phone bill is due and my insurance is due and my water bill is due
and my gas bill is due and my electricity bill is due and I have to
get to my VA appointment and I have to buy some dinners, and

there's just no way. No way I can let my goddamn car die before
I'm through writing my notes.

After a nap and a Swiffer and a brief hang-up on Helen's answering machine, I turned on the oven. I enjoy "rooster" sandwiches,
though without the tomato or lettuce that they always slop on at
restaurants. Breaded chicken patties on a white hamburger bun,
with cheese, a seep of mayonnaise, mustard, and maybe ketchup,
are mine. I realized as I sucked in the gas blast that I was missing
the season finale. I ran to the television while the oven hissed. Hit
myself in the stomach, then below. It was already six minutes into
the half-hour program! I ran back to turn off the gas, waved my
hands around to chase the excess. Hit myself again. Bun crumbs
on the linoleum had to be wiped. I turned the oven back on, pre-
heated, put the patties on a nonstick tray, and slid it in.

At the climax of the program, the phone rang. I couldn't
answer. Helen told the machine she was coming into town and
wants to talk about how she screwed up both our lives and wants
to change that and to please take a deep breath, and did I ever
think about her suggestion that I get a cat? and . . . I realized that
I would be dead before she gets here, and more directly that these
were my final finales. I pressed Volume Up on the remote.

The middles of the patties were uncooked, and strings of
chicken slag lodged in my teeth. I ended up throwing most of the
rooster away, then waited for the commercials and rushed to
the bathroom to vomit. As a child, I learned that you must flush
the toilet to get low water before vomiting, to minimize backsplash.

Conversations swirl beyond my partition, but none of them cover
the first six minutes of the finale. The clerk with the dirty khakis is
kicking the door of the copy machine. I have got to get a two-day
package together for Brendel's before close of business. I have got
to finish my notes. I have got to finish my notes.

Kattekoppen

FROM *The New Yorker*

Logar, Afghanistan

WE WENT THROUGH a number of howitzer liaisons before Levi. His predecessors, none of whose names I remember, were able to build artillery plans in support of our night raids. They were skilled enough to communicate these plans to the soldiers who would fire the howitzers. In fact, any one of them would've been perfectly fine as a liaison to a normal organization. But ours was not a normal organization. Sometimes what went on gave normal men pause. And if they paused we'd send them back and demand a replacement. After a few rounds of this, the lieutenant in charge of the howitzer battery said, "Enough."

Which was understandable, but not acceptable. So on our first night without a mission Hal and I took a walk to the howitzer camp. We set out from the dog cages under a full moon, which seemed to cast X-rays rather than light. Thus the dogs' ribs were exposed, as was the darkness below the ice on our steep climb uphill. The steel barrels of the howitzer guns were visible as shadows, and the plywood door of the howitzer camp was illuminated as if it were bone. Hal knocked on this door with an ungloved fist.

The lieutenant answered. "Hey, guys," he said.

Hal pushed past him into an empty room. "Get your men in here," he said.

The room filled with soldiers feigning indifference, but every one of them had ideas about the war. The variety of ideas among soldiers developed into a variety of ideas among units, which necessitated an operational priority scheme. As SEAL Team Six, we were at the top of that scheme. Our ideas about the war *were* the war. Therefore, we could knock on any unit's door in the middle of the night, assemble the soldiers in a room, and tell them what was what.

On this night, Hal told them that we needed a goddamn liaison. Then he searched the room for one. Levi's height—he was by far the tallest man there—made it easy for Hal to point and say, "How about you?"

You put a normal man on the spot like that and he'll get this look. Levi did not get that look. This may have been, at least partly, because Levi was Dutch, born and raised. Why he had joined the United States Army was anyone's guess.

"Yes," Levi answered. "I am available. Howeffer, I have a pregnant wife in Texas, and in two weeks' time I would like to go there for the burt of my son."

Hal, with his scar like a frown even when he was smiling, nodded my way. I nodded back.

"We can work that out," Hal said.

So Levi became our howitzer liaison. He moved into our compound and had his mail delivered to our tactical-operations center. Packages arrived from his mother in Amsterdam. Inside the packages was a variety of Dutch candy.

Levi opened these packages at his desk. He removed the Vlinders and the Stroopwafels, but he always left the licorice Kattekoppen in the box. Apparently, Levi had loved these candies as a kid, and his mother was under the impression that he still loved them. But he didn't. So he set the Kattekoppen on the shelf by the door, where we kept boxes of unwanted food.

Perhaps "unwanted" is too strong a word. Better to say that no one wanted that particular type of food at that particular time. Everyone knew that a time would come, born of boredom, curiosity, or need, when we would want some Carb Boom, squirrel jerky, or a Clue bar. But until that time, the food sat on the shelf. And the Kattekoppen sat longer than most.

American licorice was red or black. It came in ropes or tubes. Kattekoppen were brown cat heads with bewildered faces. They made me think of a bombing attack I'd been involved in, in Helmand, during a previous deployment. We'd dropped a five-hundred-pound laser-guided bomb with a delayed fuse on a group of men standing in a circle in a dusty field. The round hit at the center of the circle and buried itself, by design, before the fuse triggered the explosion. The blast killed the men instantly, crushing their hearts and bursting their lungs, then flung their bodies radially. The dead landed on their backs, and a wave of rock and dirt, loosed by the explosion, sailed over them. The dust, however, floated above. As we walked in from our covered positions, it descended slowly. By the time we reached the impact site, it had settled evenly on the dead, shrouding their open eyes and filling their open mouths. Those dusty faces, their uniform expressions of astonishment, were what I thought of when I saw Kattekoppen.

Nevertheless, the day came when I pulled a Kattekoppen out of the bag and held it up.

"How's this taste?" I asked Levi.

"Goot," he said.

So I popped it in my mouth and chewed, and I found that it did not taste goot. In fact, it tasted like ammonia. I ran outside and spat the chewed-up bits on the snow, but the bad taste remained. Thinking that snow might help, I ate some. When that failed, I ate dirt. But nothing worked.

Others who tried the Kattekoppen didn't even make it outside. They simply spat their vociferous and obscene rejections right into the trashcan next to Levi's desk. If these rebukes of his childhood favorite bothered Levi, he never let on. He just sat in his little chair, which was actually a normal chair dwarfed by his abnormal size, and with his wee M16 lying by his side, he drew circles.

In a perfect world, there would be no circles. There would be two points, launch and impact, and between them a flawless arc. But in reality our maps were best guesses, the winds erratic, and every howitzer barrel idiosyncratically bent. Not to mention the imperfect men who operated the howitzers—those who lifted the shells into the breech, who loaded the charges, who programmed the fuses. These men were exhausted, lonesome, and fallible.

So Levi's circles were graphic depictions of possible error. They described, factoring in the permutation of variables, where the howitzer rounds might fall. He drew them around our most likely targets and, since everything was subject to change, he did so in grease pencil on a laminated map. Every circle contained a potential target, along with a subset of Afghanistan proper, its wild dogs, hobbled goats, ruined castles, and winter stars.

Before a mission, I'd study the contour lines within these circles in order to understand how to navigate the rise and fall of the terrain. Similarly, I'd study the stamps on the packages sent by Levi's mother.

These stamps paid tribute to the painter Brueghel. Each stamp focused on a particular detail within a particular painting. For example, the image on the stamp featuring *Hunters in the Snow* was of the hunters and their dogs returning from the hunt. Staggering through knee-deep drifts, they crested a hill that overlooked their tiny village.

Returning from our manhunts through the snowy mountains west of Logar, I felt the weariness of Brueghel's hunters. Cresting the hill that overlooked our frozen outpost, I saw their village. And, within its fortified boundaries, I watched men go about their daily tasks as if unaware of any higher purpose.

As the time for Levi's trip home approached, the howitzer lieutenant correctly predicted that rather than work anything out, we'd simply take another of his men to cover Levi's absence. So he raised the issue with his headquarters. He did so via an e-mail to the 1st Infantry Division's command sergeant major, requesting an increase in manpower to cover our requirement for a liaison. The lieutenant forwarded us the sergeant major's response, in which the sergeant major said that the only fucking way he'd even consider this horseshit request was if we provided him with written justification ASAP.

The chances of our providing justification, written or otherwise, to anyone, for anything, were zero. So the night before Levi went home Hal and I paid another visit to the howitzer camp. That night, a blizzard clobbered Logar. I met Hal by the dog cage, as usual. The heavy snowfall had caused us to cancel that night's mission, and the dogs, which on off nights normally hurled themselves at the chainlink, setting off the entire dog population of Logar, were still. Likewise, Hal was not himself. He shivered, and his scar was barely visible. When we reached the door of the howitzer camp, he had to knock twice.

The lieutenant answered. "Hey, guys. I'm really sorry about all this," he said.

"Yeah, yeah," Hal said. He poked his head in and saw a chubby kid playing mahjong on a computer. "We'll take him."

"Uh, OK," the lieutenant said. "But the sergeant major's going to be pissed."

"Not my problem," Hal said.

Hal returned to the compound to sleep, and I waited outside until the kid pushed through the door with a variety of coffee mugs carabinered to the webbing of his enormous ruck. "Ready!" he announced. And, with his headlamp on high, we set off down the steep, icy road.

Falling snow converged to a vanishing point in the beam of the kid's headlamp. When he fell behind, I could almost reach out and touch this point. But then he'd trot up alongside me, mugs clattering, and it would recede. On one such occasion, he presented me with a handful of bullets.

"Can I trade these in for hollow-point?" he asked. "I heard you guys roll with hollow-point. I also heard you guys muj up, in turbans and man jammies and shit, with MP5s tucked up in there. Like, *ka-chow!* That must be *wicked!* And I heard you guys have makeup artists that turn you into village elders so you can drop mad PSYOP on the GENPOP. Is that true? You don't have to tell me, but *holy fuck!*"

The kid fell behind, caught his breath, and trotted up beside me again.

"So can I get an MP5?" he asked.

I ushered the kid to the TOC and showed him Levi's computer. After booting up mahjong, he was quiet.

My next task was to put Levi on the rotator at dawn. The rotator was a cargo helicopter that every morning ran a clockwise route around the AOR. From our outpost, it would fly to Bagram, where Levi could catch a transport home. With daybreak less than an hour away, I poured myself a cup of coffee and sat back to watch the drone feed.

The drone was on the wrong side of the storm that sat over Logar, and its camera, which normally looked down on our targets, was searching a dark wall of cumulonimbus for a hole. Not finding one, it punched into the thick of the storm. For a moment, it seemed like it would be OK, then ice piled onto its wings as if a bricklayer had thrown it on with a trawl, and the drone hurtled toward earth. I wrote down its grid, because if it crashed we'd have to go out and fetch its brain. But as the drone fell into warmer air, the ice peeled away, and when it leveled off, its camera remained facing aft. I watched the drone pull a thread of the storm into clear morning air. By the time I heard the rotator's approach, the storm had passed.

Outside, covering everything was a pristine layer of snow, which dawn had turned pink. I started the pink HiLux. I honked the horn and it made a pink noise. Levi emerged from his pink tent with his pink ruck. I drove him down a pink road to the pink LZ. The rotator came in sideways, and its thumping rotors kicked up a thick pink cloud. Crouching, Levi and I ran through the cloud to a spot alongside the warm machine. A crewman opened the side door and handed me the mail, which included a package from Levi's mother. Then Levi hopped aboard and was on his way home.

The sun rose as I drove back to the TOC, and the whole outpost sparkled at the edge of the war. The stamps on the package from Levi's mother featured *Landscape with the Fall of Icarus*. The detail chosen was Icarus drowning. What was not shown was how the world went on without him.

The new liaison was asleep in Levi's chair when I got back. I opened the package quietly, so as not to wake him. More Kattekoppen. I put it on the shelf with the rest and was about to go to bed when the phones started ringing.

Two soldiers on their way home from a bazaar south of Kabul had taken a wrong turn. They'd hit a dead end and been ambushed. Bloody drag marks led from the scene, which was littered with M9 and AK brass. Witnesses said that the soldiers had been taken alive, which meant a rescue operation, led by us. We received pictures of the soldiers from a search-and-rescue database. One soldier had a chin and the other did not. The TOC filled with CIA, FBI, and ODA. Then a massive helicopter slung in the missing soldiers' ruined truck. Its windows had been shot through, and bullet holes riddled the skin. The door creaked open, and blood trickled out. Their smell was still in it, along with the stuff they'd bought at the bazaar, intact in a flimsy blue bag.

The drag marks at the scene led to a tree line. The tree line opened onto a number of compounds, which we raided that night. Those compounds led to other compounds, which we raided the next day. The second set of compounds led to a village, which, over two days and one night, we cleared. That delivered us to a mountain. It took two nights and a day to clear all the caves up one side and down the other. Which led us to another village. And so on.

Time became lines on a map leading in all directions from Chin and No Chin's ambush. We searched for them night and day.

One night, we were moving along slowly, with the moon casting our shadows on the snow and the wind in our faces, when an air-raid siren blasted and a small village suddenly appeared on our left in an explosion of light. The village was just beyond a tree line. I could feel the siren in my throat. Fearing an ambush, I radioed the howitzers for a fire mission.

"Send it," they replied.

While calculating the target coordinates, I noticed that the leaves shone like silver dollars in the wind. Kids in the village, awakened by the ruckus, quit their beds to run under the streetlights. Women chased after them. Men appeared on their roofs to wave to one another, and to shout back and forth over the siren's blare: *Isn't this something!*

This, we later learned, was the unexpected restoration of power after months without—the opposite of a rolling blackout. The resulting commotion continued until one light went out, then another. Until the women had chased the kids inside and the men had waved goodbye. Until all the lights were out. Then someone shut down the air-raid siren, and its blare died to a whistle, and the whistle died to a tumble of bearings. After which all was dark and quiet.

"Send your fire mission," the howitzers repeated.

"Never mind," I said. And we continued on our search.

If we'd been asked how long we'd go on searching, our answer would have been: as long as it takes. Think of the families back home. Baby Chin. Mother No Chin. But in truth there were limits, and we had methods for determining them. From the streaks of blood found in the drag marks, we ascertained wounds. From the wounds, we developed timelines. And we presented these timelines on a chart, which read from top to bottom, best case to worst. By the time that village lit up beside us, we were at the bottom of the chart. The next night, we started looking for graves. And although it seemed as if we were forever tripping over graves, when it came time to actually locate a specific one we couldn't.

There was no time to sleep. My fingernails stopped growing. My beard turned white. Cold felt hot and hot felt cold. And soon enough, I began to hallucinate. One night, as we approached a well, I watched Chin jump out and run away, laughing. Another night, I saw No Chin ride bare-ass up a moonbeam.

Meanwhile, the Mahjong Kid had proved himself worthy by having the howitzers fully prepped for that pop-up nonambush, and for every close call since. At first, I preferred Levi's circles to MJ's hyperbolas, which opened onto an infinity that no howitzer could possibly reach. But then, as the search for our missing comrades wore on, producing only dry holes and dead ends, the idea of thrusting death somewhere beyond the finite gained a sort of appeal.

We were down to almost nothing on the unwanted-food shelf. Only the Kattekoppen and some kind of macaroni that required assembly were left by the time we found No Chin's body in a ditch outside Maidan Shar.

No Chin had a note in his pocket indicating the whereabouts of Chin. We would find Chin buried under a tree by a wall. We hiked to trees without walls, walls without trees, graveless walls, and treeless graves, until finally, by a process of elimination, we stumbled on the right combination and dug.

Under a thin layer of dirt was a wooden box. Crammed inside the box was Chin. Prior to the mission, I'd filled my pockets with Kattekoppen, which came in handy, because Chin was decomposing and covered with malodorous slime. The smell only got worse as our medic stuffed Chin into a bag. Others gagged and puked. But I popped a steady supply of Kattekoppen, which kept the smell at bay.

The next morning, when the rotator arrived, we slid Chin in one door and Levi hopped out the other.

It was a bright warm morning. The snow had melted and the sun rose on a muddy world. Levi and I got into the HiLux and, on the ride away from the LZ, I congratulated him and asked how it felt to be a father.

"It is strange," Levi said. "I have never much worried, but sef-feral times a night now I wake up afraid the boy is dead. And I sneak into his room and, like this"—he wet an index finger and held it under his nose—"I check his breeding."

From Levi, hunched over, with his finger under his nose and his knees above the dash, I looked out the windshield at the war, which, stampwise, could've been a scene from Brueghel's *Triumph of Death*—one that, even without a skeleton playing the hurdy-gurdy, or a wagon full of skulls, or a burning shipwreck, or a dark iron bell, still raised the question of salvation. At the smoldering trash pit, I turned and drove toward the artillery range.

"We will make a fire mission?" Levi asked.

"Yes," I said.

Excited, Levi got out the big green radio and started messing with freqs. I parked at the edge of the range, where the ashen hulks of what might once have been tanks had been bulldozed into a pile. Presumably, the same dozer that had cleared these wrecks had also scraped the giant concentric rings in the field of mud before us. Way out on top of the bull's-eye was our target, Chin and No Chin's truck, right where I'd asked for it to be slung.

Hal and I had met at the dog cage the night before to discuss the rise of MJ and whether or not Levi still had a place with us. While the dogs rolled around, we'd devised this test.

I sat on the hood of the HiLux as Levi shot a bearing to the target with his compass and gauged the winds by the smoke blowing off the trash pit. Then he called it in, his Dutch accent somehow thicker after two weeks in Texas. But the howitzers' read-back was good. And soon enough, I saw iron scratches against the clear blue sky. I followed them to impact, where fountains of mud ascended from white-hot flashes. The mud fell, the booms rolled by, and I saw that the hits were good: the truck was badly damaged.

Still, enough of it remained to be hit again, without question. While Levi questioned, the magnetic pole upon which his bearing was anchored drifted ever so slightly; the breeze against which he'd applied his correction stiffened, and the men cradling the heavy shells of his next barrage cursed the unknown reasons for the holdup.

BRENDAN MATHEWS

This Is Not a Love Song

FROM *Virginia Quarterly Review*

SHE WAS KITTY to her parents, Katherine to the nuns in high school, Kate when she was in college. But to anyone who knew her then—Chicago in the first years of the nineties, her hands tearing at her guitar like a kid unwrapping a Christmas present—she had already become Kat.

Like the rest of the ramen-fueled hordes of art students and rockers-in-training, we lived in Wicker Park, where rents were low and apartments doubled as studios, rehearsal spaces, black-box theaters, and flophouses. The park itself was still a rusty triangle of scalded grass littered with needles and broken bottles. It would be a few years before the new trees and the swing sets and the DIE YUPPIE SCUM stencils on the smooth-bricked three-flats, before the press would hype Chicago as "the next Seattle," and record-company types started skulking around the bars. Back then, there weren't any boutiques on Damen selling $500 sweaters—just bodegas, auto-body shops, and empty storefronts whose faded signs whispered of plumbing supplies and cold storage.

Later there would be the brief flurry of albums and magazine covers, but back then the only people paying attention to her were the music nerds on the lookout for the next band you hadn't heard of and the rock critic from the free weekly who wrote mash-note reviews of any girl with a guitar. And me, of course, but by then I'd been paying attention to her for so long that I'd started to make a career out of it.

Interior. Stairwell. Evergreen Avenue loft.

She stands in the doorway, a ghost outlined by the yawning black
of the stairwell. She looks drained, which is how she often looked
in those days. Her arms are folded across her chest and her skin
bleeds into the T-shirt, white on white. Her hair must have been
black then, because in the picture it's fused with the empty space
around her, and her face really pops: jaw set, teeth bared, eyes
canted to the side, as if the shutter caught her the second before she spit out some curse. Maybe this was the night the van
got torched by our next-door neighbors—teenage Latin Kings or
Latin Lovers or Latin Disciples, we hadn't yet figured out how to
read their tags. Maybe it was the night the bass player told Kat he
was going to law school. Or maybe she'd just been ambushed by
Zlotko the landlord wanting to know *For sure, no joking, when you
pay me my rent, huh? When you pay me my rent?* You can say that the
way her body burns a hole in the middle of the image is just a photographer's trick, a little darkroom magic to saturate the blacks
and flush everything to the whitest white, and you'd be right. But
you can't deny that she's pissed.

Interior. Basement of Kat's parents' house.
River Forest, Illinois.

If you can't imagine Kat in the gray skirt and Peter Pan collar required by the nuns at our all-girls high school, it's probably because you've never seen the pictures I took when I was the president and only dues-paying member of the photography club and
Kat was spending afternoons and weekends punching out songs in
her parents' basement and running them through the four-track
she bought with a summer's worth of babysitting money. She was
my only subject—my muse, you could say—but that was because
she was the only one who would sit still while I fussed over lenses
and light readings and angles. It wasn't patience: even then she
was focused; even then she was very good at tuning out background noise. I took rolls and rolls of film of her bent over her
guitar, her hair a veil over her eyes, her lips soundlessly counting
out the beat. Then I'd disappear for days of red-light seclusion in

my studio, which my parents insisted on calling the laundry room. A set of these pictures, soulful black-and-whites mostly, spiked with a few hallucinatory color shots, won the school art prize senior year and had the added bonus of convincing every girl in our graduating class that we were lesbians. It's too bad we weren't; maybe we wouldn't have been so lonely, so frustrated, so perpetually amped up.

Interior. Fireside Bowl. Fullerton Avenue.

Kat is onstage, surrounded by cigarette smoke and crowd steam, her eyes raked up at the low black ceiling. The smoke drifts into the shafts of light pouring from the Tinkertoy overhead rig, gives a shape to the air, makes visible the currents. You can see the way the heat from the crowd rises and then bends back on itself in ripples and swirls. For all the movement on the floor, from shoe-gazer swaying to manic pogo-ing to grand-mal moshing, the real action is above, where the air surges with color—candy-apple red and freeze-pop green, children-at-play yellow and police-light blue. Not that she ever looked at the crowd when she sang. The eyes of other people distracted her; the way those eyes begged for instant intimacy wasn't just an imposition, it was an affront. An assault, even.

She didn't look into the crowd, she looked over it, at some safe, empty spot on a far wall, or a point on the ceiling where hands and faces could not reach. When she first started playing out in clubs where there was no stage, just a space on the floor to set up, her insistence on staring at the ceiling or squeezing her eyes shut tight gave her the look of some mad, ecstatic saint. People said she was blind, or epileptic, or terminally shy. Whatever they believed, they were talking about her, and she needed that kind of an advantage—that lingering hold on the crowd's mayfly attention—if she didn't want to get lumped in with every other band thrashing through its twenty-five minutes. (*"Which band? The one with the freaky girl singer with the messed-up eyes? Oh yeah, they were pretty good."*)

Once she moved up to places with a stage that set her above the crowd, her eyes didn't have to roll so far back in her head to find that tranquil spot in the ceiling. Some people even kidded themselves into thinking that she was looking at them, in those rare moments when her eyes flicked down to check her crabbed, chord-making fingers on the neck of her guitar. But she wasn't willing to share what she was feeling with anyone, not if sharing meant locking eyes with some other face out there in the dark and exchanging a smile or some acknowledgment that, hey, we're both in this moment together. Because that would have wrecked it. For her, I mean.

Box 5, spool 3.

> MALE VOICE: What's her deal, anyway?
> KAT: *inaudible*
> M.V.: Because it's weird.
> KAT: *inaudible*
> M.V.: How am I supposed to do that? I can't turn around without her going *click click click.* It's like she's a spy or something.
> KAT: She's not spying on you. She doesn't give a shit about you.
> M.V.: Then why is she always taking my fucking picture?
> KAT: Because she's spying on *me.* You're just . . . scenery.

School portrait. Seventh grade. Ascension Elementary School. Oak Park, Illinois. Kat smiles, lips together, to hide her braces. Photographer unknown.

If you wanted to go back to the very beginning, you would have to start with the days when her brother Gerry wanted to be Jimmy Page and Robert Plant all in one and his best friend had a drum kit so there was no question who got to be John Bonham. Gerry liked Led Zeppelin because they were loud and their album covers had secret symbols and some of the lyrics made references to *The Lord of the Rings.* He explained what the symbols meant, but he said Kat wouldn't really get it until she had read all of Tolkien, including *The Silmarillion.* She hadn't been able to get through *The Hobbit.* That's practically a kid's book, he told her. It doesn't mention the Valar or Númenor or any of the important stuff.

He told Kat she could play bass or get lost. Kat knew that she was in the band only until her brother made another friend, but even at thirteen she sensed that Gerry was socially radioactive, and that this provided her with some security, bandwise.

Fast-forward ten years to when Gerry, all grown up and living on the Gold Coast, used to stop by all the time. He was in sales, though most of his job seemed to consist of taking out-of-towners to dinner at one of the steak houses that served plate-sized slabs of beef, where they practically let you select the cow to be slaughtered for your dining pleasure. Once they were glutted with porterhouse and cabernet, they would barhop the strip clubs, but if the night ever broke up early—say, before 2 A.M.—Gerry would show up at our place, half drunk and ready to be entertained.

Typical night: We would come home to find him planted on the couch, finishing off our last bottle of beer; he had swiped a key, and getting the locks changed was an enormous hassle.

"Hey," he'd say. "You're all out of beer."

Or this: "One of your neighbors gave me the stink eye. What have they got against white people?"

Or this: "You've got to let me jam with you sometime. Come on, I'm just messing with you. I know you wouldn't want me upstaging you. See, I'm still messing with you."

Another time, his clients canceled dinner. He'd taken them to a day game at Wrigley and they'd had too much Old Style, too much sun. Kat was going out to see a new band at Medusa's, and Gerry volunteered to come with.

"But you have to stop doing that 'Gerry with a G' thing," Kat told him. "Every time you meet somebody, it's 'Hi, Gerry with a G, Gerry with a G.'"

"Force of habit." He was examining the innards of the refrigerator, the augury of boredom.

"So kick the habit," she said. "You're not selling anything here."

He looked at her like he was disappointed, like she was too stupid to get it. "Kitty, I'm selling Gerry with a G."

He spent the rest of the night with a big grin on his face, telling stories about Kat when she was in grade school and clearing up any misconceptions about the band he had once led—how they specialized not only in Led Zeppelin, but in Rush, Black Sabbath, and Deep Purple. Whenever there was a change of venue, Gerry with a G would launch into the same material with a new crowd of

band dudes, hangers on, and the eyelinered riffraff who we called
friends.

Interior. Empty Bottle. Western Avenue.

She hit the stage in an English Beat T-shirt and black jeans cropped
just below the knee. Capris, you could have called them, if that
didn't seem such a kicky, genteel name for pants that had SAVE
ME painted in white on one thigh and FUCK YOU on the other.
The crowd loved it, but by then she really didn't need to try so
hard to get their attention. After every show, guys came up to her,
their fanboy hearts aflutter, and told her about a new band that
she should check out or asked what she thought about this or that
album. They always talked too loud and their eyes were bright and
unblinking, like cultists inviting her to spend the weekend at their
compound. It was just music geeks showing off, she knew that, but
she also knew that as they talked about mail-order import B-sides,
they hoped that she would be so impressed that she'd drag one of
them back to her place for a wild night of indie-rock sex. Kat had
a lot of reasons why that would never happen, and high on that
list was the conviction that these were guys who knew exactly what
song they'd want on the stereo through the whole sordid episode.
Most of them probably carried a mix tape—"Jason's Sex Mix '92"—
for just that purpose.

Later, after her first album dropped, *Spin* ran a short, front-
of-the-book Q&A with her. When they asked about some of the
dirtier, angstier breakup songs, Kat played coy and said that she
was, at twenty-five, still a virgin. A complete lie, but you should
have seen the music nerds. I told her that she had to stop messing
with the heads of her core demographic, but during the first show
after the article ran she added a revved-up cover of "Like a Virgin"
to the set list. Chaos ensued.

*Exterior. Night. Café Voltaire. Clark Street. Hand-painted
sign reads* ART TONIGHT.

There was a guy named Giles, who we used to call J. Geils whenever we thought he couldn't hear us. He wasn't an artist and he

wasn't in a band, but he was always around and he had the kind of dark energy that singers and guitarists try hard to project, and this made him both attractive and repellent, depending on your own particular polarity. I, for one, was negatively inclined, but Kat got very, very into him—so into him that she stopped calling him by our nickname and started to give me a *really?-you're-still-doing-that?* look whenever I used his alias, this thing we had made together.

Giles and his friends had money, but they didn't have jobs. They exchanged elaborate handshakes, and they had already been places—Thailand, Prague, Chile, Morocco—that marked them as secret agents or trust-fund kids or time-traveling citizens of some future world. None of this seemed to bother Kat. Soon I began to notice that when Kat said "we," more often than not she was referring to her and Giles, and not to her and me.

I was forced to cultivate other interests. I got an idea about making sound collages and let a reel-to-reel run in the loft, picking up doors slamming and the toilet flushing and stray bits of conversation. I thought about studying for some kind of professional-school exam. I started writing a play based entirely on personal ads in the *Reader,* but never got much further than the title: *Men Seeking Women.*

One night I attended an opening for the work of former rivals from the Art Institute, in a basement coffee shop where canvases covered in chewed paper and dental floss were mercilessly lit by thrift-store lamps. I smiled and cheek-kissed and appeared to ponder, but it was the lamps that demanded my attention: chipped urns of pale blue that cast jug-eared shadows, a nightmare-faced ceramic monkey in a gold-buttoned waistcoat, a rooster whose comb rose like a blood-soaked hat. I had something like a revelation: why did we keep making new art, and so much of it so bad, when we were surrounded by work that needed only the proper context to shine? So that was me: epiphanic from looking at bad arts and better crafts.

I came home and found the television on, the loft awash in noise and blue light. Kat, Giles-less, pulled the sleeve of her T-shirt tight to dab at her eyes.

I asked her if she was crying.

Kat sniffled. "It's the TV. Something on the stupid TV made me cry, OK?"

I looked at the screen: *Cheers.* "What, did Norm die?"

"Just forget it, OK?" She took a deep breath and loudly exhaled. "Giles and I had a—a fight." She rolled her eyes. Stupid. Like something from high school, if she had dated anyone in high school.

"A big one?"

"Pretty big." She turned her face to me, straight on, and I saw the red welt blazing beneath her eye. My hand went to the body of my camera, as if by instinct, before I pulled it back.

"Can we start calling him J. Geils again?"

I thought she was going to tell me to get lost or to go fuck myself. It was fifty-fifty on that one; that's how into him she had been. Instead I got that lopsided smile of hers, the one I could never catch on film, the one I'd pay a million dollars to see again.

Still life. Evergreen Avenue loft.

Call this one "a study in misguided affection": A table with a Formica top. An ashtray logjammed with cigarettes. Three mismatched glasses containing various liquids—clear, pale yellow, dark brown—in varying amounts. A pile of scattered coins: nine quarters, two nickels, one dime. A CTA fare card. A spray of keys. A stack of bills—utility, credit card, student loan—unpaid, unopened. A large manila envelope, jagged-mouthed along one edge, addressed in cursive to Miss Katherine Conboy. A folded page from the *Tribune* classifieds: circled in red is an ad for a music teacher/ band director at Northfield High School; next to the ad, also in red, Kat's mother has written "Think about it!!!! XOXO Mom."

Color mockup. Cover of the band's debut album, Chica-go-go. Kat and the others slouch against a wall, à la the Ramones.

I dated this guy Milo for longer than I should have. He was thin without being too bony. His hair was neither too shaggy nor too expensively cut. His whole wardrobe was short-sleeved buttondowns—thrift-store issue, though he had a good eye for it. The patterns were neither too dorky nor too Euro. He wasn't too bright, but he wasn't an idiot, either. That was Milo. He was neither too this nor too that. He was, for a time, just right. We called him Baby Bear.

He did something with computers during the day, and at night he played trumpet in a ska-Krautrock outfit called Rudie Kant Fail that had yet to land any of the big bookings that he believed were its due. He bemoaned "the tyranny of verse-chorus-verse" to anyone who would listen, even though it was a swipe at the music Kat was playing. Milo was the first person I knew who had an e-mail address, but since no one else had one it was pretty useless. He probably works in an office now and every time some entry-level programmer gets the grand tour of the cubicles, someone will elbow the new guy and say, *You ever heard of Kat Conboy? That singer who died? Milo over there used to date her roommate.* And the new guy will be like, *No way,* because he'll look at Milo and he'll picture Kat and he'll go, *Does. Not. Compute.* But back then, when we were young, before 99 percent of the people we knew moved on to Life Plan B, it did make some kind of sense.

Milo was in the loft on the night Kat told me that she'd met the guy from Matador, the one who would eventually sign the band and release their first album. The Matador guy had gotten hold of one of her cassettes—she had given them to two people, in other bands, and within a month they'd multiplied like rabbits. She was viral before there was viral. She had run up the stairs and her eyes were glowing when she told me, but the light went out when she saw Milo was in the loft. He'd heard everything. "Dat's da bomb!" he said.

Kat told him to pipe down. That's just what she said—*pipe down*—which was something her father used to say. Milo was loud, it was late, and Kat had grown tired of his penchant for saying things like "da bomb" or "word" or "fly" or "fresh." She thought it made him sound foolish, like the joke was on him. She told him it was a question of authenticity.

"But you're talking M to the A to the T to the Dor. That's dope."

Matador *was* dope. If they were interested in Kat, then it was a sign of good things to come.

Kat shrugged, and I could tell that she wished she hadn't said anything. Not in front of him. She looked at me like I'd tricked her, letting her share this good news when Milo was right around the corner, waiting to ruin it.

*Exterior. Daylight. Rock Island Centennial Bridge. Kat leans
over the guardrail, spitting into the Mississippi.*

This is how she explained it to me: There just aren't enough hours
in the day. But then you figure out that if you take the right pills,
there still aren't enough hours but there are more, and you need
all the time you can get. You don't take the pills to feel good, you
take them because if you don't, you'll be miserable about all of
the things you don't have the time or the energy or let's face it,
the *strength,* to do. Because working a job to pay for bad food and
a lousy apartment and banged-up equipment and posters for every show takes time, and rehearsing takes time, and touring takes
time. Oh, does touring take time. Do you know how long the drive
to the Quad Cities is? Hours in the van to be the third act at an all-
ages show in a broken-down roller rink, followed by an immediate
and equally long return trip because half the band will get shit-
canned from their nametag jobs if they miss one more shift. And
if this is an honest-to-God tour, a go-out-on-the-road-and-don't-
come-back-for-a-week-or-two tour, then you will be sapped in other
ways: sleeping on one couch after another, or on a series of floors,
getting acquainted with the many verminous regional varieties of
upholstery and shag carpet. Figuring out if there's anyone at the
show worth fucking in exchange for a night in an actual bed. Remembering where the van is parked so you don't get marooned in
Carbondale or Macomb or Terre Haute.

   And to bring this back around to the pills, and their utility: how
else does anyone stay awake at the wheel for a drive like that, a
superhuman effort necessary to keep the members of Pope Joan
from going the way of Buddy Holly, Ritchie Valens, and the Big
Bopper, albeit in a flightless, much-less-famous, not-inspiring-the-
next-"Miss American Pie" sort of way?

   So yes, pharmaceutical intervention is necessary for the drive
across the murderous midwestern prairie, and when you start to
think about it, you realize that every day asks for a kind of hero-
ism—and even, at times, for the kind of effort that would grind
lesser mortals to chalk. How else do you start a day on three hours
of sleep and then endure a double shift at your copy-shop job and
then a few hours at a sparsely peopled backroom club showing

support for a friend's latest band (and inking with your presence an unspoken contract that he will do the same for you)—and only then, after seventeen or eighteen misspent waking hours, will you finally be able to get to the part of the day that matters? Because if you don't do it—if you don't sit your ass on the busted springs of the couch with your guitar cradled in your lap and a spiral notebook in front of you bristling with gibberish that you need to wrestle into lyrics; if you don't fit words to the tune that has been ticking in your head all day long before it evaporates, leaving only a crust of failure around the bathtub rim that is your skull; if you don't do *this,* then you will go to bed—a collapse, a surrender, call it what you will—filled with the knowledge, now more apparent than ever, that you are a fraud, a faker, a failure. So if taking a handful of red or yellow or green or blue pills, administered daily, can keep that gnawing thought at bay *and* make it possible to get those sounds out of your head and into the world, you really have to ask, What's the harm in that?

Box 7, *spool 2.*

KAT: Hello? Hel—Dad, is that? Dad? Dad, it's Kat—I mean, it's Kitty. Kitty. Kit-ty. Your daughter, Kitty. Yes, like kitty cat. No, a person. I'm a person. Remember, from Christmas? I gave you . . . Uh, huh. Uh huh. Uh. Huh. Dad, is Mom there? Is she there with you? Mom. You know, the woman. The woman who lives in the house. Yes, the lady with short hair. From dinnertime, yes. No, it's not dinnertime. Not yet. No, it's not. Not yet. Is the woman—is—hello? Hello? Mom? What the hell, Mom? When did Dad start answering the phone? I didn't—I—I'm not *accusing* you of anything—

Exterior. Night. Rainbo Lounge. Damen Avenue.

One night Kat told me we needed to go out. The band had been touring the Midwest—Iowa City, Cedar Rapids, Champaign-Urbana, both Bloomingtons—and we hadn't seen much of each other. She told me she missed me. She told me she had been a bad friend. She told me the only way to drive out a nail is with another nail—that was another of her father's sayings. Her stated goal was to find me a better, post-Milo boyfriend, or at least a reasonably unembarrassing one-nighter, but sometime after all the 2 A.M. bars closed and the dirty stay-outs migrated to the last of the 4 A.M. bars, we ran into Giles. In the best of the pictures from that night, Kat had just made contact with his jaw and his head was twisted to one side like someone was trying to screw it off his neck. It had rained earlier in the evening, and behind us the neon lay on the puddles like splattered milk. To the left of Giles was his new girlfriend, the lead singer for a band called Augustus Gloop; she was wearing a silver lamé jacket that shone like woven crystal. Her face appears on film as a collage of spheres and circles: her eyes so wide that they seem lidless, her mouth rounded into a big O. If I remember it right, she was about to say "Oh, snap!" which probably made Kat want to punch her too. Authenticity, after all.

Exterior. Night. Lincoln Avenue just west of Halsted.
A line of people; a man checking IDs with a small flashlight.

Ask anyone who knew Lounge Ax and they'll tell you the place was a shoebox. If you believed the fire-marshal sign posted near the door, then it couldn't hold more than 150 people, but most nights the bodies were wedged chest to back and there could have been 300 or 400 from the window facing the street to the front of the stage. Risers lined the walls, prime spots where you could see above the bobbing heads to the back of the postage-stamp stage, and where you were less likely to get groped.

I have a picture from that night, before the really bad stuff, or the really good stuff, depending on your point of view: She has just finished her set and is standing behind the stage. The crowd is in a frenzy, screaming for the inevitable encore. She is making them wait and she is frozen in place, her hands knitted on the crown of her head and her elbows flared like wings. It's the posture of a runner at the end of a marathon, a way to open up starved lungs for a drink of pure air. She looks dazed, she looks happy, she looks like she might just lift off into the night sky, if not for the low ceiling, the apartments above, and the simple facts of matter and gravity.

OUTTAKES: Var. boxes, var. spools.

> KAT: What does this look like to you?
> ME: Yuck. What is that?
> KAT: I know, right?
> ME: How long has it been like that?
> KAT: I don't know. I just noticed it.
> ME: You should get that looked at.
> KAT: I am getting it looked at. By you.

...

> KAT: (singing) *Woke up, fell out of bed, dragged a comb across*—shit, are we really out of coffee?

...

> KAT: Not now, OK? Please? Can't you just—seriously. Stop it with the camera, OK? Stop it. Cut it OUT! Why can't you just be my friend instead of a goddamn—

Interior. Evergreen Avenue loft. Kat, backlit by windows, scissors the sleeves off a T-shirt.

People will say, isn't that wild that you two *knew* each other in high school? What are the odds? As if Kat becoming famous and me receiving some degree of—what? highly focused niche acclaim?—were independent of each other, like lightning striking the same place twice, or sisters winning the lottery one week after the other. But the truth is simpler than any of that: Kat became Kat because of the times and the tastes and the ways that her personality made her catnip for a certain breed of music fan. If she was cast as the Red Queen of post-punk pop, I was her court painter. But if we were monarch and courtier, we were also model and artist. People who know me only for my photos of Kat talk about her like she was my life's work, when she was only my first subject. If I was lucky to have a subject who became famous, even notorious, then Kat was lucky too: lucky to have someone get it all down on film, to create a public memory of who she was every step of the way.

And there's this, which gets overlooked: The pictures aren't good only because Kat is in them, they're good because I took them. She was perfecting her art while I was perfecting mine.

Interior. West Randolph Street condo.
Kat's face in profile against a black-and-white tile floor.

Someone at the party called me. Someone who knew that Kat had a roommate who might be able to put her back together and get her home, though I don't think getting her home was as much of a priority as getting her out of where she was—*where* in this case being the gut-rehabbed third floor of a former slaughterhouse west of the Loop, a place owned by a guy who called himself a club promoter, which meant he had access to enough drugs and big enough speakers to turn any room into a party. This was when Kat was losing a lot of friends. This was when Kat was making worse decisions than usual. This was when Kat had started going places without me.

I rang the buzzer and the alleged club promoter pointed to a door and he didn't say, *Hi* or *Thanks so much for coming* or *We're really worried about her,* he just said, *In there.* And in there was nothing I hadn't seen before, though maybe a little worse. She had one arm draped across the back of the bowl, and she was trying and failing to keep her hair out of her face. She had already puked a ton. I flushed the toilet, which Kat hadn't had the will or the ability to do, and she startled as the water roared in her ear. She looked at me through the sweaty fringe of her hair. I thought she was going to say my name, but she just said, *So sick* over and over again like it was her mantra. She retched and threw up, retched and spit out a little more. She looked up at me again through her bangs and her eyes were rolling in her head. She seemed like she was trying to focus. If I was a good friend or any kind of friend I would have held her hair and stroked her arm; I would have put a cool washcloth on her forehead and told her that it was going to be all right. I would have kept flushing with each heave, instead of letting the bowl fill up with a night's worth of casual poisoning. But instead I swung out my Leica—a bulletproof camera, the one they use in war photos—and started shooting. I got her leaning there using the toilet bowl like a pillow. I got her with the stuff pouring out of her like tar. I got her lying on the cool floor, the frazzled burr of her head against the smooth solid base of the bowl.

Contact sheet. Twenty-four-exposure study of an Econoline van during load-out. Location unknown/forgotten.

You should do a book, someone said. You should put them all together so people can see what she was like, before. And I could. I have thousands of pictures. Each one different. Each one telling the same story.

Kat on her first night as a blonde—her first night looking the way that most people remember her, the way she looks on the cover of the first album, with her bleached hair and black jeans spray-painted on her skeleton's legs.

Kat getting the thorn-wrapped heart tattooed at the nape of her neck, the one that she'd rub with her index finger when she was deep in thought or bored or distracted or nursing some grudge.

Kat in that ridiculous ski hat she used to wear—pompom on top and earflaps down each side. She is tottering toward me on an icy sidewalk with her arms spread wide and her lips puckered like she's about to plant a big wet kiss on my face, or on the lens.

Kat at Montrose Harbor in the bright sun with the sky so clear you could put your fist through it. It was late fall and the wind was tearing at her hair and beyond her you can see whitecaps and closer to her the lake is hurling itself against the rocks, and in the middle of all this motion and light Kat looks so. Goddamn. Tired.

This is my fear: that it would be like watching a whole carousel of slides from your neighbor's trip to the Grand Canyon. You'd ooh and aah for the first five pictures or so, but there would be another ninety on the way. Somewhere in the middle, you'd stop caring, and before you reached the end, you'd hate your neighbors, hate the Grand Canyon, hate the entire Eastman Kodak family of companies. None of this is going to make her more real for you. And none of it is going to bring her back.

Interior. ICU. Northwestern Memorial Hospital.
Close-up of Kat's hand cupping three pills: pale blue,
dull yellow, off-white.

No one agrees with me, but her last album was her best. Most
people stopped paying attention during her years in LA. They got
tired of watching her push it too far, they said the music was never
as good as those first two albums, and they all wondered why she
didn't just get it over with and die already. Instead she came back
to Chicago and after lying low for a while, she put out an album
with a small indie label run by guys too young to have been burned
by her on her way up. I imagine that recording it, playing all the
instruments herself, and knitting the tracks together must have
been like those long airless days in her parents' basement. I say
imagine because I wasn't there; I had abandoned Chicago shortly
after Kat left town. I had planned on sticking around and being
smug about how I was keeping it real, 312-style, but when I saw my
chance to go east, I went. By the time I came back to see her, after
months of promises and see-you-soon messages, she was sick and
then she was gone. Anyone who had guessed overdose or razor to
the wrist or self-immolation must have felt cheated. She got a stupid cancer, one that had nothing to do with any of her more toxic
habits, and that was it. Right before her body betrayed her that
one last time, she was tiny and bald and her skin was like cigarette
paper. I wanted to scoop her up and carry her back to our old
loft, to the couch where we had curled up all those years before,
watching reruns of *Cheers* and *M*A*S*H* and *The Mary Tyler Moore*
Show and everything else WGN threw at us. Kat had fallen asleep
on my shoulder that night. I listened to her breathe. I watched her
dreaming eyes twitch. Her face was soft and full, despite the bruise
that painted her left eye. Seeing her in that hospital bed, that's
what I wanted: to carry her back home.

That's what would happen in the dream sequence where the
best friends are reunited after the falling out, the bitter words,
the long silence, the gradual thaw. But I did not spirit her away.
When I found her in that bed, wiped out and with little left to give,
I aimed the lens and started to shoot. Because not getting those
pictures would have wrecked it—for me. And, I hope, for her.

Looking at all of the pictures now, I can pretend that she was the only one with the *what-the-fuck?* look, the *what-makes-you-so-special?* look, the *do-you-even-believe-your-own-bullshit?* look. But she's also the only one with the *thank-God-it's-you* look, the *just-trust-me-on-this-one* look, the *I'm-sorry-please-forgive-me* look, the *look-that-I-only-give-to-you* look. This is when I wish that there had been another me as devoted to me as I was to her. Someone to offer me proof that I looked at her like that, instead of just gawking with one big dumb glassy eye that only asked for more, and more, and more, and more.

MOLLY MCNETT

La Pulchra Nota

FROM *Image*

Do not love the world or the things in the world . . . For all that
is in the world, the lust of the flesh and the lust of the eyes and
the pride of life, is not of the Father, but is of the world. And the
world passes away, and the lust of it; but he who does the will of
God abides forever.
    —John 2:15–18

Sing to him a new song; play skillfully on the strings, with loud
shouts. For the word of the LORD is upright, and all his work is
done in faithfulness.
    —Psalm 33:3–4

MY NAME IS John Fuller. I am nine and twenty years of age, born
in the year of our Lord 1370, the son of a learned musician and
the youngest of twelve children—though the Lord in his wisdom
was pleased to take five brothers and two sisters back to the fold.
After a grave accident, I no longer possess the use of my hands.
Any inaccuracies in this document are not the fault of the scribe,
who enjoys a high reputation, but of my own mind. My pain is not
inconsiderable. However, I will continue frankly, in as orderly a
fashion as I am able, so that these words may accompany my con-
fession to the honorable vicar of Saint Stephen's.

My story begins as God knit me in the womb. There my knees
pressed in to form the sockets of my eyes as they do in all men.
However, my left knee—the cap of which has a sharp emboss-
ment—pressed upon the iris, pushing it to one side. While I am
able to see clearly, it appears to others that the eye looks away from

the place I have trained it. God be praised for this deformity, for it kept me close to him for the better part of my life.

My first memories are of two sounds—one ugly and one beautiful. As a child I lived in Oxfordshire in the northern Midlands. An old church stood in the center of the village, and in its center demesne what I thought must be everything the world could possibly contain: a bakehouse, granary, pigsty, dairy, an assortment of dovecotes, and a malting house. Once I recall walking on the outskirts of this enclosure with my father when there came an ugly noise, dry and papery, as menacing as a snake's warning. My father quickly lifted me to his shoulders and ran toward our cottage. Looking back, I saw a man whose skin bubbled up like a dark pudding—a leper, I later learned, required to wear a rattle to warn us of his coming. In one moment his eye caught mine from high upon my father's shoulders, and the look he gave me was so sinister that I have not forgot it. It seemed to say that only my father's body separated us, that in its absence the leper and I were one.

Our cottage was built at the edge of the village, along the banks of a tiny stream. One hot afternoon I awoke from a nap transfixed by the highest, sweetest sound I had ever heard. It was as if I could see, in my mind's eye, this sweet sound rapidly tracing the petals of a flower before plummeting down its stem. I learned later from my father that one capacity of the human voice had been described in such a way by Jerome of Moravia—as a vocal flowering. I went to the window. There my mother joined me, pointing to a nest in the bank-willow tree.

"That nest," I asked, "did you make it?" For my mother was skilled in weaving, and in fashioning all kinds of things.

"Of course not," she scolded me. "It is mother bird who builds it."

"How can she make it so?"

"God gave her the knowledge," she said. "Nothing perfect comes but it comes from God."

Then from somewhere in the tree the beautiful thick chirp came again, a trill and a sweet clucking. How I wanted to see the bird! But as much as I strained and leaned, she did not appear.

"How does she learn this song?" I asked.

"God puts the song in her breast," said my mother.

"And how can it be so sweet?"

"Tiresome boy." She smiled. "This also comes from God."

"And my eye?"

Her mouth twisted in irritation, and she dropped my hand. "From God," she muttered. "The good and the bad are from God . . ."

And perhaps I remember this day so clearly because, soon after, it pleased divine providence to take my mother to the Lord, may he be praised for all things. This was in the year of our Lord 1376, in the month of June.

After my mother's death my father accepted a position as an organist in the town of Bishop's Lynn, in Norfolk. He explained to us that an organ was a wondrous and expensive piece of equipment, and only a church of good means could acquire one. We children admired our father greatly, and as the years passed he taught us whatever he knew of music and instruments.

At two and twenty I married a woman named Katherine, nine years my elder and the daughter of a well-to-do burgher. Her father accepted my appearance. "Though thine eye may wander," he jested, "see that thy heart does not." I assured him that because of my appearance, I was a devout man and had never been burdened with lust or pride. Katherine's inheritance was more than I might have hoped for, and we did not want for money. We had a cook, a maid, and a nurse; and Katherine was wise in shopping, never fooled by watered wine or the old fish sold at market, rubbed with pig's blood to make it look fresh. We enjoyed our supper over pleasant conversation, and in the evenings I would play the gittern or the psaltery, for my father had given me a small collection of instruments and I loved nothing more than music.

Katherine herself could not keep a pitch, and sometimes when I hummed a little tune without thinking, she might ask me to stop. But no wife is without such cavils, and she was gay in demeanor then, as middling comely as befit a woman of her years, and forthcoming in wifely duties. I was pleasantly surprised in my enjoyment of these, and called myself happy in life.

In the second year Katherine was with child, and when her time came she labored through the night. Never in my life had I heard such lamentation, and I wondered how the throat could bear such pressure unscathed. The midwife came out for the rose oil and sat on the stool beside me, her head in her hands, and when hours later she fetched some vinegar and sugar, she took bits of lamb's wool and tucked them in her ears before entering the birth room again. When finally the dawn came, I heard a small cry, but most of an hour passed before finally the midwife brought the child down the stairs to me. I was happy, although it was a girl. And as I held the babe, she brought another—twin girls.

I knew Katherine to be a good and honest woman, so I could not believe that twins must be sired by two fathers. But of course many did believe it. When the days of her purification were completed, Katherine was received, according to Leviticus, back into the church, made clean to make bread or prepare food. But on the way home that day some women tore the veil and wimple from her head so that she was made to walk home as bareheaded as a harlot. In the following week our neighbors spun a yellow cross to mark her garment and left it at our door, and spat at her as she went to market, and spat upon her babes. My old father the organist would no longer speak with her, and my sisters and brothers would no longer look upon her.

Was it out of sadness that Katherine refused me my marital rights, even as a year passed? I will never know. We did have a common devotion for the sweet creatures she had borne. We employed a nurse whose breasts were large enough for two, yet not large enough to flatten the children's noses, and we took joy as these two began to smile and babble and their curls were growing long. For my part, I felt a relief and pride at their smooth kneecaps and beautiful straight eyes. For though the woman carries the seed of the child, they may have shared my deformity. Together we looked and wondered at them as one wonders at the heavens and all the beauties of nature. They were so entirely alike that only a few tiny spackles on the nose could distinguish elder from younger.

But divine providence was pleased to take the life of our dear twins two days apart from each other, the first on the fifth of June at the hour of terce, in the year of our Lord 1393. Then I too was taken sick, and woke from my fever one morning to find that the second twin had been gathered back to the Lord on the seventh of June at 5 o'clock, in the year of our Lord 1393. For this may the Lord be thanked and praised, for every devout man knows the great mercy he shows us in taking a child out of the world. Yet had they stayed with us—had even one stayed—I believe I would not have this story to tell.

Katherine was a good woman, and, until this time, perfectly ordinary. But she began to weep all the day long and into the night, and no comfort I offered was of help to her. One winter's day I could not find my wife and, looking out the window, saw her sitting in the snow with her skirt spread round her. She wore no coat. I sent the nurse, who hovered over Katherine as she rocked back and forth on her heels.

"Sir, no coaxing could get her inside," she told me. "She says she is warm inside the body, and God tells her not to fear illness."

Then she leaned in and whispered, "She wears no knickers under the skirt."

Shortly after this incident, it pleased the Lord to take to paradise my father the organist, and for this may he be praised in his wisdom. I was given the tutelage of some of my father's students who lived across the canal in the old city where there were large stone dwellings of Roman style. I found these houses impressive, for our own was timber, post and beam, and so close to its rotting neighbor that the two dwellings leaned on each other at the top like a pair of boureés.

My pupils were young girls who lived in the old quarter, from wealthy families in which the boys studied chess and hawking and the girls embroidery and singing. Most of them did not sing well, yet the lessons were pleasant for me, a diversion from our home and its growing strangeness.

Katherine no longer did the shopping. Together we went out only to church, and there she would cry. The cries began softly, and then grew to sobs, and she fell forward to the pew in front of us, and then into the aisle, writhing and groaning with a sound as great as the one she had poured forth in labor, so that it was only prudent to gather her and take her from the sanctuary. Then she smiled fiercely, her eyes gleaming in ecstasy.

"It is the Lord who makes me," she told me, later. "He speaks to me. And when I fall to the ground I cannot stop myself; it is because I hear the most beautiful music, that seems to come from heaven itself."

In truth I did not know if I could believe it. For we know of those who contract dancing fevers in the rainy season, when, for example, in Saint Vitus's dance, one town makes its way to another in a state of shivering frenzy. It seemed to be a madness of that sort. Indeed, Albertus Magnus has written that women who do not receive their husbands can become full of poisonous blood and it is better for them to expel the matter, but my wife dismissed this opinion when it was offered.

Still, she did seek the counsel of authorities, including William Southfield of the Carmelites, and Dame Julian, the anchoress, in her little cell. These agreed that God was speaking to Katherine through her fits. And so my wife had a new path to follow, this time as a woman of faith. And in time she was no longer shunned on the street. She had earned respect and her demeanor improved.

But though Saint Augustine tells us we might atone for any sin between married people by acts of Christian charity, our relations did not resume. At night we got in bed as usual, well-bedded in white sheets and nightcap. We took off our nightclothes under the covers. But when I turned to Katherine, she would feign sickness, or scratch herself.

"I have worms!" she would say, slapping my hand away.

"No," I assured her. "You have not scratched all day."

"They come out at night!"

"Let me see . . ." and smiling I would reach out to her naked-ness.

But she thrashed and spun away from me.

During this time I visited for the first time a student of my late father's who had recently recovered from illness. Her maid showed me to where she lay on the daybed still in a dressing gown of yellow silk. She looked to be sixteen, as dark haired as a Jewess, with large brown eyes and rather dark skin. I did not think of her as lovely. I suppose that those who were said to be beautiful had very white skin and light hair, so it did not occur to me to define the girl in this manner. Then too, this dark girl covered her mouth in the manner of those with rotten teeth who have been trained not to offend others. So I sometimes covered my own sinister eye with my hand, or turned my face away, to avoid the onlooker's gaze.

"I am Olivia," she said meekly. "I am happy to meet you, and I know your father is with the Lord."

I thanked her and asked her if she felt well enough to stand, for standing is the best way to sing. She nodded and, with some effort, hoisted herself up by the table stand.

"Let us begin with a recitation," I said, "for in this way I shall know what I need to teach you."

I do not remember much of the first song she sang, or even, exactly, my own reaction to it. My surprise was first that she sang a worldly song, popular in the courts of great men, and sung by troubadours. It made no mention of God.

But soon I had forgotten the song itself and marked the contrast between this girl and my typical student, who strained so on high registers; who, if she hit the note, often pushed into it like a German, or broke the tone in the manner of the French. Olivia's voice lifted to each note directly, holding on the tone without excess of ornament or vibration—the sweet sound of a child. In its simplicity there was something wondrous about it, and I wanted to laugh and delight in it, rather than find something to teach her. Yet her nurse sat embroidering on the settle, and she would report to Olivia's father. I had to begin with a suggestion, and so it came to me what I might add. For Isidore of Seville told us the voice should be "high, clear, and sweet" and indeed something was not entirely clear.

I asked, "You are aware of the epiglottis?"

Olivia shook her head. I asked the nurse to fetch ink and paper, and drew a small sketch of this leaf-shaped part. "If the tongue, perhaps swollen from sickness, is sliding backward, it may be clouding the tone of what my father—working, as you know, on the organ as he did, and noticing its similarity with the human capacity for two kinds of sound—might call the lower register."

The nurse looked up attentively from her embroidery, while the student studied my sketch with a worried expression. I suppose that I wanted to lighten this expression, though I don't remember thinking so, only that my throat ached, as it did in the moment when as a child, I raced to the window to find that the bird was not there.

"In spite of this," I told her, "your voice at times comes close to a moment of perfection—what Jerome has called *la pulchra nota*. Let us begin to listen for it. Mostly it appears with no strain whatsoever. But be attentive, for when such a note comes, if you know it, you may ever after use its sound to guide you." Then I smiled, for her brows were still knit in a childlike concern.

"Do not worry," I said gaily. "It may be only a short while."

And at this she smiled back at me quite fully and naturally. "Oh!" she said. "Do you think so?"

"Yes," I said. "I'm sure of it."

That I should not have said, I thought later. I myself had never reached such a note in singing. Why should I praise so strongly? Was there another reason to do so? In fact I went over the entire lesson in my mind for some reason, retracing what I had said and how I had said it, and I saw the image of Olivia's open face, her easy joy in singing. Perhaps I retraced our conversation only to protract the lesson in some way during the week. In this way I could avoid my circumstances at home.

For that night as I turned the psaltery, Katherine put her head in her hands and sighed, and said it would be better not to play at all. I changed my course and the next evening sang only plain-chant, making my voice as soft and comforting as possible.

But she drew her shawl about her shoulders and came to sit next to me on my stool. There she repeated to me that the music she heard in her mind, whose perfection made her yell and writhe, was not of the world, but came directly from the Lord. So worldly music and sounds were only poor imitations, distracting from worship, as all worldly pleasures do.

There was quiet that evening in our empty house, empty of the sound of children and empty of conversation, empty of music. It was a place where sound became odious to both of us—the crack of a stool, the creak of our bed as we settled there.

I tried again to approach my wife in the night, for it was cold and we slept with our clothes off as always, tucked under the foot of the bed. But she turned to me and spoke softly:

"John, I have given you sorrow. But the Lord has a remedy. We must go to the anchoress, declare celibacy, and I will again wear white."

And she smiled, petting my face as if I were a child. This soft stroking of my skin, her face and breath held near to mine were so hateful to me that my jaw tightened and I fought an urge to strike her.

"No," I told her.

"No?" she asked, as if she did not believe my refusal.

And I repeated, "No."

The next day my wife did not eat. She couldn't bear the strength of mead, she said, or of meat. And all that week and into the next she would only sip from the broth of a boiled root. She no longer spoke to me, and though it was winter she walked with no shoes, placing her toes first so that the boards would not sound when she entered a room.

After a fortnight, she was so weak that she fainted daily. Yet, leaning upon her maid, she went to church, and to the anchoress in her cell, and when they had seen her, the townspeople, including the neighbors who had shunned her, were drawn to this ethereal creature. Some came to our house to ask her advice, and for prophecy. They were embarking on a pilgrimage, they said, and wanted to know if the day they had chosen was auspicious. Would she pray for a woman on the brink of death, would she find out if this woman might indeed recover? Was another woman's husband in heaven or purgatory? And though my wife seemed happy in this role, she continued to fast.

"Eat," I coaxed her.

I knew her silent answer: I will eat again when you come with me to the anchoress and take the vow.

Olivia's strength improved as my wife's waned. I had met with her three times over the course of that month. Often we talked at length before the lesson began, and if her nurse was in the room, she too might join in our conversation. These were easy, ordinary words, concerning the season, or the news of a birth or a neighbor's pilgrimage, for example, but because I had no companion with whom to speak at home, they seemed the more delightful to me. Perhaps in any event the girl's voice would have pleased me, so high was her laugh—it tinkled like a little bell.

Now she stood without grasping and did not need to clutch the table, and her singing had become so sweet and clear I could hear it in my head at night as I lay waiting for sleep. At those times too I sometimes found myself wondering if my own left eye was not very far off its course, after all. I had been observing it in the glass of late and it seemed to have improved. Or had I exaggerated its homely effect in the past? Was there any way I could be described as handsome? I had a large gap between my front teeth, but they were good. I was not tall, but strongly built. There was some pain caused by these thoughts, for I felt in some way that the Lord had removed me from his protection.

One day, on her last lesson of that month, Olivia was just in the middle of the "Rondel d'une Dame à son Amy," from the *Chasse Départ,* in which a high sol was to be held for several measures. She smilingly ran through the notes in the early section, with no strain on her face but sometimes glancing at me, it seemed, to catch my eye:

Vivons toujours bien raisonnablement . . .
Let us always live justly
bearing our woes the most peacefully
that we can, without a single offense
to our love, for the first to fault
makes the other live inconstantly thereafter.

It was on the penultimate line, *En nostre amour, car le premier qui faut*—on its last syllable, *faut*—that Olivia soared over the high *sol*, lighting there delicately as the tone opened out into such exquisite vibrations that I cannot describe them, only that they seemed to fill the room and envelop us, so that we stood transported in their aftermath.

We rushed to each other, or really, the student to me. She threw her arms around my waist and I thought nothing of her nurse in the next room and embraced her, let myself gaze at her face turned up to mine, smilingly, and for this moment it seemed the most natural act in the world, so that there was no discomfort or thought of its being an embrace, and there was no need for words.

Still, she laughed and said, "I love you!"

I would like to end my story at this moment. I would like to linger here at the very crux of joy, where the note, and these words, were as one to me.

But I cannot. I then understood something about music that I had not learned from my father, or Jerome of Moravia, or Isidore of Seville. *La pulchra nota* is the moment of beauty absolute, but what follows—a pause, however small—is the realization of its passing. Perhaps no perfection is without this silent realization.

The wind that had lifted the bird, and the room, and those hearts within the room, grew still. I was as Adam in the garden—suddenly naked, suddenly shamed. I released her and stepped back. I remember that her smile remained, and then turned curious, so firm was her trust in the note.

"This is a good beginning," I said. "But you have been ill and should not tax yourself."

I suppose I said these words strangely. Later I wondered.

The student's head fell on its stem and she sank onto the bench as if her weakness had returned. It pained me to see that she buried her face in her hands, but I had no experience with love, and its offices, and I did not know what to do. I turned and left without speaking more to her.

In the streets of the old city—with its sturdy Roman buildings, its flowerpots, its neat sewers—every young man I passed seemed a fitting mate for a young nightingale. They wore short tunics with toggles across the front, drawn tightly across their waists. I walked on into the new quarter, past the tanners, where the offal stank in its pile near the street and my house rotted and leaned against its neighbor. In a puddle I saw the blurred vision of my form in its long shabby houppelande, its stiff, high collar hiding my jaw, which I sensed now, in comparison to these young men, was weak and undistinguished. How I wished to be the beloved in the Song of Songs, whose eyes are like *doves beside springs of water, bathed in milk, fitly set;* whose legs are *alabaster columns, set upon bases of gold!* Even in youth I had never been the object of admiration, and so I had not minded youth's passing, but I was now full of jealousy for these fashionably clothed young men. At the same time I was nearly delirious with joy. I replayed those words to myself, words my wife did not speak: *I love you.*

You may not know, if you have not been called ill formed and ugly from birth and a sweet young girl has never once looked at you in such a way, how thirsty I felt for all that had been denied me! Suddenly Olivia's smooth face, dark as the curtains of Solomon, seemed very dear; I thought of my wife and the slack skin of her neck, her visions and writhing. I did not mind the vow of celibacy as much as I felt ashamed that in exchange for a healthy dowry, I had given up my right to love.

Of course, I wondered: Had Olivia meant to say she loved me? In fact, did she love the music and the note itself, her ability to sing it? Or perhaps my small part in bringing it forth? And if I loved Olivia, what did I love? The note? The girl herself? Or my own reflection in her eyes as someone worthy of such feeling?

So my thoughts crossed from happiness to unhappiness, and I could not sleep that night. I was bound for torture, it seemed, for love itself was a sin and promised the fires of hell; and lack of love a present torture. I suffered a kind of madness that could be relieved only by some act of goodness.

There my wife sat, slumped in her rocking chair, and her bony shoulders from behind were those of an old woman. She had borne such sorrow; she was dying there in that chair, too weak to rise and take herself to bed.

"You must eat," I said softly.

"We must go to the anchoress," she whispered.

And so I answered, "Yes."

When I again crossed the canal to the old city to see Olivia, the deed had been done. My wife was at home in her white robes. She wore a special mantle and ring, having taken the vow with me through the little window carved for the anchoress to receive the sacrament.

Olivia's nurse saw me into the study, and my hands trembled as I set down my music; as I spoke my normal pleasantries I stuttered. But when the student entered, her greeting was ordinary, and calm. Though she did not meet my eye, I wondered if I had imagined what had transpired just the week before as she began further on in the "Rondel":

> *Desir mapprent telz regretz.* . . .
> Desire teaches me to know
> such sorrows that I know not what can be born of them
> And then suffering locks me in her prison
> Vexation assaults me and beats me hard and fast
> Alas, would you decrease my pain
> *Si vous pouvez.* . . .

There it was, the beautiful voice, but the tone had become slightly reedy somehow. Or was it only when compared with *la pulchra nota?* But Olivia sensed a lack too, for she stopped singing and shook her head impatiently.

I hoped silently that I was responsible for her failure. For had I not been both happy and melancholy since her declaration of love? And Jerome tells us that melancholy is an obstacle to perfection, that no sound has true beauty if it does not proceed from the joy of the heart. But I was not brave enough to console her with this information.

"I believe," I said, clearing my throat, "that you love the music because it comes from God. That is . . ."—here I began to sweat, and wiped my forehead with the long sleeve of my houppelande—"that is, you are devout, and love God, and the music comes from God. All we do well is from God, every image, every sound, and we return the glory to him. And we will continue in that vein."

Here she stood and attempted the lines again, but her voice cracked and again she fell to the daybed heavily, shaking her head.

"I am sorry," she stammered, blushing darkly. "I have told you that I love you," she said, "and you did not reply. It is shame that causes my voice to weaken." Her eyes were shining with tears.

These were the words I wanted to hear! But could I erase her shame and sadness? Yes, I should tell her that I returned her love. And I should embrace her; I should sing from the Song of Songs:

> Your teeth are like a flock of ewes
> that have come up from the washing.
> All of them bear twins;
> not one among them is bereaved.

And then she would be happy; and in this way I might hear the note again. She would love me the more for that.

The devil spoke to me thus: The note is no harm. It is beautiful, and how can beauty be harmful, when it brings such pleasure? And worldly love is not a sin, but only pleasure, of which you have been deprived.

But the Lord said, If you love the girl, would you profane her? You cannot marry her, though your own marriage be celibate. And to come each week, drawing on her hope, would be to crush and ruin her.

I blinked and regarded Olivia as if from a great distance, summoning the hate of Amnon for Tamar. "You have regressed," I said. "Or I may have misjudged your ability. You may be capable of again reaching such a note, but it is no longer within my province."

As in the beginning, before I had ever heard her sing, she lowered her head and covered her face in her hands, but this time her shoulders shook, and I saw that she hid her tears.

"I will find a suitable teacher to help you," I said.

I could hear her sobbing as I walked down the stairs, and as I walked out through the courtyard, that mournful sound carried from the open window. I tried to remember it, for I knew it would be the last I would hear that voice.

In my mind our lessons continue and I retrace every word and note and color of the voice, every dear ornament that rose naturally from her throat. I go back to the note, to recall its pitch and its perfection. Or sometimes in dreams the note comes to me, when through the open window a bird will trill and it lasts for what seems like an hour and then she rushes to me, and I wake to find that I can no longer stand or raise my hand to feed myself, and I remember.

I found that day a young minnesinger as dark as my dear student, and handsome, with good teeth and a good position. I sent him to her as a teacher, knowing full well what would happen. The note would sound, and the same feeling would well up in her heart; she would throw her little arms around this young man, and he would be free to respond. I do not know that this happened, of course. But it is written that jealousy is cruel as the grave, and that its flashes are flashes of fire. Over the bridge and crossing home I cried out in rage and frustration; at home my wife lay in her white garments, still weak though she had begun taking food. I told her I would be with her.

"You shall not, John," she responded, still softly. And still full of that cloying gentleness, she petted my head, cooing at me and speaking as if I were a small child. "You know what you have vowed."

Heretofore I had accepted my marriage on her terms, and on her father's. I was deformed, and fortunate for such a dowry. Yet in that moment my wife seemed a humbug in her wailing and prediction and prophecy, and I forgot the sympathy I had for her.

"You have tricked me," I said. "Saint Paul wrote that the husband must render his wife what is due her, and the wife her husband."

"No," she said.

And she said no again and again as I took by anger and by force what I had sworn never to take again.

This was a great sin. I cannot hope to atone for it.

When it was done I pulled my clothes on and left her there crying. I was going out, I think; and if I knew where I planned to go, I never have remembered it. Would I have left for good? Would I have gone to Olivia, to proclaim my love honestly? I would like to think so. However, it was not to be. As I began to descend, I felt something at my back.

At first I thought the stair had given way—the stairs too were rotting in that house. But later I knew it did not give way. They told me I had simply lost my footing. The neighbors found me hours later, my head twisted under me and with such deep wounds they had to be plugged in five places.

A green sapling has sprung up by the window where I have been seated, and a finch has decided to make her nest here. I can't tell why she has chosen such a place, for the branch is thin and waves terribly in the wind, but whenever I come to the window to peer out at her, the nest remains, and that bright dot of gold I discern through the tree reassures me. I wait for my wife, who comes from her visit with the anchoress to lift the spoon to my lips. For her continued attentions, I am grateful.

She tells me of Sigar, the monk of Saint Albans. He dwelt at Northaw, in the wood, where the nightingales abounded, and their song was very sweet, and his enjoyment of it immense. And so he had them killed. For he should not joy in the warbling of the birds better than the worship of God.

Yet something has happened to me, so strange and wonderful that I must tell it here in the interest of the frankness I have promised. As my world narrows, I find ethereal music in the most ordinary of sounds. My wife does not suspect the delight I take in this.

If I tell you the world is beautiful, then close your eyes; it becomes more beautiful still. The tanner's wagon has a song, and cries of children are as sweet as the brook's, and the geese are strong and shocking; and in the market square the cry of the bull is full with breath and moisture and even, it seems to me, the strength of his bones.

I lie in bed, or I sit here. And it seems at times that heaven itself has seen me at the window and comes to me before my time, as if it suspects I shall not reach it. The sun warming me, the little wind caressing my cheek, the green leaf of a katydid on the sill; these perfect notes sound everywhere, over and over again. For this, the Lord be praised. For all things praised.

BENJAMIN NUGENT

God

FROM *Paris Review*

HE CALLED HER God because she wrote a poem about how Caleb Newton ejaculated prematurely the night she slept with him, and because she shared the poem with her friends.

Caleb was the president of our fraternity. When he worked our booth in the dining hall he fund-raised a hundred dollars in an hour. He had the plaintive eyes and button nose of a child in a life-insurance commercial, the carriage of an armored soldier. He was not the most massive brother, but he was the most a man, the one who neither played video games nor rejoiced at videos in which people were injured. His inclination to help other brothers write papers and refine workouts bespoke a capacity for fatherhood. I had seen his genitals, in the locker room after lacrosse, and they reminded me of a Volvo sedan in that they were unspectacular but shaped so as to imply solidity and soundness. One morning when we were all writhing on the couches, hung-over, he emerged from the bathroom in a towel, attended by a cloud of steam. We agreed that the sight of his body alleviated our symptoms.

"If you use a towel right after Newton uses it, your life expectancy is extended ten years," said Stacks Animal.

"If a man kisses Newton, he'll turn into a beautiful woman," I said, and everyone stared at me, because it was a too-imaginative joke.

But Newton threw his head back and laughed. "You guys are fucking funny," he said. "That's why *I* don't feel hung-over anymore."

The putative reasons we named him Nutella were that it

sounded like Newton and that he was sweet. But I wondered if it was really because when you tasted Nutella you were there. You were not looking at yourself from afar.

Nutella was never angry. When we discovered the poem and declared its author God, we knew he wouldn't object. He understood that it was a compliment to him as much as to the poet. To make Nutella lose at something, to deprive Nutella of control, God was what you had to be.

We learned of the poem's existence from Shmashcock's girlfriend, who was roommates with Melanie. (That was God's real name.) She told Shmash what the poem was about, and when she went to the bathroom he took a picture of it, and though it was untitled, he mass-texted it to us with the caption "On the Premature Ejaculation of Current Delta Zeta Chi Chapter President Caleb Newton."

It was the only poem I'd ever liked that didn't rhyme. I read it so many times that I memorized it by accident.

Who is this soldier who did not hold his fire
When the whites of my eyes were shrouded
In fluttering eyelids?
I thought I knew you
Knew you were the steady hand on the wheel
The prow itself
But what kind of captain are you?
Scared sailor with your hand on your mast
Betrayed by your own body
As we are all betrayed
On your knees
Above me
Begging my forgiveness
With the muscles of a demon
And the whites of your eyes
As white as a child's?

Behind the counter at D'Angelo's/Pizza Hut, I whispered, "Muscles of a demon/And the whites of your eyes/As white as a child's" for twenty minutes because it was the perfect description of Nutella. It was as if somebody had snapped a photo of him and enlarged it until it was the very wallpaper of my mind. I loved Melanie for writing it. I also felt I was her secret collaborator, for in my head I was contributing lines. I added:

Whose hands are these?
One moment swift as a gray river
The next as still as stones

Because that was another thing about Nutella. He was a war elephant on the lacrosse field and yet capable of quietude and stillness, reading econ on the porch, his phone face-down on his knee, casting light on his groin when he received a text.

While I refined my supplement to the poem, I prepared a Santa Fe Veggie Wrap. The process demanded that I empty a plastic bag of frozen vegetables into a small plastic bucket and place the bucket in a microwave. I neglected the microwave step and emptied the bag of vegetables directly onto the wrap, with the vegetables still cold and rigid. I realized what I had done when I laid the sandwich in its basket, presented it to the girl who had ordered it, and saw the gleam of frost on a carrot rod.

Evgeny called me into the management room, which was a yellow closet straining to contain Evgeny. He said that if I kept dreaming all my days I would wind up like him, a lover of art and philosophy. He pointed to his face, with its little black mustache. I promised him that from now on my motto would be "no more spacing."

I took a pizza order and thought of all I was doing to enhance my employment prospects. Majoring in business, minoring in math, seeking internships related to data mining, building networks of contacts through Delta Zeta Chi, Campus Republicans, and Future Business Leaders. I dreamed of a consulting firm that Nutella would one day helm, staffed by brothers, known for under-promising and overdelivering, with an insignia depicting a clock-face in the talons of an eagle. This would represent efficiency and superior perception. It would be pinned on each brother upon attainment of the status of partner, by Nutella, with live chamber music in an acoustically flawless arboretum of recycled glass.

When the pizza emerged on the other side of the self-timing oven, I saw that I had neglected to sprinkle on the cheese. I used American slices intended for subs, room temperature, in the hope that they would melt on the freshly heated pizza in the course of delivery.

That night, Shmash read the poem aloud in the living room, as Nutella covered his face and grinned.

"Like you all have never detonated early," he said, as if it was a dashing crime. As if this thing that we had all most likely done, and been ashamed of, was the least shameful thing in the world. I felt that all the brothers would have stormed North Korea for Nutella then, with a battering ram of wood and stone.

"That girl is a god," said Buckhunter.

"No," said Five-Hour. "That girl is God." And that was how it started.

We spied her at the dining hall the next day at lunch, by the tray carousel.

"God," shouted Five-Hour, and then we all shouted it.

She stopped and squinted. Her friends took up defensive positions on her flanks.

Shmashcock moved his arms up and down. "You are God for writing that poem," he said.

"God," we all said, and moved our arms.

She looked at Nutella, who was smiling.

"Yeah, that's me," she said. She kicked at Stacks, who was on his knees. "I guess you guys can worship me."

That night she came to the house with Nutella to hang out with us. I didn't know the nomenclature for her clothing. She wore black tights that went on her arms, green tights that came up to her knees, and a headband with tiny teeth that made the hair that passed through it poofy when it emerged on the other side. A wrist tattoo peeked from the lace at the end of her left arm-tight. It was a picture of an old mill, a rectangular brick building. It represented Lowell, she said.

"The Venice of Massachusetts," said Buckhunter. His tone was that of an Englishman in a monogrammed paisley bathrobe, smoking a pipe.

"It's got canals," she agreed. Buckhunter cracked his knuckles and made an assertive sniffing sound.

What people often failed to realize about Delta Zeta Chi was that we were like Native Americans, in that our names referred to aspects of our personalities. Buckhunter was so named because in matters of girls he had the opposite of ADD. If a girl wandered within a certain radius of Buck, she robbed him of his faculty for reason. He couldn't assess her reactions to the things he said; he couldn't see or hear her clearly. He wanted it so bad, he never got it. That was his tragedy, to be cockblocked by his own erect cock.

Like many girls before her, God said ha-ha to Buckhunter, smiled disingenuously. I got her a beer and asked her questions. My name was Oprah because there were books in my room and I asked questions.

She wanted to work in public relations, she disclosed. She liked the Batman movies but not the X-Men movies. She was into Nutella as a friend.

God and Nutella made sandwiches in our kitchen. They were like two old men who had been in a war, or had been in a drag-out fight that neither had won. The poem, I supposed, had scoured away all pretense. Whereas the other girls who'd hooked up with Nutella, the ones who wanted him after the hookup and tried to date him, he treated with politeness and indifference. They were the undead, bumping their foreheads against our windows. They were the opposite of God.

After God and Nutella ate the sandwiches, they made carrot-ginger cupcakes for our midpoint-between-spring-break-and-summer party. In the course of so doing, they killed many ants in the kitchen and the velvety reef of mold in the sink. I offered to help with the cream-cheese frosting because I was a frosting intellectual. Nutella argued with God about welfare entitlements versus the free market as he held a mixing bowl steady and she washed it with the rough side of a sponge.

That night God gave Nutella a spot while he did a keg stand, holding his calves above her head, her arm-tights, now Easter-egg blue, taut against her forearms. God, we shouted. There were girls at the party so hot, their cheekbones so sharp, their heels so architecturally adventurous, their eyelids so thick with dark paste, they might have been the focus of male attention at a mansion with an in-ground pool. But these girls were not encircled by the brothers of our white ramshackle house. Only God was encircled.

We took turns dancing with her until Shmash asked if she wanted a beer. She declined, pivoted her way across the dance floor to Five-Hour, and humped the air near his leg. She said something in Five's ear and he said something back, and soon they were multitasking, their heads stabilized to enable conversation, their lower bodies humping on, like the abdomens of dying wasps.

Five and God went upstairs, Five leading the way, and we all watched Nutella. He threw his arms around me and Shmash and Stacks, and the blond hairs on his forearms were short and dry. His elbow slid around my neck and it was like rolling on a fresh-mowed August lawn.

"I want you guys to know," said Nutella, "that everything is completely cool. Five is the best man for the mission."

We did three Delta Zeta Chi owl hoots, and the sound was soft and Celtic against the human grunts and synthesizer belches of the music, and I wished the final owl hoot would never fade, our six arms seized up forever around our heads, our huddle rotating slowly, as all huddles do, the faces of my brothers spinning in the black light. I remembered the day my mother took me to the Boston planetarium when I was seven, how the constellations maypoled around a void.

I always woke up earlier than anyone else in the house the morning after a party because I was protective of my abs and therefore drank less beer. That morning I descended to the kitchen to make breakfast and there was Five-Hour, with the shades drawn and the song from last night's dance with God tinkling from his phone. He poured hard cider on his cereal.

"No matter what happened last night," I said, "some chocolate-chip pancakes will taste better than that." I took the bottle from his hand and poured the cider and the cereal in the almost-full garbage bag sitting on the floor by the sink. I mixed batter and chocolate chips.

"Help me," I said. "Slap some butter in a pan."

Soon there was the crackling and the smell.

"Big night?" I tried.

"Fuck you," said Five, "if you ever tell anyone else what I'm about to tell you went down."

I told him I wouldn't as long as he held the bowl so I could scoop the batter right. And he talked.

Once they were upstairs, he said, God asked him please not to call her God and call her Melanie instead. She hooked her phone to his speakers and asked him to take down the Eskimo-themed poster from the swimsuit issue. In all of this he obliged. When he tried to slide off her arm-tights with his teeth, she said, "Funny not sexy," which threw him a little. Once her bra was off, she put a yarn-shop Simon & Garfunkel song on repeat and kissed him on the lips.

It occurred to him that this girl had been Nutella's breaker. Bedding her was, for a Delta Zeta Chi brother, what bedding Shania Twain would be for a southerner or what bedding Natalie Portman would be for a Jewish person; he was belly to belly with the most major figure in the Delta Zeta Chi culture.

He thought of how Nutella, the least spastic person in the world, a man who could take a jab to the mask in lacrosse and not flinch, had burst open from her hotness, and how that explosion had been documented in a poem that was known to all our house, if not to all Greek houses. He, Five-Hour, was a champion of knights brought in to rescue a princess from a tower the king had failed to scale. I am SWAT, he thought, I am Lancelot. The more he considered it—how God was the ultimate princess, and he, therefore, the ultimate prince, deep in a forest impenetrable to others—the smaller and softer his dick became. For he could not believe that a supra-Nutellian knight was who he really was.

By this point in the telling, Shmash was loitering in the doorway of the kitchen, presumably drawn by the smell of batter. When Five and I looked up he retreated to the living room.

Five staggered to the corner of the kitchen and pressed his forehead against the wall. I turned off the stove and pinched his cheek. His face was wet. I have never cried—not once—since I was ten, and I admire people who can do it. The criers can see the admiration in my face, and it helps them talk.

"Do I just lie?" Five whispered. "Do I just act as if I fucked her, and if someone asks, say a gentleman never tells?"

I told him to tell the truth. To act like it was nothing to apologize for, because it wasn't. He fist-bumped me, weakly at first, but again and again, until the bumps acquired force. It was not what I had said, I think, because my advice was unremarkable. It was only that he could see the respect on my face, the respect for his tears, and respect, above all, was what he needed.

"I'm done telling Oprah about not getting it up last night," he called to the living room. "And he made pancakes."

Five minutes later everyone was in the sunny kitchen, eating, brewing coffee, rinsing dirty plates, taking out the trash, crushing beer cans, talking about internships. Nutella squeezed fresh OJ wearing only his Red Sox boxers and baseball cap, and juice ran down his arms. Buck proposed a toast to Five for continuing the Delta Zeta Chi tradition of almost fucking God. Dust motes frolicked in the air as if emitted by our muscles, and the kitchen smelled like garbage, chocolate, sweat, and spring. I wondered if there would come a day when I would cry.

That night I had a dream I didn't want to have. In a white hotel room, I said to Nutella, Why not? What's the reason for us not to, you and I? What harm? I woke up spattered in cum and consoled myself as I washed my abs, hunched over the sink in the bathroom down the hall, with a different question: when ten sportsmen slept beneath a common roof, the smells of their sweat joined in a common cloud, who could escape unsportsmanlike dreams?

The following evening was Otter Night at Theta Nu. We walked to the TN house with flattened cardboard boxes under our arms. To otter, you needed a cardboard box and a wet carpeted staircase. The theme of ottering was, look how brothers will pour buckets of water on a carpeted staircase, sled the stairs face-first, and be injured.

We ottered once a year at Theta Nu, but this Otter Night was remarkable for the presence of God, who'd been invited by Nutella. As soon as she climbed the stairs with the flattened box in her hand, we gave it up. None of us had seen a girl otter. To otter was to engage in a dick-bashing test of will. (Jockstraps were expressly forbidden.) To otter with tits was beyond imagining.

She stood at the top of the stairs, eyes closed, back straight. We shouted, drank, whispered that a girl wouldn't do it, filmed with our phones. She laid her box on the ground, looked at the ceiling above her, as if to consult a watchful parent. And then, to the ticking of a drum machine and the groans of a rapper and the groans of the rapper's woman floating above the rapper and the machine, she dove.

Her eyes flinched open every step. It was all quiet the three, four seconds of actual otter, but for the damp *thump-thumps*, and a collective fraternal gasp. At the end, she reached for the bannister to slow herself, a good move, and her landing at the bottom did not look unbearable. She came to a halt with her upper body on the soaked floor, her legs sprawled on the soaked stairs, her face in carpet, the cardboard sled tucked like a lover beneath her pummeled breasts.

"Give me a beer," she said, and I hugged Stacks, Nutella, and Shmash, and they hugged me back, and we all screamed God, God, God.

Throughout the night, God drank beer and touched guys' arms. And a weird thing happened: the brothers declined to put the moves on her.

No one steered her to the dance floor and freaked her. No one hovered beside her and asked her questions about her classes, holding his beer at chest height like a mantis to display his biceps.

The brothers were scared. Attempting her, Nutella had blown his load. Attempting her, Five had limp-dicked. And she ottered like a warrior.

But to me she was a secret collaborator. We were both Nutella poets, the way people we read in core humanities were nature poets. I wasn't scared of her at all.

When the music went "Biggie Biggie Biggie," I took her by the elbow and we took the floor. We humped the air between us; we collaborated.

When the two of us left early, hand in hand, stumbling down Frat Row to Delta Zeta Chi, she said, "I have to say, I'm surprised this is happening with you."

I asked her what she meant.

"Just a wrong first impression."

The house was abandoned, all the brothers at TN's post-otter party, hoping to show off their injuries to girls who had seen them be brave. Our feet creaked on the stairs as she followed me up. In my room I gave her the plug to hook her phone to my speakers and asked her to choose music. She filled the room with the yarn-shopness that Five had described, and I recited her poem from memory, with the lines I'd added, while she sat on my bed with her chin on her fist.

"Consider it your poem too," she said, and I knew I was supposed to kiss her, and I did.

I had never been to Silicon Valley, but that was where I went that night. Green grass in the shadow of silicon mountains, steel gray with chalk-white caps. Silicon wolves stalked the foothills, screen-eyed. I saw myself kneeling in that grass, doing for Nutella what God was doing for me. I made the sounds I thought Nutella would make.

I put on a condom as the yarn-shop song started over. When we were about to start fucking, I asked her to recite the poem. She looked at me for a moment. Please, I said, and she recited.

I recited with her, and it worked: when we fucked, Nutella was close, because like two lungs we had drawn him into the room. He was just out of reach, something sprayed in the air, like a poem.

I saw the blood only when we were finished. I looked at her face for an answer. She sat and sucked air through her nose, wiped her face with the back of her hand.

"Were you thinking about Nutella?" she asked.

I said no in a too-deep voice.

"You're lying to me. Why did you want us to say the poem?" She started to cry. Her shoulders jumped in rhythm to her sobs. "It's cool, but at least don't lie to me."

Cry, I ordered myself. We would cry together. I pictured tide pools in my eyes. I pictured what the funeral would look like if my little sister died, her friends crying in their glasses and braces. But I'd tried to make myself cry many times, and always the same thing happened: my eyes knew I was trying to do it, and refused. I couldn't make myself cry any better than Nutella and Five-Hour could make themselves Melanie's lovers.

I waited for a minute, listening, trying to join. Finally, I leaned over and put my lips under her eye, so that I could taste her. I wanted to tell her what I tasted: sour makeup and salt.

"I'm sorry I lied to you," I said. "I thought about Nutella but also you at the same time."

She took my hands and folded them across her ribs. And then something occurred to me.

"You can't write a poem about how I said that," I said. "About anything to do with me and Nutella. Even though it was your first time, you can't write a poem about it that you show to people."

I watched her blink in the dark.

"I might not write a poem about it," she said. "But I'm going to talk about it with my friends."

"You can't," I said. "You can't tell them I thought about Nutella."

"OK, I won't," she said, and I knew that she was now the one lying.

I pulled away from her and sat up in bed. I could see what was going to happen to me like a film projected on my wall: My life was ruined. She would tell her friends, who would tell other girls, and

Shmash or Five would find out from one girl or another. Shmash and Five would be too embarrassed to tell Nutella, but they wouldn't be able to resist telling other brothers, and one night, very drunk, a brother would tell Nutella. And nothing would happen. No one would say anything to me. No one would want to take anything from me. But brotherhood would be taken, in the end. The ease with which my brothers spoke to me, the readiness with which they spilled their guts in times of humiliation — this would be withdrawn. My place among them in the consulting firm of the clock and talons.

The arboretum full of chamber music exploded, as if God had sung a note so high it shattered four stories of green windows.

I sat there hating her. She must have hated me back, because she got out of bed, put on her clothes without speaking, and left the house by the time the brothers returned from TN. I lay awake and listened to them bang around the kitchen. They chanted in unison, a single, iambic owl: *uh-ooh uh-ooh.* It sounded like *beware, beware.*

Mastiff

FROM *The New Yorker*

EARLIER, ON THE TRAIL, they'd seen it. The massive dog. Tugging at its master's leash, so that the young man's calves bulged with muscle as he fought to hold the dog back. Grunting what sounded like "Damn, Rob-roy! Damn dog!" in a tone of exasperated affection.

Signs along the trail forbade dogs without leashes. At least this dog was on a leash.

The woman stared at the animal, not twelve feet away, wheezing and panting. Its head was larger than hers, with a pronounced black muzzle, bulging glassy eyes. Its jaws were powerful and slack; its large, long tongue, as rosy-pink as a sexual organ, dripped slobber. The dog was pale-brindle-furred, with a deep chest, strong shoulders and legs, a taut tail. It must have weighed at least two hundred pounds. Its breathing was damply audible, unsettling.

The dog's straggly-bearded young master, in beige hoodie, khaki cargo shorts, and hiking boots, gripped the leather leash with both hands, squinting at the woman and at the man behind her with an expression that seemed apologetic or defensive; or maybe, the woman thought, the young man was laughing at them, ordinary hikers without a monster-dog to pull and strain at their arms.

The woman thought, That isn't a dog. It's a human being on its hands and knees! Such surreal thoughts bombarded the woman's brain, waking and sleeping. As long as no one else knew about them, she paid them little heed.

Fortunately, the dog and its owner were taking another trail into Wildcat Canyon. The dog lunged forward eagerly, sniffing at the ground, the young man following with muttered curses. The woman and her male companion continued on the main trail, which was three miles uphill, into the sun, to Wildcat Peak.

The man, sensing the woman's unease at the sight of the dog, made some joke, which the woman couldn't quite hear and did not acknowledge. They were walking single file, the woman in the lead. She waited for the man to touch her shoulder, as another man might have done, to reassure her, but she knew that he would not, and he did not. Instead, the man said, in a tone of slight reproof, that the dog was an English mastiff—"Beautiful dog."

Much of what the man said to the woman, she understood, was in rebuke of her narrow judgment, her timorous ways. Sometimes the man was amused by these qualities. At other times, she saw in his face an expression of startled disapproval, veiled contempt.

The woman said, over her shoulder, with a wild little laugh, "Yes! Beautiful."

The hike had been the man's suggestion. Or rather, in his oblique way, which was perhaps a strategy of shyness, he'd simply told her that he was going hiking this weekend and asked if she wanted to join him. He had not risked being rejected; he'd made it clear that he would be going, regardless.

The woman had been introduced to the man seven weeks earlier, at a dinner party at a mutual friend's home in the Berkeley Hills. The friend, closer to the man than to the woman, had said to the man, "You'll like Mariella. You'll like her face," and to the woman, "Simon's an extraordinary person, but it may not be evident immediately. Give him time."

The woman and the man had gone on several walks together already. But a hike of such ambition seemed, to the woman, something quite different.

She'd said, "Yes! I'd love that."

It was late afternoon. They had been hiking for several hours and were now making their way single file down the mountain. The woman was descending first, then the man. The man, the more experienced hiker, wanted to watch over the woman, whom he didn't trust not to hurt herself. She'd surprised him by wearing lightweight running shoes on the trail and not, as he was wearing, hiking boots.

She hadn't thought to bring water, either. He carried a twenty-ounce plastic bottle of water for them both.

The man was a little annoyed by the woman. Yet he was drawn to her. He hoped to like her more than he did—he hoped to adore her. He had been very lonely for too long and had come to bitterly resent the solitude of his life.

It had been an unnaturally balmy day for late March. At midday, the temperature was perhaps sixty-eight degrees. But now, as the sun sank like a broken bloody egg, darkness and cold began to rise from the earth. The day before, the man had suggested to the woman that she bring a light canvas jacket in her backpack; he knew how quickly the mountain trail could turn cold in the late afternoon, but she had worn just a sweater, jeans, and a sun visor. (The woman's eyes were sensitive to sunlight, even with sunglasses. She hated how easily they watered, tears running down her cheeks like an admission of weakness.) And she'd confounded the man by not bringing a backpack at all, with the excuse that she hated feeling "burdened." In the gathering chill, the woman was shivering.

The trail had looped upward through pine woods to a spectacular view at the peak, where the man had given the woman some water to drink. Though she said she wasn't thirsty, he insisted. There's a danger of dehydration when you've been exerting yourself, he said. He spoke sternly, as if he were a parent she could not reasonably oppose. He spoke with the confidence of one who is rarely challenged. At times, the woman quite liked his air of authority; other times, she resented it. The man seemed always to be regarding her with a bemused look, like a scientist confronted with a curious specimen. She didn't want to think—yet she thought, compulsively—that he was comparing her with other women he'd known, and finding her lacking.

Then the man took photographs with his new camera, while the woman gazed out at the view. Along the horizon was a rim of luminous blue—the Pacific Ocean, miles away. In the near distance were small lakes, streams. The hills were strangely sculpted, like those bald slopes in the paintings of Thomas Hart Benton.

Absorbed in his photography, the man seemed to forget about the woman. How self-contained he could be, how maddening! The woman had never been so at repose in her *self*. For nearly an hour he lingered, taking photographs. During this time, other hikers came and went. The woman spoke briefly with these hikers, while the man appeared oblivious of them. It wasn't his habit, he'd told her, to strike up conversations with "random" people. "Why not?" she'd asked. And he'd said, with a look that suggested that her question was virtually incomprehensible, "Why not? Because I'll never see them again."

With her provocative little laugh, the woman had said, "But that's the best reason for talking to strangers—you'll never see them again."

At least the bearded young man with the English mastiff hadn't climbed to the top of Wildcat Peak, though other hikers with dogs had made their way there. A succession of dogs, in fact, of all sizes and breeds, fortunately most of them well behaved and disinclined to bark, several of them trailing their masters, older dogs, looking chastised, winded.

"Nice dog! What's his name?" the woman would ask. Or "What breed is he?"

She understood that the man had taken note of her fear of the mastiff at the start of the hike. How she'd tensed at the sight of the ugly wheezing beast. It had to be the largest dog she'd ever seen, as big as a St. Bernard but totally lacking that dog's benign shaggy aura. And so at the peak the woman made a point of engaging dog owners in conversations, in a bright, airy, friendly way. She even petted the gentler dogs.

As a child of nine or ten, she'd been attacked by a German shepherd. She'd done nothing to provoke the attack and could only remember screaming and trying to run as the dog barked furiously at her and snapped at her bare legs. Only the intervention of adults had saved her.

The woman hadn't told the man much about her past. Not yet. And possibly wouldn't. Her principle was *Never reveal your weakness.* Especially to strangers: this was essential. Technically, the woman and the man were "lovers," but they were not yet intimate. You might say—the woman might have said—that they were still fundamentally strangers to each other.

They'd been together in the woman's house, upstairs in her bed, but they hadn't yet spent an entire night together. The man felt self-conscious in the woman's house, and the woman hadn't been able to fall asleep beside him; the physical fact of him was so distracting. Naked and horizontal, the man seemed much larger than he did clothed and vertical. He breathed loudly, wetly, through his open mouth, and though he woke affably when she nudged him, the woman hadn't wanted to keep waking him. In truth, the woman had never been very comfortable with a man at close quarters, unless she'd been drinking. But this man scarcely drank. And the woman no longer lost herself in drink; that life was behind her.

The woman liked to tell her friends that she wanted not *to get married* but to *be married*. She wanted a relationship that seemed mature, if not old and settled, from the start. Newness and rawness did not appeal to her.

"Excuse me? When do you think we might head back?" She spoke to the man hesitantly, not wanting to break his concentration. In their relationship, she had not yet displayed any impatience; she had not yet raised her voice.

At last the man put his camera, a heavy, complicated instrument, into his backpack, along with the water bottle, which contained just two or three inches of water now—"We might need this later." His movements were measured and deliberate, as if he were alone, and the woman felt a sudden stab of dislike for him, anger that he could take such care with trivial matters and yet did not seem to love her.

There were no rest rooms on the damn trail, of course. These were serious hiking trails, for serious hikers. Longingly, the woman recalled the facilities at the trailhead. How long would it take to hike back down? An hour? Two? For male hikers, stopping to urinate in the woods was no great matter; for female hikers, an effort and an embarrassment. Not since she was a young girl, trapped on an endless, hateful hike in summer camp in the Adirondacks, had she been forced to relieve herself in the woods. The memory was hazy and blurred with shame, and humiliation at the very pettiness of her discomfort. If she'd told this story to the man, he would probably have laughed at her.

Driving to the park that day, the man and the woman had felt very happy together. It sometimes happened to them, unpredictably—a sudden flaring up of happiness, even joy, in each other's company. The man was unusually talkative. The woman laughed at his remarks, surprised that he could be so witty. She was touched that, a few days before, he'd visited the art gallery she ran, and purchased a small soapstone sculpture.

The woman slid over in the passenger's seat to sit closer to the man, as a young girl might do, impulsively. How natural this felt—a rehearsal of intimacy!

The car radio was playing a piano piece by the Czech composer Janáček, "In the Mists." The woman recognized it after a few notes. She'd played the piano cycle as a girl. Her eyes filled with tears as she remembered. The man continued talking, as if he didn't hear the music. Avidly, the woman listened to the somber, distinctive notes in a minor—"misty"—key. She didn't register the man's words, but his voice was suffused with the melancholy beauty of the music, and she felt that she loved him or might love him. *He will be the one. It's time.*

The woman was forty-one years old. The man was several years older. He had been the director of a research laboratory in Berkeley for many years. His work was predominant in his life. He was idealistic, a zealot for science education and the preservation of the environment. He was famously generous to younger scientists, a legendary mentor to his graduate students and postdocs. He'd never married. He wasn't sure he'd ever been *in love*. Though he'd always wanted children, he had none. He was dissatisfied with his life outside the lab. He felt cheated and foolish, worried that others might pity him.

He'd been upset earlier that year, while visiting one of his protégés at the Salk Institute, whose wife was also a scientist and who had several children; the young family lived in a split-level cedar house on three acres of wooded land. In this household, the man had felt sharply the emptiness of his own existence, in an under-furnished rented house near the university, where he'd lived for more than twenty years. He'd ended the visit shaken. And not long afterward he'd met the woman at a dinner party.

The woman was also lonely and dissatisfied—but primarily with others, not with herself. She'd had several relationships with men since college, but she hadn't felt much for any of them. Some she had dated simultaneously. And yet she was deeply hurt if a man wasn't exclusively involved with her. Her father had left the family when she was a child and rarely visited. All her life she'd yearned for that absent man, even as she'd resented him. She'd hated her own vulnerability.

She was an attractive woman. Within her small circle of friends, she was popular, admired. She dressed stylishly. She was social.

She'd invested wisely in her art gallery. Still, she was preoccupied with how she appeared in others' eyes. She could barely force herself to contemplate her own image in a mirror: her face, she thought, was too small, her chin too narrow, her eyes too large and deep-set. She hated the fact that she was petite. She'd have preferred to be five feet ten, to walk with a swagger, with sexual confidence. At five-three, it seemed she had no choice but to be the recipient, the receptacle, of a man's desire.

Sometimes, in the midst of buoyant social occasions, something inside the woman seemed to switch off. She could feel a deadness seeping into her, a chilly indifference. At the end of an evening, her women friends would hug her, or a friend's husband might slip his arm around her waist to kiss her, just a little too suggestively, and the coldness in her would respond, *I don't give a damn if I ever see any of you again.*

She laughed at herself. A hole in the heart.

Yet it happened, in the new man's company, that the woman felt a rare hopefulness. If she couldn't love the man, it might be enough for the man to love *her;* enough for them to have a child together, at least. (In the woman's weakest moments, she lamented the fact that she had no children, that she would soon be too old to have any. Yet children bored her, even her nieces and nephews, who she conceded were beautiful.)

What would the man have thought if he'd known about the woman's calculations? Or were these just harmless fantasies, unlikely to be realized?

Now, making her way down the trail, eager to be out of the park that had seemed so inviting hours ago, the woman felt disconsolate. The long wait at the peak had enervated her. The man's seeming indifference had enervated her. As the sun shifted in the sky, she felt strength leaking from her.

Brooding and silent, the man walked behind her, sometimes so close that he nearly trod on her heels. She wanted to turn and shout at him, "Don't do that! I'm going as fast as I can."

So absorbed was the woman with the voice inside her head that she only half realized that she'd been hearing a familiar sound somewhere close by—a wet chuffing noise, a labored breathing. The trail continued to drop, turning back on itself; another, lower trail ran parallel to it now and would join it within a few yards, and on this trail two figures were hurrying, one of them, in the lead, a large beast running on all fours.

Appalled, the woman saw the enormous mastiff stop at the junction of the two trails, unavoidable. The dog's damp, shining eyes were fixed on her, sharply focused. With a kind of indignation quickly shifting to fury, it barked at the woman, straining at its leash as the bearded young man yelled at it to sit.

The woman knew better than to succumb to panic; certainly she knew better than to provoke the dog. But she couldn't help herself—she screamed and shrank away. It was the worst possible reaction to the dog, which, maddened by her terror, leapt at her, barking and growling, wrenching the leash out of its master's hands.

In an instant, the mastiff was on the woman, snarling and biting, nearly knocking her to the ground. Even in her horror, the woman was thinking, My face. I must protect my face.

Her companion quickly intervened, pushing himself between her and the dog, even as the dog, on its hind legs, continued to attack. Futilely, the dog's master shouted, "Rob-roy! Rob-*roy!*" The dog paid not the slightest attention.

The frantic struggle couldn't have lasted more than a minute or two. Fiercely, the man struck at the dog with his bare fists and kicked it. The young man yanked at the dog's collar, cursing. With great effort, he finally managed to pull the animal away from the man, who was bleeding badly now from lacerations on his hands and arms and face.

The woman, terrified, was cringing behind him. She felt something wet on her face. Not blood but the dog's slobber. She called out, "Help him! Get help for him! He'll bleed to death."

The dog was still barking hysterically, lunging and leaping with bared fangs, while the young man struggled to hold it down, apologizing profusely, claiming that the dog had never done anything like this before—not ever. "Jesus! I'll get help." There was a ranger station a half mile down the trail, the young man said. He'd run.

Alone with the injured man, the woman cradled him in her arms as he moaned in pain. He appeared to be dazed, stupefied. Was he in shock? His skin felt cold to the woman's touch. She could barely comprehend what had happened, and so swiftly.

The dog had bitten and scratched her hands too. She was bleeding. But her fear was for the man. She fumbled in her pocket for her cell phone, tried to call 911, but the call failed to go through. She wondered whether she should make a tourniquet to stanch the flow of blood from the man's forearm. Years ago, in high school, she'd taken a course in first aid, but could she remember now? For a tourniquet, you had to use a stick? Her eyes darted about, searching for—what? Like a foolish trapped bird, her heart beat erratically in her chest.

The man insisted now that he was all right, that he could walk to the ranger station. Grotesquely, he tried to laugh. He had no idea how torn and bloody his face was.

The woman helped him to his feet. How heavy he was, how uncoordinated! His face was a mask of blood, flaps of loose skin on his cheeks and forehead. One of his earlobes was torn. At least his eyes had been spared.

The woman gripped the man around the waist, clumsily, and he was able to walk, leaning on her. She tried to comfort him—she had no idea what she was saying, except that there would be help for him soon, he would be all right. She saw that the front and sleeves of her sweater were soaked in dark blood.

By this time, the sun had sunk below the tree line. It was dusk, and the air was cold and wet, as if after a rain. They began to hear calls—two rangers were running up the shadowy trail with flashlights, shouting.

They were taken to the ranger station and given first aid. Sterilizing liquid, bandages. For the man's lacerated forearm, a tourniquet deftly applied by the elder of the rangers, who told the man how lucky he was: "The artery wasn't severed." With a dog attack, there was the possibility of rabies. It was imperative to locate the dog. It seemed that the young man had fled the park with the mastiff. Incredibly, he had not even reported the attack. But a hiker, who had witnessed it from a distance, had alerted the rangers and taken down the plate number of the young man's Jeep. The son of a bitch would be prosecuted for the attack, and for leaving the scene too, the ranger said.

Around the bandages, the man's face was ashen. His breath came quickly and shallowly. He was urged to lie down on a cot. Despite his protests, an ambulance was called. His injuries required stitches—that was clear.

Within minutes, the ambulance arrived in the now near-deserted parking lot. The woman wanted to ride with the man, but he insisted that she take his car and meet him at the hospital; he didn't want his vehicle to be locked in the park overnight.

Even with his injuries, and speaking with difficulty, the man appeared to be thinking calmly, rationally.

The woman took his keys, and his wallet and backpack, and followed the ambulance along curving mountain roads in his station wagon. She could hardly breathe, her loneliness as palpable and suffocating as cotton batting.

She still could not quite fathom the idea that the dog's owner had fled the park without reporting the attack. The young man had cared so little about their welfare; he'd fled knowing that if his dog wasn't located by the authorities, both victims would have to endure rabies shots.

She'd been told by the rangers that he would be apprehended within a few hours. The attack had already been reported to the local police. A warrant would be issued for the dog owner's arrest. She'd been assured that the authorities would find the man and check the dog for rabies, but in her distressed state she'd scarcely been able to listen or to care.

At the brightly lit clinic, the woman hurried inside as the man was carried into the ER on a stretcher. He seemed to be only partly conscious now, unaware of his surroundings. She asked one of the medical workers what was wrong and was told that the man had had a kind of seizure in the ambulance; he'd lost consciousness, his blood pressure had risen alarmingly, and his heartbeat had accelerated, in fibrillation.

Fibrillation! The woman knew only vaguely what this meant.

She was prevented from following the man into the ER. She found herself standing at a counter, being asked questions. She fumbled with the man's wallet, searching for his health-insurance card. His university ID. How slowly she moved—as clumsy in her bandages as if she were wearing mittens. One of the EMTs was telling her that she should be treated as well; her lacerated hands and wrists should be examined. But the woman refused to listen. She flushed with indignation when the woman behind the counter asked how she was related to the injured man. Sharply she said, "I am his fiancée."

*

JOYCE CAROL OATES

How long she remained in the ER waiting room the woman had no clear idea. Time had become disjointed. Her eyelids were so heavy she could barely keep them open. Several times, she inquired after the man and was told that he was undergoing emergency treatment for cardiac arrhythmia and that she could not see him yet. This news was unacceptable to her. He'd only been bitten by a damn dog! He hadn't seemed so badly injured; he'd insisted on walking. The woman was lightheaded. Her hands and wrists began to burn. She heard her thin, plaintive voice, begging, "Don't let him die!"

Looking around, she saw how others regarded her. A woman crazed with worry, fear. A woman whose voice was raised in panic. The sort of woman you pity even as you inch away from her.

She saw that her coarse-knit Scottish sweater—it had been one of her favorites—had been torn beyond repair.

In a fluorescent-lit rest room, her face in the mirror was blurred, like those faces on TV that are pixilated in order to disguise their identity. She was thinking of how the massive dog had thrown itself at her and how, astonishingly, the man had protected her. Did the man love her, then? What a coward she'd been, ducking behind him to save herself, grabbing at him desperately, cringing, crouching, whimpering like a terrified child. The man had thrust himself forward to be attacked in her place. A man who was virtually a stranger had risked his life for *her*.

The woman had the man's backpack, with his camera and his wallet. In a state of nervous dread, she looked through the wallet, a leather billfold of good quality but badly worn. Credit cards, university ID, library card, driver's license. A miniature photo of a tensely smiling middle-aged man with a furrowed forehead and thinning shoulder-length hair, whom she would have claimed she'd never seen before. She discovered that he was born in 1956—he was fifty-seven years old! A decade older than she'd guessed, and sixteen years older than she was.

Another card indicated that the man had a cardiac condition—mitral-valve prolapse. There was a much folded prescription, dated several years before, for a medication to be administered intravenously. Nearest of kin to be notified in case of emergency: a woman with the man's last name, possibly a sister, who lived in San Diego.

The woman hurried to the desk to speak with a nurse. She

pressed the prescription on the woman, who promised to report this discovery to the cardiac specialist overseeing the man's treatment.

They were only humoring her, the woman supposed. The hysterical fiancée! They'd performed their own tests on the stricken man.

"Ma'am?" The waiting room was nearly empty when an attendant came to inform her that her companion was to be hospitalized for the night, kept under observation in the cardiac unit. The cardiologist on call had managed to control the man's fibrillation and his heartbeat was near normal, but his blood pressure was still high and his white-blood-cell count was low. The woman tried to feel relief. Tried to think, Now I can go home, the danger is past.

Instead, she went upstairs to the cardiac unit. For several minutes, she stood outside the doorway of the man's room, undecided whether to enter. Inside, the man lay unnaturally still, as nurses fussed about him. His heartbeat was monitored by a machine. His breathing was monitored. The woman saw that the bandages hurriedly applied to his face at the ranger station had been removed; his numerous wounds had been stitched together and bandaged again, in an elaborate and lurid mask of crisscrossing strips of white. The man's arms and hands had been re-bandaged as well.

As she entered the room, she thought she might faint. Yet she felt gratitude for the man's courage, and for his kindness. Shame for herself, that she'd valued the man so little.

She pulled over a chair and sat beside his bed.

The man's breathing was quick and shallow but rhythmic. The bed had been cranked to a thirty-three-degree angle. His eyelids fluttered. Was he seeing her? Did he recognize her? The woman thought, He has forgotten my name.

The man was trying to speak. Or—trying to smile? He was asking her—what? His words were slurred.

She heard herself explain that she would stay with him for a while. Until visiting hours ended. She had his wallet and his camera and the key to his station wagon. She said that she would return in the morning, when he was to be discharged, and would drive him home then. If he wanted. If he needed her. She would return, and bring his things with her, and drive him home. Did he understand?

In his cranked-up bed, the man drifted into sleep. They'd given him a sedative, the woman supposed. His mouth eased open, and he breathed heavily, wetly. This was the night-breathing the woman recalled, and now felt comforted to hear. She practiced pronouncing his name: "Simon." It seemed to her suddenly a beautiful name. A name new to her, in her life, for she'd never before known anyone named Simon.

Now tears spilled from the woman's eyes and ran in rivulets down her face. She was crying as she had not cried in memory. She was too old for such emotion; there was something ridiculous and demeaning about it. But she was remembering how at the top of the steep trail the man had insisted that she drink from his plastic water bottle. She hadn't wanted to drink the lukewarm water, yet had drunk it as the man watched, acquiescing, if with resistance, resentment. In their relationship, the man would always be the stronger; she would resent his superior strength, yet she would be protected by it. She might defy it, but she would not oppose it. She was thinking of the two or three occasions when she'd kissed the man in a pretense of an emotion she hadn't yet felt.

Like the man, the woman was exhausted. She laid her head against the headrest of the chair beside the bed. Her eyelids closed. Vividly, she saw him at the peak of the Wildcat Canyon trail, holding his complicated camera aloft, peering through the viewfinder. The wind stirred his thinning silvery-copper hair—she hadn't noticed that before. She would go to him, she thought. She would stand close beside him, slide her arm around his waist to steady him. This was her task, her duty. He was stronger than she, but a man's strength can drain from him. A man's courage can be torn from him, can bleed away. But it was she who was afraid of something—wasn't she? The pale-blue rim of the Pacific Ocean. The bald-sculpted hills and exquisite little lakes that seemed as unreal as papier-mâché that you could poke your fingers through. To her horror, she realized she was hearing a panting sound, a wet-chuffing breath, somewhere beside her, or below her on the trail, in the gathering dusk, waiting.

STEPHEN O'CONNOR

Next to Nothing

FROM *Conjunctions*

Sour Sisters

THE SOROS SISTERS' eyes are the blue of lunar seas, their complexions cloud white, and their identical pageboys well-bottom black. The term "beautiful" has never been applied sincerely to either sister, though Ivy, the youngest by two years, might be deemed the better looking, because she has detectable cheekbones and a waist narrower than her hips. Isabel has very little in the way of body fat, but is square shaped from almost any angle. Even her face is square shaped. It's been that way since birth.

As soon as Isabel and Ivy slam the doors of their white van, three people in front of the pharmacy stop talking. A man whose metallic-gray pickup has just bleeped and flashed its lights feigns acute interest in a parking meter. No one looks either sister in the eye as they approach along the solitary block of the town's main street. No one raises a hand, or says hello. But once the sisters have begun to recede in the opposite direction, all four heads turn to watch. Significant glances are exchanged, but not words. There's no need.

Isabel and Ivy's parents retired to the town twelve years ago, when their father had a stroke and had to give up his orthopedic surgery practice in the city. Everybody loves Dr. Soros, who is floppy of foot and eccentric of speech, but can be counted on for a lopsided grin whenever he is spotted in public. Hilda Soros has the perpetually startled expression of a woman with too many worries, but perhaps for that very reason, with her every smile—timid, then radiantly blooming—she seems to be discovering joy for the first time in her life.

Her daughters, however, seem never to have discovered joy. They bypass even the friendliest greetings with the indifference of a bulldozer flattening a picket fence. In the rare instances when small talk is unavoidable (on the checkout line at the Food-Star, on the diving raft at the lake), they terminate it in twelve words. Or five. Their brows are always wrinkled, their mouths slot straight. They make the townspeople feel erased. They make the townspeople feel like a variety of wood louse.

Something Is Not Right

Isabel and Ivy are sociologists, and thus the beneficiaries of lengthy academic vacations. They have spent every July and August in their parents' white-clapboard house ever since each bore her first child: daughters—both eleven now. Isabel's husband is an executive at a food-processing company, and Ivy's is an investment banker. The two men cannot be in the same room without getting drunk and turning every topic of conversation into a theater of mutual disparagement. Their visits to the town never overlap and are, in fact, so fleeting and rare that many people believe that the sisters are lesbians, and that their children—six of them now; evenly divided—are the products of artificial insemination. Isabel and Ivy each have their own room, and a double bed, and their children sleep in an attic that reminds everyone of the dormitory in that old house in Paris where Miss Clavel looked after Madeline.

Tonight it is Ivy's turn to read to the children. She is sitting at the end of the aisle between the two rows of beds in a sage-green easy chair, the arms of which are frayed to their cotton batting. The children are all upright in their beds, staring at her expectantly. Although Ivy's parents are brown-eyed and both her husband and Isabel's have eyes the color of wet charcoal, each of the twelve irises turned toward her is the all-but-white blue of a lunar sea—a statistical anomaly that Ivy finds more than moderately disconcerting.

"I don't like that story," says Gwenny (Isabel's oldest child).

"I haven't even started it yet." Ivy lifts the picture book from her lap and looks at the cover, though for no particular reason.

"I don't like it either," says Jen (Ivy's oldest).

"Me too," says little Jerry (her youngest).

"We hate that book," says Gwenny.

"OK." Ivy puts the book down on one side of her chair and picks a new book from the pile on the other.

"We hate that one too," says Paulette (Isabel's middle child).

"OK." Ivy puts the second book down and picks up a third. She doesn't care what she reads. They all seem stupid to her. But the kids hate that book too, and the next.

"Tell us a story," says Gwenny.

"I'm trying to, but you won't let me," says Ivy.

"No, make one up!"

"Yeah," says Jerry. "Make us up a story, Mommy."

Ivy begins to sweat along her hairline and under her arms. For a long moment she sits in the chair, silent, swollen looking—as if she has been stuffed. Then she sighs heavily.

"Once upon a time," she says, "there was a little princess . . . or she might have been a prince"—she looks at Jerry—"only you know for sure." Jerry sticks his thumb into his mouth and slides down in his bed so that he is looking straight at the ceiling. "Anyhow," says Ivy, "the princess lived in a castle on the beach. It was a sand castle. And it had a dungeon. That was where she kept her toys."

"What kind of toys?" asks Paulette.

"She had exactly the same toys that you have," says Ivy. "One day she went down to the dungeon to play with her toys and there was a dragon there. He told her, 'This is not your castle. It is my castle. You have to leave now or I will turn you into a cinder.' 'But I've lived here all my life,' said the princess. 'It doesn't matter,' said the dragon. 'You have to go. You can take one toy with you.' So she picked up a toy and she left."

"What toy did she take?" says Jen.

"What do you think she took?" says Ivy.

"A teddy bear," says Jen.

"No. It was a plastic teepee."

"A teepee!" says Jerry, his thumb still in his mouth.

"It was her favorite toy. But as soon as she was out of the castle, she put it down on the sand and a wave washed it away." Ivy waits for a response from the children. When none comes, she continues. "For seven nights and seven days she walked, and she got so tired and so cold—because it was snowing—that she came down with a fever and fainted on the old man's doorstep."

"Which old man?" says Gwenny.

"The blind old man who lived in the cottage in the forest. He made her a bed in front of the fireplace and gave her medicine, but it was the wrong kind of medicine, so she didn't get any better."

"What kind of medicine?" says Gwenny.

"Leeches."

The children make ripping noises with their lips and teeth.

"Anyhow," says Ivy, "a prince was walking by the cottage, and when he saw the princess lying in front of the fire, he decided to go in and kiss her. The prince was so quiet that the blind man didn't even know he was there. The prince bent over the princess and kissed her on the lips. But when he lifted his head, he saw that she was dead, so he crept out of the cottage as quietly as he had come in."

"That's horrible!" says Paulette.

"Did his kiss kill her?" says Gwenny.

"Nobody knows," says Ivy. "But she was probably dead when the prince walked into the room." Ivy puts her hands on her knees and stands up. "OK, everybody—time for sleep!"

Good News

It is hurricane season. A week ago, newscasters spoke urgently about Hurricane Gigi's devastation of Haiti. Then Tropical Storm Henry earned an afternoon and evening of coverage. But now the coiffed heads on every news show talk about nothing but Hurricane Ivy, which is rolling up the Eastern Seaboard like a massive ninja star and is predicted to pass over the town as a category-four storm the day after tomorrow.

"Brace yourself," says Isabel, sitting with her laptop at a picnic table under the shade of an enormous willow. A small brook meanders just behind her, making a noise like Ping-Pong balls sliding down a plastic chute. Mosquitoes hover unsteadily around her head. She doesn't care. She takes Benadryl every night to get to sleep, so mosquito bites have no effect.

"For what?" says Ivy, who is standing directly in front of the table. A mosquito has sunk its proboscis into her left shoulder. She slaps and lifts her hand: a starburst of blood.

"You know: your name."

When Ivy still doesn't understand, Isabel adds, "Jokes."

"Oh," Ivy rubs the starburst and thready mosquito remains away with the side of her thumb. "I don't think that's anything to worry about."

It isn't.

Silence falls and eyes avert as Ivy walks into the Food-Star.

The checkout clerk looks at the name on Ivy's credit card, but only says: "Paper or plastic?"

Back outside, the sky is festively sunshiny, though gigantic clouds mount in shades of cream, blue, and gold toward the upper edge of the troposphere. One can look at those clouds and imagine monstrous forces of nature stirring within them. Ivy doesn't. The clouds are just weather.

The Food-Star has been emptied of candles and size-D batteries—the two main objectives of Ivy's expedition. She leaves the store with twenty-four cans of tuna fish, twenty-four cans of peaches, a dozen boxes of vacuum-packed milk, two giant boxes of Cheerios, and one plastic jar of yellow mustard—all items on her mother's shopping list, which bears a title: "EMERGENCY."

In the Food-Star parking lot, a young blond woman asks Ivy if she has been saved.

"What are you talking about?" says Ivy.

"Saved!" The young woman's smile brightens distinctly. "You know," she says, "have you found Jesus?"

"There's no point in talking to me," says Ivy.

When the young woman only blinks and ups her smile volume, Ivy says, "I don't believe in God."

"Why not?"

"Because I know that I am entirely insignificant, doomed to complete extinction, and I see no reason to pretend otherwise."

Isabel Tries Out Divinity

Isabel is six, Ivy four. The sky above the buildings outside their apartment windows is the color of a dusty chalkboard, and the

light coming down onto the street is exactly the color of boredom.
Nothing can move in that light. Nothing changes.

"Do you love me?" Isabel asks. Ivy says nothing. "Will you do
what I tell you to?" Isabel asks. Ivy picks up a plastic frying pan and
puts it on the pink cardboard stove. She is not looking at her sister.
"Do you want to play a game?" asks Isabel.

"What?" says Ivy.

Isabel has to think about raw liver to keep from smiling. Merely
from the way Ivy's moon-bright eyes look up at her from the floor,
Isabel knows everything that will happen.

"Hide-and-seek," she says.

Ivy looks back at her frying pan. She makes a *tick-tick-tick* in the
back of her throat, which is the sound of the cardboard burner
lighting. But Isabel knows this is only a diversionary tactic. Ivy loves
hide-and-seek.

"Only this time," says Isabel, "we will both hide."

Now Ivy looks at Isabel. In the faint pursing of Ivy's glossy, plum-
red lips, Isabel sees hope. And in the check-mark crinkle of Ivy's
right eyebrow, Isabel sees curiosity. These are weaknesses: hope
and curiosity. Isabel almost feels sorry for her sister.

"You'll hide first," says Isabel. "And while you're hiding, I'll hide
too. Then you count to twenty and try to find me."

"I want to hide first," says Ivy.

"You will," says Isabel. "That's what I just said."

"No. I want *you* to find *me*."

"I will. As soon as you find me, it will be my turn to find you."

The pursing of Ivy's lips intensifies. What was once hope is now
determination. Isabel has to move quickly or she will lose her advantage.

"I promise I'll hide in this room," she says, "so it will be easy to
find me."

"OK," says Ivy.

"Where do you want to hide?" Isabel asks. "Under the bed? In
the closet?" These are the most boring places in the world. Isabel
only asks to give her sister the illusion of choice. "What about the
trunk? You could also hide in the trunk."

The trunk is on the floor at the end of Isabel's bed, and it is the
place where their mother keeps clean sheets and pillowcases. Also,
at the very bottom is a trove of Ivy's baby clothes. It is the baby
clothes that so endear the trunk to Ivy. She likes to climb inside,

lie on the bedding, and cover her face with one of the tiny velvet dresses she wore as a newborn. When she does this, she says she is taking her "secret nap." Sometimes she closes the lid of the trunk; sometimes she doesn't.

"OK," says Ivy.

Ivy curls up inside the trunk. Isabel closes the lid and sits on top of it. "Are you counting?" she says. When Ivy doesn't answer, she adds, "I can't hide until you start counting."

Isabel hears Ivy's naptime voice counting. She waits until Ivy misses thirteen, which she always does, and then she says, "You forgot thirteen."

"You're not hiding," says Ivy.

"Yes, I am."

"You're sitting on the trunk."

"No, I'm not. I'm hiding. I'm in a special place. I bet you'll never find me. Finish counting and then come out and try to find me. Don't forget thirteen."

"Thirteen," Ivy says in her naptime voice. "Fourteen."

When Ivy reaches twenty, nothing happens. Maybe she has fallen asleep. "Come and find me," says Isabel.

Ivy's knees or elbows clunk against the trunk's side. Isabel feels the upward pressure of Ivy's hand against the lid just beneath her right buttock.

"Get off," says Ivy.

Isabel says nothing.

"Get off!" Ivy shoves the lid harder. Isabel feels the pressure, but it is entirely ineffectual. The top of the lid bulges a bit, but the lid's edges do not lift off the trunk's lip.

"Get *off!*" Now Ivy is shouting. She shoves again, still to no effect.

Isabel is smiling and working hard to keep from laughing. "Come and find me!"

"You're not hiding. You're lying!"

"I *am* hiding," says Isabel. "And you will never be able to find me. Never ever." Now she is laughing, but she doesn't care.

When Ivy flips onto her back and uses her feet to push up against the lid, it rises a quarter-inch off the lip of the trunk, so Isabel reaches down and pulls up the hinged brass lock, fastening it. Now Ivy doesn't have a prayer.

Isabel sits Indian style while her sister screams and kicks, all to no avail. After a while Ivy stops kicking, stops saying anything. Silence accumulates. Isabel thinks: "When she starts to cry, I will let her out." And a little later she thinks, "I will let her out because I am merciful."

One Leg Is Both the Same

Isabel and Ivy's natural tendency is to see human society as a pointlessly complex mechanical device of no use to anybody, and most likely broken. They know, however, that theirs is a minority opinion, and so, from a very early age, they have compared what people actually say and do to what it would be reasonable to say and do, hoping they might discover what it takes to feel at home in the world. These efforts—disappointing from the get-go and worse over time—nonetheless endow the sisters with certain intellectual habits that propel them through college, sociology graduate school, and into tenure-track jobs: Isabel at a university in Nebraska, Ivy, in Indiana.

Ivy's primary area of study is the financial futures market, where traders make billions by buying and selling absolutely nothing. Isabel investigates apocalyptic cults and is particularly interested in the notion of the apocalypse as moral reckoning. The thesis of her book, *Revenge: The Ethics of World Destruction,* is contained in its opening sentence: "As the extinction of life on earth will have no positive or negative effect on the rest of the universe, it is an event entirely without moral significance, and it is precisely this insignificance that inspires the moral furor of apocalypse cultists." *Revenge* has been submitted to seventeen university and academic publishers and so far has no takers.

"Too many mathematical formulas," says Ivy.

"Maybe you should tone it down a bit," says her mother. "After all, *some* people will care if the world ends. That's an effect, isn't it?"

"Not at all," says Isabel. "No people, no effect."

Her mother touches the index and middle fingers of her right hand to the ear stem of her glasses, as if she is listening to a secret message. Then she takes her glasses off, shrinking her eyes to the size of kidney beans. She blinks and doesn't seem to know where she is.

Field Work

Now it is Isabel's turn. Her mother insists that they have at least one set of D batteries for their solitary flashlight, which, at present, casts a faint, coppery illumination, undetectable after a yard and a half. The mission is hopeless, of course, but Isabel has undertaken it because actual failure is the only way of shutting up her mother.

Isabel is standing in front of the Food-Star, holding a plastic bag containing twenty-four cans of tuna fish, two Snickers bars, and a packet of black pantyhose. The parking lot descends partway down the hillside forming the northern edge of a valley big enough to contain an entire county—which in fact it does. On the valley's southern edge, blueberry- and plum-colored mountains rise to Isabel's eye level and higher. And above those mountains, bulbous gray and slate blue weather is stacked so precariously high, it looks as though it could topple into the valley at any minute.

"Excuse me," says a smiling young woman.

"Yes," says Isabel.

"Are you saved?" The young woman is wearing a T-shirt with the word GOD over one breast and ME over the other, and a red heart in between, more or less where her own thumping, pumping, flesh-and-blood heart is located.

"In what sense?" says Isabel. She has taken a professional interest in this young woman.

Something like the momentary disintegration of a digital image transpires on the young woman's face, and her smile intensifies. "Did I talk to you yesterday?"

"No," says Isabel.

The sheer confidence of Isabel's denial causes another disintegration in the area of the young woman's lightly freckled nose.

"'Saved' in what sense?" says Isabel.

"You know: Have you been saved by Jesus?"

"No, I haven't."

This answer seems to restore the young woman's confidence. Her smile engages in a delicate pas de deux with the sympathetic and sorrowful uptilting of her eyebrows. "Would you like to be?"

"What would I have to do?" says Isabel.

"Just let Jesus into your heart!" There is no sun out, but sunbeams ricochet off the young woman's whitened teeth.

"Is that difficult?" asks Isabel.

"It's the easiest thing in the world!"

"Are *you* saved?" Isabel asks.

"Of course!"

"How do you know?"

The sunbeams disappear from the young woman's teeth. Her uptilted eyebrows sink and collide. "I just do."

"What if I told you that I know that you are *not* saved?"

The young woman is silent. The whole time she and Isabel have been talking, she has been clutching a stack of glossy brochures in her right hand. The brochures depict periwinkle-blue skies, white doves flying, a steeple, and the faces of happy children. The young woman lifts the brochures to cover the inscription across her chest.

"I'm sorry to disturb you," she says.

"You're not disturbing me. I just want to know what you think."

"About what?"

"If I were to tell you that I know you are not saved, what would you think?"

"I would think that you are wrong."

"But how can you say that? What makes you so sure that what I 'just know' is any less reliable than what you 'just know'?"

The young woman straightens her back and lifts her chin. The closest she comes to smiling now is a sarcastic curl at the corner of her mouth. "If you have to ask me that question, then I feel sorry for you."

"Why?" asks Isabel.

But the young woman has turned and is walking toward the other exit of the Food-Star. She is wearing periwinkle sweatpants, with a single word across the twin grapefruits of her buttocks—a word that would seem to render a rather intimate detail about the condition of her genitals.

Force of Habit

Isabel and Ivy's father is a tilted man. His left eye is lower than his right; ditto the arrangement of his shoulders. And no matter what the right side of his mouth might be doing, the left is always down-turned, flaccid. He is sitting crookedly in a wing chair, looking at Ivy with his cow-brown eyes. Her mother sits in an identical chair, back straight, head upright, hands clutching the chair's upholstered arms, as if she is on a roller coaster waiting for the ride to start. Her eyes are the color of kidney beans.

"I don't understand what you are saying," says Ivy's mother.

"Fact!" says her father. "Fact! You question fact?!"

"I'm not questioning it," says Ivy. "I am only saying that, from a statistical point of view, the odds of all six having such pale eyes are so staggeringly low that sometimes, when I look at the children, I have to fight to convince myself that they are not hallucinations."

Kama Sutra

Isabel is sixteen. "How did you do it?" she asks. Ivy is fourteen. "It was easy," Ivy says.

Isabel and Ivy are sitting on a bench in Carl Schurz Park. Through a row of vertical wrought-iron bars they can see horizontally gradated strips of bluish, yellowish, and gray—with the gray being the river. Isabel is not looking at Ivy. She can't because Ivy does not look like herself. Ivy is smiling the way teenage girls smile in tampon ads.

"I knew right off the bat it had to be a loser or a nerd," says Ivy. "Neil Madbow would have been nice, but I had to be practical. Of course, I also had to be sure he was straight."

"Couldn't you just take your chances?"

"No," says Ivy. "I didn't want to waste any time. So I came up with a test."

"A test?" Isabel looks sideways at her sister. Her eyes are like two ice balls that have rolled downhill and gotten clamped under her brow.

"Yeah. Gay guys like shoes. So I started carrying around that issue of *D-Tox* with the picture of Jessamine Duff on the cover. I figured if I showed it to a guy, and he started talking about her shoes, I'd go find someone else."

"How did it work?"

"Well, I only tried it on Vince Lopez."

"Vince Lopez!" Isabel opens her nostrils and crinkles her brow. All the girls call Vince Lopez "Thermometer" because he is so skinny and his whole face is just one red zit. Isabel thinks of saying something, but doesn't.

"Yeah." Now Ivy is the one not looking at her sister.

"Did he pass?"

"Of course he passed. I wouldn't be telling you this if he didn't pass." That tampon smile is back on Ivy's face. Isabel looks away.

"So then what?" says Isabel.

"I asked him if he thought Jessamine Duff was wearing thong panties."

"What did he say?"

"He didn't say anything at first. Then he said she probably was. So then I asked him if he liked thong panties. He said he guessed he did. 'Why?' I said. And he said he didn't know, he just did. So then I asked him what was his favorite part of a girl's body."

"Don't you think that was a little too obvious?" says Isabel.

"I did worry about that a bit. Especially when he laughed and said that was a stupid question. But I decided it was too late to turn back, so I said, 'No, really, I'd just like to know.' And he said, 'Which part do you think?' And when he said that—you remember that book we found in Aunt Tessa's drawer? The one about the cowboy?"

"*The Hot Gun?*"

"Right. Remember that line about how his gaze *locked* with hers?"

"No," says Isabel.

"Well, that was exactly what happened. When Vince said, 'Which part do you think?' his gaze locked with mine. I couldn't believe it."

"So then what did you do?"

"I asked him why he liked it. And this time he didn't laugh. Just looked a little sick. Then he said, 'Because it feels good.' 'How do you know?' I asked. 'How do you think?' he said. 'Have you ever done it?' I said. He looked like he didn't know whether to vomit or run away. So I decided I had to make him relax and feel better. 'Well, I never have,' I said."

"Did it work?"

"I guess so. He started smiling then. So of course I had to go. I'd been thinking about all this for a really long time, and it was clear to me that, even though it would have been simpler to get everything over at once, the only way I was really going to get him to do what I wanted was to make him suffer. So I said I had to go to history. That was lunchtime. I saw him again last period when he was on his way to gym. He gave me this big smile. I gave him one back. But I made sure to get out of school the instant the bell sounded, because I had to make him wait twenty-four hours or it wouldn't work."

"How did you know?"

"It's obvious. Just look at any book or movie—the ones in which the boy is the hero, I mean. The boys always have at least one sleepless night before they get the girl. Anyhow, the next day I saw him in homeroom and he looked miserable, like he was afraid to look at me. I didn't say anything to him then, but when I ran into him in the hallway I told him he had a nice shirt. He didn't know what to do. His red face just got redder. 'Bye,' I said, and I walked away. Then after school I walked by his locker as if by accident. 'Hi,' I said. 'Hi,' he said. 'What you doing?' 'Nothing much.' 'Me neither.' After that it was easy. He pretended he was inviting me up to his apartment so I could listen to the Misfits, but he'd already told me his mother wouldn't be home until dinnertime. The only problem was he didn't know how to get it into me. I finally had to grab hold of it and stick it in myself."

"What was it like?"

"Well, it was really different than I thought it was going to be. It hurt more. But still, it was interesting. I'll probably do it again. They say you don't really get the full effect until you've done it a few times."

Isabel doesn't say anything for almost a minute. Then she asks if she can borrow the *D-Tox*. The next day she does everything that Ivy did, and it seems to be working perfectly. But then, when she is alone in the boy's room and her panties are already around her ankles, he tells her he doesn't want to take advantage of her.

"Maybe that's the problem," Ivy says later that night. "You can't do it with a nice guy. You have to choose someone who's a real jerk and doesn't mind taking advantage of you. That's why I chose Vince. Not only is he a nerd, but he's a total asshole."

Isabel keeps trying, but she can't get anyone to take advantage of her until she is twenty and she meets Walter Tedesco. Ivy does it three times with Vince. After that, she figures she's gotten the full effect and doesn't do it again until Isabel announces her engagement to Walter. That very night Ivy goes to a frat

party and shows her *D-Tox* to a business school student she has
never met before, Paul Henberry. He doesn't want to take advantage of her either. But eventually he changes his mind, and six
months later he and Ivy are engaged. The sisters arrange a joint
wedding.

The End Is Near

Isabel and Ivy have a private language. You might not notice at
first, but if you pay close attention you will find that many of their
words only resemble English. "Hope," for example, is a profoundly
embarrassing word to both sisters, and "discipline" has the cozy
feel of a puppy asleep in front of a fireplace.

Their language does contain wholly invented words, however,
the earliest being "lubby," a noun for a tiny part of their bodies
that—when they were five and three—they thought no one possessed but themselves. ("Lubby" also refers to the feeling evoked
by touching that part.) In elementary school, they invented
"humpless," a word for that condition—experienced most intensely at birthday and pajama parties—of not knowing who is
crazy: everybody in the room or you. A related but more recent
term is "herd dreaming," which refers to a mass of people being
possessed by the same delusion: fainting epidemics, or national-
ism, or the craze for teeth whitening. The sisters also apply this
term to the peculiar phenomenon of grown men and women—re-
positories all, ostensibly, of the capacity for rational thought—sitting in the dark, watching light flicker through strips of celluloid,
and gasping, laughing, and weeping, not merely as if they are
witnessing the tribulations of real people, but as if they are actually living those tribulations themselves. The sisters always feel
ridiculous when they accompany other people to the movies. And
bored. Though Ivy sometimes also feels panicky.

To Isabel and Ivy, the approaching hurricane is nothing so
much as an intense instance of herd dreaming. In a part of the
country where hurricanes rarely do more than blow the dead
wood out of elderly maples, flood a few basements, and leave a
solitary street without power, people are hurriedly X-ing their windows with duct tape and filling pasta pots, buckets, and bathtubs
with water. Pickup trucks loaded with sandbags, plywood, and jer-

rycans of gasoline are dopplerizing day and night, up and down
along the two-lane road in front of the Soros house, and everyone
is telling hurricane horror stories: a woman is pulverized when a
willow falls on her car; a farmer is electrocuted by the high-tension
cable writhing in his field, spewing blue-white sparks; a six-year-old
is lacerated by an imploding window. People's faces are dark with
seriousness as they tell these stories; their voices are urgent and
low—and yet they are elated. You can see it in their every word
and gesture. It's the same all over town. People dart in and out of
stores with the lightest of steps. No one seems ever to have had a
cynical thought; not a single heart has ever been touched by sorrow. Even Isabel and Ivy's own parents look a decade younger, and
their father has regained the capacity to distinguish *t* from *d* when
he speaks, and *s* from *sh*.

But if either sister even hints that catastrophe might not be
looming, people's brows ding with irritation. "Have to run," they
mutter. "No time to talk." Or they say, "Better safe than sorry." Or
"You can't be too careful." Or sometimes they just regard the sisters with slack-jawed incomprehension.

The Illusion of Choice

Little Jerry is standing in the darkness beside Ivy's bed. The house
is like a cardboard box in the middle of a field in which a pack of
wolves is having a silent wrestling match. The sound of the wind
against the sides of the house is exactly like the sound of wolf fur
against cardboard. The sound of the wind in the trees is exactly
like wolves breathing through their teeth. The big branches falling
onto the roof and lawn sound exactly like the thumping of paws
as the wolves tumble, pounce, and rear. For Jerry, barefoot on the
bare floor beside his mother's bed, there is next to nothing between the darkness where he stands and the frenzy of the universe.

"What are you doing here?" Ivy asks in her sleep.

"I'm scared."

"Why?"

"Because the wind is scary."

Ivy is not asleep now, but she has not moved from the position
she was in when she was asleep. "Were you brave enough to come
down here all by yourself?"

Jerry doesn't answer.

"Answer me."

His answer is too quiet for Ivy to hear. She tells him so.

"I'm sorry," he says.

"Of course you were brave enough to come down here all by yourself. You wouldn't be here if you weren't. And if you are brave enough to come down here all by yourself, you are brave enough to go back up to bed and go to sleep."

"I want to sleep in your bed."

"You know that's not allowed."

Jerry says nothing. Ivy cannot see him, except as a thumb shape of perfect black in the gloom of a moonless night.

"There's nothing to be afraid of," says Ivy. "It's only the wind."

"Is this the hurricane?"

"No. The hurricane won't be here until the morning."

"Are we going to die?"

"Of course we're going to die. But not in the hurricane. The hurricane is nothing. The hurricane is just a way for the television stations to expand their audiences so that they can sell advertisements for more money. It's also a way for people who have boring lives to feel that their lives are not boring. It's a fairy story, that's all it is, and fairy stories aren't real. So go back to bed."

"Paulette says the trees are going to fall on the roof and we are all going to die."

"Paulette is an idiot. Go back to bed."

"I'm scared."

Now Ivy is sitting up. She is breathing in a way that is not unlike the breathing of the wolves. "Listen, Jerry, we've been through all this before. Some children allow themselves to become afraid because of irrational ideas. But you're not going to be like those children, are you?"

Jerry makes a very small noise in his throat, but it is nothing like a word.

"Fear is an entirely useless emotion," says Ivy. "And if I were to let you come into my bed, I would be acting as if there actually were something for you to be afraid of, wouldn't I? And, on top of that, your being in my bed with me would not change one single thing. It would still be the middle of the night. The wind would still be blowing. And whatever is going to happen would still be going to happen."

"But if the trees fall on the roof, they won't hit me if I'm down here with you."

"The trees are not going to fall on the roof." Ivy had been speaking in a fierce whisper, but now her voice is loud enough to be heard in other rooms. She doesn't care. "Go back to your bed this instant."

For a long time Jerry does nothing at all. Then there is a shifting in the darkness, and she can hear his sweat-sticky feet making kissing noises along the floorboards. The door opens, then closes softly. The latch slides back into the door plate with a minute *spro-ing*.

Where Jerry was standing, there is now a larger thumb shape of perfect black. It is Ivy's mother in her nightgown.

"How could you treat your little boy like that?" says Ivy's mother.

"I'm doing it for his own good."

"I never spoke to you so heartlessly," she says. "I would never have done that in a million years. I was always careful to be sure you and Isabel knew I loved you with all of my heart."

"Do you think that made any difference?"

For a long time the only sounds in the room come from the wind against the walls. Ivy closes her eyes. When she opens them her mother is gone.

This Is This

Isabel and Ivy's father slides his left shoe along the floor as if it is filled with sand and stitched to the bottom of his empty pant leg. He moves his left arm mainly by whipping it with his shoulder. He can push the power button on the radio, but he can't turn the knob to tune in the signal. That's why the announcer sounds like he is talking through wax paper. "Hear that?" her father says, as Isabel comes into the room.

"Hear what?" says Isabel.

"Floods," he says. "Listen."

But that is the exact instant the kitchen light flickers, goes brown, goes gold, platinum, then permanently dark. The radio is silent. Some motor that is always on in the house is not on now, and the absence of its low, continuous hum makes the wind outside louder.

"Floods," says Isabel's father. "Floods, they say."

"Not here," says Isabel.

"Everywhere," says her father. "The whole county."

"But we're on high ground," she says.

She goes to the window and sees that water in the stream is racing, whitecapped and the color of her lips. It has already embraced the roots of the willow and is lapping at the southernmost leg of the picnic table where she likes to work on her computer.

"The lights are out," says Paulette, who has just entered the kitchen in her red pajamas with the feet on them and the hatch in the back.

"Go back upstairs," says Isabel, "and put on your clothes. Tell everyone that they can't come down until they are in their clothes. Shoes too."

"The wrath of Ivy," says Isabel's father.

"That's a stupid joke, Dad."

"I mean the hurricane."

"I know. But it's still a stupid joke."

It is an hour later and Isabel and Ivy's mother is sitting at the table, an empty bowl of cereal in front of her. "What are we going to do when the food goes bad?" she says. Her hair is turban shaped and the color of shredded wheat. Her kidney-bean eyes are made huge and concave by the thick lenses of her glasses.

"It's not going to go bad," says Ivy, wiping Jerry's mouth with the kitchen towel. "You are such a slob," she tells him. "The fridge will keep the food cold for days," she tells her mother.

"What about after that?"

"Tuna fish," says Dr. Soros. "Lots of tuna fish!"

"Guys," says Gwenny, standing in the doorway between the kitchen and the living room.

"I wish you had gotten some batteries," says Ivy and Isabel's mother.

"Guys," says Gwenny.

"What?" says Isabel.

Gwenny doesn't answer, just looks over her shoulder into the living room.

A braid of lip-red water is flowing across the hickory floorboards. All at once everyone can hear the sound of a cow urinating somewhere in the living room.

"It's coming right under the front door," says Gwenny.

Almost

When Dr. Soros panics, he loses all ability to coordinate his left side, so Isabel has to carry him in her arms out to the white van and buckle him into his seat.

As the family exits the house, the flood is flowing ankle deep through the front door. Gwenny, the last to leave, tries to pull the door shut behind her, but the water forms a small mountain against it, and the door flies open again and again. Finally she gives up.

Ivy is in the driver's seat. Isabel rides shotgun. The rest of the family crams into seats beside and behind Dr. Soros. The van's side door slides shut.

Ivy steers the van through the river that has covered their driveway and half their lawn and is flowing through the house. "Where should I go?" she asks.

"Up," says Isabel. "Where else?"

The road in front of their house is covered by a hissing, pinkish sheet of water. But after a few yards the road is only rainstorm wet and pocked with leaping gray drop-splashes. Ivy heads east, then turns west, then east again, then west—uphill all the while.

"We're away from the worst of it," says Isabel and Ivy's mother.

Paulette is sitting with her neck upstretched and her eyes fixed on the back of her grandfather's head. She is making swallowing noises. Warm tears mix with the raindrops on her cheeks.

Isabel and Ivy say nothing. Even through the closed windows they can hear a roar so forceful and low, it is more like the shuddering of the earth than an actual sound. Where normally there is only a cattail-clogged trickle, an avenue of red surf pours down the hillside. This is the very stream that has subsumed their yard and is rearranging the furniture inside their house. As the roar becomes louder, the sisters trade glances but still say nothing. They round a bend, mount a crest, and at last can see that the bridge crossing the stream has held. Water shoots in a pink spume out of its downhill side.

Both sisters have been holding their breath. Now their throats unclamp; air flows from their lungs. Ivy smiles, and accelerates.

A tree trunk as thick as an oil drum and as long as a salad bar bucks, rolls, and tumbles through the lip-red water. It is approaching the bridge at the exact same speed as the van. The trunk reaches the bridge first, its rooty end striking one side of the culvert, its snapped-off end slamming into the other. The torrent makes a sound like a lion clearing its throat, because now almost all of the water is prevented from flowing under the culvert, and the water that does flow there rockets over the tree flank in a blade of froth. The water blocked by the tree dithers and roils for the second or two it takes to mount the riverbank, then it surges across the road exactly where the van is driving. Had Ivy's foot depressed the gas pedal by even one more quarter-inch, the van would have made it onto the bridge and to the safety of the high ground on the other side.

Sorority

Ivy is rendered useless, as are the van's steering wheel, brakes, gas pedal, and motor. The van is swept sideways across the road, tail-wise down the embankment, and then sideways again through a cow pasture that is now a red ocean. For a very brief moment after the van has been swept back into the streambed, where the current flows most forcefully, it is pointing in the same direction that the water is flowing, and this allows Ivy to feel that she is driving on the red surf. Then the van hits a steep-sloped pyramid of rock the size of a garage and is anchored there, nose upward, by the current, which roars pinkly around its lower half, smashing all the windows and sweeping away four of the children and both grandparents before Isabel and Ivy, in the front seat, have a chance to look around.

Ivy's eyes are moon bright and blind. She is shouting something, but Isabel cannot hear what it is. The sound of the water has grown very, very large, and Ivy's voice has grown mouse small. The door next to Isabel is gone, and so is the sliding door to the back. Or maybe the sliding door is just open. For some reason Isabel finds it impossible to tell what has happened to the door, and she will never possess more than a shaky hypothesis.

Gwenny—her own daughter, her eldest child—is clinging to the post between the front and back doors with both arms, her cheek bleeding from a row of triangular punctures, her eyes also moon bright. Isabel pushes Gwenny's ribs. "Let go!" Isabel shouts. "Let go! Get out of here!"

At first Gwenny looks at her mother as if she doesn't know who she is. Then recognition dawns, and with it, that sort of pliable stupidity that is a form of trust. She lets go, slides away from the van, but at the last second Isabel shoves her with such force that she lands against the pyramid of rock with half her body out of the water. Her elbows (pointing skyward, angled like grasshopper legs) waver back and forth as she lifts herself out of the water. Then she is kneeling on top of the rock.

Little Jerry has climbed from the back seat, where he once sat next to his grandfather, and is clutching his mother around the neck. Ivy can't unfasten her seat belt. Isabel does it for her, then unfastens her own. When she slides out the door and into the water, she finds that, in fact, it is easy to clamber up onto the rock. Gwenny has vanished. There is a dense wood of black sticks and shining leaves behind the rock. Gwenny is there somewhere. Isabel knows that if she looks again, she will see her.

Ivy and Jerry slide toward the door. As their weight shifts within the van, the van shifts on the rock. They both reach for Isabel, who manages to grab one hand of each, and as the van slides out from under them and rolls with a groan and a heavy sigh into the current, she pulls them onto the rock—but not quite. The river takes hold of their legs and, in an instant, they are dragged back into the red water—Isabel too, still holding on to their hands.

All is roaring and bubbly dimness.

Then Isabel feels gravel beneath her feet and finds that she can stand, her head and shoulders out of the water. She is not sure at first, but soon she sees that she is still holding Ivy's and Jerry's hands, and they are both looking at her with the terrific seriousness of the mortally ill. Isabel realizes that she has been swept into an eddy behind the rock and that the water is only swirling idly around her pelvis and legs. Ivy and Jerry are still in the racing current, however, and Isabel is leaning backward to keep them all from being pulled downstream.

Isabel realizes three things in a single instant:

1. She is not strong enough to continue to hold her sister and her nephew; the exhaustion in her shoulders and hands has reached that point when it is searing pain.

2. Even as she is constantly stepping backward in a sort of reverse pedaling, the gravel beneath her feet is constantly giving way and she is being pulled inexorably toward the current.

3. If she lets go of Jerry, Ivy might still drag her into the flood, whereas if she lets go of Ivy and continues to hold on to Jerry, there is a chance that she might be able to lift him to safety and then climb up after him.

Isabel conveys all this information to her sister in a single glance.

As Ivy slides away on the flood, her eyes are locked on Isabel's with complete comprehension. Ivy's face grows smaller and smaller atop the current, and she seems to be shooting backward in time: not thirty-nine anymore, but thirty-five, then twenty-eight, then seventeen, twelve, five—until, just before she disappears over the falls some hundred yards downstream, her face seems to journey through something other than time, because, as small as it continues to grow, it never looks remotely like an infant's face, but more like that of an elf, then a fairy, then the bride on a wedding cake, and finally like a dotted face on a pencil-tip eraser.

Then Ivy is gone.

Isabel's back is against the pyramid rock and Jerry's back is against her chest.

"Mommy!" he cries, clawing at the red water with both hands.

"Hush," says Isabel.

"Mommy! Mommy!" Jerry strains helplessly against the rigid rings of Isabel's arms.

"Hush," says Isabel. "There's nothing we can do."

"Mommy! Mommy! Mommy! Mommy!"

"Come on," she says. "We have to get onto the rock, or we'll get washed away too."

"Mahhhh-meeee!" screams Jerry. "Mahhhh-meeee!"

"As soon as this is over, we'll come back and look for her," says Isabel. "I promise. But we have to go now or we are going to die."

"Noooo!" shouts Jerry. "Mahhhh-meeee!"

Isabel has to fight the urge to let him go too. And then she wonders if that wouldn't, in fact, be the best thing to do.

KAREN RUSSELL

Madame Bovary's Greyhound

FROM *Zoetrope: All-Story*

I. First Love

THEY TOOK WALKS to the beech grove at Banneville, near the abandoned pavilion. Foxglove and gillyflowers, beige lichen growing in one thick, crawling curtain around the socketed windows. Moths blinked wings at them, crescents of blue and red and tiger-yellow, like eyes caught in a net.

Emma sat and poked at the grass with the skeletal end of her parasol, as if she were trying to blind each blade.

"Oh, *why* did I ever get married?" she moaned aloud, again and again.

The greyhound whined with her, distressed by her distress. Sometimes, in a traitorous fugue, the dog forgot to be unhappy and ran off to chase purple butterflies or murder shrewmice, or to piss a joyful stream onto the topiaries. But generally, if her mistress was crying, so was the puppy. Her name was Djali, and she had been a gift from the young woman's husband, Dr. Charles Bovary.

Emma wept harder as the year grew older and the temperature dropped, folding herself into the white monotony of trees, leaning further and further into the bare trunks. The dog would stand on her hind legs and lick at the snow that fused Emma's shoulders to the coarse wood, as if trying to loosen a hardening glue, and the whole forest would quiver and groan together in sympathy with the woman, and her phantom lovers, and Djali.

At Banneville the wind came directly from the sea and covered the couple in a blue-salt caul. The greyhound loved most when she and Emma were outside like this, bound by the membrane of a gale. Yet as sunset fell Djali became infected again by her woman's nameless terrors. Orange and red, they seemed to sweat out of the wood. The dog smelled nothing alarming, but love stripped her immunity to the internal weathers of Emma Bovary.

The blood-red haze switched to a silvery blue light, and Emma shuddered all at once, as if in response to some thicketed danger. They returned to Tostes along the highway.

The greyhound was ignorant of many things. She had no idea, for example, that she was a greyhound. She didn't know that her breed had originated in southern Italy, an ancient pet in Pompeii, a favorite of the thin-nosed English lords and ladies, or that she was perceived to be affectionate, intelligent, and loyal. What she did know, with a whole-body thrill, was the music of her woman coming up the walk, the dizzying explosion of perfume as the door swung wide. She knew when her mistress was pleased with her, and that approval was the fulcrum of her happiness.

"Viscount! Viscount!" Emma whimpered in her sleep. (Rodolphe would come onto the scene later, after the greyhound's flight, and poor Charlie B. never once featured in his wife's unconscious theater.) Then Djali would stand and pace stiff-legged through the cracked bowl of the cold room into which her mistress's dreams were leaking, peering with pricked ears into shadows. It was a strange accordion that linked the woman and the dog: Vaporous drafts caused their pink and gray bellies to clutch inward at the same instant. Moods blew from one mind to the other, delight and melancholy. In the blue atmosphere of the bedroom, the two were very nearly (but never quite) one creature.

Even asleep, the little greyhound trailed after her madame, through a weave of green stars and gas lamps, along the boulevards of Paris. It was a conjured city that no native would recognize—Emma Bovary's head on the pillow, its architect. Her Paris was assembled from a guidebook with an out-of-date map, and from the novels of Balzac and Sand, and from her vividly disordered recollections of the viscount's ball at La Vaubyessard, with its odor of dying flowers, burning flambeaux, and truffles. (Many neighborhoods within the city's quivering boundaries, curiously

enough, smelled identical to the viscount's dining room.) A rose
and gold glow obscured the storefront windows, and cathedral
bells tolled continuously as they strolled past the same four land-
marks: a tremulous bridge over the roaring Seine, a vanilla-white
dress shop, the vague façade of the opera house—overlaid in
more gold light—and the crude stencil of a theater. All night they
walked like that, companions in Emma's phantasmal labyrinth,
suspended by her hopeful mists, and each dawn the dog would
wake to the second Madame Bovary, the lightly snoring woman on
the mattress, her eyes still hidden beneath a peacock sleep mask.
Lumped in the coverlet, Charles's blocky legs tangled around her
in an apprehensive pretzel, a doomed attempt to hold her in their
marriage bed.

II. A Change of Heart

Is there any love as tireless as a dog's in search of its master? Whenever Emma was off shopping for nougat in the market or visiting God in the churchyard, Djali was stricken by the madness of
her absence. The dog's futile hunt through the house turned her
maniacal, cannibalistic: She scratched her fur until it became wet
and dark. She paced the halls, pausing only to gnaw at her front
paws. Félicité, the Bovarys' frightened housekeeper, was forced to
imprison her in a closet with a water dish.

The dog's change of heart began in September, some weeks
after Madame Bovary's return from La Vaubyessard, where she'd
dervished around in another man's arms and given up forever
on the project of loving Charles. It is tempting to conclude that
Emma somehow transmitted her wanderlust to Djali; but perhaps
this is a sentimental impulse, a storyteller's desire to sync two flick-
ering hearts.

One day Emma's scents began to stabilize. Her fragrance became musty, ordinary, melting into the house's stale atmosphere
until the woman was nearly invisible to the animal. Djali licked al-
mond talc from Emma's finger-webbing. She bucked her head under the madame's hand a dozen times, waiting for the old passion
to seize her, yet her brain was uninflamed. The hand had become
generic pressure, damp heat. No joy snowed out of it as Emma me-

chanically stroked between Djali's ears, her gold wedding band rubbing a raw spot into the fur, branding the dog with her distraction. There in the bedroom, together and alone, they watched the rain fall.

By late February, at the same time Charles Bovary was dosing his young wife with valerian, the dog began refusing her mutton chops. Emma stopped checking her gaunt face in mirrors, let dead flies swim in the blue glass vases. The dog neglected to bark at her red-winged nemesis, the rooster. Emma quit playing the piano. The dog lost her zest for woodland homicide. Under glassy bathwater, Emma's bare body as still and bright as quartz in a quarry, she let the hours fill her nostrils with the terrible serenity of a drowned woman. Her gossamer fingers circled her navel, seeking an escape. Fleas held wild circuses on Djali's ass as she lay motionless before the fire for the duration of two enormous logs, unable to summon the energy to spin a hind leg in protest. Her ears collapsed against her skull.

Charles rubbed his hand greedily between Emma's legs and she swatted him off; Emma stroked the dog's neck and Djali went stiff, slid out of reach. Both woman and animal, according to the baffled Dr. Bovary, seemed bewitched by sadness.

This strain of virulent misery, this falling out of love, caused different symptoms, unique disruptions, in dogs and humans.

The greyhound, for example, shat everywhere.

Whereas Emma shopped for fabrics in the town.

On the fifth week of the dog's fall, Charles lifted the bed skirt and discovered the greyhound panting up at him with a dead-eyed calm. He'd been expecting to find his favorite tall socks, blue wool ineptly darned for him by Emma. He screamed.

"Emma! What do you call your little bitch again? There is something the matter with it!"

"Djali," Emma murmured from the mattress. And the dog, helplessly bound to her owner's voice—if not still in love with Madame Bovary, at least indentured to the ghost of her love—rose and licked the lady's bare feet.

"Good girl," sighed Emma.

The animal's dry tongue lolled out of her mouth. Inside her body, a foreboding was hardening into a fact. There was no halting the transformation of her devotion into a nothing.

III. What If?

"If you do not stop making poop in the salon," Félicité growled at the puppy, "I will no longer feed you."

In the sixth month of her life in Tostes, the dog lay glumly on the floor, her pink belly tippled orange by the grated flames, fatally bored. Emma entered the bedroom, and the animal lifted her head from between her tiny polished claws, let it drop again.

"If only I could be you," Emma lamented. "There's no trouble or sorrow in *your* life!" And she soothed the dog in a gurgling monotone, as if she were addressing herself.

Dr. Charles Bovary returned home, whistling after another successful day of leeches and bloodletting in the countryside, to a house of malcontent females:

Emma was stacking a pyramid of greengage plums.

The little greyhound was licking her genitals.

Soon the coarse, unchanging weave of the rug in Emma's bedroom became unbearable. The dog's mind filled with smells that had no origin, sounds that arose from no friction. Unreal expanses. She closed her eyes and stepped cautiously through tall purple grass she'd never seen before in her life.

She wondered if there might not have been some other way, through a different set of circumstances, of meeting another woman; and she tried to imagine those events that had not happened, that shadow life. Her owner might have been a bloody-smocked man, a baritone, a butcher with bags of bones always hidden in his pockets. Or perhaps a child, the butcher's daughter, say, a pork chop–scented girl who loved to throw sticks. Djali had observed a flatulent Malamute trailing his old man in the park, each animal besotted with the other. Blue poodles, inbred and fat, smugly certain of their women's adoration. She'd seen a balding Pomeranian riding high in a toy wagon, doted on by the son of a king. Not all humans were like Emma Bovary.

Out of habit, she howled her old courtship song at Emma's feet, and Emma reached down distractedly, gave the dog's ears a stiff brushing. She was seated before her bedroom vanity, cross-examining a pimple, very preoccupied, for at four o'clock Monsieur Roualt was coming for biscuits and judgment and jelly.

A dog's love is forever. We expect infidelity from one another; we marvel at this one's ability to hold that one's interest for fifty, sixty years; perhaps some of us feel a secret contempt for monogamy even as we extol it, wishing parole for its weary participants. But dogs do not receive our sympathy or our suspicion—from dogs we presume an eternal adoration.

In the strange case of Madame Bovary's greyhound, however, "forever" was a tensed muscle that began to shake. During the Christmas holidays, she had daily seizures before the fireplace, chattering in the red light like a loose tooth. Loyalty was a posture she could no longer hold.

Meanwhile, Emma had become pregnant.

The Bovarys were preparing to move.

On one of the last of her afternoons in Tostes, the dog ceased trembling and looked around. Beyond the cabbage rows, the green grasses waved endlessly away from her, beckoning her. She stretched her hind legs. A terrible itching spread through every molecule of her body, and the last threads of love slipped like a noose from her neck. Nothing owned her anymore. Rolling, moaning, belly to the red sun, she dug her spine into the hill.

"Oh, dear," mumbled the coachman, Monsieur Hivert, watching the dog from the yard. "Something seems to be attacking your greyhound, madame. Bees, I'd wager."

"Djali!" chided Emma, embarrassed that a pet of hers should behave so poorly before the gentlemen. "My goodness! You look possessed!"

IV. Freedom

On the way to Yonville, the greyhound wandered fifty yards from the Bovarys' stagecoach. Then she broke into a run.

"Djaliiiiii!" Emma shrieked, uncorking a spray of champagne-yellow birds from the nearby poplars. *"Stay!"*

Weightlessly the dog entered the forest.

"Stay! Stay! Stay!" the humans called after her, their directives like bullets missing their target. Her former mistress, the screaming woman, was a stranger. And the greyhound lunged forward, riding the shoals of her own green-flecked shadow.

In the late afternoon she paused to drink water from large cups in the mossy roots of unfamiliar trees. She was miles from her old life. Herons sailed over her head, their broad wings flat as palms, stroking her from scalp to tail at an immense distance—a remote benediction—and the dog's mind became empty and smooth. Skies rolled through her chest; her small rib cage and her iron-gray pelt enclosed a blue without limit. She was free.

From a hilltop near a riverbank, through an azure mist, she spotted two creatures with sizzling faces clawing into the water. Cats larger than any she'd ever seen, spear-shouldered and casually savage. Lynxes, a mated pair. Far north for this season. They were three times the size of the Bovarys' barn cat yet bore the same taunting anatomy. Analogous golden eyes. They feasted on some prey that looked of another world—flat, thrashing lives they swallowed whole.

Gazehound, huntress—the dog began to remember what she'd been before she was born.

Winter was still raking its white talons across the forest; spring was delayed that year. Fleshless fingers for tree branches. Not a blade or bud of green yet. The dog sought shelter, but shelter was only physical this far out, always inhuman. Nothing like the soft-bodied sanctuary she'd left behind.

One night the greyhound was caught out in unknown territory, a cold valley many miles from the river. Stars appeared, and she felt a light sprinkling of panic. Now the owls were awake. Pale hunger came shining out of their beaks, looping above their flaming heads like ropes. In Tostes their hooting had sounded like laughter in the trees. But here, with no bedroom rafters to protect her, she watched the boughs blow apart to reveal nocturnal eyes bulging from their recesses like lemons; she heard hollow mouths emitting strange songs. Death's rattle, old wind without home or origin, rode the frequencies above her.

A concentrated darkness screeched and dove near her head, and then another, and then the dog began to run. Dawn was six hours away.

She pushed from the valley floor toward higher ground, eventually finding a narrow fissure in the limestone cliffs. She trotted into the blackness like a small key entering a tall lock. Once inside she was struck by a familiar smell, which confused and upset her. Backlit by the moon, her flat, pointed skull and tucked abdomen cast a hieroglyphic silhouette against the wavy wall.

The greyhound spent the next few days exploring her new home. The soil here was like a great cold nose—wet, breathing, yielding. To eat, she had to hunt the vast network of hollows for red squirrels, voles. A spiderweb of bone and fur soon wove itself in the cave's shadows, where she dragged her kills. When she'd lived with the Bovarys, in the early days of their courtship, Emma would let the puppy lick yellow yolks and golden sugar from the flat of a soft palm.

Undeliberate, absolved of rue and intent, the dog continued to forget Madame Bovary.

Gnawing on a femur near the river one afternoon, she bristled and turned. A deer's head was watching her thoughtfully from the silver rushes—separated, by some incommunicable misfortune, from its body. Its neck terminated in a chaos of crawling black-flies, a spill of jeweled rot like boiling cranberries. Its tongue hung limp like a flag of surrender. Insects were eating an osseous cap between the buck's yellow ears, a white knob the diameter of a sand dollar. A low, bad feeling drove the dog away.

V. Regret

Regret, as experienced by the dog, was physical, kinetic—she turned in circles and doubled back, trying to uncover the scent of her home. She felt feverish. Some organ had never stopped its use-less secretions, even without an Emma to provoke them. Hearth and leash, harsh voice, mutton chop, affectionate thump—she wanted all this again.

There was a day when she passed near the town of Airaines, a mere nine miles from the Bovarys' new residence in Yonville; and had the winds changed at that particular moment and carried a certain woman's lilac-scented sweat to her, this story might have had a very different ending.

One midnight, just after the late April thaw, the dog woke to the sight of a large wolf standing in the cave mouth, nakedly weighing her as prey. And even under that crushing stare she did not cower; rather, she felt elevated, vibrating with some primitive species of admiration for this more pure being, solitary and wholly itself. The wolf swelled with appetites that were ancient, straight-forward—a stellar hunger that was satisfied nightly. An old wound sparkled under a brittle scabbard on its left shoulder, and a young boar's blood ran in torrents from its magnificent jaws. The greyhound's tail began to wag as if cabled to some current; a growl rose midway up her throat. The predator then turned away from her. Panting—*ha-ha-ha*—it licked green slime from the cave wall, crunching the spires of tiny amber snails. The wolf glanced once more around the chasm before springing eastward. Dawn lumbered after, through the pointed firs, unholstering the sun, unable to shoot; and the wind began to howl, as if in lamentation, calling the beast back.

Caught between two equally invalid ways of life, the greyhound whimpered herself toward sleep, unaware that in Yonville Emma Bovary was drinking vinegar in black stockings and sobbing at the exact same pitch. Each had forgotten entirely about the other, yet they retained the same peculiar vacancies within their bodies and suffered the same dread-filled dreams. Love had returned, and it went spoiling through them with no outlet.

In summer the dog crossed a final frontier, eating the greasy liver of a murdered bear in the wide open. The big female had been gut-shot for sport by teenage brothers from Rouen, who'd then been too terrified by the creature's drunken, hauntingly prolonged death throes to wait and watch her ebb out. In a last pitch she'd crashed down a column of saplings, her muzzle frothing with red foam. The greyhound was no scavenger by nature, until nature made her one that afternoon. The three cubs squatted on a log like a felled totem and watched with grave maroon eyes, their orphan hearts pounding in unison.

Still, it would be incorrect to claim that the greyhound was now feral, or fully ingrained in these woods. As a fugitive the dog was a passable success, but as a dog she was a blown spore, drifting everywhere and nowhere, unable to cure her need for a human or her terror at the insufficiency of her single body.

"Our destinies are united now, aren't they?" whispered Rodolphe near the evaporating blue lake, in a forest outside Yonville that might as well have been centuries distant. Crows deluged the sky. Emma sat on a rock, flushed red from the long ride, pushing damp woodchips around with her boot toe. The horses munched leaves in a chorus as Rodolphe lifted her skirts, the whole world rustling with hungers.

In the cave, the dog had a strange dream.

A long, lingering, indistinct cry came from one of the hills far beyond the forest; it mingled with Emma's silence like music.

VI. A Break

The dog shivered. She'd been shivering ceaselessly for how many days and nights now? All the magic of those early weeks had vanished, replaced by a dreary and devoted pain. Winter rose out of her own cavities. It shivered her.

Troubled by the soreness that had entered her muscles, she trotted out of the cave and toward the muddy escarpment where she'd buried a cache of weasel bones. Rain had eroded the path, and in her eagerness to escape her own failing frame, the mute ruminations of her throbbing skeleton, the dog began to run at full bore. Then she was sliding on the mud, her claws scrabbling uselessly at the smooth surface; unable to recover her balance, the greyhound tumbled into a ravine.

An irony:

She had broken her leg.

All at once Emma Bovary's final command came echoing through her: *Stay.*

Sunset jumped above her, so very far above her twisted body, like a heart skipping beats. Blood ran in her eyes. The trees all around swam. She sank further into a soggy pile of dead leaves as the squealing voices of the blackflies rose in clouds.

Elsewhere in the world, Rodolphe Boulanger sat at his writing desk under the impressive head of a trophy stag. Two fat candles were guttering down. He let their dying light flatter him into melancholy—a feeling quite literary. The note before him would end his love affair with Emma.

How shall I sign it? "Devotedly"? No . . . "Your friend"?

The moon, dark red and perfectly round, rose over the horizon.

Deep in the trench, nostalgias swamped the greyhound in the form of olfactory hallucinations: snowflakes, rising yeast, scooped pumpkin flesh, shoe polish, horse-lathered leather, roasting venison, the explosion of a woman's perfume.

She was dying.

She buried her nose in the litterfall, stifling these visions until they ebbed and faded.

It just so happened that a game warden was wandering in that part of the woods, hours later or maybe days. Something in the ravine caught his eye—low to the ground, a flash of unexpected silver. He dropped to his knees for a closer look.

"Oh!" he gasped, callused hands parting the dead leaves.

VII. The Two Huberts

The greyhound lived with the game warden, in a cottage at the edge of a town. He was not a particularly creative man, and he gave the dog his same name: Hubert. He treated her wounds as those of a human child, with poultices and bandages. She slept curled at the foot of his bed and woke each morning to the new green of a million spring buds erupting out of logs, sky-blue birdsong, minced chlorophyll.

"Bonjour, Hubert!" Hubert would call, sending himself into hysterics, and Hubert the dog would bound into his arms—and their love was like this, a joke that never grew old. And like this they passed five years.

Early one December evening Hubert accompanied Hubert to Yonville, to say a prayer over the grave of his mother. The snow hid the tombstones, and only the most stalwart mourners came out for such a grim treasure hunt. Among them was Emma Bovary. From within her hooded crimson cloak she noticed a shape darting between the snowflakes—a gray ghost trotting with its lips peeled back from black gums.

"Oh!" she cried. "How precious you are! Come here—"

Her whistle crashed through the dog's chest, splintering into antipodal desires:

Run.

Stay.

And it was here, at the margin of instinct and rebellion, that the dog encountered herself, felt a shimmering precursor to consciousness—the same stirring that lifted the iron hairs on her neck whenever she peered into mirrors or discovered a small, odorless dog inside a lake. Suddenly, impossibly, she *did* remember: Midnight in Tostes. The walks through the ruined pavilion. Crows at dusk. The tug of a leather leash. Piano music. Egg yolk in a perfumed hand. Sad, impatient fingers scratching her ears.

Something bubbled and broke inside the creature's heart.

Emma was walking through the thick snow, toward the oblivious game warden, one golden strand of hair loose and blowing in the twilight.

"Oh, monsieur! I too once had a greyhound!" She shut her eyes and sighed longingly, as if straining to call back not only the memory but the dog herself.

And she very nearly succeeded.

The greyhound's tail began helplessly to wag.

"Her name was Deeeaaaa . . . Dahhh . . ."

And then the dog remembered too, callused hands brushing dead leaves from her fur, clearing the seams of blackflies from her eyelids and nostrils, lifting her from the trench. Their fine, sturdy bones clasped firmly around her belly as she flew through evening air. The rank, tuberlike scent enveloping her, the firelight in the eyes of her rescuer. Over his shoulder she'd glimpsed the shallow imprint of a dog's body in the mud.

With a lovely amnesiac smile, Emma Bovary continued to fail to remember the name of her greyhound. And each soft sound she mouthed tugged the dog deeper into the past.

It was an impossible moment, and the pain the animal experienced—staring from old, rumpled Hubert to the absorbing, evanescing Emma—did feel very much like an ax falling through her snow-wet fur, splitting down the rail of her tingling spine, fatally dividing her.

"My dog's name is Hubert," Hubert said to Madame Bovary, with his stupid frankness. He glanced fondly at little Hubert, attributing the greyhound's spasms in the cemetery drifts to the usual culprits: giddiness or fleas.

Writhing in an agony, the dog rose to her feet. She closed the small, incredibly cold gulf of snow between herself and her master.

"Sit," she then commanded herself, and she obeyed.

LAURA VAN DEN BERG

Antarctica

FROM *Glimmer Train*

I.

IN ANTARCTICA THERE was nothing to identify because there
was nothing left. The Brazilian station at the tip of the Antarctic Peninsula had burned to the ground. All that remained of my
brother was a stainless steel watch. It was returned to me in a sealed
plastic bag, the inside smudged with soot. The rescue crew had
also uncovered an unidentified tibia, which might or might not
have belonged to him. This was explained in a cold, windowless
room at Belgrano II, the Argentinian station that had taken in the
survivors of the explosion. Luiz Cardoso, the head researcher at
the Brazilian base, had touched my shoulder as he spoke about the
bone, as though this was information intended to bring comfort.

Other explanations followed, less about the explosion and more
about the land itself. Antarctica was a desert. There was little snowfall or rain. Much of it was still unexplored. There were no cities.
The continent was ruled by no one; rather, it was an international
research zone. My brother had been visiting from McMurdo, an
American base on Ross Island, but since it was a Brazilian station
that had exploded, the situation would be investigated according
to their laws.

"Where is the bone now? The tibia?" I'd lost track of how long
it had been since I'd slept, or what time zone I was in. It felt very
strange not to know where I was in time.

"In Brazil." His English was accented but clear. It had been less than a week since the explosion. "It's not as though you could have recognized it."

We stood next to an aluminum table and two chairs. The space reminded me of an interrogation room. I hadn't wanted to sit down. I had never been to South America before and as Luiz spoke, I pictured steamy Amazonian rivers and graveyards with huge stone crosses. It was hard to imagine their laws having sway over all this ice. It was equally hard to believe a place this big—an entire fucking continent, after all—had no ruler. I felt certain that it would only be a matter of time before there was a war over Antarctica.

"It's lucky the explosion happened in March." Luiz was tall, with deep-set eyes and the rough beginnings of a beard, a few clicks shy of handsome.

"How's that?" My brother was dead. Nothing about this situation seemed lucky.

"Soon it will be winter," he said. "It's dark all the time. It would have been impossible for you to come."

"I don't know how you stand it." The spaces underneath my eyes ached.

My husband hadn't wanted me to come to Antarctica at all, and when our son saw where I was going on a map, he cried. My husband had tried to convince me everything could be handled from afar. *You're a wife,* he'd reminded me as I packed. *A mother too.*

"Did you know about your brother's work?" Luiz said. "With the seismograph?"

"Of course." I listened to wind batter the building. "We were very close."

I couldn't stop thinking about him as a boy, many years before everything went wrong: tending to his ant farms and catching snowflakes in his mouth during winter. Peering into a telescope and quizzing me on the stars. Saying tongue twisters—*I wish to wish the wish you wish to wish*—to help his stutter. We had not spoken in over a year.

Luiz clapped his hands lightly. Even though we were indoors, he'd kept his gloves on. I had drifted away and was momentarily surprised to find myself still in the room.

"You have collected your brother's things, such as they are. There will be an official inquiry, but you shouldn't trouble yourself with that."

"I'm booked on a flight that leaves in a week. I plan to stay until then."

"The explosion was an accident," he said. "A leak in the machine room."

"I get it." Exhaustion was sinking into me. My voice sounded like it was coming from underwater. "Nobody's fault."

I had flown from JFK to New Zealand, where I picked up a charter plane to an airstrip in Coats Land. There had been gut-popping turbulence, and from the window I could see nothing but ice. Luiz had been the one to meet me on the tarmac and drive me to Belgrano II in a red snow tractor. I'd packed in a hurry and brought what would get me through winter in New Hampshire: a puffy coat that reached my knees, a knit hat with a tassel, leather gloves, suede hiking boots. I'd had to lobby hard to come to Antarctica; the stations weren't keen on civilians hanging around. When I spoke with the director of McMurdo, I'd threatened to release a letter saying that details of the explosion, the very information needed to properly grieve, were being kept from the victims' families. I knew Luiz was looking me over and thinking that the best thing I could do for everyone, including my brother, including myself, was just to go on home.

"Are there polar bears here?" I felt oddly comforted by the idea of spotting a white bear lumbering across the ice.

"A common mistake." He drummed his fingers against the table. He had a little gray in his eyebrows and around his temples. "Polar bears are at the North Pole."

"My brother and I were very close," I said again.

There was a time when that statement would have been true. We had been close once. During our junior year of college, we rented a house in Davis Square, a blue two-story with a white front porch. Our parents had died in a car accident when we were in middle school—a late spring snowstorm, a collision on a bridge—leaving behind the grandparents who raised us, and an inheritance. My brother was in the Earth Sciences Department at MIT, and I was studying astronomy at UMass Boston. (I was a year older, but he had been placed on an accelerated track.) Back then I thought I would never grow tired of looking at the sky.

When it was just the two of us, we did not rely on language. He would see me cleaning chicken breasts in the sink, and take out breadcrumbs and butter for chicken Kiev, our grandmother's recipe. After dinner we watched whatever movie was on TV. *E.T.* played two nights in a row, and *Maybe it was just an iguana* became something we said when we didn't know what else to do, because even though we had been close, we never really learned how to talk to each other. Sometimes we didn't bother with clearing the table or washing dishes until morning. We went weeks without doing laundry. My brother wore the same striped polos and rumpled khakis; I showed up for class with unwashed hair and dirty socks. His interest in seismology was taking hold. He started talking about P-waves and S-waves. Fault lines and ruptures. He read biographies of Giuseppe Mercalli, who invented a scale for measuring volcanoes, and Frank Press, for whom land in Antarctica, a peak in the Ellsworth Mountains, had been named.

It was at MIT that he met Eve. She was a theater arts major. They dated for a semester and wed the same week they graduated, in the Somerville courthouse. I was their only guest. Eve wore a tea-length white dress and a daffodil behind her ear. She was lithe and elegant, with straight blond hair and freckles on the bridge of her nose. When the justice of the peace said "man and wife," she called out "wife and man!" and laughed, and then everyone started laughing, even the justice. I wasn't sure why we were laughing, but I was glad that we were.

There were three bedrooms in the house. It might have seemed strange, brother and sister and his new wife all living together, but it felt like the most natural thing. Our first summer, we painted the walls colors called Muslin and Stonebriar and bought rocking chairs for the porch. We pulled the weeds that had sprung up around the front steps. All the bedrooms were upstairs. When I was alone in my room, I played music to give them privacy. At dinner I would watch my brother and Eve—their fingers intertwined under the table, oblivious—and wonder how long it would take them to have children. I liked the idea of the house slowly filling with people.

That fall my brother started his earth sciences PhD at MIT. He kept long hours in the labs and when he was home, he was engrossed in textbooks. Eve and I spent more time together. She lived her life like an aria—jazz so loud, I could hear it from the sidewalk; phone conversations that sprawled on for hours, during which she often spoke different languages; heels and silk dresses to the weekend farmers' market. She always wore a gold bracelet with a locket. I would stare at the oval dangling from her wrist and wonder if there were photos inside. I helped her rehearse for auditions in the living room, standing on a threadbare oriental rug. I got to be Williams's Stanley Kowalski and Pinter's Max, violent and dangerous men. I started carrying slim plays around in my purse, the way Eve did, even though I had no plans to write or perform; the act alone felt purposeful. I learned that her father was an economics professor and she had majored in theater to enrage him, only to discover that she loved the stage. I'd never met anyone from her family.

One afternoon I went to see her perform in *The Tempest* at a community theater in Medford. My brother had been too busy to come. She was cast as Miranda. Onstage she wore a blue silk dress with long sleeves and gold slippers. In one scene Miranda argued with her father during a storm; somewhere a sound machine simulated thunder. Everything about her carriage and voice worked to convey power and rage—"Had I been any great god of power, I would have sunk the sea within the earth . . ."—but for the first time I noticed that something was wrong with her eyes. Under the lights, they looked more gray than blue, and her gaze was cold and flat.

Afterward we drank at the Burren. The bar was bright and crowded. A band was unpacking instruments from black cases. We jammed ourselves into a small table in the back with glasses of red wine. Eve was depressed about the production: the turnout, the quality of the lighting, and the costumes.

"And the guy who played Prospero," she moaned. She had left a perfect lip print on the rim of her wineglass. "I would've rather had my own father up there."

When the waitress came around, she ordered another drink, a martini this time. She took an eyebrow pencil out of her purse and drew hearts on a cocktail napkin.

"What do squirrels give for Valentine's Day?" she asked.

I shook my head. My hands were wrapped around the stem of my glass.

"Forget-me-nuts." She twirled the pencil in her fingers and laughed the way she had during her wedding, only this time I caught the sadness in her voice that I'd missed before.

She put down the pencil and leaned closer. At the table next to ours, a couple was arguing. The band tuned their guitars. When she spoke, her voice was syrupy and low.

"Lee," she said. "I have a secret."

In Antarctica I shared a bedroom with a meteorologist from Buenos Aires. Her name was Annabelle and she talked in her sleep. Every morning, I had a three-minute shower in the communal bathroom (it was important to conserve water). I took my meals in the mess hall, with its long tables and plastic trays and harsh overhead lights. I sat with the ten Argentinean scientists who worked at the base; we ate scrambled eggs and canned fruit and smoked fish. They spoke in Spanish, but I still nodded as if I could follow. The five scientists from the Brazilian station always sat at their own table, isolated by their tragedy, which I understood. After my parents died, it took me months before I could carry on a conversation with someone who had not known them, who expected me to be young and sparkling and untouched by grief.

Four of the Argentinean scientists were women. They had glossy dark hair and thick, rolling accents. In Antarctica I'd found that personalities tended to match the landscape, chilly and coarse, but these women were kind. There was a warmth between them, an intimacy that made me miss being with Eve. They lent me the right clothes. They let me watch the launch of their meteorology balloon from the observation room, a glass dome affixed to the top of the station. The balloon was white and round and looked like a giant egg ascending into the sky. In broken English, they told me what it was like during the darkness of winter: *The sun,* they said. *One day it's just not there. There are no shadows. You have very strange dreams.* They included me in their movie nights in the recreation room, which had a TV, a small library of DVDs, a computer, and a phone. Once it was *Top Gun,* another time *E.T.* Everything was dubbed in Spanish, and when I didn't get to hear the iguana line, I started to cry. I didn't make a sound, didn't even realize it was happening until I felt moisture on my cheeks. The women pretended not to notice.

I started wearing my brother's watch. No matter how much I cleaned the metal, it kept leaving black rings around my wrist. With my calling card I phoned McMurdo, only to be told that the scientists who worked with my brother had departed in anticipation of winter; all they could offer was the date he left and that their reports indicated he'd been in good health. I started pestering Luiz for a meeting with everyone from the Brazilian station, with the hope that they had more to tell.

"An interview?" he asked, frowning.

"No." By then I'd been in Antarctica for three days, though I felt it had been much longer. "A conversation."

The day of the meeting, I dressed in thermals, snow pants, wool socks, fleece-lined boots, a hooded parka, and thick red gloves that turned my hands into paddles. I added a white ski mask that covered everything but my eyes. From Annabelle I'd learned it was called a balaclava. She had given me a laminated sheet with a drawing of a human body. Arrows pointed to what kind of layer should cover each part, to avoid frostbite.

When I first stepped onto the ice, I felt like an astronaut making contact with the surface of the moon. I wandered around the trio of heated research tents and the buzzing generators and the snow tractors. The sky was blue-black; the period of twilight, which seemed to grow smaller each day, would soon begin. By April, Antarctica would be deep into winter and there would be no relief from the dark.

I found all five of the Brazilians in the middle research tent, standing by a long white table covered with black rocks. With the snowsuits and the balaclavas, it was hard to tell who was who, though I always recognized Luiz by his height. Some of the rocks on the table were the size of a fist, others the size of a grapefruit. One was as large as a basketball.

"Meteorites," Luiz said when he saw me looking. Apparently the ice in Antarctica preserved meteorites better than any climate in the world. His team had discovered ones that were thousands of years old.

I touched the basketball-sized rock—it was the color of sand and banded with black—and remembered how much my brother had loved the moon rock collection at MIT.

"So what did you want to ask?" Luiz wore an orange snowsuit. His goggles rested on top of his forehead.

I stopped touching the meteorite. Red heat lamps were clamped to the top of the tent. Standing before the other scientists, I suddenly felt like the one about to be questioned. It was hard to breathe through the balaclava.

"What do you remember about him?"

Not much, it turned out. One scientist volunteered that he often ate alone; another said he never participated in group activities such as evening card games and Ping-Pong. He sang in the shower on occasion, an American song no one recognized. He had a stutter, though sometimes it was barely noticeable.

"What about the other times?" I asked.

"He could barely say his own name," Luiz said.

"How much longer was he supposed to stay with you?" I wished I had a notepad. I would remember everything, of course, but writing it down would have made me feel official and organized, like I was asking questions that might lead us somewhere.

"Two more weeks," Luiz said.

"And when did you last see him?"

There was silence, the shaking of heads. Someone thought they saw him the morning of the explosion, pouring a cup of coffee in the break room.

"Nothing else?" These weren't the questions I came with, not really, but maybe if we kept talking a door would open and I could ask something like *Did you know he had a sister?* or *Did he seem happy?* or *What did he love about being here?*

"I crawled out of the station." The words came from the woman in a sharp burst, like a gunshot. The hood of her parka was down and auburn hair peeked through the top of her balaclava. Bianca, that was her name.

"On my stomach, through fire, smoke. This is what I remember." She swept her hand toward the group. "No one was thinking about your brother. We barely knew him. We can't understand what you're doing here."

She pulled up her hood and walked out of the research tent. The other three scientists looked at Luiz, who shrugged and said something in Portuguese before following her.

I watched them go. The tent flapped open, revealing a pale wedge of sky. Already I was failing as a detective.

"I didn't mean for it to go like that," I said.

"You want to know the truth?" Luiz said. "Your brother was a beaker."

"A what?"

"A beaker. A scientist who can't get along with the others. It wasn't a privilege for him to be at our station. They were tired of him at McMurdo."

At breakfast Annabelle had bragged that she could teach me to say *asshole* in any language. If you spent enough time in Antarctica, you learned a little of everything.

"*Ojete.*" I picked up a meteorite the size of a grape and threw it at his feet. "*Ojete. Ojete.*"

Luiz looked down at the rock, unfazed. I left the tent and walked away from the station. I tried to run but kept slipping on the ice. When I finally stopped and looked back, the U-shaped building was minuscule against the vastness of the land. It was like standing in the middle of a white sea—ice in all directions, stretching into infinity. I pulled at the balaclava. I wanted to take it off but couldn't figure out how. The thought of venturing any farther was suddenly terrifying.

Annabelle had explained that most researchers came for short stints, a handful of months. Few stayed as long as a year, as my brother had. There was the feeling that nothing but the elements could touch you out here, and I understood that was something he would have appreciated. Since we had been close, I could make these kinds of calculations.

I turned in a circle, still looking. I imagined my brother trekking across the ice, fascinated by the world that existed beneath. My throat ached from the cold. My breath made white ghosts in the air. It was impossible to distinguish land from sky.

II.

It happened right after Eve's seventeenth birthday, in Concord, where she had grown up. She had been reading Jane Austen in a park and was just starting home. She remembered the soft yellow blanket rolled under her arm, the page she had dog-eared, the streaks of gold in the sky. She was on the edge of the park when she felt an arm wrap around her chest. For a moment she thought someone was giving her a hug, a classmate or a cousin. She had lots of cousins in Concord. But then there was the knife at her throat and the gray sedan with the passenger door flung open. She dropped the Jane Austen and the blanket on the sidewalk. Somewhere, she imagined, those things were in a collection of crime scene photos.

At the Burren, she stopped there. Her martini glass was empty.

The band was playing a Bruce Springsteen cover. She balled up her cocktail napkin and asked if I wanted to dance. She was wearing a silk turquoise dress and T-strap heels. Her bracelet shone on her wrist. She took my hand and we dipped and twirled. Men watched us. One even tried to cut in.

Two days later I woke to the sound of my bedroom door opening. It was midnight. Eve stood in the doorway in a white nightgown. She got into bed with me and started telling me the rest, or most of the rest. She lay on her back. I watched her lips move in the darkness and wondered if my brother had noticed that his wife was no longer next to him. Soon he would be departing for a month-long research trip to study the Juan de Fuca Plate in Vancouver, leaving us in each other's care.

The man was a stranger. He was fat around the middle. He had a brown beard and a straight white scar under his right eye. In the car, he turned the radio to a sports station. He told her that if she did anything—scream, jump out—he would stab her in the heart. He drove them to a little house on a dirt road in Acton, where she stayed for three days.

Her parents had money. She told herself that he was just going to hold her for ransom; she didn't allow herself to consider that maybe he had other things in mind. The thing she remembered most vividly from the car ride was the radio, the sound of a crowd cheering in a stadium.

"That and one of those green, tree-shaped things you hang from the rearview mirror," she said. "To freshen the air." This explained why she hated Christmas trees, why the scent alone made her lightheaded and queasy. On our first holiday together, she'd told us she was allergic to pine and we'd gotten a plastic tree instead.

"How did you get away?" I asked.

"I didn't." She blinked. Her eyelashes were so pale, they were almost translucent. "I was rescued."

Eve had been half right about the man's intentions. After holding her for forty-eight hours, he placed a ransom demand; it didn't take long for the authorities to figure out the rest. The police found her in a basement. Her wrists were tied to a radiator with twine. She was wearing a long white T-shirt with a pocket on the front. She had no idea where it had come from or what had happened to her clothes. Right before she was rescued, she remembered tracking the beam of a flashlight as it moved down the wall.

In the months that followed, the man's attorney had him diagnosed with a dissociative disorder, something Eve had never heard of before. He hadn't been himself when he had taken her, hadn't been himself in Acton. That was their claim. He got seven years and was out in five due to overcrowding. Her parents advised her to move on with her life. *He's been punished,* her father once said. *What else do you want to happen?* Now she just spoke to them on the phone every few months. They didn't even know she had gotten married.

"Where is he now?" I asked. "Do you know?"

"I've lost track of him." She tugged at the comforter. Her foot brushed against mine.

This was not a secret Eve had shared with my brother. I should have been thinking about him — how I couldn't believe he did not know about this, how he needed to know about this — but I wasn't. Instead I was trying to understand how anyone ever ventured into this world of head-on collisions and lunatic abductors and all the other things one had little hope of recovering from.

"I never went to therapy, but acting is having a therapeutic effect," she said next.

"How so?" During one of her epic phone conversations, I'd glimpsed her sprawled out on the living room sofa, painting her toenails and speaking in French. I'd picked up the landline in the kitchen, curious to know who she was talking to, but there had just been her voice and the buzz of the line. I'd wondered if it was some kind of acting exercise.

"Getting to disappear into different characters. Getting to not be myself."

I remembered her face on the stage in Medford. She was supposed to be Miranda, but her eyes had never stopped being Eve.

In time, I would learn it was possible to tell a secret but also keep a piece of it close to yourself. That was what happened with Eve, who never told me what, exactly, went on during those three days in Acton. The floor was damp concrete. He fed her water with a soupspoon. I never got much more than that.

Of course, I could only assume the worst.

*

The aurora australis was Luiz's idea of a peace offering. We met in the observation room after dinner. It had been dark for hours. Despite my studies in astronomy, I couldn't get over how clear the sky was in Antarctica. I'd never seen so many stars, and it was comforting to feel close to something I had once loved. Annabelle and the others had gone back to work. I still hadn't forgiven Luiz for calling my brother a beaker.

"I've had too much ice time," he said. "I've gotten too used to the way this place can swallow people up." In his first month in Antarctica, two of his colleagues hiked to a subglacial lake and fell through the ice into a cavern. By the time they were rescued, their bodies were eaten up with frostbite. One lost a hand, the other a leg.

"So it's Antarctica's fault you're an asshole?" I said.

"I blame everything on Antarctica," he said. "Just ask my ex-wife."

"Divorced!" I said. "What a surprise."

Luiz had arrived with two folded-up lounge chairs under his arms. They were made of white plastic, the kind of thing you'd expect to see at the beach. In the summer months, when there was no night, the scientists lounged on them in their snow pants and thermal shirts, a kind of Antarctic joke.

"I got them out of storage." He had arranged the chairs so they were side by side. "Just for you."

We reclined in our lounge chairs and stared through the glass. Since we were indoors, I was wearing my New Hampshire gear, the tassel hat and the leather gloves. A wisp of green light swirled above us.

"Tell me more about the explosion," I said, keeping my eyes on the sky.

The early word from the inspectors had confirmed his suspicions: a gas leak in the machine room. They were alleging questionable maintenance practices, because it was impossible to have a disaster without a cause. When the explosion happened, the three people working in the machine room were killed, along with two scientists in a nearby hallway. A researcher from Rio de Janeiro died from smoke inhalation; she and Bianca had worked together for many years. Others were hospitalized with third- and fourth-degree burns. But my brother, he should have made it out. His seismograph was on the opposite end. He'd been sleeping next to it, on a foam mattress, for God's sake. Everyone thought he was crazy.

The green light returned, brighter this time. It was halo-shaped and hovering above the observation room. I hadn't stayed with astronomy long enough to see the auroras in anything other than photos and slides. I thought back to a course in extragalactic astronomy, to the lectures on Hubble's law, and the quasars that radiated red light and the tidal pull of super massive black holes, which terrified me. In college, I had imagined myself working in remote observatories and seeing something new in the sky.

"He thought he'd found an undiscovered fault line," Luiz continued. "He was compiling his data. No one believed him. The peninsula isn't known for seismic activity. He was the only one with an office in that part of the building who didn't survive."

"Where were you during the explosion?" I watched the circle of light contract and expand.

"Outside. Scraping ice off our snow tractor."

So that was his guilt: he hadn't been close enough to believe he was going to die. He couldn't share in the trauma of having to save your own life, or the life of someone else; he could only report the facts. My brother had been too close, Luiz not close enough.

"We hadn't spoken in a long time." The halo dissolved and a sheet of luminous green spread across the horizon, at once beautiful and eerie.

"I asked him about family," Luiz said. "He didn't mention a sister."

I closed my eyes and thought about my brother in that hallway. I saw doorways alight with fire and black, curling smoke. His watch felt heavy on my wrist.

"Luiz," I said. "Do you have any secrets?"

"Too many to count." Silence fell over us in a way that made me think this was probably true. I pictured him tallying his secrets like coins. The sky hummed with green.

Later he explained the lights to me, the magnetic fields, the collision of electrons and atoms. I didn't tell him this was information I already knew. He reached for my hand and pulled off my glove. He placed it on his chest and put his hand over it.

I sat up and took the glove back from him. He held on to it for a moment, smiling, before he let go.

"Of course," Luiz said. "You are married."

That afternoon I'd e-mailed my husband from the recreation room: *Still getting the lay of the land. Don't worry: polar bears are at the North Pole.* He was a real estate agent and always honest about his properties—what needed renovating, if there were difficult neighbors. He believed the truth was as easy to grasp as a baseball or a glass of water. That was why I had married him.

"Yes," I said. "But it doesn't have anything to do with that."

As it turned out, Eve had lied about losing track of the man who had taken her. After his release from prison, she had kept very careful track, aided by a cousin in Concord, a paralegal who had access to a private investigator. It was February when she came to me with news of him. We were sitting in a window seat and drinking tea and looking out at the snow-covered lawn. A girl passed on the sidewalk, carrying ice skates and a pink helmet.

"He's in a hospital," she said. "Down on the Cape. He might not get out. Something to do with his lungs." She sighed with her whole body.

"And?" I said.

"And I want to see him."

"Oh, Eve. I think that's a terrible idea."

"Probably." She blew on her tea. "Probably it is."

In the weeks that followed, she kept at it. She talked about it while we folded laundry and swept the front steps. She talked about it when I met her for drinks after her rehearsals—she was an understudy for a production of *Buried Child* at the American Repertory Theater—and while we rode the T, the train clacking over the tracks whenever we rose aboveground to cross the river. Eve explained that her parents had kept her from the court proceedings. She had wanted to visit him in prison, but that had been forbidden too. Now he was very sick. She was running out of chances.

"Chances for what?" We were waiting for the T in Central Square, on our way home from dinner. On the platform a man was playing a violin for change. Eve had been in rehearsals earlier and was still wearing the false eyelashes and heavy red lipstick.

"To tell him that I made it." She raised her hands. Her gold bracelet slid down her wrist. "That I'm an actress. That I got married. That he wasn't the end of me. That I won."

"How about a phone call?" I said. "Or a letter?"

The T came through the tunnel and ground to a stop. The doors opened. People spilled onto the platform. A woman carrying a sleeping child slipped between me and Eve. My brother had been in Vancouver for two weeks and called home on Sunday mornings.

"You don't understand," she said as we boarded the train. "It has to be done in person."

I missed the perfect chance to tell my brother everything. The day before he left for Vancouver, I went to see him at MIT. His department was housed in the Green Building, which had been constructed by a famous architect and was the tallest building in all of Cambridge. From the outside you could see a white radome on the roof. The basement level was connected to the MIT tunnel system. The first time I visited him on campus, he told me you could take the tunnels all the way to Kendall Square.

"How about some air?" I had found him hunched over a microscope. He was surprised to see me. I hadn't told him I was coming.

"I'm gone tomorrow." He gestured to the open laptops and the stacks of notebooks and the empty coffee mugs that surrounded him. Eve had been trimming his hair, and there was an unevenness to the cut that made him look like he was holding his head at a funny angle. The lenses of his glasses were smudged.

"I know," I said. "That's why I'm here."

We left campus and walked along Memorial Drive. By the river it was cold and windy. We pulled up our coat collars and tightened our scarves. We turned onto the Longfellow Bridge and kept going until we were standing between two stone piers with domed roofs and tiny windows. They reminded me of medieval lookout towers. We leaned against the bridge and gazed out at the river and the city skyline beyond it.

I should have had a plan, but I didn't. Rather, the weight of Eve's secret had propelled me toward him the way I imagined a current tugs at the objects that find their way into its waters.

"The house," my brother said. "Is everything OK there?"

Without his realizing it, I felt he had become an anchor for me and Eve; we always knew he was there, in the background, and with his departure I could feel a shift looming: subtle as a change in the energy, the way the air gets damp and cool before a storm.

But this was before Eve had brought up going to the Cape. I didn't know how to explain what I was feeling, or if I should even try. I couldn't imagine what the right words would be.

"Everything's fine."

"Eve says you've been like a sister," he said.

"We'll miss you," I said. "Don't forget to call."

A gust nearly carried away my hat. I pulled it down over my ears. Snow clouds were settling over the brownstones and high-rises. My brother put his arm around me and started talking about the Juan de Fuca Plate, his voice bright with excitement. I could detect only the slightest trace of a stutter. The plate was bursting with seismic activity, a hotbed of shifts and tremors. I wrapped my arms around his waist and leaned into him. With his free hand he drew the different kinds of fault lines—listric, ring, strike-slip—in the air.

The near-constant darkness of Antarctica made my body confused about when to rest. At three in the morning, I got out of bed and pulled fleece-lined boots over my flannel pajamas. I put on my gloves and hat. Annabelle was babbling in Spanish. At dinner, under the fluorescent lights of the mess hall, I'd noticed a scattering of freckles on her cheekbones and thought of Eve. I had to stop myself from reaching across the table and touching her face.

The station was quiet. The doorways were dark and shuttered. I peered through shadows at the end of hallways and around corners like I was searching for something in particular—what that would be, I didn't know. I drifted to the front of the station. In the mudroom I surveyed the red windbreakers hanging on the wall, the bundles of goggles and gloves, the rows of boots. The entrance was a large steel door with a porthole window. I thought about opening the door, just for a moment, even though the temperature outside would be deep in the negatives; I imagined my hair turning into icicles, my eyes to glass.

Through the window the station lights illuminated the outbuildings and the ice. The darkness was too thick, too absolute, to see anything more. When Luiz first told me that the rescue crew hadn't found any remains, there had been a moment when I'd thought my brother hadn't died in the explosion at all. Maybe he hadn't even been in the building. Maybe he had seen smoke rising from the land and realized this was his chance to vanish. I could picture him boarding an icebreaker and sailing to Uruguay or Cape Town. Standing on the deck of a ship and watching a new horizon emerge.

For a long time I kept watch through the window, willing myself to see a figure surface from the night. Who was to say he hadn't sailed to another land? Who was to say he wasn't somewhere in that darkness? For him, I would open the door. For him, I would endure the cold. But of course nothing was out there.

In the observation room, after the aurora australis had left the sky, I'd turned to Luiz and said, *Here's what I want.* The idea had come suddenly and with force. I wanted to go to the Brazilian station, to the site of the explosion. At first Luiz said it was impossible; it would involve chartering a helicopter, for one thing. I told him that if he could figure out a way to make this happen, I'd be on the next flight to New Zealand. I didn't care how much it cost. He promised to see what he could do.

I left the window and slipped back into the hallway. A light had been left on in the recreation room. I sat in the armchair next to the phone. I'd tucked my calling card into my pajama pocket, thinking I might phone my husband. Instead I dialed the number of the house in Davis Square, which I still knew by heart. The phone rang five times before someone answered. I'd thought a machine might come on and I could leave whoever lived there now a message about polar bears and green lights in the sky. For a moment I imagined my sister-in-law picking up. *Où avez-vous été?* she would say. *Where have you been?*

A woman answered. Her voice was high and uncertain, not at all like Eve's. I pressed the phone against my ear. I pulled on the cord and thought about fault lines. I could see a dark streak running down my ribs, a fissure in my sternum.

"Hello?" she said. Static flared on the line. "How can I help you?"

III.

It was a military hospital, just outside Barnstable. The morning we left, Eve talked to my brother on the phone and said we were going to see the glass museum in Sandwich. I drove. She was dressed in jeans and a gray sweatshirt, unadorned by jewelry, the plainest I'd ever seen her. She rested her socked feet on the dashboard and told me what her cousin had discovered about this man. He'd been in the military, dishonorably discharged. Years ago he'd been part of a real estate scam involving fraudulent mortgages and the elderly, but pleaded out of jail time. He had two restraining orders in his file.

"I'm surprised someone hasn't killed him already." She cracked the window. The air was heavy with moisture and salt.

We drove through Plymouth and Sandwich. From the highway I saw a billboard ad for the glass museum. At the hospital—a labyrinthine gray building just off the highway—we learned he was in the ICU. We pretended to be family.

He was in a room with two other men. A thin curtain hung between each of the beds. Eve slowly walked from one to the next. The first patient was gazing at the TV bolted to the wall. The second was drinking orange juice from a straw. The third was asleep. He wore a white hospital gown. His gray hair was shorn close to the scalp. One hand rested on his stomach, the other on the mattress. I followed Eve to his bedside. His face was speckled with broken capillaries, his cheekbones sharp, his slender forearms bruised. He was on oxygen and attached to a heart monitor. I smelled something sour.

"Are you sure this is him?" I asked Eve, even though I could see the scar. It was just as she had described it: a thin line of white under his eye.

"Don't say it." She walked over to the window and looked out at the parking lot.

"Say what?"

"That's he's old and frail and defenseless." Eve turned from the window. "He's not like that at all. Not on the inside." She pressed her fist against her chest.

She slumped down on the linoleum floor. A nurse was attending to the patient next to us. I watched her shadow through the curtain. She carried away a tray with an empty glass on it. She told the man who had been drinking the juice to have a nice day.

"So what do we do now?" I asked. "Wake him up?"

"I'm thinking," Eve said. "I'm thinking of what to do."

It took her a long time to do her thinking. I listened to the din of the TV. I thought a game show was on from the way people kept calling out numbers.

Finally Eve jumped up and started digging through her purse.

She took out a tube of lipstick, the garish red color she wore on-stage, and raised it like a prize.

"OK," she said. "I have my first idea."

She uncapped the lipstick and went to the sleeping man. She smeared color across his mouth. I stood on the other side of his bed and stared down, trying to see the evil in him. Eve used the lipstick to rouge his cheeks before passing it to me. I drew red half-circles above his eyebrows. We waited for him to wake up, to cry for help, but he only made a faint gurgling sound. His hand twitched on his stomach. That was all.

"Now I have another idea," Eve said.

For this second thing she wanted to be alone. I looked at the clown's face we had given this man. My stomach felt strange. On the intercom a doctor was being paged to surgery.

"Five minutes. Three hundred seconds." Her face was free of makeup, her freckles visible. She'd had her teeth bleached re-cently and they looked unnaturally white. "That's all I'm asking for, Lee."

After what had happened to her, wasn't she owed five minutes alone with him? That was my thinking at the time. On my way out of the ICU, the same nurse who had picked up the juice glass asked me if I'd had a pleasant visit.

I waited on the sidewalk. I watched people come and go through the automatic doors. An old man on crutches. An old man in a wheelchair. A nurse in lavender scrubs. What was the worst thing these people had done?

Eve stayed in the hospital for fifty-seven minutes. I couldn't bring myself to go back inside. I paced in the cold. I had forgotten my gloves and my hands were going numb. Even though I'd never smoked in my life, I asked a doctor smoking outside if I could bum a cigarette.

"These things will kill you." The doctor winked and flipped open his cigarette pack.

When Eve emerged from the hospital, she took my hand and pulled me toward the car. We drove in silence. She rested her head against the window. When I tried to turn on the radio, she touched my wrist. Her fingertips were waxy with lipstick.

"Please," she said.

After a half-hour on the road, I exited at Sagamore Beach. The

silence felt like a pair of hands around my throat. Eve didn't object
when I parked in the designated beach lot, empty on account of
its being February, or when we climbed over dunes and through
seagrass. Cold sand leaked into our shoes. I didn't stop until I
reached water.

We were standing on the edge of Cape Cod Bay. The water was
still and gray. Clusters of rock extended into the bay like fingers. A
white mist hung over us. A freighter was visible in the distance.

"Why didn't you come out when you said you would?" The
freighter was moving farther away. When it vanished from sight,
it looked like it had gone into a cloud. "What were you doing in
there?"

"We were talking." Her face was dewy from the mist. Her pale
hair had frizzed. She picked up a white stone and threw it into the
water.

"So he woke up?"

"Yes," she said. "He did and then he didn't."

She picked up another stone. It was gray with a black dot in the
center. She held on to it for a little while, turning it over in her
hands, before it went into the bay.

In Cambridge she wanted to be dropped at the Repertory Theater. She had to tell the director that she couldn't make rehearsal;
she promised to come home soon. Her hair was still curled from
being at the beach. Her cheeks and forehead were damp. I tried
to determine if anything had shifted in her eyes.

I idled on Brattle Street until Eve had gone into the theater.
Her purse swung from her shoulder, and somewhere inside it was
that lipstick. I kept telling myself that the most dangerous part was
over. We were home now. Everything would be the same as before.

But no. Nothing would be the same as before. Eve never talked
to her director. She never returned to the house. I had to call
my brother and tell him to come home from Vancouver. When I
picked him up at the airport, it was late. I waited in baggage claim.
Long before he noticed me, I spotted him coming down the es-
calator, a duffel bag slung over his shoulder. He had lost weight.
His hair had grown out. I remember thinking that I wished I knew
him better, that I wished we'd taken the time to learn how to talk
to each other. When he finally saw me, he tried to call out, *Lee*,
but his stutter was as bad as it had been in childhood. It took him
three tries to say my name.

A report was filed. Eve's parents—a frail, bookish couple—came into town from Concord. The investigation went on for weeks. There was no sign of Eve, no sign of foul play. As gently as he could, the detective asked us to consider the possibility that she had run away. Apparently women—young mothers, young wives—did this more frequently than people might think. I told everyone I'd dropped Eve at the theater, but the truth stopped there. Every time I tried to say more, I felt like a stone was lodged in my throat.

Because I was his sister, because we had been close, my brother knew I was holding something back. He pressed me for information. Had she been taking an inordinate amount of calls? Had anything peculiar arrived in the mail? Was she having an affair with a cast mate? Had we really gone to the glass museum in Sandwich? I submitted to these questions, even though I didn't—couldn't, I felt at the time—always tell the truth. And I knew he was confronting his own failing, the fact that he hadn't cared to know any of this until after his wife was gone.

We waited months before we packed up her belongings: the silk dresses, the shoes, the jewelry, the plays. Her possessions had always seemed rich and abundant but filled only three cardboard boxes. My brother kept them stacked at the foot of his bed. When he moved, two boxes went to Eve's parents, and he took the other one with him. I don't know what happened to her things after that.

The last time he asked me a question about Eve, we were on the front porch. It was late spring. The trees were blooming green and white. I was in a rocking chair. My brother was leaning against the porch railing, facing the street.

"Do you think you knew her better than I did?" he said.

"No." Once I had come upon them in the upstairs hallway: they were pressed against the wall, kissing, and he was twisting one of Eve's wrists behind her back. It was clear that the pleasure was mutual, which led me to believe that she might enjoy a degree of pain. Only my brother could say how much.

He stared out at the glowing streetlights. I could tell from the way he licked his lips and squeezed the railing that he did not believe me.

By summer we had moved into separate apartments: his on Beacon Hill, so he could be closer to MIT; mine in the North End, scrunched between a pastry shop and a butcher. I bounced from one entry-level lab job to another, my ambition dulled, while I watched my brother pull his own disappearing act: into his dissertation, into the conference circuit, into one far-flung expedition after another. The Philippines, Australia, Haiti. Antarctica. The phone calls and postcards turned from weekly to monthly to hardly at all.

I got married the year I turned thirty. My brother came but left before the cake was served. It was too painful, watching the night unfold; I understood this without his ever saying so. I told my husband only that he had been married briefly and, years ago, we'd all lived together in Davis Square. Soon I had a child. I worked part-time as a lab assistant, sorting someone else's data, and cared for him, which was not the life I'd imagined for myself, but it seemed like a fair exchange: I hadn't kept sufficient watch over Eve, hadn't kept her from danger. This was my chance to make it up. I tried to tell myself she was someplace far away and happy. I tried to forget that she might have been in trouble, that she might have needed us. When I looked at my son, I tried not to think about all the things I could never tell him. I tried to shake the feeling that I was living someone else's life.

In the years to come I would start so many letters to my brother, each one beginning in a different way: *Eve was not who you thought,* and *I don't know how it all started,* and *How could you not have known?* I never got very far because I knew I was still lying. The letter I finally finished—addressed to the McMurdo station but never mailed—opened with *None of this was your fault.*

Another thing I never told him: before leaving the house in Davis Square, I cut open one of Eve's boxes and found her gold bracelet in a tiny plastic bag. The chain was tarnished. I popped open the locket; the frames were empty. I took the bracelet and resealed the box with packing tape. I held on to it—never wearing it, always hiding it away, even before there were people to hide it from. My husband found it once, and I said it had been a gift from my mother. I imagined other people discovering the bracelet through the years and how I would tell each one a different story. I would carry it with me to Antarctica, tucked in the side pocket of my suitcase, though I was never able to bring it out into the open.

Not long after Eve's disappearance, I looked up the name of her abductor on a computer: Randall Smith. I'd only heard her say it aloud once, in the hospital. After a little searching, I found an obituary. He had died the day after our visit, survived by no one. The obituary said it was natural causes, which explained nothing.

It was twilight when we flew over Admiralty Bay. Luiz said that if I watched the water carefully, I might see leopard seals. The pilot was from the Netherlands, hired for a price that would horrify my husband when the check posted. Luiz's boss had gotten wind of our expedition and wasn't at all pleased; that morning he'd called from Brazil and told Luiz that he was not in the business of escorting tourists. Soon I would have to get on the plane to New Zealand, like I had promised, but I wasn't completely out of time.

The landscape was different on the peninsula. The ice was sparser, exposing the rocky peaks of mountains and patches of black soil near the coastline. When the explosion site came into view, it looked like a dark scar on the snow.

The helicopter touched down. Black headsets swallowed our ears, muffling the sound of the propellers. The helicopter swayed as it landed. I could feel the engine rumbling beneath us; it made my skin vibrate inside my many layers of clothes. Luiz got out first, then helped me onto the ice. The pilot shouted something in Dutch, which Luiz translated: soon the twilight would be gone; he didn't want to fly back in the dark.

Together we approached the wreckage. Luiz still had his headset on. I had taken mine off too soon and now my ears buzzed. Up close, the site was smaller than I'd expected: a black rectangle the size of the swimming pool I took my son to in the summer. Nothing of the structure remained except for metal beams jutting from ridges of ash and debris. The sky was a golden haze.

"I told you there wasn't much to see." He slipped off his headset. His face was covered except for his eyes. I was wearing a balaclava too and knew I looked the same.

"Tell me what it was like before."

The station had been shaped like a horseshoe. He pointed to the empty spaces where the mess hall used to be, the dormitories, the bathroom, my brother's seismograph. Their base had been smaller than Belgrano. They didn't have an observation room or heated research tents. Everything had been contained under one roof.

I stepped in the ash and listened to it crunch under my boots. I

passed black spears of wood and warped beams. One section of the
site was even more charred, the ground scooped in. I stood inside
the depression and looked at the bits of metal glinting in the ash.
I picked up something the size of a quarter. I wasn't sure what it
had been before; the fire had made it glossy and flat. I slipped it
into my pocket and kept walking. I told myself it was evidence; I
just didn't know what kind.

The wind blew flurries of ash around my legs. On the other end
of the site, I looked for some sign of my brother's seismograph. I
came across a spoon, the handle melted into a glob of metal, and
a lighter. I put those things in my pockets too. More evidence.
Luiz was still on the edge of the site. By then I understood he was
someone who had no desire to go searching for things. He didn't
even collect the meteorites; his only concern was classifying them.
The helicopter would be ready for us soon, but the sky still held a
dull glow.

There were so many times when I wanted to tell my brother
everything—when, in the middle of the night, I wanted to kneel
by his bed and whisper, *I have a secret.* In Cambridge, I'd told myself these were Eve's secrets to keep or expose; it was her life to
walk away from, if that's what she wanted. And the more time that
passed, the more unimaginable the truth seemed. To admit one lie
would mean admitting another and then another.

I imagined myself at home in New Hampshire, arranging everything on the living room floor. A map of Antarctica, with stars
to mark the bases: McMurdo, here, Belgrano. My brother's watch.
Eve's empty locket. The photo he mailed, without a note, when
he first arrived in Antarctica. He was wearing a yellow snowsuit
and standing outside McMurdo, surrounded by bright white ice.
Around these materials I would place the metals I had collected
at the site and try to see something: a pattern, a sign. Or maybe I
would just read aloud the last letter I wrote to him. Or maybe, in
the helicopter, I would turn to Luiz and tell him everything.

The sky was almost dark. I was back inside the depression. I
was sitting down in it and hugging my knees. I had no memory of
walking over there and stepping into the hole; I had just done it
automatically. Luiz was calling to me. The wind carried his voice
away.

Maybe it was just an iguana, I heard my brother say.

In Antarctica I did not know if he had denied himself the

chance to get out of the burning building. I did not know what he believed I knew, or what would have changed if I'd given him the truth. I did not know if I would ever see Eve again. I did not know what had happened in that hospital room, or in Acton. Some of these things I did not know—not because they were unknowable, but because I had turned away from the knowledge. In Antarctica I decided that was the worst thing I'd ever done, that refusal.

The stars were coming out. Luiz was crossing the site, waving and calling my name. The temperature was dropping. My eyes watered. I sank deeper into the hole.

In Antarctica I did not know that a month after I left, Luiz would become trapped in a whiteout and lose two fingers to frostbite. I did not know that the tibia would turn out to have belonged to my brother, that it would be shipped back to America in a metal box. I did not know if one day I would disappear and no one except a missing woman and a dead man would be able to tell the people who loved me why.

Contributors' Notes

CHARLES BAXTER is the author of twelve books of fiction and nonfiction. His most recent collection, *Gryphon: New and Selected Stories*, was published in 2011. "Charity" will appear in *There's Something I Want You to Do*, to be published in February 2015. "Bravery," from last year's *Best American Short Stories*, is also part of that collection. He lives in Minneapolis and teaches at the University of Minnesota.

· I have been writing stories about virtues and vices, a kind of decalogue, and I found myself thinking about charity. At first nothing suggested itself, and I sat for a few days with my head in my hands in front of the big stupid blank face of the desktop computer. It occurred to me that I had just written a story called "Chastity," in which my protagonist, Benny Takemitsu, gets mugged, and I thought, "I wonder who did that?" Whoever did it had to be desperate. Whoever it was, I thought, might be a good soul in the grip of something truly terrible. So I wrote it that way. The ending was nowhere in sight until I remembered something a diplomat once told me about a certain custom at African weddings to honor those who are no longer with us. The events of several sections of the story take place in the part of the city of Minneapolis where I walk every day. Most of the story was improvised, based on what I knew about the characters.

Harry Albert, who narrates "Charity," appears in another story of mine, "Vanity," in which his younger and more vain self appears.

I have always wanted to write a story that begins, "He had fallen into bad trouble." This is that story.

ANN BEATTIE is assembling a new collection of stories. *The New Yorker Stories* was chosen by the *New York Times* as one of the top ten books of 2010.

· I surprised myself by writing this because I thought the central incident—which does not even appear in the story—was strange and haunting, and it has bothered me for years. Maybe I'll write that another time. Once I started piecing together the story, I realized that the truth mattered not at all, but that a conflation of people and places served my purposes better. Is this oblique? Probably I didn't want to write the one moment I so vividly remembered from real life, since writing isn't about getting down on paper what I remember, and also because I still don't know what to make of it. So I made something else, which my agent responded to in part by saying that she recognized X in the story, and only then did I realize that she was quite right, and that I'd conflated X with Y. Lest I seem to be writing about chromosomes, let me say that this is a story I decided to keep hidden from myself, but that the goings-on seemed to happen of their own accord and that this story exists in a parallel universe with the story I didn't write. I'd been to Philadelphia (which I don't know well) recently with my husband, and somehow the visuals were there for me like a painted back-drop—those (forgive me) repurposed buildings, the restaurants so unlike those in New York, the fact that I'd walked by an apartment building that seemed anonymous yet attention-getting—and it made me wonder what kind of people lived there.

T. C. BOYLE is the author of twenty-five books of fiction, including his collected stories, *T. C. Boyle Stories* (1998) and *T. C. Boyle Stories II* (2013), as well as the forthcoming novel *The Harder They Come*. He is a member of the American Academy of Arts and Letters and is writer in residence at the University of Southern California, where he founded the undergraduate program in creative writing.

• As if we didn't have enough to worry about in a world ruled by chance and festering with terrorists, Walmart outlets, and mutating diseases (and the scaremongers of the press to keep it all fresh for us, 24/7)—now we have to look to the sky as well. I wrote "The Night of the Satellite" while wearing a crash helmet and flame-retardant suit, certain that the decaying NASA weather satellite adduced in the story was going to defy all odds and come hurtling through the roof of my house to pin me like an insect to the concrete slab in the basement. Again, what next? We are kept in a state of perpetual anxiety along the information highway, and I wonder, really, how much good it's doing us.

That said, this is a story, like many of mine, that slams two scenarios together in order to see what the result will be. As a student at Iowa I was the guy on that country road while the "lovers' quarrel" played out before me, and I've wrestled for many years with the notion of personal respon-sibility—mores—in view of the larger picture. Chance brought Paul and Mallory to that road on that day and to the darkened field at night. There is cosmic debris out there (as in my earlier story "Chicxulub," which deals with the comet that resulted in the mass extinctions of 65 million years ago) and manmade junk too, and the most we can hope for is to duck it, or, to quote Calvino: "You know that the best you can expect is to avoid the worst." Still, we are grounded and we live our tribal lives in a state veering from placidity to agitation, everything personal and interactive, and the earth is our home. Woe to those bleeding sheep, woe to our relationships, woe to us all! Indeed, you never can tell what's going to come down next.

PETER CAMERON is the author of six novels, including *The City of Your Final Destination* and *Someday This Pain Will Be Useful to You,* and three collections of stories. His fiction has appeared in *The New Yorker, Yale Review, Rolling Stone, Paris Review,* and *Subtropics.* He has worked for the Trust for Public Land and Lambda Legal Defense and Education Fund and has taught at Columbia, Sarah Lawrence, Yale, and the New School. He lives in New York City, where he runs Shrinking Violet Press, a small private press that publishes limited-edition chapbooks.

• I rarely write short stories these days and so go about it differently from when I was a young writer and ideas for short stories came to me frequently and unbidden. Now I have to set myself some kind of assignment or problem to solve in order to call forth or jump-start a story, and hope that this forced inception won't adversely affect the finished piece—that the story will transcend its deliberateness. After all (I tell myself), some arranged marriages are happier and more successful than those unions formed by passion or romance.

In the case of "After the Flood," I set out to write a story based upon the not-very-original notion of a home or a family being disturbed or altered by the sudden presence of strangers. A story about what happens when people who aren't meant to live together live together. And it occurs to me now that perhaps all the stories I write are about that.

NICOLE CULLEN was raised in Salmon, Idaho, and earned an MFA in writing from the Michener Center for Writers at the University of Texas–Austin in 2011. She was the 2011–2012 Carol Houck Smith Fiction Fellow at the Wisconsin Institute for Creative Writing and a 2012–2014 Stegner Fellow at Stanford University. She lives in Boise, Idaho.

• I wrote the first draft of "Long Tom Lookout" in 2010 during the aftermath of the Deepwater Horizon oil spill. That summer I drove from Texas to Idaho, but the news coverage of the oil spill made it hard to leave the Gulf of Mexico in the rearview. I was researching wildfires when I came across two stories: a bit of folklore about the drowned miner Long Tom, who was too tall for his casket, and a 1993 *Post Register* article about a woman working as a fire lookout on Long Tom Mountain with her two young sons. A few weeks later, while visiting the Lochsa Historical Ranger Station, I was able to get my hands on an old Osborne Firefinder, and the story started from there.

CRAIG DAVIDSON is the writer of *Rust and Bone, The Fighter, Sarah Court, Cataract City,* and a forthcoming collection of stories that will include "Medium Tough." He also writes horror fiction under the name Nick Cutter. He lives in Toronto with his fiancée and their son.

• I've always been interested in broken characters. Mine are often physically broken, in addition to their attendant emotional pains (I like 'em good and beaten down!): boxers with chronically brittle hands, whale trainers with gnawed-off legs, that kind of deal. Dr. Railsback falls into that tradition. But I also like characters—really, I like *people*—who just keep on trucking despite whatever cosmic belittlements and mockeries life throws at them. There's that Hemingway line about bones being strongest at their broken point . . . I don't buy that. I'm sure it's true in a physical sense, but the whole "what doesn't kill you makes you stronger" jazz doesn't carry water with me. I think what doesn't kill you can make you weaker and more frail and fearful, but despite that fact most of us still summon the will to carry on after life breaks us in the little ways life tends to—carry on to do good things, to tamp down those weaknesses when we can, and in our best moments, do right for others. Jasper Railsback and Penny Tolliver and the other broken people in this story are the kind of characters I find myself drawn to over and over. I can't say why. A therapist probably could, but I can't afford one.

JOSHUA FERRIS is the author of three novels, including *To Rise Again at a Decent Hour,* published in 2014. His first novel, *Then We Came to the End,* has been translated into twenty-four languages and was a finalist for the National Book Award. Ferris was chosen for *The New Yorker's* 20 Under 40 list in 2010. He lives in New York City.

• A lot of people don't understand how I could have written this story, or any story, or anything at all, on my phone. The phone is cumbersome and represents, in the life of the mind best exemplified by the writing of short stories, pretty much everything that's soulless and antagonistic. There's the prevailing notion that if a story (or a novel) can be written on a phone, it must not have been very hard to write, and so can't possibly merit the attentions of the reader. Some people are threatened by it, because the written story is already no competition for the smartphone, which makes the smartphone the unintegratable enemy; and if just anyone can use the phone to doodle away, how far are we from the elevation of texts and tweets into high literature? That would be a galling attack on a conservative tradition. But I did use my phone to write this story, which means I sat hunched over its torture screen and tiny little keyboard for however long it took—two or three weeks of steady work—and when I was done had the knotted shoulder, the crimped neck, and the carpel tunnel to prove it. Writing fiction on the phone, compared to the tranquility of computer-composing or the gentlemanly custom of pen and paper, is a full-contact blood sport. Why do I write under these conditions? Do I not have a desk, and a comfortable chair to sit in, and several empty notebooks waiting? I must like the pain. I must find it fitting. But the real answer is this: I wish I could tell you. I wish I could tell you why I write at all.

NELL FREUDENBERGER is the author of the novels *The Newlyweds* and *The Dissident,* as well as the story collection *Lucky Girls.* A recipient of a Guggenheim Fellowship, a Whiting Award, and a Dorothy and Lewis B. Cullman Fellowship from the New York Public Library, she was named one of *Granta*'s Best of Young American Novelists and one of *The New Yorker*'s 20 Under 40. She lives in Brooklyn with her family.

 • I was on my way to pick up my daughter from school when I had an idea about a mother who could fly. By "fly," I mean occasionally lift off the ground in an awkward, unplanned way, a miraculous skill that would be absolutely useless to her. That's what motherhood often feels like to me. I've never written a story with a supernatural element before, and I found that it allowed for a certain distance from the details of daily life that made them flexible enough for fiction. There was also a very compelling boy in my daughter's class, by the name of Jack, with a strong attachment to a bag of white flour.

DAVID GATES is the author of the novels *Jernigan* and *Preston Falls,* and *The Wonders of the Invisible World,* a collection of stories. "A Hand Reached Down to Guide Me" is the title story of a new collection, to be published in 2015. He teaches at the University of Montana and in the Bennington Writing Seminars.

 • This story came out of an image I don't remember myself: a friend with whom I played in a band for many years told me he first saw me on-stage in a coffeehouse in New Haven, Connecticut, in 1965, playing mandolin while wearing a full-length cast on my leg. I was a high school kid then. The mandolin player in the story has some superficial resemblances to me—the cast, the day job as a writer at *Newsweek*—but I've never been much of a mandolin player: improbable legends would hardly have accrued around me as they did around him. His TR-6, by the way, actually belonged to a fellow student of mine at Bard College, who played in a rock-and-roll band with me; I've never forgotten riding with him once from New York City up the Taconic State Parkway. The mandolin player's death shares some details with the death of my father, and like the story's hero-worshiping narrator, I kept chickens at one point. The rest of the story is invented—that is, patched together from this and that bit of memory and fantasy. Like my narrator, I'm over-immersed in nineteenth-century British novels, but I've been to Yorkshire only by way of Google, and I've never aspired to write about *Wuthering Heights;* any proper nineteenth-century scholar is welcome to take the title of his book, *Cathy's Caliban,* and run with it. In a passage I cut from the story's final version, the narrator is at work on a second book, about *Mansfield Park* and *Bleak House,* to be called *Castles of Indolence.* That is a project I can imagine taking on—though perhaps in another life.

LAUREN GROFF is the author of a short story collection, *Delicate Edible Birds,* and two novels, *The Monsters of Templeton* and *Arcadia,* a finalist for the Los Angeles Times Book Prize for fiction. Her stories have won the Push-cart Prize and the O. Henry Prize and have appeared in magazines, including *The New Yorker, The Atlantic, Tin House, One Story,* and *Ploughshares,* and in the 2007 and 2010 editions of *The Best American Short Stories.* She lives in Gainesville, Florida.

• A story arrives in me either as a flash or as a slow underground confluence of separate fixations. This story was of the second type. I have lived in north-central Florida for eight years and have struggled with the place the whole time: my overwhelming love for aspects of Florida is balanced with an equal and opposite dread. I believe, also, that fiction writers should read as much poetry as they read fiction, and this story showed itself at a time when I was reading John Donne's (astonishing) "Holy Sonnet 7" every morning. This is a poem capable of wrecking a writing day or filling it with light. Thanks to John Donne's long-moldering bones, there is no copyright, so here it is:

> At the round earth's imagin'd corners, blow
> Your trumpets, angels, and arise, arise
> From death, you numberless infinities
> Of souls, and to your scatter'd bodies go;
> All whom the flood did, and fire shall o'erthrow,
> All whom war, dearth, age, agues, tyrannies,
> Despair, law, chance hath slain, and you whose eyes
> Shall behold God and never taste death's woe.
> But let them sleep, Lord, and me mourn a space,
> For if above all these my sins abound,
> 'Tis late to ask abundance of thy grace
> When we are there; here on this lowly ground
> Teach me how to repent; for that's as good
> As if thou hadst seal'd my pardon with thy blood.

RUTH PRAWER JHABVALA was a German-born screenwriter and novelist. She was the author of twelve novels, eight short story collections, and twenty-three screenplays. Known for her work with Merchant Ivory Productions on such films as *Room with a View* and *Howards End,* she is the only author to have won both a Booker Prize and an Oscar. Jhabvala died at the age of eighty-five on April 3, 2013.

O. A. LINDSEY'S writing appears in *Iowa Review, Forty Stories: New Writing from Harper Perennial, Fourteen Hills, Columbia,* and *Yalobusha Review.* He holds an MFA in writing from the School of the Art Institute of Chicago and an MA in southern studies from the University of Mississippi. Lindsey lives in Nashville.

· I spent years trying to ignore my combat experience, and then years trying to write about it. I failed at both. For many of us, there's a catch with Operation Desert Storm, 1991: nothing much happened, perhaps, but whatever did happen still shades your thoughts most every day. (The best thing I ever read about Desert Storm was Aimee Bender's "The 20th-Century War Veterans Club." I mean, she nailed it.) Ultimately, thankfully, I chose to pursue different war stories, such as the tectonic roles of female soldiers, or the impact of nonstop media. I also refocused on the mundane postwar assaults, e.g., what it was like to go from logging SCUD missile strikes to delivering Papa John's pizza—and being worried sick about screwing up the latter. So that's the gist of Evie's story: a nontraditional soldier faces the barrage of postwar pinpricks, and the anxiety related to each.

WILL MACKIN is a veteran of the U.S. Navy. His writing has appeared in *DIAGRAM, Tin House,* and *The New Yorker.* He lives in New Mexico with his wife and two children and is currently at work on a collection of short stories titled *Task Force Blue,* due out in 2015.

· I'd spent years trying to join this particular unit. Once I joined I never wanted to leave. It was everything I'd imagined: that rare place where I got to do my job with almost zero interference. Downsides were that failure was catastrophic, personally and professionally, and the pace. If I wasn't training to go on deployment to Iraq or Afghanistan, then I was elsewhere in the Third World on an unrelated contingency. Regular deployments in support of big-name operations provided, paradoxically, opportunities to refocus and regroup. The deployment on which the events of this story are based was, however, the exception. I never really got my bearings. I made rookie mistakes. I dreaded calling home because I didn't know what to say. I couldn't sleep. Night after night became one long exercise in crisis management.

During one of those crises I fell asleep on my feet and somehow got into an argument. The body odor of the guy I was arguing with seeped into my dream the way a ringing phone will, and it woke me up. I remember looking at this guy, who despite lack of hygiene in other areas always used product in his hair. He was so mad his hair was jiggling. With hindsight I think of the rage I saw in his face as the thing that kept that unit, and its mission, going. But at the time I didn't know what to think. I excused myself, saying something like "I need to get back to work," though I never really did. From that moment on, I wondered how much longer I could stay. Meanwhile packages arrived from the Netherlands at regular intervals, and Levi's disavowal of his childhood favorite struck a chord.

BRENDAN MATHEWS'S stories have appeared in *The Best American Short Stories 2010* and in *Virginia Quarterly Review, Cincinnati Review, Five Chapters, Glimmer Train,* and other magazines. He teaches at Bard College at Simon's Rock and in fall 2014 will be a Fulbright U.S. Scholar in Cork, Ireland. He lives in western Massachusetts with his wife and their four children.

• This story may not be a love song, but it is a love letter of sorts to the city of Chicago, where I lived from 1992 to 2003. It's where I met my wife, where my oldest daughter was born, and where I started figuring out how to drag stories out of the margins of my notebooks and into the world. This one in particular lurked on my hard drive for years. In one draft, Kat and her brother were the central characters; their back-and-forth arguments filled fourteen pages. In another version, Kat and Milo were a couple (their arguments filled only eight pages). The story wasn't going anywhere. Then, late in 2011, I was invited to give a reading at Y Bar in Pittsfield, Massachusetts. I was asked to talk about writing, and rather than lecturing a bar full of friends and strangers on the finer points of writerly craft, I decided to read a busted story and talk about why it wasn't working. With the reading approaching, I gutted and stitched up the draft du jour (then titled "Badges, Posters, Stickers & T-Shirts") and gave it its first public airing. The draft was a mess, but I left that night knowing that the story had a chance. The breakthrough came when, in a mad rush, I wrote the scene where the narrator finds Kat sick in the bathroom. I finally knew what she was willing to do—and what I had to do—to make this story work. I had plenty more to figure out, but that scene gave me what I needed: a point of view. For the final sprint to the finish line, I give credit to Jon Parrish Peede at *VQR,* who asked all the right questions and pushed me to find the ending that had long eluded me.

MOLLY MCNETT lives on a farm in Oregon, Illinois, with her husband and children. Her book *One Dog Happy* won the 2008 John Simmons Award for short fiction from the University of Iowa Press, and her stories have appeared in *The Best American Nonrequired Reading, New England Review, Missouri Review, Crazyhorse, Fifth Wednesday,* and many other journals. Thanks to the composer Robinson McClellan and the rogue pastor Mike Shea for their help on this story.

• I was writing a contemporary story in which a high school choir director falls in love with his student's beautiful voice, but I was a little anxious that it might seem like an episode of *Glee*. One day I found a textbook on singing, with a brief history of vocal instruction that mentioned Jerome of Moravia and his theory of *la pulchra nota*, or teaching from the perfect note. Why not set the story in a time when this theory might be applied? In my research I came across a diary of a man who lost his whole family within a month, and his trust in divine providence at each death was deeply touching to me. I wanted the voice teacher to have that kind of faith, though I can't claim to share it or even fully understand it.

BENJAMIN NUGENT is the author of *Good Kids*, a novel, and *American Nerd*, a cultural history. His essays have appeared in the *New York Times Magazine* and on the op-ed page of the *New York Times*. An assistant professor at Southern New Hampshire University, he teaches creative writing at the undergraduate level and in the low-residency MFA program. He divides his time between Manchester, New Hampshire, and Brooklyn, New York.

• Last year, one of my best creative writing students, Megan Kidder, a well-mannered girl from rural Maine with dyed black hair, a silver nose ring, and a studded belt, dropped by my office. "I wrote a poem about how this one guy prematurely ejaculated," she said, "and he told his frat brothers about the poem and now they call me God. They're like, 'Hey, God.'" A few days later, I was pacing, whispering things, and the first sentence of "God" presented itself. It took the perspective of one of the boys. I didn't think about how that perspective might open or foreclose storytelling possibilities. I just liked the way it fell into iambic pentameter: "We called her God because she wrote a poem," and so on.

I can write lyrically only by accident. Whenever I think "I'm going to sit down and write some poetic lines about my characters now," the result is hideous. That's why I like to write about frat boys. I never expect their lives to lend themselves to lyricism.

In its plot, "God" is a bit like *The Sword in the Stone*, which was my favorite movie when I was seven. It's Disney's adaptation of T. H. White's novel *The Once and Future King*, itself an adaptation of *Le Morte d'Arthur*. At the time I didn't think of my debt to Malory but rather to Megan Kidder. It was as if she had stepped from a mist-crowned lake and handed me a sword.

JOYCE CAROL OATES is the author most recently of the novel *Carthage* and the story collections *High-Crime Area* and *Lovely, Dark & Deep*. A long-time faculty member at Princeton, she has been visiting professor at the University of California–Berkeley, at which time the story in this volume,

"Mastiff," was written, as well as visiting professor at NYU in 2014. In 2011, she was awarded the President's Medal in the Humanities and, in 2013, the Lifetime Achievement Award of PEN Center USA.

• "Mastiff" grew out of a protracted and arduous hike undertaken by my husband and me in Wild Cat Canyon near Berkeley, California, in March 2013. The relationship between the (initially unnamed) man and woman hikers is not unlike, but not fully identical with, the relationship between the actual hikers, on that actual hike. The scientist who is also a photographer—this is a type with whom I am intimately acquainted, though the individual in "Mastiff" is not in fact—not actually—my husband, a neuroscientist-photographer with hiking skills and a strong sense of what should, and should not, be done on the trail. And the giant, threatening dog that becomes the very emblem of death, against which some sort of human bond must be the protection, as thin woolen gloves are some sort of protection, however inadequate, against the freezing cold—this terrifying creature too sprang from that actual hike on Wild Cat Canyon Trail. So vivid was the experience, and so intense the emotions (felt by the writer/hiker), it was not difficult to find a language in which to "tell the story"—though it should be reiterated that "Mastiff" is fiction, whatever its wellsprings in actual life.

STEPHEN O'CONNOR is the author of two collections of short fiction, *Here Comes Another Lesson* and *Rescue,* and two works of nonfiction, *Will My Name Be Shouted Out?,* a memoir, and *Orphan Trains,* a biography/history. His fiction and poetry have appeared in *The New Yorker, Conjunctions, One Story, Missouri Review, Poetry, Electric Literature, Agni, Threepenny Review, The Quarterly,* and *Partisan Review,* among many other places. His story "Ziggurat" was read by Tim Curry on *Selected Shorts* in October 2011 and June 2013. His essays and journalism have been published in the *New York Times, DoubleTake, The Nation, Agni,* the *Chicago Tribune,* the *Boston Globe, New Labor Forum,* and elsewhere. He teaches in the MFA programs at Columbia and Sarah Lawrence. For additional information, please visit www.stephenoconnor.net.

• In all likelihood "Next to Nothing" would never have been written if it weren't for Hurricane Irene. I spend weekends and vacations just under three hours northwest of New York City, in an area particularly hard hit by the storm. Our house was spared, fortunately, but on either side of the shoulder of land on which it is built, massively engorged streams of red water roared through culverts like spumes from gigantic fire hydrants. At the height of the storm, the entire valley we overlook became a red sea, with huge waves and frothing pink "whitecaps." And I really did stock up in advance of Irene at a supermarket, from the parking lot of which one can look out across a valley big enough to hold an entire county—and, in fact, parts of two or three others. But the real inspiration for the story came from an image that just popped into my head of two sisters with black pageboys and eyes of such a pale blue that they were almost the color we sometimes imagine the moon to be. The image wasn't entirely static. I saw the sisters from the shoulders up, rocking slightly, as if they were walking—or, more likely, lumbering. I also understood, maybe as a function of their freakishly pale eyes, that this pair would be entirely lacking in what is sometimes called "fellow feeling." They would be extremely intelligent and absolutely rational, but have no emotional attachment to any human being—not to their parents, their children, or each other, and not really even to themselves. I had probably gotten about a page and a half into my first draft when it occurred to me that there was a parallel between the sisters and nature—which is also consummately rational and absolutely indifferent to human concerns. And thus it was that I decided that my protagonists should confront Hurricane Irene.

I am an atheist and the child of atheists. For as long as I have been able to think in such terms, I have always tried to anchor my beliefs in reason and fact. Starting sometime in adolescence, however, it became clear to me that certain things I want desperately to believe simply cannot be justified by rational interpretations of fact. Is romantic love real, for example, or only a sentimental delusion? Does it make any sense at all to say that human life is sacred? As a result of this realization, I became aware of the paradox that, atheist though I may be, I too must live by faith—not in spiritual terms, but in the sense that in order to be a happy and decent human being, I must cherish "beliefs" that can never be verified. Much of my writing over the years has explored the absurd and possibly delusory nature of many of our most essential values. And when I decided to have the Soros sisters confront a hurricane that shared a name with one of them, I knew that I would be able to explore the significance of our absurd beliefs through negative means—that is, through a pair of protagonists in whom they are entirely lacking. Beyond that, I had no clear idea of what course the story would take, and I intentionally tried to keep myself off balance by making each new segment of the story go off in a direction I hadn't anticipated. While I knew for a long while that the Soros sisters would end up in floodwaters, I had no idea what would happen at the climax until I was actually writing it. And I still have no idea what happens at the very end of the story—or at least what would have happened in the two or three unwritten sentences that might have followed my final line.

KAREN RUSSELL, a native of Miami, is the author of two short story collections, *St. Lucy's Home for Girls Raised by Wolves* and *Vampires in the Lemon Grove*. Her first novel, *Swamplandia!*, was a New York Times 10 Best Books of the Year selection, a finalist for the Pulitzer Prize, and winner of the

New York Public Library Young Lions Fiction Award. She is a 2012 Guggenheim Fellow and a 2013 MacArthur Fellow.

 • Sometimes I think it can be perversely liberating to commit to a premise that seems too goofy to work, or basically foredoomed from the outset. I remember looking up at a certain point while drafting "Madame Bovary's Greyhound" and blinking into the light of a hard truth: OK, I thought, I am writing Flaubert fan fiction, about a heartbroken dog. But I don't think I could have told a story about the vertigo of falling out of love, that terrible inertia, or the gravity that first love can continue to exert on a life, except obliquely, from Djali's low-to-the-ground animal vantage point. In *Madame Bovary*, the newlywed Emma receives a greyhound puppy as a gift from her husband, Dr. Charles. I loved the deep green haunted quality of the pair's twilight walks in Tostes, this dog and her mistress, and the way the animal serves as a screen onto which Emma projects every dream and ambivalence. She rehearses her hopes and her fears, using the animal as a sounding board. You sort of feel for the little puppy. As I tried to write the greyhound as a character, I returned to chapters 7–9 and began at the moment of Madame B's hilarious exhalation, "Mon Dieu, why did I ever get married?" In that scene, her "vagrant" thoughts stray here and there, as if connected by some tether to the dog's manic pursuit of yellow butterflies; at sunset, she is overcome by formless dread, which she transmits to the dog. It was great fun to try to thread some of Flaubert's language into this story. Several chapters later, Emma sets out for Yonville and the affair that will end in her suicide; the carriage pauses, and the little dog runs off into the woods, escaping the pages of this novel, never to return.

This struck me as a wildly surprising event: we expect infidelity from one another, but a dog's love we assume to be unconditional and eternal. A space opened up in the treeline of the original story, one that I was happy to enter: what on earth happened to this greyhound who abandoned her owner?

The greyhound's flight also gave me a physical alphabet to explore the weightlessness, pain, exhilaration, and terror that can follow the dissolution of a bond. And to represent Djali's escape from the shelter of one relationship, and into an unfamiliar landscape, as a kind of survival story.

A huge thank-you to Michael Ray of *Zoetrope,* a brilliant editor with an uncanny sympathy for every kind of story and protagonist—child and adult, animal and monster.

LAURA VAN DEN BERG is the author of the story collections *What the World Will Look Like When All the Water Leaves Us,* a Barnes & Noble "Discover Great New Writers" selection and a finalist for the Frank O'Connor International Award, and *The Isle of Youth,* which received the Rosenthal Family Foundation Award from the American Academy of Arts and Letters. Her first novel, *Find Me,* is forthcoming in early 2015. She currently lives in the Boston area and is a 2014–2015 Faculty Fellow in Fiction at Colby College.

• I have long been fascinated with Antarctica—the isolation, the extremity of weather and landscape, even the cadence of the word itself, *Ant-arc-ti-ca*—and thus had been trying to write a story set in Antarctica for years. But my drafts, written always from the perspective of a research scientist living in Antarctica, kept withering on the page.

In 2012, on the news I learned about an explosion at the Comandante Ferraz research base in Admiralty Bay. Two men were killed. The story stayed with me. A few weeks later, a line got stuck in my head: "There was nothing to identify in Antarctica because there was nothing left." This line soon became the first line of a new story and eventually two interlocking narratives emerged: a present thread set in Antarctica, where the narrator has come to investigate the mysterious death of her scientist brother, who perished in an explosion, and a past thread set in Cambridge, Massachusetts.

In hindsight, I can see why those earlier Antarctica stories kept failing. Not only am I not an expert on Antarctica, I am also not a scientist (and by "not a scientist" I mean barely able to name an element on the periodic table). The gap in knowledge was too great; I had been coming up against the limits of what I could convincingly imagine.

In "Antarctica," the narrator is a stranger in a strange land, an outsider—outsider I knew; outsider I understood. And while I have never been to Antarctica, I know Cambridge intimately, and in the end it was the collision between the radically familiar and the radically foreign that helped this story take shape.

Other Distinguished Stories of 2013

Editorial Addresses of American and Canadian Magazines Publishing Short Stories

Able Muse Review
467 Saratoga Avenue, #602
San Jose, CA 95129
$24, Nina Schyler

Adroit Journal
www.adroit.co.nv
Peter LaBerge

African American Review
http://aar.expressacademic.org
$40, Nathan Grant

Agni
Boston University Writing Program
Boston University
236 Bay State Road
Boston, MA 02115
$20, Sven Birkerts

Alaska Quarterly Review
University of Alaska, Anchorage
3211 Providence Drive
Anchorage, AK 99508
$18, Ronald Spatz

Alimentum
www.alimentumjournal.com
$18, Paulette Licitra

Alligator Juniper
http://www.prescott.edu/alligator
_juniper/
$15, Melanie Bishop

American Athenaeum
www.swordandsagapress.com
Hunter Liguore

American Letters and Commentary
Department of English
University of Texas at San Antonio
One UTSA Boulevard
San Antonio, TX 78249
$10, David Ray Vance, Catherine Kasper

American Reader
779 Riverside Drive
New York, NY 10032
$54.99, Jac Mullen

American Short Fiction
P.O. Box 302678
Austin, TX 78703
$25, Rebecca Markovits

Amoskeag
Southern New Hampshire University

2500 N. River Road
Manchester, NH 03106
$7, Michael J. Brien

Antioch Review
Antioch University
P.O. Box 148
Yellow Springs, OH 45387
$40, Robert S. Fogerty

Apalachee Review
P.O. Box 10469
Tallahassee, FL 32302
$15, Michael Trammell

Apple Valley Review
88 S. 3rd Street, Suite 336
San Jose, CA 95113

Arcadia
9616 Nichols Road
Oklahoma City, OK 73120
$13, Benjamin Reed

Arkansas Review
P.O. Box 1890
Arkansas State University
State University, AR 72467
$20, Janelle Collins

Armchair/Shotgun
377 Flatbush Avenue, #3
Brooklyn, NY 11238

Arts and Letters
Campus Box 89
Georgia College and State
University
Milledgeville, GA 31061
$15, Martin Lammon

Ascent
English Department
Concordia College
readthebestwriting.com
W. Scott Olsen

The Atlantic
600 NH Avenue NW
Washington, DC 20037
$39.95, C. Michael Curtis

Baltimore Review
P.O. Box 36418
Towson, MD 21286
Barbara Westwood Diehl

Barrelhouse
www.barrelhousemag.com
Dave Housley

Bayou
Department of English
University of New Orleans
2000 Lakeshore Drive
New Orleans, LA 70148
$15, Joanna Leake

The Believer
849 Valencia Street
San Francisco, CA 94110
Heidi Julavits

Bellevue Literary Review
Department of Medicine
New York University School
of Medicine
550 First Avenue
New York, NY 10016
$15, Danielle Ofri

Bellingham Review
MS-9053
Western Washington University
Bellingham, WA 98225
$12, Brenda Miller

Bellowing Ark
P.O. Box 55564
Shoreline, WA 98155
$20, Robert Ward

Blackbird
Department of English

Virginia Commonwealth University
P.O. Box 843082
Richmond, VA 23284-3082
Leia Darwish

Black Clock
California Institute of the Arts
24700 McBean Parkway
Valencia, CA 91355
Steve Erickson

Black Warrior Review
P.O. Box 862936
Tuscaloosa, AL 35486-0027
$16, Emma Sovitch

Blue Lyra Review
bluelyrareview@gmail.com
B. Kari Moore

Blue Mesa Review
The Creative Writing Program
University of New Mexico
MSC03-2170
Albuquerque, NM 87131
Samantha Tetangco

Bomb
New Art Publications
80 Hanson Place
Brooklyn, NY 11217
$22, Betsy Sussler

Bosque
http://www.abqwriterscoop.com/
bosque.html
Lisa Lenard-Cook

Boston Review
P.O. Box 425
Cambridge, MA 02142
$25, Joshua Cohen,
Deborah Chasman

Boulevard
PMB 325
6614 Clayton Road

Richmond Heights, MO 63117
$15, Richard Burgin

Brain, Child: The Magazine for
Thinking Mothers
P.O. Box 714
Lexington, VA 24450-0714
$22, Jennifer Niesslein,
Stephanie Wilkinson

Briar Cliff Review
3303 Rebecca Street
P.O. Box 2100
Sioux City, IA 51104-2100
$10, Tricia Currans-Sheehan

Byliner
hello@byliner.com
Mark Bryant

Callaloo
Callalloo.tamu.edu
$50, Charles H. Rowell

Calyx
P.O. Box B
Corvallis, OR 097339
$23, the collective

Camera Obscura
obscurajournal.com
M. E. Parker

Carolina Quarterly
Greenlaw Hall CB #3520
University of North Carolina
Chapel Hill, NC 27599
$24, the editors

Carve Magazine
Carvezine.com
$39.95, Matthew Limpede

Catamaran Literary Reader
1050 River Street
Santa Cruz, CA 95060
$30, Elizabeth McKenzie

Chariton Review
Truman State University
100 E. Normal Avenue
Kinesville, MO 63501
$20, James D'Agostino

Chattahoochee Review
www.chattahoochee-review.org
Anna Schachner

Chautauqua
Department of Creative
Writing
University of North Carolina,
Wilmington
601 S. College Road
Wilmington, NC 28403
$14.95, Jill and Philip Gerard

Chicago Quarterly Review
www.chicagoquarterlyreview.com
$17, S. Afzal Haider

Chicago Review
935 E. 60th Street, Taft House
University of Chicago
Chicago, IL 60637
$25, Ben Merriman

Cicada
70 East Lake Street, Suite 800
Chicago, IL 60601
$33.95, Marianne Carus

Cimarron Review
205 Morrill Hall
Oklahoma State University
Stillwater, OK 74078-4069
$32, Toni Graham

Cincinnati Review
Department of English
McMicken Hall,
Room 369
P.O. Box 210069
Cincinnati, OH 45221
$15, Michael Griffith

Coe Review
Coe College
1220 1st Avenue NE
Cedar Rapids, IA 52402
Emily Weber

Colorado Review
Department of English
Colorado State University
Fort Collins, CO 80523
$24, Stephanie G'Schwind

Columbia
Columbia University Alumni Center
622 W. 113th Street, MC4521
New York, NY 10025
$50, Michael B. Sharleson

Commentary
165 East 56th Street
New York, NY 10022
$45, Neal Kozody

The Common
Thecommononline.org/submit
$30, Jennifer Acker

Confrontation
English Department
C. W. Post College of Long Island
University
Brookville, NY 11548
$15, Jenna G. Semeiks

Conjunctions
21 East 10th Street, Suite 3E
New York, NY 10003
$18, Bradford Morrow

Crab Orchard Review
Department of English
Faner Hall 2380
Southern Illinois University at
Carbondale
1000 Faner Drive
Carbondale, IL 62901
$20, Carolyn Alessio

Crazyhorse
Department of English
College of Charleston
66 George Street
Charleston, SC 29424
$20, Anthony Varallo

Cream City Review
Department of English
University of Wisconsin, Milwaukee
Box 413
Milwaukee, WI 53201
$22, Ann McBree

Crucible
Barton College
P.O. Box 5000
Wilson, NC 27893
$16, Terrence L. Grimes

CutBank
Department of English
University of Montana
Missoula, MT 59812
$15, Josh Fomon

Daedalus
136 Irving Street, Suite 100
Cambridge, MA 02138
$41, James Miller

DailyLit
Plympton Inc.
28 2nd Street, 3rd Floor
San Francisco, CA 94104
Yael Goldstein Love

December
P.O. Box 16130
St. Louis, MD 63105
Gianna Jacobson

Denver Quarterly
University of Denver
Denver, CO 80208
$29, Laird Hunt

Descant
P.O. Box 314
Station P
Toronto, Ontario M5S 2S8
$28, Karen Mulhallen

descant
Department of English
Texas Christian University
TCU Box 297270
Fort Worth, TX 76129
$15, Dan Williams

Drash
2632 NE 80th Street
Temple Beth Am
Seattle, WA 98115
$11, Wendy Marcus

Ecotone
Department of Creative Writing
University of North Carolina,
Wilmington
601 South College Road
Wilmington, NC 28403
$16.95, David Gessner

Electric Literature
electricliterature.com
Andy Hunter, Scott Lindenbaum

Eleven Eleven
California College of the Arts
1111 Eighth Street
San Francisco, CA 94107
Hugh Behm-Steinberg

Epiphany
www.epiphanyzine.com
$20, Willard Cook

Epoch
251 Goldwin Smith Hall
Cornell University
Ithaca, NY 14853-3201
$11, Michael Koch

Esquire
300 West 57th Street,
21st Floor
New York, NY 10019
$17.94, fiction editor

Event
Douglas College
P.O. Box 2503
New Westminster
British Columbia V3L 5B2
$29.95, Christine Dewar

Fantasy and Science Fiction
P.O. Box 3447
Hoboken, NJ 07030
$39, Gordon Van Gelder

Farallon Review
1017 L Street, #348
Sacramento, CA 95814
$10, the editors

Fiction
Department of English
The City College of
New York
Convent Avenue at
138th Street
New York, NY 10031
$38, Mark Jay Mirsky

Fiction International
Department of English and
Comparative Literature
5500 Campanile Drive
San Diego State University
San Diego, CA 92182
$18, Harold Jaffe

The Fiddlehead
Campus House
11 Garland Court
UNB P.O. Box 4400
Fredericton
New Brunswick E3B 5A3
$30, Mark Anthony Jarman

Fifth Wednesday
www.fifthwednesdayjournal.org
$20, Vern Miller

Five Points
Georgia State University
P.O. Box 3999
Atlanta, GA 30302
$21, David Bottoms and
Megan Sexton

Fjords Review
www.fjordsreview.com
$12, John Gosslee

Florida Review
Department of English
P.O. Box 161346
University of Central Florida
Orlando, FL 32816
$15, Jocelyn Bartkevicius

Flyway
206 Ross Hall
Department of English
Iowa State University
Ames, IA 50011
$24, Genevieve DuBois

Fourteen Hills
Department of Creative Writing
San Francisco State University
1600 Halloway Avenue
San Francisco, CA 94132-1722
$15, Kendra Sheynert

Free State Review
3637 Black Rock Road
Upperco, MD 21155
$20, Hal Burdett

Fugue
uidaho.edu/fugue
$18, Warren Bromley-Vogel

Gargoyle
3819 North 13th Street

Arlington, VA 22201
$30, Lucinda Ebersole,
Richard Peabody

Gemini
P.O. Box 1485
Onset, MA 02558
David Bright

Georgetown Review
400 E. College Street, Box 227
Georgetown, KY 40324
$5, Steven Carter

Georgia Review
Gilbert Hall
University of Georgia
Athens, GA 30602
$40, Stephen Corey

Gettysburg Review
Gettysburg College
300 N. Washington Street
Gettysburg, PA 17325
$28, Peter Stitt

Ghost Town/Pacific Review
Department of English
California State University,
San Bernadino
5500 University Parkway
San Bernadino, CA 92407
Tim Manifesta

Glimmer Train
1211 NW Glisan Street, Suite 207
Portland, OR 97209
$38, Susan Burmeister-Brown,
Linda Swanson-Davies

Gold Man Review
P.O. Box 8202
Salem, OR 97303
Heather Cuthbertson

Good Housekeeping
300 West 57th Street

New York, NY 10019
Laura Matthews

Grain
Box 67
Saskatoon, Saskatchewan
57K 3K9
$35, Rilla Friesen

Granta
841 Broadway, 4th Floor
New York, NY 10019-3780
$48, Ella Allfrey

Green Mountains Review
Box A58
Johnson State College
Johnson, VT 05656
$17, Neil Shepard

Greensboro Review
3302 Hall for Humanities
and Research Administration
University of North Carolina
Greensboro, NC 27402
$14, Jim Clark

Grey Sparrow
P.O. Box 211664
Saint Paul, MN 55121
Diane Smith

Grist
University of Tennessee
English Department
301 McClung Tower
Knoxville, TN 37996
$33, Christian Anton Gerard

Guernica
P.O. Box 219 Cooper Station
New York, NY 10276
Meakin Armstrong

Gulf Coast
Department of English
University of Houston

Houston, TX 77204-3012
$16, Nick Flynn

Hanging Loose
231 Wyckoff Street
Brooklyn, NY 11217
$27, group

Harper's Magazine
666 Broadway
New York, NY 10012
$16.79, Ben Metcalf

Harpur Palate
Department of English
Binghamton University
P.O. Box 6000
Binghamton, NY 13902
$16, Barrett Bowlin

Harvard Review
Lamont Library, Harvard University
Cambridge, MA 02138
$20, Christina Thompson

Hawaii Review
Department of English
University of Hawaii at Manoa
P.O. Box 11674
Honolulu, HI 96828
$12.50, Stephanie Mizushima

Hayden's Ferry Review
Box 807302
Arizona State University
Tempe, AZ 85287
$25, Sam Martone

High Desert Journal
P.O. Box 7647
Bend, OR 97708
$16, Elizabeth Quinn

Hobart
P.O. Box 11658
Ann Arbor, MI 48106
$18, Aaron Burch

Hotel Amerika
Columbia College
English Department
600 S. Michigan Avenue
Chicago, IL 60657
$18, David Lazar

Hudson Review
684 Park Avenue
New York, NY 10065
$36, Paula Deitz

Hunger Mountain
www.hungermtn.org
$12, Miciah Bay Gault

Idaho Review
Boise State University
1910 University Drive
Boise, ID 83725
$15, Mitch Wieland

Image
Center for Religious Humanism
3307 Third Avenue West
Seattle, WA 98119
$39.95, Gregory Wolfe

Indiana Review
Ballantine Hall 465
1020 East Kirkwood Avenue
Bloomington, IN 47405-7103
$20, Katie Moutton

Inkwell
Manhattanville College
2900 Purchase Street
Purchase, NY 10577
$10, Todd Bowes

Iowa Review
Department of English
University of Iowa
308 EPB
Iowa City, IA 52242
$25, Harilaos Stecopoulos

Iron Horse Literary Review
Department of English
Texas Tech University
Box 43091
Lubbock, TX 79409-3091
$18, Leslie Jill Patterson

Isotope
Utah State University
3200 Old Main Hill
Logan, UT 84322
$15, the editors

Italian Americana
University of Rhode Island
Providence Campus
80 Washington Street
Providence, RI 02903
$20, Carol Bonomo Albright

Jabberwock Review
Department of English
Drawer E
Mississippi State University
Mississippi State, MS 39762
$15, Michael P. Kardos

Jelly Bucket
Bluegrass Writers Studio
467 Case Annex
521 Lancaster Avenue
Richmond, KY 40475
F. Travis Roman

Jewish Currents
45 East 33rd Street
New York, NY 10016-5335
$25, editorial board

The Journal
The Ohio State University
Department of English
164 W. 17th Avenue
Columbus, OH 43210
$15, Kathy Fagon

Joyland
joylandmagazine.com
Emily Schultz

Juked
220 Atkinson Drive, #B
Tallahassee, FL 32304
$10, J. W. Wang

Kenyon Review
www.kenyonreview.org
$30, the editors

Kugelmass
http://firewheel-editions.org/
kugelmass
$26, David Holub

The Labletter
3712 N. Broadway,
#241
Chicago, IL 60613
Robert Kotchen

Lady Churchill's Rosebud Wristlet
Small Beer Press
150 Pleasant Street
Easthampton, MA 01027
$20, Kelly Link

Lake Effect
Penn State Erie
4951 College Drive
Erie, PA 16563-1501
$6, George Looney

The Literarian
www.centerforfiction.org
Dawn Raffel

Literary Review
Fairleigh Dickinson University
285 Madison Avenue
Madison, NJ 07940
$24, Minna Proctor

Little Patuxent Review
6012 Jamina Downs
Columbia, MD 21045
Laura Shovan

Little Star
107 Bank Street
New York, NY 10014
$14.95, Ann Kjellberg

Los Angeles Review
redhen.org/losangelesreview
$20, Kate Gale

Louisiana Literature
SLU-10792
Southeastern Louisiana University
Hammond, LA 70402
$12, Jack B. Bedell

Louisville Review
Spalding University
851 South Fourth Street
Louisville, KY 40203
$14, Sena Jeter Naslund

Lumina
Sarah Lawrence College
Slonim House, One Mead Way
Bronxville, NY 10708
Lillian Ho

Madison Review
University of Wisconsin
Department of English
H. C. White Hall
600 North Park Street
Madison, WI 53706
$25, Elzbieta Beck

Make
www.makemag.com
Sarah Dodson

Mānoa
English Department

University of Hawaii
Honolulu, HI 96822
$30, Frank Stewart

Massachusetts Review
South College
University of Massachusetts
Amherst, MA 01003
$29, Ellen Doré Watson

Masters Review
1824 NW Couch Street
Portland, OR 97209
Kim Winternheimer

McSweeney's
826 Valencia Street
San Francisco, CA 94110
$55, Dave Eggers

Memorious
521 Winston Drive
Vestal, NY 13850
Rebecca Morgan Frank

Meridian
Department of English
P.O. Box 400145
University of Virginia
Charlottesville, VA 22904-4145
$12, Julianna Daugherty

Michigan Quarterly Review
0576 Rackham Building
915 East Washington Street
University of Michigan
Ann Arbor, MI 48109
$25, Jonathan Freedman

Mid-American Review
Department of English
Bowling Green State
University
Bowling Green, OH 43403
$9, Abigail Cloud

Minnesota Review
ASPECT Virginia Tech
202 Major Williams Hall (0192)
Blacksburg, VA 24061
$30, Jeffrey Williams

Mississippi Review
University of Southern
Mississippi
118 College Drive, #5144
Hattiesburg, MS 39406-5144
$15, Andrew Milan Milward

Missouri Review
357 McReynolds Hall
University of Missouri
Columbia, MO 65211
$24, Speer Morgan

Montana Quarterly
2820 W. College Street
Bozeman, MT 59771
Megan Ault Regnerus

n + 1
68 Jay Street, #405
Brooklyn, NY 11201
$35, Keith Gessen, Mark Greif

Narrative Magazine
narrativemagazine.com
The editors

Nashville Review
331 Benson Hall
Vanderbilt University
Nashville, TN 37203
Matthew Maker

Natural Bridge
Department of English
University of Missouri, St. Louis
St. Louis, MO 63121
$10, Mary Troy

New England Review
Middlebury College

Middlebury, VT 05753
$30, Carolyn Kuebler

New Letters
University of Missouri
5101 Rockhill Road
Kansas City, MO 64110
$22, Robert Stewart

New Madrid
www.newmadridjournal.org
$15, Ann Neelon

New Millennium Writings
www.newmillenniumwritings.com
$12, Don Williams

New Ohio Review
English Department
360 Ellis Hall
Ohio University
Athens, OH 45701
$20, Jill Allyn Rosser

New Orphic Review
706 Mill Street
Nelson, British Columbia V1L 4S5
$30, Ernest Hekkanen

New Quarterly
Saint Jerome's University
290 Westmount Road
N. Waterloo, Ontario N2L 3G3
$36, Kim Jernigan

New South
www.reivew.gsu.edu
$8, Matt Sailor

The New Yorker
4 Times Square
New York, NY 10036
$46, Deborah Treisman

Nimrod International Journal
Arts and Humanities Council
of Tulsa

600 South College Avenue
Tulsa, OK 74104
$17.50, Francine Ringold

Ninth Letter
Department of English
University of Illinois
608 South Wright Street
Urbana, IL 61801
$21.95, Jodee Rubins

Noon
1324 Lexington Avenue
PMB 298
New York, NY 10128
$12, Diane Williams

Normal School
5245 North Backer Avenue
M/S PB 98
California State University
Fresno, CA 93470
$5, Sophie Beck

North American Review
University of Northern Iowa
1222 West 27th Street
Cedar Falls, IA 50614
$22, Grant Tracey

North Carolina Literary Review
Department of English
Mailstop 555 English
East Carolina University
Greenville, NC 27858-4353
$25, Margaret Bauer

North Dakota Quarterly
University of North Dakota
Merrifield Hall, Room 110
276 Centennial Drive Stop 27209
Grand Forks, ND 58202
$25, Robert Lewis

Northern New England Review
Humanities Department
Franklin Pierce University

Rindge, NH 03461
$5, Edie Clark

Northwest Review
5243 University of Oregon
Eugene, OR 97403
$20, Ehud Havazelet

Notre Dame Review
840 Flanner Hall
Department of English
University of Notre Dame
Notre Dame, IN 46556
$15, John Matthias,
 William O'Rourke

One Story
232 Third Street, #A111
Brooklyn, NY 11215
$21, Maribeth Batcha,
 Hannah Tinti

Orion
187 Main Street
Great Barrington, MA 01230
$35, the editors

Oxford American
201 Donaghey Avenue, Main 107
Conway, AR 72035
$24.95, Marc Smirnoff

Pak N Treger
National Yiddish Book Center
Harry and Jeanette Weinberg Bldg.
1021 West Street
Amherst, MA 01002
$36, Aaron Lansky

Parcel
parcelmag.org
$20

Paris Review
62 White Street
New York, NY 10013
$34, Lorin Stein

Passages North
Northern Michigan University
Department of English
1401 Presque Isle Avenue
Marquette, MI 49855
$13, Jennifer A. Howard

Pearl
3030 East Second Street
Long Beach, CA 90803
$21, Joan Jobe Smith

Pembroke Magazine
pembrokemagazine.com
Jessica Pitchford

PEN America
PEN America Center
588 Broadway, Suite 303
New York, NY 10012
$10, M Mark

Phoebe
MSN 2C5
George Mason University
4400 University Drive
Fairfax, VA 22030
$12, Brian Koen

The Pinch
Department of English
University of Memphis
Memphis, TN 38152
$28, Kristen Iverson

Pleiades
Department of English and
Philosophy
University of Central Missouri
Warrensburg, MO 64093
$16, Wayne Miller

Ploughshares
Emerson College
120 Boylston Street
Boston, MA 02116
$30, Ladette Randolph

PoemMemoirStory
HB 217
1530 Third Avenue South
Birmingham, AL 35294
$10, Kerry Madden

Post Road
postroadmag.com
$18, Rebecca Boyd

Potomac Review
Montgomery College
51 Mannakee Street
Rockville, MD 20850
$20, Julie Wakeman-Linn

Prairie Fire
423-100 Arthur Street
Winnipeg, Manitoba R3B 1H3
$30, Andris Taskans

Prairie Schooner
201 Andrews Hall
University of Nebraska
Lincoln, NE 68588-0334
$28, Kwame Dawes

Prism International
Department of Creative
Writing
University of British Columbia
Buchanan E-462
Vancouver, British Columbia
V6T 1Z1
$40, Anna Ling Kaye

Progenitor
595 W. Easter Place
Littleton, CO 80120
Kathryn Peterson

Provo Canyon Review
www.theprovocanyonreview.net
Chris and Erin McClelland

A Public Space
323 Dean Street

Brooklyn, NY 11217
$36, Brigid Hughes

Puerto del Sol
MSC 3E
New Mexico State University
P.O. Box 30001
Las Cruces, NM 88003
$20, Evan Lavender-Smith

The Quotable
www.thequotablelit.com
Eimile Denizer

Redivider
Emerson College
120 Boylston Street
Boston, MA 02116
$10, Matt Salesses

Red Rock Review
English Department, J2A
Community College of
Southern Nevada
3200 East Cheyenne Avenue
North Las Vegas, NV 89030
$9.50, Richard Logsdon

River Oak Review
Elmhurst College
190 Prospect Avenue
Box 2633
Elmhurst, IL 60126
$12, Ron Wiginton

River Styx
3547 Olive Street, Suite 107
St. Louis, MO 63103-1014
$20, Richard Newman

Roanoke Review
221 College Lane
Salem, VA 24153
$5, Paul Hanstedt

Room Magazine
P.O. Box 46160

Station D
Vancouver, British Columbia
V6J 5G5
$10, Rachel Thompson

Ruminate
140 N. Roosevelt Avenue
Fort Collins, CO 80521
$28, Brianna Van Dyke

Salamander
Suffolk University
English Department
41 Temple Street
Boston, MA 02114
$15, Jennifer Barber

Salmagundi
Skidmore College
Saratoga Springs, NY 12866
$20, Robert Boyers

Salt Hill
salthilljournal.com
$15, Kayla Blatchley

Santa Clara Review
Santa Clara University
500 El Camino Road, Box 3212
Santa Clara, CA 95053
$16, Nick Sanchez

Santa Monica Review
1900 Pico Boulevard
Santa Monica, CA 90405
$12, Andrew Tonkovich

Seattle Review
P.O. Box 354330
University of Washington
Seattle, WA 98195
$20, Andrew Feld

Sewanee Review
735 University Avenue
Sewanee, TN 37383
$25, George Core

Shenandoah
Mattingly House
2 Lee Avenue
Washington and Lee University
Lexington, VA 24450-2116
$25, R. T. Smith, Lynn Leech

Slice
www.slicemagazine.org
Elizabeth Blachman

Sonora Review
Department of English
University of Arizona
Tucson, AZ 85721
$16, Astrid Duffy

So to Speak
George Mason University
4400 University Drive
MSN 2C5
Fairfax, VA 22030
$12, Kate Partridge

South Carolina Review
Center for Electronic and
Digital Publishing
Clemson University, Strode Tower
Box 340522
Clemson, SC 29634
$28, Wayne Chapman

South Dakota Review
http://southdakotareview.com
$40, Lee Ann Roripaugh

Southeast Review
Department of English
Florida State University
Tallahassee, FL 32306
$15, Brandi George

Southern Humanities Review
9088 Haley Center
Auburn University
Auburn, AL 36849
$18, Chantal Acevedo

Southern Indiana Review
College of Liberal Arts
University of Southern Indiana
8600 University Boulevard
Evansville, IN 47712
$20, Ron Mitchell

Southern Review
3990 W. Lakeshore Drive
Louisiana State University
Baton Rouge, LA 70808
$40, Cora Blue Adams

Southwest Review
Southern Methodist University
P.O. Box 750374
Dallas, TX 75275
$24, Willard Spiegelman

Sou'wester
Department of English
Box 1438
Southern Illinois University
Edwardsville, IL 62026
Stacey Lynn Brown

Subtropics
Department of English
University of Florida
P.O. Box 112075
Gainesville, FL 32611-2075
$21, David Leavitt

The Sun
107 North Roberson Street
Chapel Hill, NC 27516
$39, Sy Safransky

Sycamore Review
Department of English
500 Oval Drive, Purdue University
West Lafayette, IN 47907
$16, Jessica Jacobs

Tampa Review
The University of Tampa
401 W. Kennedy Boulevard

Tampa, FL 33606
$22, Richard Mathews

Third Coast
Department of English
Western Michigan University
Kalamazoo, MI 49008
$16, Emily J. Stinson

Thomas Wolfe Review
P.O. Box 1146
Bloomington, IN 47402
David Strange

Threepenny Review
2163 Vine Street
Berkeley, CA 94709
$25, Wendy Lesser

Timber Creek Review
8969 UNCG Station
Greensboro, NC 27413
$17, John Freiermuth

Tin House
P.O. Box 10500
Portland, OR 97296-0500
$50, Rob Spillman

Transition
104 Mt. Auburn Street,
3R
Cambridge, MA 02138
$43.50, Tommy Shelby

TriQuarterly
629 Noyes Street
Evanston, IL 60208
$24, Susan Firestone Hahn

Unstuck
unstuckbooks.submittable.com
Matt Williamson

Upstreet
P.O. Box 105
Richmond, MA 01254

$10, Vivian Dorsel

Vermont Literary Review
Department of English
Castleton State College
Castleton, VT 05735
Flo Keyes

Virginia Quarterly Review
5 Boar's Head Lane
P.O. Box 400223
Charlottesville, VA 22903
$32, W. Ralph Eubanks

Wag's Review
313 Sackest Street, #3
Brooklyn, NY 11231
Sandra Allen

War, Literature, and the Arts
Department of English and
Fine Arts
2354 Fairchild Drive, Suite 6D45
USAF Academy, CO 80840-6242
$10, Donald Anderson

Washington Post Magazine
1150 15th Street NW
Washington, DC 20071
David Rowell

Water-Stone Review
Graduate School of Liberal Studies
Hamline University, MS-A1730
1536 Hewitt Avenue
Saint Paul, MN 55104
$32, the editors

Weber Studies
Weber State University
1405 University Circle
Ogden, UT 84408-1214
$20, Michael Wutz

West Branch
Bucknell Hall
Bucknell University

Lewisburg, PA 17837
$10, G. C. Waldrep

Western Humanities Review
University of Utah
255 South Central Campus Drive
Room 3500
Salt Lake City, UT 84112
$21, Barry Weller

Willow Springs
Eastern Washington University
501 N. Riverpoint Boulevard
Spokane, WA 99201
$18, Samuel Ligon

Witness
Black Mountain Institute
University of Nevada
Las Vegas, NV 89154
$12, Maile Chapman

World Literature Today
The University of Oklahoma

630 Parrington Oval, Suite 110
Norman, OK 73019
Michelle Johnson

Yale Review
P.O. Box 208243
New Haven, CT 06520-8243
$36, J. D. McClatchy

Zoetrope: All-Story
Sentinel Building
916 Kearney Street
San Francisco, CA 94133
$24, Michael Ray

Zone 3
APSU, Box 4565
Clarksville, TN 37044
$15, Barry Kitterman

ZYZZYVA
466 Geary Street, #401
San Francisco, CA 94102
$40, Laura Cogan

THE BEST AMERICAN SERIES®

FIRST, BEST, AND BEST-SELLING

The Best American series is the premier annual showcase for the country's finest short fiction and nonfiction. Each volume's series editor selects notable works from hundreds of magazines, journals, and websites. A special guest editor, a leading writer in the field, then chooses the best twenty or so pieces to publish. This unique system has made the Best American series the most respected—and most popular—of its kind.

Look for these best-selling titles in the Best American series:

The Best American Comics

The Best American Essays

The Best American Infographics

The Best American Mystery Stories

The Best American Nonrequired Reading

The Best American Science and Nature Writing

The Best American Short Stories

The Best American Sports Writing

The Best American Travel Writing

Available in print and e-book wherever books are sold.
Visit our website: *www.hmhbooks.com/hmh/site/bas*